D1044425

"Should not be missed."

—Robert Crais, *New York Times*
bestselling author of *Hostage*

"Green tells an emotionally provocative story while keeping readers on edge with suspense."

—*South Bend Tribune*

"An indelibly etched mood piece."

—*Kirkus Reviews*

"Fast, stylish, and morally centered, *Shooting Dr. Jack* is an auspicious debut from a gifted writer who wears his rough edges proudly."

—*The News-Press* (Florida)

"Crackles with enough good lines to have been saved up for a life-time . . . Even considering the sharp New York scene setting and fast-paced plotting, the best thing about *Shooting Dr. Jack* is the characters."

—*Tampa Tribune*

"This novel mixes elements of *The Sopranos* and *Traffic* and comes up with the best qualities of both. . . . Green's greatest triumph is the development of three realistic characters readers can relate to."

—Associated Press

"With his debut novel, *Shooting Dr. Jack,* Norman Green eloquently puts into words the struggle we all face: getting through the day, getting one step closer to love and happiness, and if possible making a few bucks along the way."

—*Sun Herald* (Biloxi, Mississippi)

"This gritty urban tale is a strong debut."

—*Seattle Times*

Brian DeFiore

About the Author

NORMAN GREEN is the author of *Shooting Dr. Jack,
The Angel of Montague Street, Way Past Legal,* and
Dead Cat Bounce. He lives in New Jersey with his
wife. For more information, visit him on his Web
site at www.normangreenbooks.com.

DEAD CAT BOUNCE

A NOVEL

NORMAN GREEN

HARPER

NEW YORK · LONDON · TORONTO · SYDNEY

HARPER

This book is a work of fiction. References to real people, events, establishments, organizations, or locales are intended only to provide a sense of authenticity, and are used fictitiously. All other characters, and all incidents and dialogue, are drawn from the author's imagination and are not to be construed as real.

HarperCollins books may be purchased for educational, business, or sales promotional use. For information please write: Special Markets Department, HarperCollins Publishers, 10 East 53rd Street, New York, NY 10022.

FIRST EDITION

Designed by Nancy Singer Olaguera, ISPN Publishing Services

Library of Congress Cataloging-in-Publication Data

Green, Norman.
    Dead cat bounce : a novel / Norman Green.—1st Harper pbk. ed.
      p.   cm.
    ISBN-13: 978-0-06-085169-9
    ISBN-10: 0-06-085169-4
    1. Italian American families—Fiction. 2. Brooklyn (New York, N.Y.)—Fiction. 3. Organized crime—Fiction. I. Title.

PS3607.R44D43 2006
813'.6—dc22   2005054549

06 07 08 09 10 ISPN/RRD 10 9 8 7 6 5 4 3 2

To Christine, as always

It is not the strongest . . . that survives,

nor the most intelligent. . . .

It is the one that is the most adaptable to change.

—CHARLES DARWIN

Stoney leaned against the end of the bar and watched the bartender fix his drink. Ice in a tall glass, seltzer water, squeeze the lime, goddammit, don't just throw it in there. The guy put it down in front of him without comment, picked up the five-dollar bill lying there, and went to make change. It had been eight months since Stoney had touched alcohol, and somewhat to his surprise, Seagram's had not gone out of business, nor had Budweiser, Miller, Bushmill's, or any of the rest. The bartender brought back his change, turned away without asking him if he was sure he didn't want a chaser, how about a Dewar's on the side, nothing. There were a half dozen other people in the place, and not one of them, as far as he could tell, cared what he was drinking.

Benny would care. Stoney could hear the guy's voice in his head. "Keep playing on the tracks, kid, don't be surprised when you get hit by the train." Stoney figured that Benny would be right about that, Benny was right about most things that had to do with not drinking, and with living your life like you gave a shit. Stoney glanced at his watch. Another twenty minutes until it was time to meet his daughter. Stoney did not know why he was standing in this bar in the bowels of New York City's Grand Central Station. Wait upstairs, asshole, he told himself. What is wrong with you? You really think you need something to fortify yourself? She's just a kid, for chrissake. He left the seltzer and the change on the bar and walked out.

Grand Central Station's main waiting room is a vast open space, it's the kind of vaulted stone hall that no one builds anymore, a cathedral to all that railroads had once been. Stoney was there because his daughter, Marisa, had left a voice mail on his cell phone. "Meet me under the clock in Grand Central," she'd said, gave him the date and time and nothing else. Surprised the hell out of him, he didn't even know how she'd found his number. She must have gotten it off one of the old bills, back when they were still sending them to the house. Back before his wife, Donna, had thrown him out.

There was nothing for him to do but stand there, Marisa hadn't told him what train she'd be on. He tried to figure it out from the schedule but he gave up on that pretty quickly. He found that he did not know enough about his daughter to be able to do more than guess. How old is she? he asked himself. Do you even know? He came up with an answer to that, though, because he'd driven to the hospital to pick up Donna and the new baby in the Buick Grand National he'd bought in '86. He'd smacked up the car a year later, so Marisa had to be around sixteen. Seventeen. Something like that. Jesus.

She came striding across the floor of that enormous room, longish brown hair, brown eyes, tall but not too tall, thin, but not out of the ordinary, pretty, but not a knockout. Physically, she put him in mind of Donna, his wife, but he could see from the look in her eyes that she was her father's daughter. She's not gonna be easy to deal with, he thought.

He had spent most of the previous evening talking to Benny about this meeting. Stoney might have been a while without a drink, but his head was still all fucked up. Benny supplied him with perspective, judgment, purpose. Benny told him which AA meetings to attend. "Go to Liberty Street tonight," he would say. "Get there around eight and help them put the chairs out." Stoney followed the instructions. Sometimes he'd see Benny there, sometimes he wouldn't. Stoney had quit trying to make sense of it. Just do what the little bastard tells you, he told himself. Working so far, isn't it?

"So let her come meet you," Benny had told him. "Just try not to overreact. She might be coming to tell you she hates your guts and never wants to see you again, or she might want to tell you she misses you. Either way, you gotta take it, you owe her that."

"What about this business of making amends?" Stoney asked him. "Don't I have to say something about that when I see her?"

"You ain't up to that part yet," Benny told him. "No jumping ahead. Look, just go meet her, okay? Don't chase her away by running after her. And try not to act like an asshole. Call me after."

She was wearing jeans and a T-shirt that came several inches short of meeting at her waist. The part of the jeans that would have held belt loops was missing, torn off, leaving a ragged fringe. She had a diamond tennis bracelet on one thin wrist. Stoney could sense the men passing by regarding his daughter as a sexual being, and that primal father thing started up in his head. He couldn't help himself.

She stopped about six feet away and looked at him without expression. "Where's the rest of your pants?" he asked her, but he almost smiled when he said it, and that saved him.

She gave him a look. "That's the way they make them

now," she told him. He could tell that she was trying to
suck in her stomach the way females do, but she didn't really
have one.

"You hungry? You feel like something to eat?"

She shook her head. "Show me where you live," she said.

He wondered if Donna had put her up to this, if she
wanted to know where he lived so she could serve papers on
him or some shit, but he immediately felt bad for thinking
that. Donna was not that underhanded, her mind did not
work that way. And even if it did, so what? There was no way
he could win, either way. "Come on," he said, nodding his
head at the doors to the street. "Let's take a cab."

"All right." She crossed the space between them and they
headed for the exit. She hooked her arm around his elbow. He
wondered if she did it out of habit, or did she feel something?
She didn't say anything, but that was all right. He concentrated
on the sensation of her arm on his. Live in the moment, that
was one of the things Benny kept telling him. Take what life
gives you.

She belted herself in when they got into the cab. Stoney gave
the driver his address, leaned back in the seat as the guy took
off. He noticed her staring at him.

"What?"

"You don't wear seat belts?"

"This country is becoming a nation of sheep," he told her.
"Government tells you you gotta fasten your seat belt, so you
all do it."

She shook her head, looked out the window.

"How is everybody," he asked her.

"Pissed off," she said. "Dennis, especially. He thinks

you're a real shit. He's only thirteen, though. He doesn't know anything."

"How about your mom?"

She glanced at him, looked away. "She doesn't cry as much anymore, but she's still pretty mad. She had to start looking for a job last week, and that didn't help. She says you hid all the money." She was looking at him, her brow furrowed. "Is that true?"

"Well, I didn't leave it in the desk drawer, for chrissake." He shook his head. Donna had never concerned herself much with finances, not in all the years they had been married. "Why didn't she call me? I would have told her what to do."

"Maybe she was waiting for you to call her." He could hear the resentment in Marisa's voice.

"She didn't want me to. She made that pretty clear."

"Is that what she told you?"

"Oh yeah." He started to elaborate, thought better of it. "You better believe it."

"Women change their minds sometimes, haven't you heard that?"

"That right?" He considered it. "Okay," he said. "I'll try calling her." He could hear the doubt in his own voice.

Marisa exhaled, as though she'd been holding in more air than she should have. "Fine. Don't wait around too long, though. Mr. Prior told her she should go see a lawyer."

"Who's he?"

She pursed her lips in distaste. "He's a jerk." She stared out the window for about a block, then turned back to him, shaking her head. "He's just this guy. I think he's from her support group."

"Oh." She sleeping with him yet? He was aching to ask the

question, but he knew it would be a terrible mistake. "What's his first name?"

"Look, just pretend I didn't tell you, okay?" The resentment was back in her voice. "Don't even say anything. I shouldn't have told you about him. Mom says you'll kill him."

He thought about that. Let it go, he told himself. At least for now. But all his regrets came back to him in a flood, all the things he needed to make up for, all the rotten, joyless years. He had been hoping that things would still work out somehow, that Donna would still take him back, or at least that she'd give him another shot. He didn't understand how it could be that she still owned him so completely.

Marisa had been watching him intently. "All right," he told her, trying to keep the dismay out of his voice. "I never heard of the guy. Fair enough?"

She was still watching him, gauging his reactions. "You still care about her, don't you."

He nodded. "Always did."

She sat back and looked out the window. "Mr. Prior says you're a common criminal."

He laughed at that, a short, staccato burst of sound. "You tell Mr. Prior," he said, "there ain't nothing common about me."

"I already did," she said. "Where the hell are we going?"

"East Village," he told her.

"Oh," she said. "Charles. His name is Charles David Prior." She wrinkled her face in distaste. "He uses all three names. But don't forget, you promised."

"I won't forget."

The building vestibule, where the mailboxes were, smelled like vomit, but that receded once you got inside and got the door closed behind you. The place was on Twelfth Street, between Avenues B and C. It had once been a tenement, but the residents had gotten together, bought the place, and fixed it up. The rest of the block, though, still looked like shit. They climbed the stairs to the fourth floor in silence. Stoney unlocked the door to his apartment, held it open for Marisa to precede him inside.

"Good grief," she said, looking around the living room. There was an antique Bokhara on the floor, Oriental prints on the walls, shoji screens blocking off the small kitchen.

"What?" he said. "You thought I was sleeping in the backseat of an abandoned car?"

"There's an idea," she said. "Actually, I thought you'd be living with Fat Tommy."

"Tried that for a few weeks. Me and Tommy, we been partners forever, but we couldn't coexist in the same space. We got different schedules, you know what I mean? Tommy has to get his nine, ten hours every night, and I hardly sleep at all. I like it quiet, he has to have the goddamn radio or the television on all the time. Besides, I think I was cramping his style."

She smiled, thinking of Tommy. She's just like all the rest of them, Stoney thought. It was irritating, how the females always seemed to like Fat Tommy, aka Tommy Bagadonuts, aka Thomas Rosselli. She looked up at her father and her smile went away. "So how'd you find this place?"

"Belongs to a friend of Tommy's. She doesn't use it much anymore, so she's letting me stay here for a while."

"She's got good taste," Marisa said, and she went over to sit by a window. "You still going to AA?" She didn't look at him.

"Yeah. You want something to drink? Soda, coffee, tea?"

"You have seltzer?"

"I got everything. Except, you know . . ."

"I didn't think you'd offer me a beer."

"No. Maybe not."

"How many meetings you go to?"

He went around behind the screens and into the kitchen to get her water. He filled a tall glass with ice cubes, took the glass and the bottle of seltzer back out into the main room. She took them from him. "How many meetings?"

"One a day," he said. "What do you know about it?"

"I had a boyfriend in NA," she said.

"Had?"

"Last I heard, he was back in a long-term rehab." She scowled at him. "You got a sponsor?"

"Yeah. Guy name of Benny."

"You gonna make it? The counselor at school says the odds are something like thirty to one against."

"Yeah, I heard that. Benny says the odds are bullshit. He says if I do what he tells me, I'll be okay."

"I hope he's right," she said, and then turned away. "You have any idea what it was like, living with you?"

"I got the feeling you're gonna tell me."

"You remember those people down the street, used to have that Doberman?" Her voice was getting louder and angrier. "I couldn't understand why anyone would keep a dog like that. He was so mean, he hated everyone."

He went and sat on the couch across the room from her. "Maybe he didn't hate everybody. Maybe he was afraid." He watched her thinking about it. "Look, I'm sorry, but I can't go back and change the past. It is what it is."

She sighed. "What happened?"

"What do you mean?"

"With you and Mom? What happened? What did you do?"

He looked her in the eye. "What did I do. I'm an addict," he said. "Do you know what that means?"

"I know what it looks like," she said, staring back. "Maybe I don't really know what it means."

"It means I did what I had to do to get what I needed. You were standing in the way, I bulldozed you. I'm not making any excuses for it. But when I finally stopped using and drinking, I thought we'd get better. You, me, her, Dennis . . . All of us. Didn't work out that way. I didn't expect any medals, okay, but I didn't know things were going to fall apart. I don't exactly know what to do next."

"How about apologizing? You gonna tell Mom you're sorry?"

"Talk is cheap," he said. "Your boyfriend, the one back in long-term rehab. How many times he apologize to you? How many times he promise you he'd never touch it again?"

She snorted, a humorless noise freighted with derision and resignation.

"So you really want to hear him say it again?"

"No," she said. "But you could start by just calling her up. You could help her out with the money."

"Okay. You're right. I should have done that before. I never even thought about the bills."

"Look, don't go nuts, okay? Let her go get a job, at least that would get her out of the house. Just, like, try to help out a little bit."

"I get you."

She looked at him, shook her head. She's more adult than I am, he thought. He resisted the urge to say it.

"Dad?"

"Yeah?"

"What's gonna happen to us?"

He shrugged. "Life," he said. "Life's gonna happen to us. Just like everybody else."

"Like everybody else? I'm not sure I would know what that is. I've been aiming for medical school, Dad. Should I forget about that? Should I start looking for a job, too?"

"Don't you have to go to a regular college first?"

She didn't answer that, she just glared at him.

"Look," he said, "don't worry about the money. You worry about getting in. I can pay for school."

She sucked in a big breath, held it, blew it out. "This has to happen regular, Dad. You know what I mean? Normal, like everyone else. I don't want you visiting the dean of students with a baseball bat."

"I don't know what you're talking about."

She gave him a look. "Oh, please. Sometimes I feel like my whole life fell off the back of a truck."

"Count your blessings," he said. "I been feeling like the truck fell on me."

They walked the long avenue blocks across Fourteenth Street to Union Square. She'd gone quiet on him, and he let her brood. He'd never been much of a conversationalist, and he found himself wondering if he ought to bring her down to see Fat Tommy, just so they wouldn't have this silence hanging between them. He didn't have to, though, he could sense that she had something on her mind, that she was working her way around to it, getting ready to tell him. It was an ungenerous thought, but he figured she was going to ask him for money. Why would she come, otherwise? It's a long trip from the New

Jersey burbs into Manhattan, and she was just a kid. Would she do it just to say hello? Just to get him talking to Donna again? But you compare everyone else to yourself, he thought. Maybe she feels something for you, maybe she's not dead inside, maybe she's not as big an asshole as you.

They stopped to watch the skateboard kids working on their moves on the steps of the park in the middle of Union Square.

"Dad?" she said. She hated to do it, he could tell. "I have to ask you a favor."

"Okay." He watched the muscles in her jaw working.

"You have to promise me you won't do anything to him, okay? But I want you to check out this guy, Mom's friend, Mr. Prior."

"What do you want to know about him?"

She shook her head. "There's something funny about the guy, Dad. He's got a weird way of looking at me, and I don't like it. It's not just like leering, either. There's something wrong with the way he stares. I mean, I sort of expect middle-aged guys to look, and everything, but this guy is not about just looking. And Mom is such an idiot right now, pardon me for saying it, but I mean . . ."

She had been right to be so careful, making him promise not to touch Prior. He didn't want to lose her, and he didn't want to give Donna yet another reason to hate him, but . . . "What?"

She looked away from him. "She's got her head up her ass, okay? Somebody wants to be her new best friend, all they have to do is smile at her, for God's sake. I mean, she's so much smarter than this, I knew this guy was a creep the first time I saw him, okay, and I learned how to do that from her, but right now she can't see it. If you give me something on the guy, I can probably get her away from him. But you have to promise me you'll let me do this. She won't listen to you right now. Okay? And you have to be careful."

"Careful of what?"

"Mr. Prior is connected. I asked around a little bit, and I was told he knows all the cops in town, he gives money to all the local politicians, his lawyer is some big shot in the county government." She looked up at him, took a piece of paper out of her pocket, and gave it to Stoney. It had Prior's name and address written on it. The town was Alpine, New Jersey, more of an enclave than a town, a haven for rich people who valued their privacy. He looked up from the paper at his daughter. She opened her mouth to say something, then shut it again.

"What?"

"I don't want to say it," she said, her voice small.

"No, go on."

He watched her thinking it over. "I'm sorry, Dad. I'm sorry for how this is gonna sound, okay, but you're the only person I know who's a mean enough bastard to take this guy on."

He laughed.

"I said I was sorry."

"You know," he said, "my sponsor, Benny, he says I have to change. Can't be what I was anymore or I'll go back to drinking again."

"Maybe," she said. "But do this for me first, all right? Then get better."

He laughed again, threw his head back, and let it go. She looked at him, appraisal in her eyes. "You're different already," she said. "Listen, I'm sorry I compared you to the Doberman down the block."

"That's all right," he said. "Even bad dogs have their uses."

He saw a flash of white teeth then, an actual smile, but it was quickly replaced with a fierce scowl. "Dad?"

"Yeah?"

"Mom's having a graduation party for me next week. Will you come?"

"You want me to?"

She nodded at him without changing her expression. She didn't seem happy, and he began to feel like a guy invited to his own hanging. "All right," he said. "Sure."

It was a lonelier place when he got back to the apartment. He couldn't remember feeling that way about it since he'd moved in. Another one, he thought, another new sensation I can't quite identify. He'd gotten used to not feeling much of anything at all, unless you counted the sudden rage that enveloped him when his temper snapped, and now he didn't know what to do with these resurrected emotions. They had been dead for so long he'd forgotten all about them. Since he'd been sober, though, they'd come raging back to life and they would roar through his head like some new disease to which he had no natural immunity. There seemed to be no medium for him; no mild euphoria, no slight depression. Benny had warned him that this would happen, but knowing it was no defense. His moods seesawed madly between idiotic heights of exhilaration and black depths of suicidal despair. I should be used to this, he thought, I ought to have expected it. He hadn't, though. It had been so good to see his daughter, pissed off or not, and now that she was gone, Mrs. Cho's studio, where he was living, seemed colder and meaner than he could remember it ever being. He stared at the mute television set. He had an urge to turn it on, if only to fill the empty space with human sounds. He sat there looking at it, and it stared back with its blank gray face. He couldn't muster up enough interest to get up out of his chair and go look for the remote.

The telephone was right next to him, so he picked it up and punched in Benny's number. He knew almost immediately that Benny wasn't home, because Benny was an old-fashioned guy, he didn't have voice mail or an answering machine, Benny either picked up the phone or he didn't, and in this case he didn't. Stoney counted six rings, and then two more just in case Benny was in the bathroom, but there was still no answer.

TWO

Seeing Stoney made Tommy Rosselli feel old. It wasn't Tommy's fault, he'd been shot in a robbery the previous year and he was still recovering. The doctors who had saved his life had taken a bullet out of his back, but there was another one still in there, lodged too close to the spine for the doctors to remove. A third one had hit him high in the back of his shoulder and passed on through, and now the healing exit wound was an angry red and white puckered scar that he didn't like looking at. On cold days he swore he could feel the bullet that was still in him, dull and heavy with the malice of the man who had put it there. The thought of it made him feel tired, discouraged, disappointed. It was hard for him to take, because Tommy had always been a man who embraced life, even in the midst of trouble and strife he found things to savor in almost every experience that passed his way. Fat Tommy Rosselli was a man who loved, in no particular order, young women, Dame Joan Sutherland, fine food, fat women, Luciano Pavarotti, good wine, middle-aged women, expensive cars, the company of competent men, women with gray hair who still knew how to take care of themselves. Thin women made him nervous, as did the concept of denying oneself until the very shape of one's body was changed.

This thing with the bullet was different, though, and even though the constant ache was more of an annoyance than a real pain, it reminded him of his own fragility. The pills the doctor prescribed for him eased his discomfort but they also dulled his mind, and so he didn't like to take them.

Stoney, his partner, was not a source of sympathy. "You gotta get out and walk around, you fat fuck. It's summertime, for chrissake, you stay up in that loft much longer, the cleaning lady is gonna put you on her list of shit that gets dusted once a month." Stoney was right, of course, though it would not have killed him to show a little bit of human feeling. Understanding. He'd never do it, though. Stoney had changed, somewhat, since he'd put down the booze and the dope, but he hadn't changed that much.

Tommy had the cabdriver let him out around the corner from his destination. Another useless subterfuge, because Stoney knew him too well to ever believe that Tommy would be out walking, following his doctor's orders without someone yelling at him first. He did it anyway, tipped the driver a five, and watched the guy drive away. He walked slowly to the corner, pausing to consider the image looking back at him from a store window.

He might be feeling down but he still looked good. He was wearing a new suit, Italian wool with a subtle pinstripe cut to fit his ample frame perfectly, gray silk collarless shirt. The shirt wasn't Italian, it had been made in Hong Kong. You can't have everything, though, and it was a good shirt nonetheless. He leaned on his cane and winked at his reflection. An extra-large Don Johnson, he thought. Very cool.

Stoney was sitting at a table in a sidewalk café on Seventh Avenue South, down in the Village, smoking a cigarette. New

York City's billionaire mayor didn't smoke, didn't like cigarette smoke or the people who produced it, and as a result you weren't supposed to light up anywhere except inside your own house or your own car, preferably with the windows rolled up. Stoney, however, didn't give a shit what the mayor liked, and he exhaled gray smoke out of his nose as he eyed Tommy making his unhurried way up the sidewalk. He kicked out a chair when Tommy got close.

"Good to see you out in the sun," he said. "Bet you forgot what it looked like."

Tommy puffed his chest out, tried to look insulted. "Every day," he said, "I take a lilla walk. Just like the doctore wasa tell me."

"Yeah, sure you do. You walk from your couch to your refrigerator. How you feeling?"

Tommy sat down, leaned his cane against the table, and straightened the creases in his trousers. "I gonna be okay," he said. "Just take time."

"You still taking those Percocets?"

Tommy shook his head. "I don't like," he said. "They makea me tire."

"That's too bad. My daughter came in to visit me yesterday."

"Marisa?" Tommy brightened. "How old is she now?"

"Seventeen."

"Oh my God, seventeen." Tommy shook his head. "You tell her, next time she gonna come see me. Seventeen, very danger to be seventeen. How she'sa do? She's okay with this thing between you and Donna?"

"I don't know." Stoney took a last drag on his cigarette, flicked it in the general direction of the gutter. "Marisa's not like her mother. You only get to see what she wants you to see."

"Smart girl," Tommy said, nodding his head. "Grown up now. Become a woman."

"I suppose. She says I should call Donna."

Tommy watched his friend's face, said nothing. He himself would have called long ago, he would have sent flowers, candy, singing telegrams, he would have campaigned, he'd have waged war to win his way back into her bed, but what worked for him might not work for Stoney. He knew that Stoney had not given up, though, because he did not yet have that melancholy and eviscerated look common to newly single men. Stoney just looked pissed off. He watched as Stoney reached for another cigarette. He wondered at the guy sometimes. For years, he had watched his friend drink, smoke, snort and generally abuse himself, and yet the bastard was in disgustingly good health. "So? You gonna call?"

Stoney stuck the new cigarette in his mouth and clicked it alive with a plastic lighter. "I guess I have to," he said. "I hate to do it, though, you know what I mean? She's just gonna rip me a new asshole all over again. I don't know how to get past that."

"Marisa must think she's ready," Tommy said. "Maybe worth a try, but you're right, too easy to scream at somebody onna phone. Phone isa no good." He thought about it for a minute. "In case it was me," he said, "I'ma send a car to get her. Bring her to meet me at a nice fancy restaurant. You know, flowers, music, wine . . ." He looked up at Stoney. "Wine for her. Water for you. But you know, nice, nice. She don't gonna yell at you too much inna nice place. Maybe then you could talk."

Stoney was nodding. "Good idea," he said. "Much better than calling."

The waiter came, looked disapprovingly at Stoney's cigarette, took their order. They both waited until the guy was out of earshot before resuming their conversation. "You smoke too much," Tommy said, happy to find some defect in Stoney to talk about. Stoney eyed him for a second, then shrugged.

"Yeah," he said. "I know. It's not so bad now, believe it or not. I cut down a lot. I was going nuts for a while, there, you know, crawling outta my own skin. Benny told me not to worry about it. 'One thing at a time,' he told me. Anyway, better to kill yourself with butts than with dope and alcohol, it's a much easier way to die. You don't lose everything first."

Tommy had never met Benny, but Stoney spoke of him often. He didn't know much about AA, but he knew that Benny was Stoney's AA rabbi, he was the guy who had taken Stoney under his wing, showed him the ropes. Tommy was naturally suspicious of new relationships and new confidences, but this AA thing Stoney was into seemed to be a vast improvement over the self-destructive, suicidal course he had been on before, so Tommy kept his misgivings to himself. He had made discreet inquiries when Stoney first told him about joining. Some of the cops watching over him in the hospital had been acquainted with AA, and they had given the program mixed reviews. "Yeah, sure," one cop told him. "They'll help him quit drinking, all right. But just be ready, 'cause he's gonna cut you loose. They won't let him hang with you no more." It hadn't happened yet, but Tommy was waiting and watching, observing the ongoing metamorphosis in his friend. Tommy was a keen student of human behavior and a master of the art of subtle manipulation, but this new aspect of Stoney's personality continued to surprise him. "Maybe you gonna quit next year?"

Stoney shrugged. "Yeah, maybe. Listen, I need your help with something. I need somebody to check out a guy over in

Jersey for me, somebody good. You know a guy?" He handed
Tommy a card with a name and an address written on it.

Tommy read the name off the card. "Charles David Prior,"
he said. "Alpine, New Jersey. Okay. No problem. I gonna
check." He left his questions unasked.

Stoney stared out into the street. "Town the guy lives in is
like Beverly Hills East, serious money. Real serious."

A rich guy, Tommy thought, and his predatory instincts
were aroused, but he gave no sign of it. He did wonder,
briefly, what Charles David Prior had done to attract Stoney's
attention. "Okay. Don' worry, I think I know the right guy, he
gonna find out everything."

"Thanks, Tommy."

"De nada. You gonna meet with Donna?"

Stoney nodded. "I have to."

"Everything gonna be okay, you'll see. Just do me one
favor."

"Yeah? What's that?"

Fat Tommy wrinkled up his face in distaste. He gestured at
Stoney's clothes, filling the movement with contempt as only a
native-born Italian can. "Dress up, lilla bit. Try to look nice. Alla
time, blue jean, sweatshirt, sneaker. What's wrong with you?"

Stoney looked down at himself. "I don't even know if I got
a suit, Tommy. If I do, it's at the house."

Tommy shook his head. *"Minghe,"* he said. "After we
eat, I gonna take you to a nice tailor I know. You look like a
fucking bum." He paused. "You need my help with this other
sommanabitch, you gotta tell me."

"Fine."

THREE

It was just three in the afternoon, barely the beginning of the evening rush hour, but the cab Stoney was in got stuck in a traffic jam down in lower Manhattan. It was on Chambers Street, about four blocks from the Brooklyn Bridge, when Stoney ran out of patience and decided to walk the rest of the way.

There is a wooden walkway across the bridge, it runs high above the cars in between the two traffic lanes. It's about a mile across, and Stoney figured it might be another mile through Brooklyn Heights, the neighborhood on the far side, over to the building where Tuco lived. No reason not to walk, he thought, late spring day, warm, what the hell. Besides, he'd never done it before, might as well cross it off the list.

He had come to enjoy walking again during the months he'd been living back in the city, after all of those years in the Jersey suburbs. Not all New Yorkers do, though. Tommy Bagadonuts kept his car in a garage two blocks from his loft, and when he wasn't driving, he rode in cabs. Guy likes taking care of himself, Stoney thought, but his weight and health had begun to impose limitations on him that Stoney would not have been able to tolerate. It was frustrating, because Stoney was relatively sure that, if Tommy could just once experience how good it felt to be in shape, he would go nuts for it the way he went nuts for everything he liked. Fat Tommy was the kind of guy, if he liked opera, it wasn't enough to collect the CDs and go see it at Lincoln Center. He wasn't happy until he was sleeping with one of the singers. He'd brought a woman home shortly after Stoney moved in with him, a coloratura soprano, whatever that was, thirtyish, a bit heavy, but she had a nice shape and a gorgeous round face that broadcast rosy happiness. The two of them had rampaged through the loft like a pair of rutting Clydesdales. Jesus.

It was maddening, watching the fat son of a bitch limp around feeling sorry for himself, because Stoney could picture him after a couple of weeks in the gym, he'd have his own nutritionist, his own personal trainer, he'd buy every workout gizmo that he could find, and he would tear a swath through the sea of aerobics instructors like Sherman marching through Georgia. Tommy Bagadonuts rarely did anything at less than full throttle. Thus far, however, Stoney had not managed to get him interested.

He stopped right at the top of the arch, the midpoint between the two stone towers. From there he could see the tip of Manhattan on his right, the residential neighborhood of Brooklyn Heights on his left, Governors Island, low, green and improbably empty, close to the Brooklyn side. The Statue of Liberty was out on her island in the bay, and Staten Island and Jersey were off in the distance. He could feel the bridge vibrating under his feet, almost as though it moved in harmony with the heartbeat of the city. He became conscious of the low rumble, the collective undercurrent of the ceaseless human activity that was New York. He had never really noticed it before. I been unconscious, he thought. I been right here all along, but I missed everything.

• • •

Tuco was the superintendent of a five-story building on Clark Street in Brooklyn Heights. It was a nice gig, especially for a poorly educated Hispanic kid who was not yet twenty years old. It came with a one-bedroom apartment that was nicer than anyplace he'd ever lived before, even if it was in the basement. The work was easy, he could do it with half his brain tied behind his back. It's the best job you ever had, he told himself that for the umpteenth time. You could stay here for the rest of your life. . . . The very thought of that made him want to go up on the roof and throw himself off.

His friend Tommy Bagadonuts had gotten him the job, he'd introduced Tuco to Ms. McKinnon, the real estate agent who managed the building. The previous super had died, and they needed someone to mop the halls, take out the garbage, and so on. Tuco had been in need of a place to live, and it had seemed like a decent trade-off. A short time later, Tuco came into some money, and Fat Tommy had convinced him to keep the job and invest the money in real estate. Now Tuco owned a couple of co-op apartments in a building around the corner from where he lived. One of the initial problems had been that his windfall had come in the form of cash, but Tommy had winked at him, told him not to worry, everything would work out. Tuco didn't even think of the places often anymore, he didn't really have anything to do with them. Ms. McKinnon took care of renting them out, and rents came in, mortgage payments and management fees went out, all just numbers on a piece of paper. He couldn't read very well, but numbers, he had no problem with.

There was a couple that lived on the fourth floor of his building, and they'd caught his eye as soon as he moved in.

He'd been told by someone else in the place that the woman had just recently moved in with the man, but it seemed clear to Tuco that a victor had already been declared. The guy was thirtyish, he worked in international finance, and he seemed to have everything that marked a man as successful in Brooklyn Heights. He drove a late-model Volvo, traveled on business often, carried a PDA and a cell phone everywhere he went. He spoke several languages, wore exquisite clothing, beautiful shoes. His army, however, was in rout, his cannons spiked, his balls taken, held in escrow by his diminutive blond girlfriend. He smiled nervously in her presence, was solicitous of her well-being and state of mind, deferred to her opinions. You could almost watch the air leaking out of the guy, you could see him turning into a pale and flaccid imitation of what he had once been. Tuco wanted to shake the guy, yell at him. Run, you stupid bastard! Or else throw the bitch out. But it was no good, he knew that. The guy was in love. For her part, she exercised her authority firmly, but without a lot of unnecessary fireworks. Tuco had heard them argue a few times, but in each instance the firefight was brief, sharp, and followed by a strategic withdrawal on the part of the financier. When the guy brought his garbage downstairs, he would linger in the alley, lean back against the cool masonry wall, mop his forehead, close his eyes, but just for a minute or so. Then he would hurry back.

She, on the other hand, altered her regal pace for no man. It fell to her to take the garbage out when her financier was out of town, and it seemed that every time she did so, she went out of her way to find Tuco. He was in the habit of leaving his apartment door open, with just a screen between him and the common spaces when he was home, and she would rap on the door, call out his name, offer her comments on the repaint that he was doing on his living space. Each time it happened, Tuco would wonder, afterward, what it was he had been supposed to do, what cues he had missed, what it was that she really wanted from him. Tuco had always been intrigued by the ways in which people affiliated, how they attached themselves to this group or that, and in particular, how they paired themselves off into couples. Whether they got married or just lived together, whether they were straight, gay, or some combination of the two, their behaviors seemed, to him, remarkably uniform. The first phase of a relationship was love, or failing that, at least a period of unwarranted optimism during which they tried hard to ignore the other person's flaws, because they had their own, after all. Didn't they? But that initial promise rarely lasted. You could watch it decay, if you were around them long enough. This one liked Leno, the other preferred Letterman. He wanted a new Acura, she would rather spend the money on plastic surgery and European holidays. The contest of wills signaled the end of the first phase, and the beginning of the struggle for supremacy that would last, generally, until there was a clear winner. And a clear loser. If the couple stayed together after that, you could always tell which was which. The winner became a bit louder, a bit more confident of their opinions, while the loser, by degrees, surrendered their capacity for independent thought, their personality withered, faded away until they became a poor and dog-eared carbon copy of their dominant partner, to whom they began to look for opinions, ideas, desires, and ultimately, permission to be.

When he pressed himself for examples of what he thought a healthy relationship might look like, he could not think of any. It was discouraging, because he wanted to fall in love, he wanted that mad infatuation, that ecstatic high, but he could not abide the thought of the battle for control that seemed inevitably to follow. He emphatically did not want to be responsible for some other person's life, he could barely manage to be responsible for his own. On the other hand, he didn't know how much of himself he was willing to surrender in order to gain someone else's conditional approval.

In the first week of the fourth month of his tenure as superintendant, she had come to him with a problem. Her financier was in Singapore, and therefore unavailable. The thingy in the tank part of the toilet must be broken, because the water would not stop running. She didn't like to bother anybody, normally she would wait, but the noise was making her nuts, she couldn't sleep. Did he know anybody? Or could he, by chance, fix it for her himself? He would be such a lifesaver. . . .

She was a white girl. Technically she was no longer a girl, but she had flawless skin, and she spoke in a junior-high-school voice which fostered the impression, so that's how he thought of her. Five foot four or so, with breasts that seemed a bit large for her thin frame. There was something about her lips, too, they may not have been precisely what God had given her, but Tuco didn't really know much about such things, and she looked fine, either way. "Yeah, I can probably fix it," he said. He had a closet full of repair parts, left over from the previous administration. "Would you like me to come have a look?"

"Oh, that would be great," she said. She started in on him during the elevator ride upstairs. "So, Tuco," she said. "Tell me about yourself."

It was the question he hated most in life. It wasn't what she really wanted to know, he was sure of that, it was just the opening step in a verbal ritual dance that would continue until she had him pigeonholed. She wouldn't be direct, either, it would be, "What kind of work do you do?" and "Where do you come from?" and "What kind of music do you listen to?" In the part of Brooklyn where he had grown up, your physical stature and your reputation for toughness went a long way in establishing your manhood, and he had grown comfortable with himself, measured by those standards. In Brooklyn Heights, though, what they really wanted to know was how much money you had, and how you had gotten it.

"I'm the super," he told her. That was the first answer his brain handed him, along with a tickle of self-loathing, every time the subject came up. I'm a custodian. I mop floors, I coax that ancient boiler to send you heat, I brought the garbage out to the curb. There were other things he could say. He was a mechanic, and a gifted one at that, he was an investor, he was a student in search of a teacher. And when he worked with Fat Tommy and Stoney, he was a liar, a thief, and a con artist. Any of those answers were true, but his mouth did not seem to want to form the words that would make him look better in her eyes.

He didn't understand why he felt ashamed. He made a nice living, he sent a few bucks home to his mother, what was wrong with that? The problem was, he knew that he had potential, he just didn't know how to unlock it, so he condemned himself to loser status. A custodian in a neighborhood of stockbrokers and lawyers. Short-dick motherfucker . . . It seemed that everyone else could unzip and lay it out there. "Hey, kid, look at this. You see this? This is a man, by God . . ." And he was just a boy.

"I know that, silly," she said, reaching out, touching him on the shoulder. "It says so right on your doorbell. But you only do that to pay the bills." The elevator reached her floor, the doors opened, and she preceded him out and down the hall. She stuck her key in her front door. "This isn't what you do for your spirit," she said.

"I suppose not," he said. "What do you do, for your spirit?"

She turned, looked at him over her shoulder, grinned. "Come on inside," she said. "You want a beer?"

He never got an answer to his question.

He didn't think of it until later, how odd it was that a woman could have such large breasts and yet be so thin you could count her ribs. He found her tan lines incredibly sexy, though, he'd never seen such a thing before. He tried to apologize after he came the first time. "You young guys," she told him. "You're always in such a hurry." She held him there, kept him occupied until he came back to life, then she showed him things he had never dreamed of. It was like being in the hands of an accomplished mechanic, a technician who knew how to coax every last ounce of torque out of an engine. Tuco was nothing if not a student, he dropped his inhibitions on her floor next to his clothes and dived in. She did not, however, give up on her attempts to classify him, she would choose what seemed like the most inopportune moments to stop what the two of them were doing to ask him another question. "I should have put some music on," she said, at one such time, holding him in a disbelieving state of suspended animation. "What kind of music do you like?"

He held on, reeling. "Don't need music," he croaked. She laughed that teenage laugh of hers, and then she posed, a little bit, lay back on her pillows, looking like an adolescent's wet dream, before she continued. She left no doubt in his mind, though, who was driving, and who was the passenger.

She didn't bother to get dressed, afterward, she strolled naked into her kitchen for two more beers while he put on his clothes. She handed him one when she got back. "You can fix the water some other time," she told him, and laughed her schoolgirl laugh. "Give me a couple of days to recover."

"All right," he said.

"I'll call you," she said, walking him out to the front door. "I'll let you know when to come back."

"Okay," he said, wishing he could think of something else to say to her, but he could not. She let him out, closed the door behind him. All in all, a nice friendly fuck, he thought, waiting for the elevator. Still, he felt strangely unsettled. Are you crazy, he asked himself, what's wrong with you? What more could anybody ask for? But it seemed like there ought to be more to it.

"It ain't like it's a bad job or nothing." Tuco and Stoney walked down the slate sidewalk, past the brownstones and carriage houses of Brooklyn Heights. Stoney looked thinner than Tuco remembered him, and his face was different, too, but he was still big, still intimidating. Tuco always thought of him as looking like a guy who had a toothache and was pissed off about it. Something is happening to him, he's different now, Tuco thought. He'd known it for sure as soon as Stoney told him he preferred walking to sitting. "I mean, it ain't any work to speak of, especially in the summer. Couple more months, there won't be no boiler to run, half the people in the building will have went off to the Hamptons for the summer. It's really nothing, all I gotta do is take the trash out, mop the hallway once in a while. And for that, I get a free place to live in a nice neighborhood. They even pay me a few bucks. I know I oughta be happy with that."

"So? You bored?"

"Stoney, I keep thinking like there's something else I'm supposed to be doing, and I don't know what it is."

"Yeah? What are you doing about it?"

The question surprised him. I suppose, he thought, it is up to me. "Nothing," he said.

"Why not?"

"I don't know what to do."

"Well, that's a problem. Don't feel bad, you ain't alone. There's a lot of people walking around, don't know what they wanna be when they grow up. Lotta people die without ever figuring it out."

"Serious?"

"Yeah. Ain't life a bitch?"

"You been a big help, you know that?"

"Look, what are you, nineteen? You're still just a kid. Lotta directions you could go in. All you gotta do is figure out what it is that you like, okay? Once you find something that winds your clock, then you find out what the process is, how you get from where you're at to where you wanna go. You break that process down into steps, you start taking the steps one at a time. You don't give up and you don't die, sooner or later you'll get there."

"Yeah, but I got this other problem."

"What's that?"

"Dyslexia. It makes it hard for me to read. I don't see what everybody else sees when they look at a newspaper."

Stoney did not look surprised. "So?"

Tuco's stomach was churning. He knew better than to expect sympathy from Stoney, but he had expected compassion. "It makes things more hard. It means there's a lot of stuff I can't do."

"Look, kid, everybody's got something. Everybody's got some kinda monkey on his back. Look at it this way: this thing you got, at least you know what it is, right? It's got a name, you could look it up in the dictionary."

"Maybe you could."

"Whatever. But it's in there, ain't it?"

"So what if it is?"

"Well, if it's in the dictionary already, then you ain't the first motherfucker to get it, are you?"

Tuco blinked. "No," he said.

"Fine. So somewhere, somebody's working with you assholes that have this thing. You get me? Someone, somewhere, can show you how to work with it. All you gotta do is find the guy."

"How the hell do I do that?"

"Easy. You ask for help." He looked over at Tuco's face, saw the doubt there. "Although," he said, "asking for help used to be the hardest thing in the world for me to do. I had to pick something up, right, I would rather break my back than ask you to help me. I don't know why that is, but I would strain until my dick fell off and my balls ran down my pant leg before I asked somebody to give me a hand. Now, my problems are different from yours, okay, but I wasn't asking anybody for anything. Fuck you, I'm fine, maybe I got blood coming out of every orifice in my body, okay, but I can handle my own shit. That's what I thought. It was just through sheer stupid fucking luck I ran into a guy who had the answer I needed." They walked on in silence for a half a block, and Tuco began to think Stoney was done, but he wasn't. "I tell you what," Stoney finally said. "I'll talk to Tommy about it. You know Tommy, if he don't know the right guy, he knows somebody who does." He looked over at Tuco. "Once you find the right guy, ninety-nine times out of a hundred, he's happy to help you. Sometimes, you even find out he was waiting for you. You get me?"

Tuco wasn't sure what to say to that. What Stoney said might be true, but it ran counter to his experience. In his lifetime, Stoney and Fat Tommy were just about the only guys he could remember who had showed any interest in helping him at all. "All right," he said, feeling the butterflies in his stomach. "Thanks."

"You taking care of my car like I asked you?"

"Yeah, 'course. I told you before, it's in a parking garage over on Henry Street."

"You had it out lately?"

"Couple of weeks ago, I took it for a ride out on the Island."

"Okay. I guess it ought to start, then. I gotta borrow it for a few days."

"You get your license back? You want me to drive you?"

"I didn't exactly get it back. What I got is a new one. I found the right guy, he works at a New York State Motor Vehicles place up in the Bronx. He fixed me up. What I gotta do, I got this thing I gotta do over in Jersey."

"You need a hand?"

Stoney shook his head. "Not right now. There's this guy I gotta check out, but I don't know what I'm gonna do with him yet. It ain't business, anyhow, it's personal."

"Whatever," Tuco said. "You need me, you just yell."

"All right," Stoney said. "I'll get back to you."

FOUR

It was a strange sensation, driving again after all the months of walking. The only cars he had been in for ages had been taxicabs, and they were usually beat. Plus, it's different, being the driver instead of the passenger. A thought struck him, and he pulled the Lexus over to the side of the road and got out, reached down underneath the driver's seat and felt around. It seemed like a previous life, but not that long ago he had kept a pint bottle of scotch under there. It was gone, though, along with the accumulation of trash that had been in the back, last time he saw the car. Tuco, in his intensely serious way, must have cleaned it all out. The car looked clean, too, and Stoney could not remember ever washing the thing. The kid probably changed the oil, too, Stoney thought. And paid for the garage. Be just like him. I'll have to remember to ask what I owe him.

He got back in the car, drove to the on-ramp to the Brooklyn Bridge, looked at the wall of traffic. Ain't nothing for it, he told himself, go on and get in line. What's your hurry, anyhow?

It took about an hour and a half to get to Jersey. He felt like he hadn't been out of the city in ages, he'd almost forgotten what New Jersey looked like. He thought back to when he and Donna had first moved out. All he'd known about the

place then was what you saw when you drove out of the
Lincoln Tunnel and headed for Newark Airport: it had been an
otherworldly landscape, a ruined canyon of polluted marshes,
empty warehouses, oil refineries, and power plants, nothing but
a stinking industrial desert that could not have looked more
devastated if you dropped an atomic bomb on the fucking place.
He knew better now, though. Cross the George Washington
Bridge, get off the highway and into the little towns, and you
felt like you were on another planet, quiet streets, green grass,
trees, houses with lawns and hedges all around, whitetail deer
eating your wife's plants. Just like your house, he told himself.
Just like the one Donna threw you out of.

It took fifteen minutes, driving through the local streets,
before he found the address in the town of Alpine for Charles
David Prior. It was an enormous old mansion, set well back in
the woods off Route 9W, a two-lane state road that paralleled
the Palisades Parkway. There were no other houses in sight,
just trees, with an iron perimeter fence up next to the road.
The driveway to the place ran between two stone pillars that
buttressed an iron gate, back to a two-story carriage house that
had room for at least four cars. The house beyond was a stone
and timber monstrosity of the kind rich people sometimes erect
for themselves, simple materials and a rustic style taken to such
heights that the building almost became a parody of itself. This
guy isn't just wealthy, Stoney thought, he's beyond that. The
dude has to be filthy. Forget what the house is worth, Stoney
thought, the land alone must be worth millions. This guy is ten
minutes from the bridge, but the son of a bitch has as much
privacy as if he were living in the middle of a wilderness. There
were no cars or people in sight behind the fence, nothing to be
gained by sitting there looking. Stoney drove on past.

Past the fence that marked the end of Prior's property, a tract of undeveloped forest ran for about a half mile before he got to the next sign of human habitation. It was a small development of nearly identical houses, accessed by a short street just off the main road. They were McMansions, two-story stucco fashion statements with two-car garages attached, separated from the street and from one another by smallish, improbably green carpets of manicured grass. Stoney turned in, pulled over in front of one which had a "For Sale" sign in the middle of its front lawn. He got out, walked up to the front door, and rang the bell. There was no answer, the place was empty. It had no curtains in the windows, no furniture inside. The house is probably worth a couple million, he thought, but who the hell would want to live in it? There were houses just like it, springing up all over Jersey. They were built out of sheet metal two-by-fours, fabricated floor trusses instead of wooden beams and rafters, vinyl windows, veneer floors. Even the stucco was phony, it was a plastic compound made to look like the real thing, applied over an exterior of foam insulation. The place might look like a stone castle from the street, but you could probably kick your way through the wall if you wanted to. Nothing about it was real, none of it looked like what it really was.

He looked around the micro-neighborhood. There were no signs of life, no trikes in the driveways, no cars outside, no children's toys on the lawns, not a human being in sight except for him. They're all at work, he told himself, they're paying the price it takes to live in this sterile place. Just what I'm looking for, he thought, a place where nothing has to mean anything, not really, it just has to appear as though it might. He walked back to his car, wrote down the real estate agent's name and phone number before driving away.

He spent the next hour cruising around the neighborhood, if you could call it that, looking for a road that might run behind Prior's house. He didn't find one, though, as close as he could make out, the woods ran down a long hill behind the place. There was a golf course at the bottom of the hill. There wasn't much else up on the hill, just a few other widely scattered houses, lots of trees, an empty field here and there. There was a plaque by the side of the road, halfway around a blind curve. Curious, Stoney found a place to park and walked back to read it. It told the story of Skunk Hollow, a pre–Civil War community of freed blacks, but it had been obliterated when the parkway was built. Robert Moses, let my people go. The plaque didn't say anything about what had happened to the denizens of Skunk Hollow when they put the road in.

It was getting dark. Stoney headed down the hill, out of Alpine and into Closter, the neighboring town where Donna and their children still lived. It was nowhere near as plush as Alpine, but it was still solidly upper-class white, populated by prosperous folks who favored Mercedes, Jaguars, hulking SUVs, and, yes, Lexuses. Donna had gotten him the car about a year ago. Stoney had figured that she was embarrassed by the old Pontiac he'd been driving. It hadn't bothered him, he didn't much care what his neighbors thought. He knew he had enough money socked away to buy all the Jaguars the local dealer had, so he hadn't needed one. Donna was different, though, she wanted to fit in. That's because she's become a part of all this, he thought. This is her world, this suburban wonderland, this quiet, green, forested place that lay a short commuter's bus ride from midtown Manhattan. This is what she is. You were never more than a foreigner. You only slept here.

He followed the streets automatically, his mind seemingly

on autopilot. What will you do if she sees you? he wondered. She would recognize the car, she's the one who bought it, after all. She'd know it was you from a mile away. Will you stop to talk to her, will you look at her, or will you pretend not to see her and drive away? He still hadn't come up with an answer when he turned down his street. There was no one outside, though. Most of the houses had lights on inside, including the one he had once lived in with Donna, but you couldn't see any of the occupants from the street. He wanted to stop but he did not, he continued on past, berating himself for his lack of courage. What are you afraid of, he wondered, what do you think she's gonna do to you? But she had more power to hurt him than anyone alive, she could stick a knife through his heart with just a look. He got to the end of the block, pulled a U-turn, went back on past. Donna, he thought, Donna . . . God, he missed her. It made him despise himself all the more for what he was going to do. You wouldn't, if you really loved her, he told himself. You'd go sit down with her, ask her what she really wanted. And if her answer really is this guy Prior, you should turn your back and walk away, leave her to him.

Still, the primitive in him was strong enough to know that they had better not ever let him see the two of them together. And Donna would know that, too.

The guy was waiting right where Fat Tommy said he would be, in a chrome-and-glass diner in Westwood, New Jersey. It was one of those places that never close. The P.I. was just a kid, tall, skinny, zits on his face. His skin was pasty white, like he never went out in the daylight, and he had large gnarly hands with fingernails chewed all the way down. If he found it strange to meet Stoney at this place on such short notice, he did not

show it. They took a table in the back room. The waiter left a
pair of menus on the table. Stoney paged through it while the
kid opposite fidgeted. They had everything, at least in theory,
steak and lobster, Greek and Italian, burgers and a salad bar,
breakfast all day and all night. When the waiter came back,
Stoney handed him a ten. "Two coffees," he said. The waiter
nodded, took the menus, and departed.

Stoney looked over at the kid, watched him for a minute.
"Friend of mine told me you're good," he finally said. "Says
you do good work and you know how to keep your mouth
shut." The kid nodded nervously and said nothing. It's no
wonder he's afraid, Stoney thought. He knew that he had been
unable to keep the pain and rage off his face. The waiter came
back with the coffees.

"What can I do for you?" the kid said, after the waiter left.

"Two things," Stoney said. "One, this guy Charles David
Prior, lives up on the hill in Alpine. I wanna know who he is,
what he does, where he came from."

"Sure, okay," the kid said. "Gimme a day, two at the most.
What's the other thing?"

Stoney looked at the cup in front of him. He didn't want
to taste what was in it, he was already filled with acid. He didn't
even want to smell it. "I want you to follow my wife." He
hated himself for saying it. He could feel the tension building
inside, he felt like ripping the table off the wall and flinging it
across the room.

"All right." The kid spoke in a soft voice, looked away, out
through the open doorway into the main part of the diner.
"Do you want the full treatment?"

"What's that?"

"Well, it starts with round-the-clock surveillance. I can

drop some spyware on your computer if you want, it'll record every keystroke anyone makes on it, e-mail, Web surfing, the works. I can tap your phones, too. If your name's on the deed, it's legal but probably not admissible in court."

Stoney's breath felt like it was burning his nose as he exhaled. "We're not going to fucking court," he said. "All right. Do the phone and the computer. You don't need to stay on her all night, she's generally had it by ten-thirty. She gets going early, though."

"All right. Do you need pictures? I mean, if I find something. You said you weren't going to court, but . . ."

There's no clean way to do this, Stoney thought, you drop something in the toilet, you can't get it back without getting slimed. What a fucking life. "Yeah," he said. "Just so there's no questions. Time-stamped, I guess." He felt like he needed to take a shower.

The kid looked away again. "All right," he said.

"Just make fucking sure," Stoney said, staring straight at him. "You understand me?"

"Yes, sir." He cleared his throat. "You got a name? I mean, the guy you think is, ahh . . ."

"Yeah, I got a fucking name, but I don't want to give it to you. You just tell me what you find."

The kid shrugged. "Okay by me."

"You need a key?"

"Huh?" He looked at Stoney blankly.

"To my house."

"What? Oh, for the phone and all. No, sir, I don't need to go anywhere near your house."

"You're kidding me. How do you do it?"

"At the phone-company switching station. I'll just call in

like a regular phone-company lineman would. You just need to know the nomenclature."

"I see. Well, that's it, then."

"Ah, yeah, except, um, you gotta pay me a retainer, and you gotta tell me how long, you know . . ."

Stoney nodded. "Gimme a week," he said. They worked out the finances. Stoney paid the kid in cash, and the kid folded the bills up in his big hand and stuck them in his pocket.

FIVE

Benny was a short guy, he had to take two steps for every one of Stoney's just to keep up. He never looked as though he minded, though, because Benny was one of those guys who seemed to have more energy than everyone else. His eyes were never still, he seemed to devour the landscape as he walked through it, he was like a man who'd been in prison for a long time, with nothing to look at but concrete walls. Stoney had the feeling that it wasn't the walking Benny loved, it was the spectacle and the splendor of ordinary life as it played out on the Manhattan sidewalks. "How'd it go?" Benny said. "How'd it go with your daughter?"

"I guess it went all right," Stoney said. He wondered how much of it he should tell Benny. Benny didn't have the attention span for long, complicated stories. He decided to omit the stuff about the investigator he'd hired, and about Charles David Prior. "She was a little torqued off at me, at first, but I think we did okay anyhow. She wants me to call up Donna, help her out with some financial shit. Fat Tommy says, instead of calling, I should surprise her, you know, send a limo to pick her up and bring her to a fancy restaurant, you know, dinner, flowers, and like that. Romantic. Put her in a better mood."

"Set her up, you mean."

"Yeah. All right, basically, set her up. Play her."

"She's not a mark," Benny said. "Why be so underhanded? I don't understand what all the subterfuge is gonna get you."

"Subterfuge is one of my best things," Stoney told him.

"Yeah? How's it working so far?"

Stoney shook his head. "I see your point, at least as far as dealing with Donna is concerned. But I'm telling you, Benny, last time I talked to her, she wanted to bite my head off. I don't wanna do anything to make it worse. Fat Tommy thought . . ."

"Fat Tommy's your partner, right?"

"Yeah. He's known Donna for years. He thought it might be better if I met her in a public place, somewhere she's gotta dress up to go, you know, fancy. That's Fat Tommy's style. Champagne, music, all that shit."

"Stoney, you can't scam your way out of this. If Donna is pissed off at you, she's gonna want to have her say, and all of this bullshit manipulation is just your way of cheating her out of it. You could buy her a diamond ring or something, right, it's not gonna change what she really feels, and sooner or later you're gonna have to hear about it anyhow. Why not just get it over with?"

They reached the Greek coffee shop on Twenty-third Street that was their normal meeting place. It took a minute for them to get inside and seated. Stoney waited until the waiter had taken their order and gone away. "So you think I should just call her, right?"

Benny shrugged. "I would. I don't think it helps to try and weasel your way out of things. Call her, meet her someplace if you want, let her have her say. The best thing you can do here is be a stand-up guy, let her know you're trying to do the right thing."

"Jesus, Benny, she's never gonna believe something like that." The two of them laughed, and Benny eyed Stoney, shaking his head.

"You are some piece of fucking work," he said.

Benny had taken him to a meeting up in the Bronx, and it was ten-thirty by the time Stoney got back to his apartment. He went inside and sat on the couch in the dark. Outside on Twelfth Street things were gearing up, the night creatures were coming out. There had been a conflict brewing on the stoop of his building when he'd gotten there, he'd had to shoulder his way past two women who were having a loud disagreement over something. Each of them had the support of a couple of friends, and from the sound of it, the backers were now joining in. Stoney had not understood the mixture of Spanish and English they had been arguing in, and he didn't care what it was about anyhow. The confrontation on the stoop was escalating, though, growing steadily louder. The problem was, it was an odds-on favorite that at least one asshole in the crowd carried a gun, and pretty soon they were going to use it, Stoney could feel it coming. That would probably mean that the cops would be around for a day or so, asking questions, and who needed that? He got up and fished the trash can out of the broom closet, removed the plastic bag and its contents, and set them to one side. He filled the empty bucket with cold water from the bathtub. About six gallons, he figured. He carried the bucket to the front window, opened it, and dumped the water out into the night air.

They had been hard to miss, hanging on the steps directly below his window, and the noise they had been making was nothing compared to what erupted when the water hit. Stoney closed the window and sat back down, laughing silently, listening to people screaming invective at the front of the building. At least now they had a common opponent. After another fifteen minutes of empty threats and curses, they seemed to tire of it. Five minutes later, they were gone.

He went back to rehearsing what he would say to Donna. He'd been doing it, on and off, ever since he'd had the visit from Marisa. He knew what Benny would say: "Don't have conversations with people who ain't in the room with you." It was a futile exercise anyhow, because who the hell could tell what kind of mood he'd catch her in, she might say anything at all. He'd built it up in his mind, though, knowing, even as he did it, that he was making it harder and harder for himself to make the call.

Coward, he told himself. You're afraid of her.

"Fuck it," he said, and he picked up the phone and called his home number. He listened to it ring four times, then five. He breathed a sigh of relief, prepared to hang up. She answered it, though, just as he'd been about to put the phone down.

"Hello?"

She sounded tired. He felt like a teenager, tongue-tied, afraid to ask the girl next door out on a date. "Hello," he said, and he could hear the fear in his own voice. He hoped that she couldn't. "Hiyadoin'?"

She exhaled into the phone once, twice. He waited, silent. Then he thought, Maybe she doesn't recognize you. . . . "Donna?"

"Yeah," she said. "Hello, Stoney."

"I'm sorry," he said. "I know you told me not to call, but I wanted to hear your voice."

"I shouldn't have said that," she said. "I'm glad you called. I mean, I guess I am. I was pretty nasty, last time."

"That's okay—"

"No, it's not," she said, cutting him off. "I just get so mad at you sometimes, and then I say things I don't mean, and I have to go around feeling shitty over it."

He didn't know what to say to that, so he kept his mouth shut.

"How did we get to this, Stoney?"

"I don't know."

"I don't, either. Why is it, how could we have went for such a long time, we made it through all those years of craziness and nothing ever seemed to change, then you quit drinking and we fall apart? Can you tell me why that is?"

"I heard a story," he said. "Probably not true. Probably just one of those things that gets repeated over and over. But the story goes, you put a frog in a pan of water on your stove, you heat the water up very slowly, he won't notice it getting warmer. He'll sit there until he boils."

"Is that how it was? Things just kept getting worse, and I didn't see it?"

"I don't know," he said. "Maybe you didn't want to see it. Maybe you wanted to believe that everything was all right."

"Maybe I did," she said. "Are you working?"

He shook his head. She really had no idea, she couldn't, not if she was asking a question like that. He and Fat Tommy had been partners for years, using a succession of scams to prey on people who should have known better. In the shadowier, seedier neighborhoods of capitalism, far from the eyes of the law, a smart and ruthless person could make himself wealthy. "Vultures," that's what Fat Tommy called the two of them. Stoney didn't like the word, but maybe that's how it really was. He hated to think of himself that way, though.

He had considered talking to Benny about it a couple of times, but he hadn't been ready. And what the fuck would Benny know about it, anyway? Benny had been a plumbing inspector before he retired, a guy who went around making sure you got the hot water on the left and the cold water on the right, for chrissake. But that's not the way it worked. AA was a collective, a distillation of the hard-won experiences of a couple million desperate motherfuckers who had, beyond everything else, taken the hardest punches that life could throw at you, and had gotten back up again. You find the right guy in AA, he can save you oceans of grief. Find the wrong one, he'll cosign your bullshit, you both wind up dead. But Stoney was pretty sure Benny was the right guy. "If you're a thief," Benny had told him once, early on, "we'll make you a better one." Stoney always wondered how much the guy really knew.

Donna cleared her throat. "I had to get a job, you know." Stoney could hear the kernel of resentment in her voice. Donna had never been much interested in the particulars of Stoney's complex financial gerrymandering. She didn't know what the two of them had, how could she? Not if she had gotten a job. And what the hell did she know how to do, anyhow? He recognized that for an ungenerous thought, and he rephrased it carefully in his mind before giving it voice.

"Yeah? Doing what?"

"I'm a personal assistant." He could hear the mixture of defensiveness and pride in her voice. "For a judge. She needed someone to run her house for her."

"A judge? Are you shitting me?"

"What?" She was angry, insulted. "Do you think I'm so stupid that I can't—"

"No, no, no," he said, interrupting her. "Easy does it, okay?

I didn't mean that. It's just that, I mean, a judge? You sure go from one extreme to the other."

She didn't see the humor in it. "I had to do something, Stoney. The bills are piling up around here."

"I understand. We need to get together to talk about this, Donna. There are things we can't go into over the phone."

"Okay."

Jesus, was it going to be that easy? "I could meet you somewhere. . . ." You screwed up already, he told himself. You were supposed to have a place picked out ahead of time, with flowers and shit.

"Yeah . . ." She sounded doubtful.

"We'll meet at some restaurant in Closter. Say Monday night."

She thought it over for a few seconds. "All right. But not in Closter."

He tried to calm himself and keep his nervousness out of his voice. "All right. How about that steakhouse up on the river, just over the New York state line? What's the name of that town?"

"Piermont," she said. "All right, that's fine. Marisa's graduating soon, you know."

"Yeah, she told me."

"Marisa talked to you?"

He could hear it in her voice, Donna felt betrayed by her own daughter. That's twice you messed up, hasn't even been two minutes, he told himself. What's wrong with you? "Look," he said quickly, "maybe I shouldn't have said. Did I screw up by telling you? I don't want to get her in trouble with you." She didn't say anything, and he sat listening to the sound of her breathing. "Donna, gimme a break. Don't make this worse than it already is. Cover for me. Can you do that?"

"Stoney, this is so fucked up."

We can save it, babe, oh man, he ached to tell her that, but he was afraid to, he hesitated too long, and the opportunity was lost. "I'm doing the best I can."

"All right." She didn't sound like she believed him, she sounded like she had settled for what she could get instead of holding out for what she needed. "Anyhow, some of the other parents and I got together, we're going to throw a big graduation party for the kids. Maybe you should come." She told him the day and the time.

He didn't tell her that Marisa had invited him already. He felt a great weight lifting from his shoulders, though, and his spirit rose up, leaving him breathless, wordless, afraid to move. "I'll be there." He could sense her, silent, on the other end of the line, and he knew he should say something more but he had no idea what that something was.

"I'll see you later, then," she said. Waiting for him to say it, that elusive right thing.

"Okay. Talk to you Monday night. Call my cell number." He became afraid, then. Do I tell her that I love her, he wondered, or would that scare her away? Would it be presuming too much to say how much I miss her? Maybe she doesn't want to hear about that. Or that he saw her face a dozen times a day, superimposed on the women walking down the streets of the city, standing on a subway platform, dancing, once, at Kelleher's, naked as the day she was born. God, what a sight that had been, until the smells of beer and scotch had driven him out.

"Okay," she said. "Well, all right, then. Good-bye."

"Good-bye," he said, making no move to hang up. He listened to her, doing the same, for a few seconds, then he heard the click as she put the phone down.

SIX

Stoney had seen her a few times, going in and out of the apartment across the hall from his. The thing he noticed about her most of all was her condescending smile. Every time they passed in the hallway she would give him this look, like she knew something funny about him but had promised not to tell what it was. It was the kind of look that made you check the zipper on your pants, just in case. She could have passed for her late twenties, early thirties, but he really couldn't tell how old she was. The two of them had fallen into a sort of nodding acquaintance, hi, how are you. He didn't think she actually lived in the place, she usually left late at night, returned around noon the next day. He'd noticed a succession of male callers, mostly middle-aged white guys who wore suits and carried a little extra weight. She was quiet, though, and he supposed that it was none of his business how she made her living.

"Who was that girl I saw you with?" She had been coming down the hall, heading for her door just as he was leaving. It was the first time she'd ever asked him anything. There might have been an edge to her voice, but he hadn't spoken with her enough to be sure. "She looked awfully young."

"That was no girl," Stoney told her. "That was my daughter."

"Ah," she said, with what could have been relief. "I see. For a while, there, I thought you were one of those raincoat perverts."

"Not me," Stoney said. He noticed that she was wearing some kind of black eye makeup that went all the way around her eyes, the way young girls and Ozzy Osbourne were wearing it. "I may be a pervert, but I don't think I own a raincoat."

"Well, that's a relief," she said, and she flashed that patronizing smile of hers. She was wearing a tight white sweater that spoke volumes about the wonders hidden inside. Normally he would not have been affected, but it had been a long time. He turned and locked his door behind him.

"So you're divorced," she said, making it a question.

"No. Separated, I guess. You?"

"Oh, I'm single," she said. "Divorced two years ago, for the second time. I love men, but I just can't find one I can live with."

"Hah," Stoney said. "I saw this show on albatrosses the other night. They mate for life, right, but they're not up each other's ass all year long. They meet once for mating season, and to raise baby albatrosses. The rest of the year they leave each other the fuck alone."

She laughed. "Sounds like an intelligent system. That's probably why human beings can't do it that way. We have to make everything so goddamn complex. Wouldn't it be great if we could take the sentimental bull out of relationships? Just get together once in a while, give each other what we need. Let the rest of it slide." She had her door open, and she stood in the doorway. "I like the albatross thing, except for the once-a-year part." She smiled at him again, what the hell was it about that smile? "You gonna be around today?"

"No," he said. "I got something I gotta do out in Jersey."

"Too bad." She stepped inside. "Well, knock on my door sometime," she said, and she closed it, left him standing there in the hall, wondering.

When the realtor showed up, she looked pretty much how Stoney had imagined her. She was emphatically buxom, suspiciously blond, way past twenty-one. She had an Al Gore bumper sticker on the back of her Volvo 4X4. Stoney waited until she'd parked it in front of the McMansion's garage and got out before sauntering over and sticking out his hand. "You must be Ms. Garrett," he said. "I'm the guy who called you yesterday. Thanks for coming out."

"Oh, it's my pleasure," she said, and she shook his hand. "Shall we go inside and have a look around?"

"Absolutely," he said, and he looked past her, out across the short expanse of lawn to the edge of the woods. It was a half a mile, more or less, through those trees to the edge of Prior's property. It would take ten minutes of hard going to get from one to the other. Maybe twenty. A lot of things could happen in twenty minutes.

"Mr. Ross?" She was looking at him quizzically.

Was that the name he'd given her? "Ma'am?"

"Would you like to look inside?"

"Yes," he said. "Yes. I was just admiring the, ahh, forest, there. Still an amazing thing to a city kid like myself."

"Oh, it is beautiful," she gushed. "This property really is a rare opportunity. Not many houses up here on top of the hill come on the market, and there is no new development on the horizon. Not up here." She stepped up to the front door, stopped to wrestle with the lockbox hanging from the doorknob. It held the key to the front entrance.

"Anybody wants to build up here, spends ten years in court, I bet," he said.

"At least," she said. She got the key out and opened the door. "Believe me, it would take an act of God, at this point, to get approval to build anything new around here."

The front door opened into a soaring entryway. The room had a larger footprint than Stoney's entire apartment. It was open to the second floor, and semicircular stairways on either side of the room led to the upper level. A chandelier the size of a small automobile hung down in the center of the room. "Wow," Stoney said.

Ms. Garrett glanced at him, then up at the chandelier, cleared her throat. "Well, yes," she said. "Wow." Stoney got the impression that she did not want to render an opinion about the house, or even imply that she had one. Stands to reason, he thought. How many houses you gonna sell if you go around telling your customers they got no taste?

"There are closets all along this back wall," she said, her steps echoing as she walked across the empty room and pushed on a panel that sprang open to reveal one of the promised closets. It was as empty as the rest of the place. "Down this corridor," she said, pointing to her left, "is the gourmet kitchen. . . ."

There was, indeed, a gourmet kitchen, along with a butler's pantry, a breakfast nook, a formal dining room, a great room, a living room with a fireplace large enough to roast a pig in it, a study, an entertainment room, a laundry, maid's quarters, five bedrooms, and four bathrooms, not counting the one in the master suite. It also had a panic room in the basement, a steel-doored vault the size of a walk-in closet. The maker's name was posted on a metal tag affixed to the inside of the door. Stoney followed her from room to room, listened to her spiel without comment. Eventually they found their way back down to the kitchen.

"Well," she said. "What do you think?"

"Big house," he said.

"Yes," she said, somewhat uncertainly. "Yes, ahh, it is."

"Ms. Garrett, let me ask you something. You live in town?"

"Yes, I do." She stared at him. "I bet I have the smallest . . . I, ah, live in a small house, down near the Closter town line. Why do you ask?"

"You like Alpine?"

"Alpine is a treasure," she said. "I love it here."

"So you don't want to see it change," he said.

"I would hate to see it developed," she said. "You don't care for the house, do you?"

"Hate it," he told her. "The place is hideous. Can't imagine what kind of moron would want to live in it."

She fought off a smile. "So?"

He pointed out across the empty dining room, where the woods were visible through the glass sliding doors. "Can you imagine," he said, "about four hundred town houses just down over the hill, there? Imagine what that would do to this town. Not to mention the strain on the environment."

"That will never happen." She sounded, all of a sudden, a bit less sure of herself.

"That's gonna happen quicker than you think," he said. "You know the old saying 'A good lawyer knows the law, a great lawyer knows the judge.'"

She stared at him, openmouthed. "Do you know something I don't? There's no way . . ."

"This is New Jersey," he said. "We've gotten word that the fix is in."

"You have to be kidding. My God. How could this have happened?"

"You ever hear of a place called Skunk Hollow?"

"Well, I've seen the sign, but it's just a mile or so north of here. I have never stopped to read it. What does that have to do with—"

"We believe the sign is misplaced," he told her. "We believe that Skunk Hollow was right down there in those woods. I work for a very wealthy individual who holds the same opinions about development in this town that you do, Ms. Garrett. Now, briefly, not to bore you too much, Skunk Hollow was a pre–Civil War settlement of freed African-Americans. I think that archaeological evidence of that settlement must still exist on that property, but I have been unable to gain access, due to the developer's concerns about his project. In point of fact, I was threatened with arrest for trespass twice in the past month."

"Lord," she said. "Well, if they're smart, they'll bulldoze whatever's left before anybody sees it. And if you do find something, you'll have gained that knowledge unlawfully, won't you? You won't be able to use it in court."

He nodded. "They will destroy the evidence if they know what to look for. I don't know how much time I have left. And it doesn't matter whether it's been found legally or not, once it gets out that there's something historically significant on that property, we've won. The developer will be forced to sell to the state. Anyhow, now you understand my interest in this house."

"But . . . Surely you can't be serious. Would you actually buy this place, just to . . ." She gestured at the woods.

"My employer's generosity does have its limits," he said. "You still have this property under exclusive contract, am I right? If we were to compensate you for your forbearance, could you be persuaded not to show this house for, say, another week to ten days? Or is the market too hot for such a thing?"

"The top end of the market has plateaued," she said. "Yours is the first call I've gotten on the place. But what you're proposing is unethical and against the law. I would be acting contrary to the interests of the current owner."

"I understand," he said. "Can I ask you who the current owner is?" She looked at him, unsure. "I'm sure it's a matter of public record. You'd hardly be giving away state secrets."

"Sony," she said. "One of their executives owned it, and they took it off his hands when they transferred him back to Japan."

"Ahh," he said. "Well, that's a relief. All is not lost, corporate property managers are notoriously corrupt."

"Well, in that case," she said, and she cleared her throat. "How much are we talking about?"

"I can go ten thousand," he said. "In cash, of course. For a week." He nodded his head in the direction of the front door. "I came prepared," he said. "The money is out in my car."

"Lord have mercy," she said. "Here's the key. I'll give you two weeks. How's that? Is there anything else you need?"

"Yes," he said. "I'll need the garage door opener."

He stepped through the woods carefully, taking his time, doing his best to walk south in a straight line, which would keep him parallel to the road and the parkway beyond. The sound of the traffic was muffled, but steady and unceasing. Once out of sight of the McMansions, there was nothing to look at but the trees, the carpet of leaves under his feet, the occasional stone ledge shouldering its way up through the earth, a dead tree here and there, prone on the forest floor. Three times he crossed narrow trails that meandered across his path. Kids, he thought, coming into the woods to drink beer, but there were no empty beer cans anywhere, no footprints, and the trails were too narrow to have been made by a bunch of undisciplined humans. That's not the way we walk, he thought. We wander off the trail, we throw shit on the ground to let everyone know we've been here, empty bottles and candy wrappers and cigarette butts. He saw none of that. Deer, he thought, or coyotes. This part of New Jersey had plenty of both.

He stopped next to a giant elm. The tree was a monster, it completely dwarfed its neighbors. He stood there, leaning by one hand against the deeply ridged bark of the tree as he looked down the slope in front of him. There was a clearing about a hundred and fifty yards ahead. He could see the bright green of cultivated grass shining between the tree trunks, the glint of a galvanized metal chain-link fence. A dog sat just inside the fence, small in the distance, tan and dark brown, lean and hungry-looking. Doberman, he thought. The thing knows you're up here, and he wants a piece of you. . . . He moved forward carefully, slowly halving the distance between himself and the dog before finding a clump of bushes to hide behind.

The dog became agitated when Stoney dropped down out of sight. He stood up, pointed his snout skyward, and howled. *"Yourrrrr!"*

A moment later the Dobie was joined by another dog, similar in color but heavier. Probably a Rottweiler, Stoney thought. The second dog sniffed at the first, then lay down in the grass next to it. A moment later, two men showed up, probably guards. Stoney crouched, motionless, behind his bushes as one of them scoped the woods with a pair of binoculars.

"Anything?" The second guard's voice carried clearly up the hill.

"No."

"Stupid mutt. Probably some goddam turkeys again." He cuffed at the dog. "Get on back up to the house, you!"

The Doberman looked at the guard, trotted a few steps away, and yowled again. "G'wan, I said," the guard yelled. "Fuckin' pain in my ass. Get goin'." The guard with the glasses gave up, and the two men walked back in the direction they'd come from, followed by the Rottweiler. The Doberman was last, and he paused, turned and looked back at Stoney.

Yeah, Stoney thought. I see you, too.

He made his way back north again, came out of the woods almost exactly where he'd entered them. Halfway across the McMansion's backyard, he noticed a tick crawling up his forearm. He watched it negotiate the hairs on his skin, moving slowly and deliberately. After a few seconds, he flicked the thing off into the grass. Should have killed you, he thought. When he got back inside, he went into one of the bathrooms and examined himself carefully. He found one more, crawling resolutely up his sock. It didn't squash when he stepped on it, so he wound up flushing it instead. Friggin' bloodsuckers, he thought. You got to watch yourself every minute. . . .

SEVEN

Stoney stepped out of the elevator and into the front corner of Tommy Bagadonuts' loft. Straight ahead and to his left, a row of windows looked down on the narrow street, several floors below. To his right was the kitchen area, an island of cabinets, appliances, and countertops in the middle of a long narrow room. Beyond that lay the rest of the living spaces.

"Hello?" He craned his neck out, looked around. "Tommy?"

"Come on in." Tommy was in the office area at the other end of the loft, maybe forty feet away. He got up and hurried across the space between the two of them. Even at home, Stoney thought, the guy always looks well put together. Fat Tommy was wearing a hand-knit wool sweater that emphasized his height and minimized his girth, a carefully creased pair of gray slacks, Italian loafers. Stoney handed the flowers he was carrying to Fat Tommy.

"Where's your opera singer?"

"On tour," Tommy said, accepting the flowers, holding them out at arm's length, the better to admire them.

"She coming back?"

"'Oo knows," Tommy said, shrugging expansively. He carried the flowers over to his kitchen and rummaged around in a cabinet, fished out a clear glass vase about ten inches high. He filled it with water at the sink, put the flowers in it. He came back, set it down on the end of the counter, and fussed with the flowers until they were arranged to his satisfaction. "Don' worry," he said. "I gonna take a nice picture, senda to her the e-mail. Tell her you wasa think about her."

Stoney looked at him. "You got e-mail?"

Tommy drew back. "Yeah, I got e-mail. I wasa buy the compute, maybe two months ago. Tuco wasa come over, set up everything, show me how to use. I tol' you, very smart boy."

"Yeah, no kidding. Especially for a kid who couldn't read a year ago."

"He gonna be okay, Stoney." Fat Tommy tapped a thick finger against his temple. "Very smart boy. You an' me, we wasa do something good with him. You gotta see now, he figure his own way to do everything. Just needed, you know . . ." He looked at the ceiling, searching for the right English words.

"A little encouragement."

"Yeah," Tommy said. "*Exactamente.* You want a nice coffee?"

"Nah, that's all right."

Fat Tommy ignored Stoney's answer. "Hey, I gotta nice Italian roast. You gonna like." He busied himself measuring water, grinding beans, pouring cream into a little ceramic pitcher. "So? You calla you wife yet?"

"Yeah. We're supposed to meet at a steakhouse up by the Tap tomorrow night."

"Tappan Zee Bridge? Nicea place?"

"Yeah."

"Good. Don'a you worry, everything gonna come good."

"I hope you're right, Tommy, but I don't have your confidence. Donna's been in a pretty strange head ever since I quit drinking. I don't get it. I don't know if she's got too many birds on her antenna or what."

"Listen to me," Tommy said. "Everything different, all of a sudden. Everybody wasa worry about you. I know you stoppa to drink, stoppa to smoke ju-ju weed, sniff powders, alla that stuff you wasa do. That'sa nice, you make everybody happy, maybe we don' gonna bury you so soon. But you become different guy now, you understand? Nobody understand exactly what to do with you. I wasa think, maybe you gonna find the baby Jesus, go find another line of work."

Stoney squinted at him. "What the fuck are you talking about?"

Fat Tommy shrugged. "Well, I'ma ask around, you know, what's gonna happen. Here'sa this guy, used to be alla time drink, get high, now he'sa go to meeting instead. 'Watch out,' they tolla me. 'Everything gonna change now.' I don' know what to do. I don' wanna be the guy, you know, make you go back. Me an' Donna, I think we do the same lilla dance. Check, you know, peek, he's okay? I don' know, what he'sa do now? You hear me? You gotta have some patience. Gonna take time."

"Yeah, all right. Listen, don't be surprised if Donna calls you sometime in the next few days."

Tommy nodded. "She wanna talk about money."

Stoney looked at him, surprised. "Money? Is that what she said? She call you already?"

"No. But I know she gonna call. Everybody don' gonna be like you, Stoney."

"I don't get it. What do you mean?"

Fat Tommy shook his head. "Every year," he said, "tax time, I make a nice report. Marty Cohen used to help me do.

This year I hadda find a new guy. Anyway, nice report, show everything, almost. So much over here, so much over there, this building, that company, all that stuff. Plus, I tell you few things we don' gonna write down, some cash over here and over there. I give to you, along with tax paper, you don' even look. You sign the name, hand back. Am I right?"

"I suppose. But it's been a while since you and I needed to worry about money, Tommy."

"Stoney, people don' worry about money because they need. You go hungry in this country, you don' try very hard. People worry about money because they wanna new house, new car, new fur coat."

"Or because they gotta put their kids through school."

Tommy tilted his head, looked at Stoney. "Okay, that, too. But usually, they want, they no need. But I know you don' think about, too much, so I take care. No problem."

"I trust you, Tommy. With my money, anyhow."

Tommy snickered. "Everybody got his limitation. Listen to me. Donna is like a woman who wasa sleep for a long time. You understand? But now she'sa wake up, she'sa look around, she start to worry about everything. For so many years, she wasa just trust you, now she wanna see for herself. So don't worry, when she'sa call me, I gonna make everything okay."

"You can tell her the truth, Tommy."

Tommy snickered again. "Don' worry, she gonna like. Okay?"

"Okay. Next topic. You remember the guy I was checking out? Charles David Prior? I'm gonna make a move on him. I got a feeling he's too fat to pass up."

"Yeah? Whatta we know about thisa guy?"

"So far, not much. We know he lives in a big house in the

woods in Jersey, got a fence all the way around, got security guards and dogs. But that kid you put me onto is checking into him for me, we'll see what the kid comes up with."

"Okay by me." Tommy brightened. "Hey, wait," he said. "I got another idea. I know thisa guy, in case we aska him, he gonna find out a few things only a thief would wanna know. You know what I mean? I gonna give him a call."

Stoney trudged up the stairs and down the hallway, glanced at the door across the hall from his on the way past. He ignored the impulse to knock and went on past. He had barely gotten through his own door when the phone rang. It was the kid from Jersey, the investigator he'd hired. "I'm off your case," the kid said.

Stoney held the phone away from him, stared at it in disbelief, then put it back to his face. "Are you nuts? I hired you to do a job, pal."

The kid was adamant. "I'm off your case."

"Look, man, you can't do this to me, you hear me? You can't hang me up like this. What happened, somebody get to you? You gotta tell me what happened, you fucking weasel. What's the goddam problem?"

"The goddam problem is this." Stoney gritted his teeth and listened while the kid got himself together. "I don't know what you're into, and I don't want to know, but I'm not getting killed for you. Do you understand me? I am done with your case."

Stoney took a breath. "What are you talking about? Somebody threaten you or what?"

"Not verbally, but the message was pretty clear. There's a man in the morgue this morning, and he's there because I was turning over rocks, looking into your guy, Prior. I don't know what you think I am, okay, but I told you before, I deal in information, not violence. I'm finished. Matter of fact, I'm gonna be out of town for a couple of weeks."

"You are unbelievable. All right, look, you wanna bail on this, I suppose I can't blame you, but you gotta meet with me and tell me how far you got. If you got some shit stirred up, you owe me that much. You can't run away and leave me here in the dark."

The kid was silent for a few seconds. "All right," he said finally. "Meet me tomorrow morning, and I'll give you what I got."

"Fine. Where?"

"I'll call and tell you in the morning. And come alone." He hung up.

EIGHT

The place had been a service area once, but now it was nothing more than a bus station standing solitary guard in the middle of a massive parking lot. It was favored by commuters, they drove in from all over North Jersey, parked in the lot, and rode the bus into Manhattan. The lot was surrounded by the Jersey Meadowlands, a swampy expanse of pale brown marsh reeds. Stoney sat on the hood of his Lexus, trying to stifle his irritation.

A two-year-old Toyota Camry in need of a wash circled the parking lot once, then again, the driver seemingly unable to locate a parking spot to his liking. Finally, the car slid up to where Stoney waited, and the passenger side window rolled down. The kid was behind the wheel. "Get in," he said.

Stoney slammed the door shut and fought to keep control of his tongue. Careful what you say to this guy, he told himself, careful what you call him, because you need as much cooperation out of him as you can get. "Tell me what happened," he said, his voice unnaturally flat and calm.

"First of all, I got nothing on your wife. It's too soon to say anything for sure, but up to now I got squat."

Stoney wanted to be relieved, but he wasn't. Just because the kid didn't find it, didn't mean it wasn't there. "So what's the problem?"

"Let me get out of here first," the kid said. He looked around, nervous, then stepped on the gas and headed for the entrance for the Jersey Turnpike. He watched his rearview mirror as they hit the ramp. "Anybody behind us?"

Stoney glanced over his shoulder. "Half of New Jersey is behind us."

"Well, keep your eyes open," the kid said. He got onto the turnpike, but took the next exit, followed it through the tollbooths and out onto local streets.

"Where we going?"

"I don't know. This is Secaucus. I'm not going anywhere in particular, I just want to keep moving. Look, here's what happened. Something told me I needed to be extra careful with this job, and it's a damned good thing, too. For me, at least. You know anything about computers?"

"Not a lot."

"All right. Basically, a computer leaves tracks, just like your feet. When I go digging through somebody's dirty laundry, okay, I don't want the tracks going there to be mine, you get me? So what I do, I piggyback on a server at a bank in Jersey City. There's a back door on the server . . . well, anyway, from the server I access a computer in a law office in Newark, and I run my shit from there. You get me?"

"Yeah," Stoney said, irritated.

"They had a break-in at the law office. The place got trashed, but the only thing missing was a couple of hard drives."

"You musta hit a trip wire of some kind. What were you doing, you were running searches on Prior, am I right? Were you doing anything else?"

"No. Just Prior." They passed a truck dealership, turned into an industrial park behind it. In the distance, the turnpike soared on green legs high up and over the marsh. The kid drove past the last of the warehouses, down to where the road ended in a small parking lot. Beyond the end of the parking lot, the waters of the Jersey Meadowlands lay turgid and motionless. A few men stood fishing from a ledge at the water's edge, right past a sign that warned anglers not to eat any fish they pulled out of the marsh due to the toxic nature of the environment the fish lived in. The kid parked, sat there watching the fishermen. "There was a security guard at the office building in Newark. Someone grabbed him from behind, and they stuck a knife up under his rib cage. Right through his heart."

"Shit."

The kid didn't look at him. "I can't think of a reason to kill the guard, other than to send a message."

"So I guess you got the message."

"I'm not taking any chances."

"What did you find on Prior?"

"Some of the standard info. I mean, I got the same shit you can get on anyone in about two hours. Couldn't get his Social Security number, though, which is, like, unheard of. The guy is supposed to be some kind of businessman, but I never found out what he does. There was no evidence of any business-type activity on his part anywhere. There's no credit history on the guy past the last three years, either, and the college he supposedly graduated from up in Massachusetts never heard of him. No kids, no wives, no ex-girlfriends. I couldn't find a thing that made me think that Charles David Prior is the name this cat's mother gave him."

"So you're telling me he's a rich guy, but you don't know how he got the money, and you don't know who he really is."

The kid swallowed. "Yeah. He owns that house in Alpine,

bought it outright three years ago. Keeps some money in an index fund, but that's just his walking-around money. Working capital. He plays with commodities, that's a crapshoot, you can win big or lose it all in a big hurry, but he's just playing. You and me, we might put a C-note on the Jets game, this guy drops ten grand trying to guess which way the euro dollar is gonna bounce tomorrow morning."

"How's he do at it?"

"I only saw his last few trades, and he was one and four. But like I said, I think he's just fooling around. Oh, and his golf handicap is three."

"What's that mean?"

"I'd say it means he's got it all."

"Got the world by the balls, huh? So how much money does this guy have?"

"I don't know." The kid shook his head. "Listen, what I got on this guy is basically the top layer. Anything more than that, he's got it buried, and he's standing guard. Sorry."

"Shit. All right. Whoever hit the office building, do they have any way of tracing the searches back to you?"

"Yeah. Yeah, they do, if they have somebody good enough, they can follow me back to the server at the bank, and if they can get into that, they've got me."

"Why don't you smoke the server before they can get to it? Didn't you say there was a back door?"

"Yeah, I did. I thought I could wipe the drive, but the bank has gotten smart, and their security shut me down when I tried." One of the fisherman on the boulder leaned back, and his fishing rod curled into an arc as his catch fought for its life.

"I suppose that doesn't mean that they can't get in, whoever they are."

"Hey, I'm not going to kid you. I'm pretty good, okay, but there's always somebody better. You can design the best security system money can buy, but there's always someone, somewhere, smart enough to beat it. If these people want it bad enough, okay, they can get into the server, and that means they can get to me."

"And you're gonna run."

The kid's voice rose. "Fucking right I'm gonna run! After I drop you back at the lot, I'm going straight to the airport."

"So you're giving me nothing, am I right?"

"Not quite nothing," the kid said. He reached into the backseat, dragged a briefcase into his lap, opened it, and rooted around inside. He fished out a manila folder, handed it to Stoney, shut the briefcase, and chucked it back behind him. "There's everything I got on Prior. It's who he is now, where he goes, all that kind of shit. You might be able to do something with it, I don't know. At the very least, if you find someone else to do this for you, it'll give them someplace to start. And your money's in there, I'm refunding your retainer."

"If that's the way you feel about it." In front of them, the lucky fisherman dragged an eighteen-inch carp out of the brown water, and it flapped spastically on the ground. "What about my wife. What can you tell me about her?"

The kid shook his head. "You want my opinion, you're wasting your time. I put this girl I know on your wife, and last I heard she was bored stiff."

"What do you mean, the last you heard? This girl, she work for you? She know you're leaving?"

"I left a message on her voice mail, okay? She didn't get back to me."

"Yeah, great job, dude, way to go. You really know how to take care of your own."

The kid turned and shouted at him, red-faced. "Hey, man, she's freelance, okay? I pay her off the books, if it's any of your business. There's nothing that ties her to me! And she didn't have nothing to do with Prior, anyhow, just your old lady." He turned away. "I told you, I left a message on her voice mail."

"What's your girl's name."

"Oh, now look, man, why can't you just leave her out of this?"

"What's her name."

"Ain't you got any fucking heart? Ain't you got any soul? One dead body ain't enough for you? Why can't you just leave her alone?"

"Yeah, like you give a fuck. Look at you, you're shitting your pants, you're running for the hills, and you spared this girl of yours one lousy phone call. Look, I need to talk to her. I promise I'll give her a better heads-up than you did."

The fisherman had filleted his catch, and he stood up and tossed the entrails back into the water. Two of the other fishermen had started a fire, and a third was wrenching the metal sign, the one that detailed the contaminants in the fish, off its pole. When he got it off, he took it over and laid it on top of the fire. After the painted warning burned off, he took a half stick of butter out of his beer cooler and put it on the metal surface, and a minute later they were all gathered around the sign, drinking beer and watching their contaminated breakfast cooking.

The kid exhaled heavily. "Tina Finbury," he said. "I'm gonna call her again, when I get where I'm going. She decides to do something for you, it's on her."

"What a guy," Stoney said. "What's her phone number?" Stoney entered the numbers into his phone's memory.

"All right," the kid said. "I'll drive you back."

"Great."

He sat in his car, watched the kid's Toyota fade into the distance. He flipped his phone open, dialed Tina Finbury's number, listened to the phone ring, then waited through the standard message. "Listen, Tina," he said. "You were looking into something for me, but indirectly. Your, ahh, associate, the guy I hired, has taken off, and for just cause, I guess. I don't know if you're in harm's way here or not, but we should talk." He left her his number.

There were a lot of mirrors in the Closter Diner, with a little luck you could watch a reflection of a reflection of just about anybody there and still appear to be minding your own business. Stoney sat in his booth over next to a window in the corner of the place and watched Charles David Prior order his lunch from his seat at the counter on the other side of the room. He was tall, on the thin side, silver hair, tan, carefully put together. Nothing about him was loud, his clothes, his haircut and his shoes all whispered "money," instead of shouting it. A heavily muscled white guy wearing a gray suit and a black T-shirt sat at the end of the counter, sipping coffee. His eyes passed over Stoney twice, but the guy was watching everyone in the place.

The waitress obviously knew Prior, she chatted with him for a few minutes before she departed with his order. Prior watched her as she walked away. She was a middle-aged woman, slightly overweight, but he watched her anyway, transfixed. One of the other waitresses passed by, stopped to say hello. She was a bit younger than the first one, and Prior brightened, smiled at her, engaged her in conversation. Stoney could not read lips, not in a mirror, anyway, but he really didn't need to know what the man was saying to understand what was going on.

The females in the place loved the guy. Rich guy, loves the broads, probably a great tipper.

Prior was a creature of habit, he ate his lunch in this diner most weekdays, that was one of the tidbits the kid had come up with. The second waitress moved away, and Prior started talking to the guy sitting next to him.

Stoney pretended to be interested in his copy of the *Daily News*. The freaking Mets had assembled another collection of overpriced veterans, mixed in a few young kids, and the general manager kept talking about his master plan, how he needed a few more pieces to put the team over the top. It looked like it was going to be another long season. Across town, the Yankees had an all-star at almost every position, and they were in the market for more. A little more proof, in case he needed it, that life was not fair. He'd said that to Benny once, who had looked at him disdainfully and told him that a man in his position ought to feel grateful that such was the case.

Something to be said for that.

Stoney's waitress came by and refilled his coffee cup. She was the best-looking broad in the place, young, tall, nice rack, proud face. She walked back over to replace the coffeepot behind the counter. Prior followed her in the mirror, Stoney wondered if the guy was going to notice him watching, but Prior was completely focused on the woman. She walked past Prior, ignoring him, and he looked down at the counter in front of him as she passed.

He must have made a play for her, Stoney thought, and whatever happened, she had nothing to say to the guy now, and he didn't want to look her in the face. He still had it bad, though, he couldn't resist eyeballing her as she went off into the kitchen. Some guys are like that, Stoney thought, they live to chase pussy, and even though some of them develop amazing social skills, they learn how to smile and engage and ask the right questions, they really have only a peripheral interest in the woman in question, and that simply because she is attached to what they really want. Fat Tommy had a touch of that, but the thing that kept it from being sick, at least in his case, was that Tommy really was interested in almost anyone who had a story to tell.

God, he thought, Donna must be a real mess. She's got to be fucked up in the head to be giving this guy the time of day. . . . He turned back to his newspaper, stared at the pages for a while. The guy was so transparent, how could she not see through him? One of the things he'd always admired about her was her ability to face up to the truth, to refrain from pretending to herself that things were better than they really were. It doesn't fit, he told himself, I can't picture Donna staying in the same room with this asshole for more than five minutes. Could she really have become so unhinged by the changes the two of them had gone through in the past year? It was almost flattering, in a way, to think that she needed him that way, but after toying with that thought for a few minutes, he discarded it. Please, he said to himself. Get serious.

He drank coffee and read the paper while Prior finished his lunch. He silently cursed whoever was calling the shots over at Shea, why they kept chasing over-the-hill ballplayers was beyond him, particularly when it was obvious what they needed. Stick Michael was the guy they needed to go after, and they could get him, too, all they had to do was wait until the next time Steinbrenner took a piss on the guy's shoes, then call him up and make his day.

Prior stood up to go, said good-bye to the two waitresses who were still talking to him, left some money on the counter. Stoney could see why they'd be attracted to him, some women wouldn't be able to see through the act. This guy could model clothes for Brooks Brothers, Stoney thought, or play a rich doctor in one of the daytime soaps. Prior took a heavy leather biker jacket off the rack and put it on, fished a thin pair of driving gloves out of a pocket, and walked out the back door as he put them on. The guy in the gray suit got up and followed him out.

There was an old Italian motorcycle parked next to a stretch Lincoln Town Car in the lot behind the diner. The bike was a vintage Ducati 750SS, it was beautiful, and just like the man who owned it, rich, easy on the eyes, and probably had a few good moves. The thing was a classic, a piece of mechanical jewelry, exceedingly rare and positively gorgeous. It really belonged in a museum. Prior nosed it out of the parking lot, took off, the bike bellowing that unmistakable Ducati roar. The Town Car, piloted by the man in the gray suit, followed close behind.

Stoney waved to his waitress for the bill. Who is this guy, he wondered, and why should I care? Why not just smoke the bastard and be done with it? But he had promised Marisa . . . Got to be a way to find out who you are, he thought, looking out the window, in the general direction Prior had taken. Got to be.

You open the door to the place, you're looking down the length of the bar, dark paneling, brass rail, big mirror, rows of bottles, tall beer taps, TV down at the end where the fat bartender and a couple of waiters were watching a baseball game. It was preseason, the grapefruit league was playing, and a lot of kids with names nobody knew were out there taking their shots. It was long odds that any of them were going to make the bigs, but they were doing the best they could. They were in the game.

Stoney could feel his heart trying to crawl up into his throat. Nice, quiet place to sit and get a load on. It would have felt just like home to him, once, this place and a thousand others just like it. Heaven on earth, and he had never intended to leave, never aspired to anything better, never thought he could find any greater happiness. That familiar barroom smell filled his head as he stood in the inner doorway. It was the perfume of a beautiful woman who had once loved him, and a hint of that scent started the images rolling, what she had looked like, how she had taken him in her arms, the way she had been able to blow all that shit out of his mind, open his cage door and set him free. . . .

Yeah, never mind the way she'd tried to cut your throat, last time out. Nostalgia for the gutter, that's what Benny called it.

"Help you, sir?" Stoney was standing in the doorway to The Landing, a steakhouse in Piermont, New York, and the maître d' was looking at him quizzically.

"Yeah." The dining area was to the right, in a different room. Away from the bar. "Yeah, I'm meeting someone here." Two steps took him to the threshold of the dining room. She was sitting all alone, over by a window on the far side of the room. Their eyes met and he was sixteen again, getting ready to ask her out for the first time, his stomach sinking because he knew she was out of his class, she would never go out with a guy like him. He'd been so sure she'd say no, laugh at him with her friends later on. She hadn't, though. He felt a little unsteady, put a hand on the door frame. How am I gonna do this? he wondered. God, can I go through this again? "I'm with her," he said.

"Right this way, sir." The maître d' had a large leather-bound menu under his arm, and he headed across the room. Stoney would have preferred to stand where he was for another minute, to wait for his heart to go back down where it belonged, maybe catch his breath, but he did not, he followed the guy over to her table.

She looked tired, but he knew better than to tell her that. The maître d' laid the menu on the table and departed. Stoney stood there looking at her, she sat there looking at him. Neither of them was exactly young anymore. Stoney never thought much about time's erosion of his own face, but looking down at Donna, he could see faint lines and shadows where once there had been none. It didn't matter to him, didn't affect the way he felt about her. She was the only woman he had ever loved, and the first human being who had ever really loved him. "Hello, beautiful. Mind if I sit down?" He smiled as he said it, trying to project a confidence he did not feel.

"Please do," she said. She waited until he was seated. "You've lost weight," she said. "I can see it in your face. You look nice. Did Tommy buy you that suit?" She looked down at herself. She was wearing a plain white blouse, khaki pants, and a blue blazer hung from the back of her chair. She probably came straight here from work, he thought. Better stay away from that. . . .

"I missed you," he said.

She had to think about it for a minute. "I missed you, too," she said. "Sort of."

He wondered what that meant, but the waiter came just

then, rattled on about his specials, a fish from here and a filet from there, prices to go with them, all of that. Stoney didn't listen, he watched Donna stare at the menu. She seemed reluctant to order, as though she had no appetite, or maybe she didn't want to be beholden to him. She did, though, finally, and so did he, and the waiter took their menus and went away.

"Oh," she said, in sudden alarm, turning to look at the waiter's departing back. "I ordered a wine spritzer. . . ." She turned back to face him. "I'm sorry, I forgot. I didn't think."

"It's all right," he said. "It won't bother me, just as long as you don't get all sloppy."

She glared at him. "I should," she said. "I should get loaded, just so you'll have to drive me home. Maybe I could throw up in the backseat of your car."

Try to make a little joke, he thought. Mistake. "I'd have to have Tuco clean it out for me."

"Sounds like you," she said, still angry. "Pass your problems along for someone else to take care of."

He just nodded.

"That was mean," she said after a minute. "I apologize." She didn't look at him when she said it, she just stared out the window.

"It's all right," he said.

"It's just that—" She stopped, shaking her head, and then went on in a quieter tone. "I keep getting this urge. This impulse to pay you back. I just don't know what I could do to hurt you. Nothing ever touches you. You never feel anything."

If you only knew, he thought. "Stay away."

She stared at him. "That's it? That's all it takes?"

"Yeah."

They sat in silence for a couple of minutes. Donna looked

around, finally, at the other tables. The place did most of its business on the weekend. At that moment it was almost empty. "You know," she said, "all of the years we've been married, I never knew how much money we had. I didn't know how much you made, or anything." She paused. "I sort of know what you do. You and Tommy."

"You were never—"

"Hush. Please. Let me get this out before you start poking holes in it, okay?"

"All right." I wasn't going to poke any holes, he wanted to say, wanted to defend himself, but he kept silent.

"All this time," she said, a little bit louder. "All these years, if I wanted something, I had to ask you first. 'Stoney, can we afford this? Stoney, can I have one of those?' Just like a little kid . . . I thought the children were my job. That was the deal we made, you and I, even though we never talked about it. But then, we never talked about anything, did we? I needed you for everything. I needed you to check the oil in my car, to tell me what color to paint the kitchen, to figure out what schools the kids should go to . . . I was, I was like a toy, you kept me in the house next to your fishing rods. I always needed you for everything, and you never needed me at all."

He couldn't remember owning any fishing rods. "That isn't true," he said. "I always needed you. I need you now."

"Yeah, to keep your house clean," she snapped. "To wash your underwear. And for sex."

Every time I open my mouth, he thought, I make this worse.

"Were you drunk at our wedding?" she asked. "Were you drunk when you married me?"

The few other patrons in the place were starting to pay the

two of them a bit more attention. Stoney inhaled. "No," he lied. "Not at the wedding. Afterward, maybe."

"Oh, I remember that," she said. "And all during the honeymoon."

"Well . . ."

"And when Marisa was born? You really wanted to be there, that's what you said, but you had some cockamamie story, what was that all about?"

He couldn't remember. He hadn't been there for Dennis's birth, either. She'd had to take a cab to the hospital, both times. "What do you want me to tell you?"

"Well, let's start with an easy one. You've been under the influence of one thing or another the whole time I've known you. Is that fair to say?"

He hadn't been fucked up the whole time, that was ridiculous . . . But it had been there all along. His best friend, his crutch, as omnipresent as the air he breathed. He sighed. "Fair enough."

"I feel like my whole life with you has been a lie," she said. "You and I never had a real relationship. We were more like roommates than lovers. You had your life, and I never knew very much about it. I had my life, and you never cared much about that." She saw the waiter headed for their table bearing plates of food, so she fell silent while he served them.

"When did you talk to Marisa?" she said, when he was gone.

"She came to see me last week."

Donna pursed her lips. "She went in to see you? In the city?"

"Yeah. I met her at the train station."

"That girl," she said, shaking her head. "She looks so innocent, but she never tells me anything."

She told me plenty, Stoney thought. She told me about this guy you're seeing. He almost said it, but then he bit it back, swallowed the words and the bile. Not now, he told himself. Not here. He felt it, though, the anger of it coming up, and the pain of forcing it back down. Was this all me, he wondered, is this all my fault? He remembered asking Benny if it was his fault he was an addict. "*Fault* is a word for school yards," Benny had told him. 'Doesn't matter whose fault it is. It's your responsibility. You gotta deal with it.'

". . . did she want?" Donna was asking him something. "Did she just want to see you?"

He assumed they were still talking about Marisa. "I guess. She wanted to talk." He swallowed Prior's name again, and it tasted just as bitter going down the second time. "She wants to go to school, says she wants to be a doctor. She wanted to know about tuition."

Donna passed a hand across her forehead. "I've been afraid to even think about that," she said, her voice unsteady. "What did you tell her?"

"Told her not to worry. Told her I could pay for it."

Her eyes were on him then, hard and bright. "You told her you could pay for it." She emphasized the word *you,* leaned on it hard, both times. Should have said "we," he thought. You and I. It was too late, though.

"Yeah."

"Just how much money do you"—she did it again— "have?"

"We." He threw it out there, for what it was worth. "We have assets, you and I. Not just the house, either. Not what's in the bank."

He could see her anger building. "In the bank?" she said, her voice rising. "There isn't enough money in the bank for me to even use my ATM card anymore. I had to go get a job, just to try and stay somewhere near current on the bills, for chrissake."

He was mad enough to take pleasure in that, loved her enough to feel guilty about it. "Don't you ever look at bank statements?"

"As a matter of fact, I did look," she said. "The checking account had something like four hundred bucks in it when you left."

When you threw me out, you mean. "What about the money-market account?"

He had her complete attention. "What money market account?"

"Farther down on the page," he said, but he didn't manage to keep all of the sarcasm out of his voice. "You transfer money out of one into the other when you need it. I usually keep about twenty grand in it."

She was leaning forward, her face red, but then she sat back abruptly and looked away. "Well, I'm an idiot, then," she said. He could see the muscles working in her jaw. "And where do you get it from? When your twenty grand runs low, where does the money come from to fill it back up?"

He shrugged. "Here and there," he said. "Tommy and I, and you, have a very complicated financial situation. But we're doing okay."

"How okay?"

He shrugged again. "I'd have to talk to Tommy, go over it all. Or you could do it yourself. Go sit down with him, let him tell you everything."

"You know I love Tommy," she said, "but he's your friend. He'd protect you."

"Tommy wouldn't lie to you."

She looked unconvinced. "So Marisa's tuition isn't a problem."

"No."

"What about the mortgage on the house? Could we . . ." She threw the word in his face. "Could we afford to pay that off?"

"Yeah," he said, "but it would be stupid. That mortgage is cheap money. Besides, a mortgage makes us look normal."

"Is that so." Her face was dark red again. "I've been killing myself to pay that bill every month, did you know that? I've been so afraid of losing the house because you, because you . . ." She swallowed then, and didn't finish her sentence. "How have you been getting by? Have you been taking money out of your money-market account?"

"No." This is not going to go over well, he thought. He'd been drawing cash out of one of his safe-deposit boxes, and he couldn't, in honesty, say "we" again. She was right. They were his.

"Well?"

Try it anyhow, he thought. "We have other resources."

"Do we now." She was holding a fork in her right hand, but more like a weapon than an eating utensil. She put it down carefully, next to her plate, and she picked the cloth napkin up off her lap and dumped it on her untouched food. "Fine," she said. "Maybe I will talk to Tommy after all. And maybe this exercise has been useful for at least one reason."

He was almost afraid to ask. "Yeah? What?"

"I found out I can make it without you," she said, and she stood up, knocking her chair over behind her, and she walked away.

"Donna . . ." He stood up too, but he only watched her. What are you gonna do? he asked himself. Go grab her by the hair and drag her back to the cave? The restaurant was silent, all he could hear was the blood roaring in his ears. The other patrons turned away when he looked at them, out the windows or down at their food. He stood there in the silent room. "Hey," he said, loud, addressing them all. "That went well, don't you think?"

NINE

It was a close thing, Benny." It was not yet light out. Benny had told him, long ago, to call him anytime, day or night, and Stoney was taking him up on it. It had to be something like five in the morning, but Benny sounded like he always did.

"So? What happened?"

"I went to see Donna last night."

"Yeah? How'd it go?"

"Not good. You were right, I guess. She had some hard things to say, she said them, and then she walked out."

"What she said, was it true?"

"Yeah. Yeah, Benny, I guess it was."

"So maybe that's not entirely bad. Maybe she felt like she had to get it out there, and she did. You make any progress on the money issue?"

"Nah, I don't think so. She had questions, but I don't know if I had any answers."

"What do you mean?"

"It's complicated, Benny. My shit is all tied up with my partner, Fat Tommy. It ain't like it's on a spreadsheet somewhere."

"That don't sound too smart to me."

"I trust the guy, Benny. We been friends for a long time."

"Okay, so you trust the guy. What would you do if he died, God forbid?"

"God forbid." Stoney thought about it for a minute. "Most of it's legal, and on paper somewhere. It's just that I don't spend a lot of time thinking about it. Once in a while Tommy comes to me, says, we ought to sell this, buy a piece of that. That's kind of like his end of things, I let him do it."

"I bet you don't even know how much money you got, you dumb fuck. How do you get paid?"

"I got a good idea how much there is, more or less." Stoney could hear the defensive tone in his own voice. "Tommy and I pay ourselves a salary, you know, the IRS gets their vig and the whole bit. But it ain't like I work for a regular corporation or anything."

Benny was chuckling. "No wonder your wife don't believe you. Here's what I would do, I was you. I would set up a meeting between Donna and your partner. I assume he's a little sharper than you when it comes to finance."

"Yeah."

"So let her find out from him what she needs to know. Are you okay with that, or are you afraid she'll do something stupid?"

"I guess it doesn't matter, if she does or if she doesn't. Money ain't the issue, not on my end."

"Well, there you go, then." Benny was silent for a minute. "What did you mean, exactly, when you said it was a close thing? You weren't talking about your wife."

"No. The restaurant we were in last night had a bar attached. Nice place, Benny, quiet, dark . . . After Donna walked out, I was gonna go for it, you know what I mean?"

"Yeah, I do. So?"

"Well, I went to the men's room first. I don't know if I was gonna try to talk myself out of it, or into it. I'm telling you, Benny, everything inside of me was saying, fuck it, man, half a dozen single malts and I'll forget all about the bitch. So anyhow, I'm splashing water on my face, right, and one of the Spanish kids they got working in the kitchen comes out of a stall and starts washing his hands. He's got the AA logo tattooed on the back of his left hand, so I asked him about it. He knew a little English, and I knew a little Spanish, so I kinda told him what was up."

"So what'd he say?"

"I don't know. Called me a lot of names. I think he was saying, you know, drink tomorrow if you still want to, just not now. Not tonight. He got me out of there, took me out the back door so I wouldn't have to pass the bar. Got me into my car. Once I was rolling, you know, I focused on getting home, I guess I was all right. But it's funny, ain't it, how there's always a cliff handy when you got the urge to jump."

"Yeah. You gonna be all right, or you want to meet for breakfast or something?"

"Nah, I'm here now, I'm okay." He was silent for a minute, worked on formulating his question. Such a stupid thing to ask, how would Benny know, anyway, and how to ask him without sounding like a little kid? "What the fuck do I do now? What's gonna happen, Benny?"

"I can't tell you that. All I can tell you is what happened to me, and what I've seen in the past."

"Yeah?"

"Yeah." It took him a minute to come around to it. "Look, if the two of you, you and Donna, I mean, if you two really are friends, you know, beneath it all, you'll probably come out of this all right. If you're not, if this thing between you and Donna is really dead, you'll be able to give it a decent burial. The thing is, right now, there's nothing you can do about it either way. The only thing you can do is take care of your own side of the street. Did you actually consider drinking over this?"

"Consider? I didn't think about it, Benny, but for about twenty minutes, I was right fucking there. You know what I mean? I was ready to blow everything just for a couple hours' worth of oblivion."

"No guarantee you'd get a couple of hours. You gonna make a meeting tonight?"

"Yeah."

"Good. Call me later, maybe I'll meet you there."

"All right."

Tina Finbury was cautious, she borrowed a conference room at the corporate headquarters of one of her bigger customers, an insurance company, and insisted on meeting him there. The place was surrounded by a tall iron fence, you had to go through security to get in, and the guard ran a metal detector over Stoney, then patted him down. Stoney stood there, his arms out and his legs spread as the guy checked him for weapons. "You can't be too careful these days," he said, but the guard didn't react, he just finished what he was doing, then gave Stoney a brief mechanical smile.

"Thank you, sir," the man said. "Wait right there, your escort will be here shortly."

He was taken to a small room, generic corporation chic, tasteful conference table, comfortable chairs, fluorescent lighting. She was waiting for him there. "Sorry for the rigmarole," she said. "I asked them to make sure you weren't armed. I hope you don't mind. You must be Stoney."

"Tina," he said. "Nice to meet you. I guess I'd wonder about you if you didn't take some precautions."

She didn't look anything at all like what Stoney had expected. Hearing her voice on the phone, knowing what she did for a living, his imagination had assembled a variety of images, and had even ranked them in order, from most to least likely. He'd bet on a Jewish Kathleen Turner, mostly because of the voice, but he lost. She stood up and held her hand out.

Her hand was warm and dry. "Nice to meet you," she said. She had Suburban Jersey Matron written all over her. She had short gray hair, a round face, and she looked at him over half-glasses. "You look surprised."

"I guess I pictured you . . ."

"Hah," she said. "Some shrew, you thought you were gonna find. Sam Spade in drag. You know something? One of the things that makes me good at what I do is that I look just like a million other old broads from New Jersey. You saw my face in a crowd, would you remember me? I don't think so."

"Maybe not. Listen, like I started to tell you on the phone, I got your name from your boss. . . ."

"Boss? I got no bosses, honey."

"Well, then, this guy you were working for."

"With."

"Okay, with. He was doing a couple of things for me, but he got scared off. But he did say . . ." Jesus, how could he give voice to this? "He told me he used you to watch my wife."

She shrugged. "Yes," she said. "There really isn't much to say. I know where she works, where she sleeps, who she talks to on the phone, and none of it is very interesting, if you get what I mean. So it's good news, am I right? At least, so far it is."

"Maybe. And maybe it's just my paranoia, but . . ."

She stared at him for a few seconds. "Listen, if your nose tells you there's something wrong inside your house, you're probably right, but I was only supposed to follow your wife. Usually in these situations I listen to my intuition. In your case, I would think about casting my net a little wider."

"What do you mean?"

"Well, I don't want you to think I'm trying to milk this job, but you don't look like you're starving to death. Why don't you let me off the leash? I won't lie to you, it'll cost you more than a simple surveillance job, but whatever's going on, I'll find it."

He thought about that. "Yeah," he said. "Whatever you wanna do. Listen, I, ahh . . ." He sighed. "I just wanna be sure. You know what I mean?"

"I can handle that for you," she said. "Tell me, first, what was it that caused all of this fuss? People hiding, leaving messages on my phone, 'ooh, you better watch out,' and all like that? What's that all about?"

"It doesn't have anything to do with my wife. At least, I don't think it does. Your, ahh, associate was checking into something else for me, and it got sticky."

"Something else? Something else like what? If I'm going to work for you, I need to know what's going on, so I can watch where I put my feet."

"A guy. I asked him to check into a guy for me. It turns out, the man values his privacy. His name is Charles David Prior, and he lives up on the hill in Alpine. Do us both a favor, okay? Stay away from him."

"All right," she said, and she handed him her card. "I'll call you in a day or so."

• • •

They met at the Greek restaurant on Montague Street, about six blocks away from Tuco's building in Brooklyn. It was early in the afternoon, too late for the lunch crowd and before the evening rush. The place served old-country peasant food, pungent with garlic. Tuco dug in with relish while Stoney toyed with his own lunch.

"So," Tuco said, between bites. "What's up?"

Stoney gritted his teeth. He hated having to lean on anybody. "I need your help."

"Okay."

"Don't just say 'okay,'" Stoney said. "Listen to what I got to say, first."

Tuco looked at him and shrugged. "Okay."

Stoney stared at him and shook his head. "All right, listen. I need you to do something for me, but I don't want to answer a lot of fucking questions about how come I want you doing it. You get me?"

Tuco shrugged. "Whatever you say."

"I need someone to keep an eye on my daughter, and I can't do it, I got too many other things to do."

"All right." Tuco put his fork down. "I know you don't wanna talk about why, but, like, what am I looking for?"

Stoney shook his head. "I don't know. That's why I'm asking you to do it, instead of hiring somebody I don't know. I know you can use your fucking head for something besides holding your hat up off your neck."

"I ain't even got a hat."

"This is probably just paranoia, okay? But I want to know where she goes and what she does in between the time school lets out and whenever she gets home at night. You up for that?"

Tuco nodded. "Yeah. Sure. She walk home from school?"

"No, she rides home with her girlfriend. Girlfriend drives a green Toyota. I got a picture of my daughter here." He handed it across the table. "Her name is Marisa."

Tuco looked at the image on the picture, than pocketed it. "You gotta give me something more than this," he said. "You know what I mean? You gotta give me a hint."

"Just look for whatever it is that's got the hairs on the back of my neck standing up. There's one other thing. This might turn out to be a lot more dangerous than following somebody around." Stoney told Tuco what he knew about Charles David Prior.

"I'll watch for him," Tuco said.

"All right. You should know that Marisa might not be thrilled to have you around."

"She don't want no babysitter, huh?"

Stoney stabbed at a piece of meat with his fork, held it up and examined it. "She's, ahh . . ." He put the fork back down on his plate. "I know you're a good kid, and it ain't like I don't trust you, but I gotta say this anyhow. She's only seventeen."

"Yassuh, boss. Keep my dick-skinners off'n her. I got it."

"Listen, I appreciate this."

Tuco waved him off. "Ain't nothing to it."

"Okay. One last thing. There's this female, looks like a little old yenta from Forest Hills. She's, ahh, she's watching the house. You might see her around, just pretend you belong there."

"Gotcha."

Jack Harman lay on the hotel bed holding the phone to his ear with his shoulder. He was five foot ten, blond and blue,

California tan and a gymnast's overbuilt shoulders and arms. "Mrs. Martinelli? Hi, this is Jim Carson, Midtown Branch. I wonder if you could help me out. I'm new here, this is only my second day on the job, and my workstation keeps freezing up. Yes, I know, and I'm sure they'd do their best, but they were here all day yesterday, and they're very busy, besides. Hey, you know what, I'm just trying not to look like a total dweeb in my first week at the bank. Thanks. Yes, well, what I'd like to know is if you have a contact in I.T. who's a bit sharper than average. . . . Oh, wow, that's really great. Does she have a direct line? I'd look it up, but you know what? My workstation's frozen up. . . . That's great, Mrs. Martinelli, I appreciate that. No, I won't tell her it was you." He snapped the phone shut, ending the call, and looked at the telephone in his hand. "Where did you get this thing, Tommy?"

Fat Tommy was sitting in a chair by the hotel room's only window. "RadioShack, just like you wasa say," he said. "Prepaid."

Harman nodded. "Good. I don't know what kind of guy would kill a security guard just to make a point, but I don't want him looking for me." He punched numbers on the phone and held it to his ear. "Hi. Is this Valerie in I.T.? Hi, Val, my name is Purgatory. I'm calling you to let you know that one of your servers has been compromised. You can expect a black-hat assault through a back door. It might be under way already. I'm sorry? Oh. Well. Let's just say I have a dispute with one of the parties involved. No, sorry, I'm not sure which server, but what I would do if I were you, I would examine all administrator traffic in the past, say, five days. Look for someone using a password that's either dormant or not listed in your directory. Good-bye." He ended the call.

"You slam the back door shut?" Tommy said.

"Well," he said, "assuming Valerie's half on the ball, and assuming your target didn't already get in and get what he wanted, yeah, we slammed the door."

"Pretty smart," Tommy said.

"Hey, I'm just getting warmed up. What did you say this guy's name is?"

"Charles David Prior." Tommy handed Harman a sheet of paper on which was written all that he knew about Prior. "Rich guy, lives in Jersey, lotta security."

"Alpine? Is that the name of the town he's in?"

"Yeah."

"Okay. Gimme the Jersey phone book." Tommy handed it across. "Alpine is up by the bridge, right? So that's got to be Bergen County." He opened to the blue pages, the ones that gave you government phone numbers. "Here it is," he said. "Building department. Okay, here we go." He placed another call.

"Teresa? Hi, Teresa, how are you? This is Martin Wills, Twelfth District Court, Investigations. No, Teresa, don't worry, you're cool, but maybe you could bail me out. My boss is seriously steamed at me, and I don't want to get canned. Yeah, aren't they all? Like he never makes a mistake. Well, what happened, he's doing a field inspection, but someone sent the wrong prints, and when they got here, I stuck them in the file without double-checking. No, it was totally my fault, if I had looked at them first, none of this would have happened. Anyhow, Ethelred the Unready is pitching a fit. What we're looking at is a residence, in Alpine." He read her Prior's address. "There should be a set of plans for that residence in the permits section. Could you do me a giant favor and take a look? Oh, you got that on microfiche?" He paged through the phone book while he talked. "Wow, if you would fax that over to me, I might not have to look for a new job after all. Oh, Teresa, that's great. Hey, wait, I've got a better idea. Fax it to the UPS store in Westwood, and I'll call his majesty and tell him he can pick 'em up there. Teresa, you're a lifesaver, I can't tell you how much I owe you." He gave her the number. "Great. Thanks again."

Fat Tommy was smiling. "I'll send someone over. . . ."

"No need," Harman said. "Hang on one second." He went back to the phone book, then dialed again. "Hi. Is this the UPS store in Westwood? Yeah, hi, I'm Craig, in the Main Street store in Yonkers. I've got a customer standing here, and he's about to blow a cork. He's been waiting for a set of drawings of some sort, and he just called up his source to find out where they are, only to find out the guy faxed them to you guys by mistake. What? Oh, great. Hold on one sec." He winked at Tommy. "Ah, sir? He says they're just coming out of the machine now." Tommy shook his head in admiration. "Listen," Harman said. "Can you stick those back in the machine and forward them to us here? You've got the number, right? Thanks, man. Great." He ended the call. "UPS store, Tommy, it's a couple blocks down on Main. The plans to Prior's house will be waiting for you."

"Damn," Tommy said. "Hey, how come you wasa don't con some messenger service to bring 'em over?"

Harman grinned. "You want me to?"

"No," Tommy said. "I gonna go take a walk. You keep working on Prior. You wanna nice coffee?"

"Sure," Harman said. He went back to the phone book. "Okay, Social Security Administration," he said. "They got an eight-hundred number, should be in here somewhere . . ."

• • •

Stoney pulled up to the garage at the McMansion in Alpine. It was the middle of a quiet afternoon, and none of the neighbors had yet returned from the salt mines. A lawn-service guy working the yard next door fogged the air with blue two-cycle smoke and noise as he herded some lawn clippings out to the curb. He glanced up once as Stoney opened the garage door, then went back to his work. Stoney parked inside, shut the garage door behind him, and sat in his car, waiting. Twenty minutes later he heard the honk of Fat Tommy's Mercedes, he opened the door again, and Tommy pulled inside.

"Stoney," Fat Tommy said as he maneuvered himself out of the driver's seat, "this is Jack Harman."

"Hello, Jack." Stoney squinted at the guy. "I know you?"

"No." Harman shook his head. "I did something for Tommy about six years ago. I don't know where you were."

"You remember the guy," Tommy said, "had a home movie of me anna that nice lady lawyer from the Brooklyn D.A.'s office? Jack wasa break into the guy's office, steal his camera, film, compute, file cabinet, steal everything."

Stoney remembered the story. It seemed like a lifetime ago. "Yeah. I'm a little foggy on the details. You took the whole file cabinet?"

"Two of 'em," Harman said. "Dude had an office in a converted warehouse building in Brooklyn, down in Fort Greene. I had two guys in a van parked in the alley behind the place, I lowered all his shit down the outside wall with a climbing rope. I even reset the alarm after I left, if I remember right."

"How'd you get the alarm code?"

"Dude had this broad working in the office, she was temping from some big agency. Guy treated her like shit. I gave her five grand, she gave me the code, the layout, the guy's schedule, the whole megilla."

"Ain't it funny," Stoney said. "You act like a dick, it'll come back and bite you in the ass every time. I remember now." Bagadonuts had been impressed with the man's abilities to gather information on his targets ahead of time. "Come on into the house."

They stood around the island in the middle of the kitchen and drank tepid Dunkin' Donuts coffee. "All right." Harman glanced at Stoney. "Charles David Prior, whoever he really is, is gonna be a hard nut to crack. First of all, he's something of a 'flat-earther.'"

"What's that mean?"

"Means he's stuck in the past. He doesn't have Internet access from his house, he doesn't even have cable television. I can't say for sure if he has a computer or not, but I'd guess probably not. No e-mail. That means there's no way to hack him because there's nothing to hack into. He doesn't use phone accounts, either. The guy does business in person, face-to-face, in private. He gets a check, he puts the thing in his pocket, takes it to his bank. He's got some investment stuff with a broker, I'll get to that guy in a minute. Okay, Prior travels with security, sometimes one guy but usually two, and they don't look like your average rent-a-cops, either. Rides in the back of a limo, unless he's on his motorcycle, in which case they follow behind. And when he's in public, he treats his guards like trained monkeys."

"What do you mean?"

"He doesn't talk to them, he uses hand signals. He'll move them around with gestures, you know, he'll point at a guy, then point where he wants the guy to go. Very formal."

"Very strange."

"Well, yeah, the guy ain't Mr. Warmth. What else? Ah, the dude is an adrenaline junkie. Likes to skydive, once a month or so he goes up to this place in Connecticut, hires out the plane and the pilot, him and his guards all jump. Or he'll fly an ultralight, or go rock climbing, but whenever he does anything, he goes private. Hires the whole place, so it's just him, the guards, and maybe an instructor or two."

"He don't like rubbing elbows with the great unwashed."

"Something like that. You could chalk it up to security, but you ask me, the guy's a banana. Same thing when he goes to a store. He goes after hours, somewhere where they'll open up just for him. What else do I know for sure? He vacations in Mexico, same place every year, private villa, very remote, on the coast of Baja. He belongs to some pistol club in Tenafly, couple towns south of here. Dude that works there told me Prior is the quickest shot he's ever seen, on a combat range the guy is in a league all by himself. Now, when a gun nut tells you something like that, you gotta remember the guy probably spends hours and hours practicing this shit, so Prior must really be off the charts. And, oh yeah, I got prints of his house, if you're thinking of going in. There was a panic room in the place when he bought it, but he had the fucking thing completely ripped out and replaced after he moved in."

"How'd you get all this stuff?"

"People will usually talk to you if you use the right approach. The panic room, for example, the building permits were on file with the county. I got the name and phone number of the contractor who did the work, but I'd be very careful about approaching the guy. That's the stuff I'm sure of, the rest is guesswork."

"All right. Go ahead and guess," Stoney said.

Harman nodded. "My opinion, Prior is suffering from Howard Hughes syndrome."

"Got long fingernails?"

Harman shrugged. "In a manner of speaking. The guy's got nobody close enough to him to tell him when he's getting weird, or when he's full of it. The dude is too isolated, he's self-referential. If he's thinking something, if he's into something, it must be right, because there's no one else whose opinion means anything to him. So the longer he stays locked away from the world, the stranger he becomes. He's got nothing to measure himself against, nothing to conform to. That's one thing. Here's another: his cover story is that he's a European businessman, but I didn't see any evidence of him ever going to Europe, or even calling overseas on the phone. My best guess, this guy's ex-military. He's paranoid as hell, he's sitting up there in that house just waiting for someone like you or me to climb through his bedroom window, and when you do, he's gonna put a hole in your skull and you'll wind up buried in those woods down behind his house. I don't have a clue who he really is or how he got his money. And what's really interesting is the stuff you can't find on him."

"Such as?"

"Such as his Social Security number, for one thing. Usually getting that is a snap, you can buy it off the Web for ten bucks or you can scam it out of the local office, if you know the right lingo, but I couldn't come up with his no matter what I did. He doesn't have any personal history, either, just the same two lines he feeds anyone who asks."

"European businessman."

"Yeah, basically. No family, no wife, no ex-wives, no

girlfriends, nothing like that. I don't know where he goes to
get laid, that's not the kind of thing people will talk about on
the telephone. Now. Burglar's instinct? This is not the kind of
man who keeps serious money in a bank, he won't trust the
banker much farther than he trusts anyone else. You can bet
your house he's got his assets close at hand, probably in that
panic room, and he'll have it in something liquid and easy
to transport. Stamps, fine art, gems, whatever, but nothing
heavy and nothing that won't fit in the back of a van. And
he has a van, incidentally, a white cargo van, it's registered to
the security outfit he uses but they keep it in his garage. Add
it all up. This guy's in terrific shape, he likes firepower, and
he's dialed in, man, he's forted up, and he'll cap anybody who
comes over the wall after him. My personal opinion, I would
take a pass, at least for now. Give the guy another year or two,
I'm guessing the guy will deteriorate over time, mentally, and
when he gets warped enough, he'll be easier to handle. But
right now? Forget it."

"You think we gonna take a big chance," Tommy said.

Harman shrugged. "Plenty of softer targets."

"Maybe." Stoney looked at Fat Tommy. "I can't forget it. I
have a personal interest in Charles David Prior."

"I kinda figured that," Harman said. "Listen, you just
wanna wax the guy, probably easier to take him out than to
rob him."

"That don' makea no sense," Tommy said. "In case you
got a problem with a rich man, it's only right you should take
his money first. It'sa the civilized way. Then you step on him.
In case you decide to do him," he asked, looking at Harman,
"what's your approach?"

"I ain't like you guys," Harman said. "I'm just a burglar, and a retired one, at that. But I would chart his movements for a week or so. Then I'd pick a time when I knew he was gonna be out of his house, and then I would do what I do." He looked from Stoney to Fat Tommy. "I'm assuming you want more than that."

"I do," Stoney said. "I want his ass."

"Well, then, his broker is the obvious approach. The guy has an office in Haworth, about ten minutes from here. Dude used to be a broker, but he lost his license, now he calls himself a 'professional finance counselor.' Something like that. Prior goes down to see him twice a week, Tuesdays and Fridays, seven in the morning, like clockwork."

"Every week?" Tommy asked.

"Absolutely. The guy's like a machine."

"Why did the broker lose his tag?" Stoney said.

"Money laundering."

"So his broker is a crook."

"Ain't they all? The guy is a capitalist, that's for sure. Dude's an addict, too, for whatever that's worth. Kid that cleans his office told me the dude is up to a bottle of JD and a half a gram of blow a night."

"Goddam," Tommy said. "How come Prior gonna use a guy like that?"

"Hard to say," Harman said. "Prior may not know much about dope, he might be so focused on himself, you know, if he isn't into something, it doesn't exist, not for him. And the broker still keeps his act together at work. Never takes a day off, doesn't start doing anything until the closing bell. Then he's off to the races. Your only worry, given Prior's paranoid nature, is that he might be using this broker as a sort of canary in the mine shaft. You know what I'm saying? Give yourself an obvious flaw, then watch to see who tries to use it."

"You might be giving the guy too much credit," Stoney said. "Hard to imagine the son of a bitch doing a background check on everyone he does business with. He might just be more comfortable doing business with someone who's a crook. You think the broker will work with us?"

"You kidding?" Harman said. "The guy's a cokehead, he'll work with anyone for the right price. But if you guys are thinking of running a game on Prior, you really gotta find out who he is, first. Otherwise, you'll never know for sure what you're dealing with. Poker's only a good game when you know what cards the other guy is holding. And from here on in, you're probably gonna have to find somebody smarter than me to get your information from. I think I already got everything I know how to get."

"You did great," Stoney said. "I appreciate it. I haven't talked this over with Tommy yet, so I don't know how he feels about all this. We're gonna figure out something in the next day or two. You interested?"

"Depends on what you come up with," Harman said. "I'm retired. I'm just helping out an old friend, so far. I can't take another fall."

"Neither can I," Stoney told him. "Nobody planning to go to jail. Tommy tells me you're just in town for a few days."

Harman nodded. "Visiting my sister. They've got her locked up in Downstate Medical. It's kind of tough for me to get in to see her."

"Why's that?"

Harman sighed. "Family stuff, you know how it is. There are a couple of old warrants out on me, and if my father knew I was here, I'd be wearing bracelets before the day was out."

"Nobody can do you like your family," Stoney said. "I'm thinking this will only take a few more days."

"I just have to stay out of the line of fire."

Stoney glanced at Fat Tommy, who nodded. "Tell you what," he said. "Before we move, we'll lay it all out, and then you can decide how you feel about it."

"Fair enough," Harman said.

Tuco wanted to hate the car, but it was impossible. Sure, the thing was a rolling cliché, it seemed that every second teenager in the wealthy Jersey burbs was driving one, maybe it was the upwardly mobile yuppie vehicle of choice, and yeah, you could buy two perfectly serviceable Hondas for less money, but still, the three-series BMW that Stoney had rented for him was beautiful, it was fast, and it seemed almost telepathically in tune to his intentions. He pointed it north on Route 17, sliding effortlessly through the throng of soccer moms driving elephantine SUVs. The dark blue Corolla he was tailing, six cars ahead, put its turn signal on and shouldered its way into the lane for the next exit, and Tuco followed suit behind it.

He had picked up the two girls at their high school. The school itself looked nothing like the ones Tuco had sporadically attended in Brooklyn. The place was a modern red-brick building that stood back from the street behind a wide spread of green lawn. From his spot under a tree on the far edge of the students' parking lot, Tuco could see the athletic fields out behind the place, where a bunch of kids in football uniforms ran up and down a practice field. Yellow buses were parked in a long half circle along the driveway out front. A flag flapped in the stiff breeze, and a bunch of flowers planted in a bed by the street out front nodded their heads to the cars passing by. God, he thought, what a fucking place. It didn't look anything like the five-story blockhouse he remembered on Pennsylvania

Avenue, surrounded by chain-link fences, with razor wire on the roof to keep the kids from throwing one another off.

He kept his eye on the blue Corolla. Stoney had pointed it out to him before he'd gone on his way. The kids came flooding out at the appointed time of their release, streaming past in groups, some headed for the parking lot, some for the buses, and more than a few straggling away on foot. There were none that looked like Tuco, they were predominantly white, with a smattering of Asians. But it wasn't Tuco's skin color or his economic status that separated his world from theirs, he knew that. If they had given you a free pass to this place, he told himself, it wouldn't have made any difference. You still couldn't cut it. The familiar bitterness rose up in his throat, and he fought to choke it back down, to keep from hating these children of privilege, these lucky souls trooping past on their way back to houses on quiet streets, off to their appointed and preordained futures on Wall Street, or wherever the hell else they might be going. So they caught a few more breaks than you did, he told himself. So what?

Get over it.

Growing up in Brooklyn, who knew that places like this even existed? It looked just like television out here, just like that neighborhood on *Desperate Housewives,* it was like a fantasy world, the kind of place where everyone seemed to have already gotten everything they wanted. How could you not hate them? Wasn't it only human to want to come out here and take something away from them, just so they could see how it felt, just that one time?

Two girls approached the Corolla. One of them was big, not fat but big, the kind of female that caught your eye, tall, long legs sticking out from under a short skirt, thick blond hair that ran down over her shoulders. The other one was a little shorter, and thin, with pale skin and dark hair. He knew immediately that the thin one was Stoney's daughter. He would have known even without the picture Stoney had given him, he would have known from those eyes, from the expression on her face that told you nothing. She didn't look much like her father, but she had definitely gotten some of his DNA. She got into the Corolla on the passenger side while the blond slid behind the wheel. A moment later the car pulled away. Tuco gave them a thirty-second head start, then followed.

He had assumed, at first, that they were headed for a mall, because Route 17, the road they headed for, seemed to split the very center of the retail universe, but they continued past the thicket of new car dealerships, rug stores, diners, giant bookstores, and furniture outlets. Finally they got off the highway and headed into the neighborhoods.

The town they wound up in, Ridgewood, had a main drag that rose gently up a hill as it stretched from east to west. It was a long street, lined on both sides with stores that sold the kinds of things Tuco had never known he needed. The Corolla pulled into a parking spot as Tuco drove past. He took the next spot, a block and a half farther up the hill. He spent the next several hours tailing the two girls, pretending to be interested in store-window displays while he waited. Neither of the girls seemed to buy anything. Recreational shoppers, he thought, with some derision. And they've probably already got at least one of everything that's for sale in this stupid place.

He paid four bucks for a cup of coffee, parked himself on a bench in a vest-pocket park while Stoney's daughter and her friend ogled a jewelry-store window. The stuff was bitter and tasted burned, but he sipped at it anyway.

He heard a phone ring, saw Stoney's daughter reach into her bag, pull out a cell phone, and answer it. Her body stiffened and she held the phone out away from her ear. Tuco couldn't hear her voice, but as he watched, her pale face flushed and she stood rigid, Tuco could not tell whether from anger or fear. After a minute, her voice got loud enough for him to hear. "No," she said. "Will you please stop?" She looked around, her eyes passing over but not stopping to rest on Tuco. "Just leave me alone." She snapped the phone closed, ending the call. She glanced around again, checking behind her on the street, a frightened impala trying to locate the lions before she dares take a drink. Tuco looked around, too, wondering if anyone there besides him did not belong in this suburban Jersey paradise. She won't stay out here now, he thought, she's gonna head for cover. That call spooked her. He dropped his coffee in the trash can.

TEN

Stoney sat in the AA meeting next to Benny and wondered what in hell he was doing there. I don't know any of these people, he thought, I hardly even know Benny, truth be told. The speaker was up front, telling a story about his twin brother, who had, one month previous, hung himself from a rafter in his garage out in Islip, Long Island. "I don't know why he didn't call me," the guy said. "But he couldn't get it. He kept relapsing, and I guess he got tired of it."

Stoney's mind wandered. He could still hear the guy's voice but was no longer conscious of what the guy was saying. He wondered if he had gotten "it," whatever it was, and what good it had done him if he had. He got up and went to the back of the room to refill his coffee cup. He stood there next to the big silver pot, turned, and looked at the backs of all the heads. It was an early morning meeting, and the place was full of people on their way to work. I know why the guy did it, he thought. I'm not on my way anywhere, and neither was he. He tossed his empty cup in the trash and walked out.

There was a bar just up the block, on the far side of the street. The sign over the door proclaimed it to be MCGLOIN'S TAVERN. There was an unlit neon beer sign in the single window. Apart from the sign, the place was dark, there was nothing else to see, nothing to tell you if the joint was open or what kind of place it was. Yeah, you bet your ass the place is open, he thought, and you know exactly what kind of place it is. It was a place for serious drinking. It would be dark in there, and quiet, and he could camp out at the end of the bar all day long. He'd have to say 'Old Grand-Dad' to the bartender just one time, and after that he wouldn't have to pass another single word to another living soul. Whenever he wanted a refill, a raised finger would do. Instant serenity, however short-lived it might be . . .

He walked straight on past the place. A sign in a bank window on the corner told him it was 7:45 A.M. God, he thought, I don't have to meet Tommy until two this afternoon, Jesus, what am I gonna do until then? He turned when he got to the corner, walked north on the avenue, headed nowhere.

Tuco watched Stoney's house from the church parking lot at the end of the block. There was an old station wagon in the lot, and Tuco parked on the far side of it and watched through the wagon's back windows. He'd been there almost an hour when the Toyota Corolla turned up Stoney's street, stopped in front of the house, and honked the horn. Marisa came out carrying an overnight bag and jumped into the car. He had a feeling it was going to be a long day. No way I would do this, he thought, for anybody besides Stoney or Tommy. Whatever else they might have done, those two had rescued him from the street, they had taken him in, given him his chance to break out. He shuddered, thinking what might have become of him if they hadn't done it. He let two cars pass by before pulling out to follow the Corolla.

• • •

The sound of leaf blowers echoed throughout the empty house in the enclave of McMansions up on the hill in Alpine, New Jersey. "Sorry to drag you back out here," Harman said.

I could have walked here, Stoney thought, and had time to spare. "Don't worry about it," he said. "Tommy explain what we came up with?"

"Yeah," Harman said.

"I wasa just cover the basics," Tommy said. "Better to talk about when everybody's in one place."

"We need five people, minimum," Stoney said. "Maybe a few more, depending on how things break."

"Sounds complicated," Harman said. "Most I ever worked with was five, and it didn't turn out very good for four of them. I wouldn't want to have to go through something like that again."

"I think you'll find us a civilized bunch," Stoney said wryly.

"Easy to say that now," Harman said. "Who would I be? Mr. A, Mr. B, or Mr. C?"

"I'm thinking you're a natural Mr. C."

"Okay. And I would guess Tommy is your Mr. B."

Stoney glanced at Fat Tommy, who nodded his assent.

"And who would you be?" Harman said, looking at Stoney. "You can't be Mr. A, you aren't even close to the right type. None of us is."

"No," Stoney said. "But a guy like Mr. A don't go far without his lawyer. It's the modern equivalent of carrying a six-shooter. I can be Mr. A's lawyer."

"You don't look much like a lawyer, either."

"Listen," Stoney said. "All I have to do is stand there while Mr. A screams at me, anyhow. Nothing to it."

"So who's Mr. A? You got anybody in mind?"

"Not yet," Stoney said.

"Yes," Tommy said, at almost exactly the same time. Stoney and Jack Harman both turned and looked at him. "Georgie Cho," Tommy said.

"Mrs. Cho's nephew?" Stoney said. "You think he'll go for it?"

Tommy nodded his head. "I gonna ask. But he gonna do, you wait and see."

"There's still one thing in all of this that makes me nervous," Harman said. "We still don't know who this guy really is. I'd feel a lot better if we knew exactly what kind of animal we were dealing with."

"We can still work on that," Stoney said. "We do know a few things about him. Rich guy, living under an alias. He's got to be hiding from something or somebody, so that makes him vulnerable. We know he's a plunger, otherwise he wouldn't be into commodities. And we know he's got the bucks. Plus, at any time in this process, we can pull the plug if things start to get sticky. I have a plan B to fall back on."

"Yeah, I'll bet you do," Harman said. "Well, Prior's a candidate, all right. Bored, greedy, rich, and in hiding. But remember, he's willing to kill to protect his identity."

"And good at it, apparently," Stoney said. "I agree with you, it would be better if we knew exactly who he is, but it's not critical. And we do have some time, because we're gonna be rehearsing for a while, especially with Georgie. His part is the most important."

"Georgie gonna be fine," Fat Tommy said. "You wait and see."

"So," Stoney said. "We ready to go to Defcon One?"

Jack looked at Stoney, then at Fat Tommy. "I'm not

breaking in anywhere," he said. "And I'm not putting on a mask and sticking a gun in anyone's face, either."

"Yeah," Stoney said. "I know, you said you were retired. That stuff is not our style, anyhow. The object of this game is to induce the mark into handing his money to you, and thanking you afterward for showing him a good time."

"Nice work if you can get it," Jack said. "I just want to make sure you understand, ahead of time, I have my limits. There are places I won't go any more. You know what I mean?"

"I don't have a problem with that," Stoney said. "I'm not down for storming the barricades, either. Why don't we do this? Let's walk through it a few times, and you let us know if we're getting you into places where you're not comfortable."

"All right," Harman said. "Get everybody together, and we'll do a couple of dry runs. See how it feels. Won't cost nothing to do that."

"No," Stoney said. "It won't cost us much until we sink the hook in Prior's lip. That's when it gets expensive. Couple hundred thou, I'm guessing."

"Maybe not that much," Tommy said. "I gonna buy for you wholesale. Don' worry, you gonna like."

"All right," Stoney said. "Jack, do you need to work from a script?"

"No," Harman said. "We'll just keep running over it until everybody's got it down cold."

She paused just inside the back door, her heart pounding. Jeannette was still on, but Marisa didn't like to wait inside after her set, she preferred sitting in the car. They paid her in cash, it saved everybody trouble, and she had the bills tucked into the side pocket of her bag.

Prior had been there tonight. He'd almost swallowed his tongue when he saw her walk out on the stage. He usually had two guards with him, but she'd only seen one, the one who shaved his head. Prior had moved up to the edge of the stage, stared at her with that sad-faced dog look of his, sat there rubbing himself and getting redder and redder.

It had felt so good, watching him watch her, up on the stage.

She put her hand on the crash bar that would open the back door. Fear and exhilaration, adrenaline and noise, money and the joy of letting loose, finally, they all swirled around in her mind as she took one last look around, wondering if she'd ever see the inside of the place again. You can't keep doing this, she thought. This has to be it, really. She nodded to herself. Last time.

I'm done with it. I have to be.

She shoved the door open and went through.

Mercury-vapor floodlights bathed the parking lot in an eerie blue glow. Jeannette's car was on the far side of the lot. She paused in the shadows by the corner of the building, listening. The last thing she needed was to get pawed by some half-loaded loser who wanted more than he could get inside. She couldn't hear anything over the hum of the cars out front on Route 46 and the drone of a small plane vectoring in for a landing at Teterboro Airport, just on the other side of the highway. Her heart was beating wildly. God, she thought, please get me though this, get me to bed safe tonight and I'll never come back here again. I promise. . . .

But you love it, she thought.

She started out across the parking lot, her shoes clicking on the pavement. She was just past the corner of the first row of cars, the ones parked up against the building, when she felt him grab her. His hand clamped down on her shoulder before she even knew he was there. It was the bald one, she knew it from his aftershave. She dropped her bag as his voice rasped in her ear. "Mr. Prior wants to talk to you."

She struggled, but she could sense the steel in his grip. "Let me go!" she said, looking wildly around the parking lot. She could see the cars going by on Route 46, but she did not see another human being out and walking. "I'm not talking to him!"

The guy chuckled. "You're not showing Mr. Prior much respect," he said. "Shut up and come with me."

"Let me go!" This guy could kill me, she thought, and her strength and will to resist seemed to drain out of her. God, what if I never gonna see my mother again, or Dennis, or even my father. . . . She began to think about all the terrible things men did to women, and she felt her knees go weak.

"Hey, asshole." She heard the unfamiliar voice, then felt the impact. Then she heard the bald man's explosive grunt as something heavy hit him in the back. His arm flew off her and his momentum catapulted her away from him, throwing her down onto her hands and knees on the coarse pavement. She could feel small pebbles and grains of sand embed themselves in the skin of her palms as she fought to absorb the impact of the fall with her hands and not her face. She rolled over, wrenching her shoulder and banging the back of her head on the ground in the process. "Lady said to let go," the voice said. She still didn't know who the speaker was, but she saw Prior's man swarming to his feet, turning to face a stocky figure that had stepped out of the shadows.

"Goddammit!" the guy yelled. "This is none of your business! You'd better hit the fucking road, pal!"

Get up, she thought, her anger returning, get up, goddammit. She struggled to her feet, slightly unsteady. The newcomer was shorter than her father, looked like he was in his early twenties. He had that same broad build her father did, that same physical presence. He had black hair, pale brown skin, and the face of a cruel Incan deity, the kind you saw carved into a temple wall. His nose started high up on his forehead and ran straight down, hooking slightly at the end, where it flared out at the tip. His eyes were so dark she could not distinguish pupil from iris, all she could see was black. He was just a kid compared to the guard, though, and now she was worried that Prior's guard was going to kill the kid, whoever he was. The bald guy seemed to wave his hand, and a black-bladed knife materialized in his fist. "I will cut you, boy. You hear me?" He sliced at the kid's midsection, but the kid danced aside, and suddenly he had the hand holding the knife in his grip. He bent the bald guy's wrist back at an unnatural angle, then, as the man shouted in pain, the kid punched him hard in the face. Prior's man staggered back, lost his footing, and went down, eyes wide.

Marisa stared at the kid. "Who are you?" she shouted.

Behind her, the side door to the limo opened and Prior's other guard got out. She half expected to see Prior, too, but he didn't show. "Run!" the kid yelled at her. "Go! Get outta here!" She kicked herself into awkward motion, saw the bald man on the ground latch onto the kid's leg as she went past. He's got two of them to deal with now, she thought, and she stopped and turned back. The driver was coming fast, and the bald one was struggling to maintain his grip on the kid's leg as he rolled up onto his hands and knees. She felt the rage rising up in her throat. It was two quick steps back to them, and she put all of her anger in the kick. The guy let go of the kid and howled, curling himself into a ball just like a spider landing on a candle flame.

The second guard dropped one shoulder and dove into the kid's chest, and the two of them tumbled down onto the pavement. Baldie had a pistol in his armpit, she could see the checkered black grip stark against his white shirt. He was in no shape to resist, so she reached down and pulled it out. She'd never held a gun before, but she'd seen it in the movies a thousand times. She racked the slide back to chamber the first round, guessed that the tiny lever by her thumb was the safety. She flipped it up, exposing a tiny red dot.

Had to be.

The two fighting on the ground were still ignoring her, so she pointed the pistol at the limo and pulled the trigger. It went off, twisting skyward in her grip. They quit struggling, then, and she walked over and rested the end of the pistol against the side of the guard's head.

The kid extricated himself, stood up, and took the gun away from her. "Gimme that," he said. He stepped back, dragging her with him. "Shots fired," he said to the driver. "Cops got to be on the way. You wanna be here when they show?"

The driver glared at the two of them, then grabbed Baldie and heaved him to his feet. He glanced back at them once more. "I'll see you around," he said.

"Okay, *pato*," the kid told him.

Marisa felt her face flaming red. She looked at the kid standing there with Baldie's pistol in his hand. "Who are you?"

"Your father sent me," he said, without looking at her, and she felt a chill run throughout her body. "This way, come on."

"My girlfriend's car . . ."

"No time for that," he said. "Come on."

He was parked in a lot behind a warehouse a short distance away. He had the car started and moving before she even got her door closed, but he stomped the brake before he got to the street. "Where's your bag?"

"Back . . . Back there."

"Shit. What's in it?"

Her costume, the one she kept in Jeannette's trunk, along with the money she'd made. "Nothing," she said.

"You sure? Nothing with your name on it?"

"Nothing. Go."

He parked next to an all-night drugstore in Hackensack, and the two of them went inside for first-aid supplies for Marisa's bleeding hands. They stood outside by the car in a pool of light from the drugstore window while he used tweezers to pick the pebbles out of her palms, dabbing iodine on the holes they left behind. "You didn't tell me your name," she said, biting her lip as he probed with a pair of tweezers.

"Tuco."

"Tuco? Is that your real name?"

"The name my mother gave me is Eddie. Nobody but her uses it."

"Do you mind if I call you Eddie?"

"Whatever," he said. "Gimme your other hand."

"Did you go inside, Eddie? Back at the Jupiter?"

"What difference does it make?"

"I just want to know how rotten I should feel," she said.

He looked up at her and nodded. "Hadda pay the door guy an extra twenty to let me in, on account of being underage."

"Oh," she said in a small voice. She winced as he dabbed iodine on one of the deeper cuts. "I'm sorry you saw that."

"Me, too," he said. "If it bothers you, why do it?" She didn't answer.

"Who were those two guys?"

"Bodyguards," she said. "They work for a man named Prior. He's obsessed with me."

"Why?"

"I don't know. Before me, he was all over this girl from Colombia, until she disappeared. Everybody thinks she went home, but nobody knows for sure."

"You think he could have did something to her?"

"If he wanted to. He does whatever he wants."

He finished with her hands, took the rest of the first-aid stuff, and dumped it in a trash can over by the pharmacy door. She stood by the car and waited for him to come back. "What now?" she said.

"Now I take you home."

"No!" she said, alarmed. "You can't! My mother thinks I'm staying at Jeannette's house. If I go back now, she'll . . . She'll have all sorts of questions."

"You're in too deep," he told her. "Your parents gonna find out anyhow. Might as well get it over with."

"Oh, come on, Eddie! Can't you give me a break? I'll never go back to that place, I swear to you. . . ."

"You don't gotta swear nothing to me," he said, turning away.

"If my father finds out, he'll kill me."

"If he finds out I knew about it and didn't tell him, he'll kill us both. Besides, those two assholes will be ready for me next time around. You won't be so lucky."

"I can take care of myself."

"Oh yeah?" His voice rose in disbelief. "Is that what you was doing back in that parking lot? Is that what that was? Because if it wasn't for me, you'd probably be in the back of that fucking Lincoln right now, sugar, and telling your mother how you spend your nights wouldn't be your number one problem."

"I know, but . . ."

"But what? This is fucking stupid, you know that?"

She looked around the darkened street, but there was no one else in sight.

"Let me ax you something," he said. "What do you got up in that head of yours, anyhow?"

She stood there, looking off down the empty street.

"Look at yourself," he said. "You got everything." She could hear a kernel of resentment in his voice. "I seen that house you live at, and I seen that that country-club school, too. You got everything, but you wanna piss it all away to go dance in some fucking hoochie joint?" He shook his head. "I been through this before." He turned away from her. "I can't do it again. It's too hard."

"What are you talking about?"

"You think you're the first empty-headed female to piss her life away?" He turned back to face her. "I wouldn't care, you know, if I didn't, already like, talk to you and all that. But I can't take this shit." He shook his head. "I'm gonna tell your father I can't do this anymore. He's gonna have to lock your ass up in a convent or some shit."

"Come on, Eddie. So I messed up. Haven't you ever done anything stupid in your life?"

He stared at her. "That's it? You think this is just, some

little thing, like you bought the wrong color shoes, and now you got to take 'em back to the store?"

"Was it really that terrible?"

He shook glanced at his watch. "Anybody gonna be looking for you tonight?"

"Jeannette, maybe," she said. "My girlfriend. I can leave a message on her voice mail."

"Get in the car, then," he said. "Somebody I want you to meet."

It was well after midnight when they cruised down Troutman Street, just west of the Brooklyn/Queens border. The junkyards, sweatshops, garages, and factories were all boarded up tight for the night, but the whores and the dope dealers were still out, and commerce was still being conducted. Tuco cruised slowly past the small groups of neighborhood kids, waving off the few that approached the car. "She probably be down here somewhere," he told her.

"Who is she?" Marisa asked him. "How do you know her?"

He didn't answer.

"You live here?"

"Not anymore," he said. "But my mother still lives right around the corner. I slept on her couch my whole life, almost."

They passed a double-parked car. A man leaned his butt against the grille, his hands behind him on the hood. Marisa turned to look at him as they passed by, and the girl on her knees on front of the man paused to stare back. "What's she doing?"

"What's it look like? Hey, there's someone, I think I know that kid." He pointed to a knot of teenagers on the next block.

"I only been gone a little while, but I was beginning to think everybody was gone." He glanced at Marisa. "Lotta turnover in their business. Your father told me that." He paused at the red light on the corner, then cruised through the intersection and pulled over, rolling his window down. "Yo, Mario," he said. "That you?"

"Tuco!" One of the kids detached himself from the group and sauntered over. He looked like he was about fourteen, but Marisa had the impression that this kid was the real thing, and the guys in the rap videos were the poor copies. "Hey, muthafucka, wassup, bro? That look like yo lawyer's car. You want some rims for that piece a shit, I could hook you up," he said, laughing.

"No thanks, Mario."

The kid peered past Tuco at Marisa. "You shoulda stuck around, back after you whacked out half a Dr. Jack's crew," he said, looking back at Tuco. He peered into the empty backseat. "You coulda stepped right up, bro, you coulda been the man round here. You coming back now, the shit is all tight. You gonna have some people up in yo face."

"I don't do retail, Mario. Listen, man, you know who I'm looking for. You seen her?"

"Miguel's bitch? That ho is dead, yo."

Tuco exhaled, leaned back in his seat. "What happened? She OD?"

Mario shook his head. "Somebody cut her up. Cops found her down on Flushing, they took her to Woodhull, but you know how it is. You want me to find out who did her?"

Tuco looked like he was thinking it over. "No," he said, after a minute. "She wasn't mine. I was just trying to help her out."

"Bitch was beat, anyhow," Mario told him. "Used and abused, bro. Not like that sweet little white piece you got right there. Why you looking for some skank when you got that one?"

"She was no skank when she started out, Mario."

"Well, she ain't nothing now," Mario said. "She ain't even a whisper no more."

"No," Tuco agreed. "Thanks, Mario. I'm rolling."

Mario pushed himself off the car, shot Tuco with an index finger as Tuco rolled up the window and pulled away. "Ain't it nice?" he asked her, looking straight ahead. "This is what your father and Fat Tommy saved me from. Just makes me all homesick and shit."

"Who's the girl you were looking for?"

"The one that got sliced up?" Tuco turned left, headed up the hill. "She was as pretty as you are, once." He exhaled, glanced over at her. "She didn't come from Jersey, she grew up out on the island. Oyster Bay. Beautiful, out there. I wanted you to see her. I think—" He stopped, waited a moment. "I thought she really wanted to get out of it. I thought she was probably a good person, you know, besides being a addict. Maybe she was. Too late, now. Anyway, I wanted you to see her. She would have told you, you know, what she hadda do for ten bucks. Just so you'd know. You know what I'm saying? Because that business you're in, it ain't like it looks on television." He looked away. "And I wanted to see her again, myself. Twist the knife one more goddam time." He stopped at a red light, actually waited for it to turn green.

"Would you have wound up like Mario?" she said, after a minute.

"No," he told her. "Mario's way smarter than I was at his age. I probably woulda wound up dead. Anyhow, I could drop you on a good corner, that's what you want. Might as well get right to it."

"Stop it, Eddie," she said. "Knock it the fuck off, okay? And take me home."

It was still dark when Tuco slid the BMW up into Stoney's driveway. He shut the car off, sat there listening to the engine ticking as it cooled down. Marisa put her hand on the door handle. "What did Mario mean," she asked him, "when he said you whacked out half of Dr. Jack's crew?"

"My cousin," Tuco said. "My cousin Miguel."

"Did you really kill him? And his crew?"

"He did it to himself," Tuco said. "Listen, I'll give you the day, all right? I'll lie to your father one time for you. But work it out. Tell him straight up, that's the best way. Because I owe him too much. You hear what I'm saying?"

"Yes," she said. "All right."

"You going to school today?"

"No," she said.

"Well, do me a favor. Stay away from that other stupid cow, what was her name?"

"Jeannette?" She didn't know whether to be outraged or not.

"Yeah, that's her. From now on, I'm your dog. You wanna go somewhere, anywhere at all, you call me, I'll take you. Can we do that?"

"Yes, Eddie," she said. "Give me your phone number."

"You got something to write on?"

"Just give me the number," she told him. "I'll remember it. I'm not as stupid as you think I am."

The light over the garage door went on, and she got a good look at Tuco's face, haggard in the stark white glare. "Oh, shit, that's got to be my mother," she said, and she opened her door. "I'm in for it now. I'm sorry about your friend, Eddie. The one they found on Flushing Avenue."

"Me, too," he said, and he gave her his phone number.

The front door opened, and she saw her mother standing in the doorway. "Eddie? Can you do me a favor? One more, I mean. I think you'd better come inside."

ELEVEN

When Stoney called Tina Finbury, she suggested that they meet for a late breakfast. Stoney had resisted the impulse to grill her on the phone, but the two hours he had to wait before he saw her had been bad, and now he sat across from her in a booth at the Westwood Pancake House, sick to his stomach.

She reached across the table and put a hand on one of his. "You know, honey, this is not always such a nice business. But you can stop worrying, your wife isn't seeing anybody."

His head swam, he felt as though the chair he sat on and the floor under it were suddenly unsteady. Tina was still talking, and after a few seconds Stoney held up a hand to stop her. Relief and nausea washed over him in waves. God, it wasn't true, what the hell had Marisa been talking about? But you still can't assume that Donna feels anything for you. He closed his eyes, brought himself back under control. He took one of the paper napkins off the table and wiped his face with it. "All right," he said. "Sorry."

"It's fine," she said. "You ready? Your wife seems to be celibate. She goes to work, she goes home, she talks to her girlfriends on the phone. Attends some Al-Anon meetings. There are a few guys at those, but not many. Two *alte kakhers* in one of the meetings she goes to, some teenagers in another one. She didn't talk to any of them, except to say hello."

"How do you know that?"

"I went in," she said. "I been, plenty of times, believe me. Okay, she uses her computer, but like an old woman. No chat rooms or any of that."

"So what does that tell you?"

She smiled at him. "Try to keep up, honey. It means she's not into any online funny business. She looks at the same stuff every time she logs on. She stays on for five, ten minutes, looks at the market, reads her e-mail and her horoscope, pulls the plug. That's it. Now maybe, it's remotely possible, she is seeing someone, or has in the past, and maybe they didn't talk to each other this past week. But I'm telling you, my opinion, she's an angel."

Stoney leaned back in his chair. "God."

"So that's a good thing. But we're not finished yet."

"No?"

"No." She shook her head. "Not quite. This next part is not so nice. I'm just gonna tell you straight out. On the nights your wife is out of the house, someone uses her computer to surf porn sites and adult chat rooms. At first, I assumed it was your son, you know?" She shrugged. "I mean, boys are boys, and they're gonna look, if they think they can get away with it, and sometimes, even if they know they can't. That's how God made them. But he's just thirteen, he's all the time with the skates, I couldn't see it. Didn't feel right. And that only leaves you, honey, and your daughter, and you haven't been home. Plus, your daughter spends a lot of time out of the house. Her girlfriend comes to pick her up, she walks out with schoolbooks and an overnight bag. Nobody said yes and nobody said no, but I thought I should go have a look."

Stoney sighed. "Okay."

She reached down into a bag at her feet, pulled out a red file folder, placed it on the table between the two of them. "Your daughter has been, aah, performing in what they like to call a 'gentleman's club' these days. She's a dancer." Tina's expression told him another word would have been more accurate, but she hadn't used it, on his account. "There's a written report in here, my name's not on it anywhere, but it'll tell you everything you need to know. Names, dates, phone conversation transcripts." She hesitated, touched the folder with her fingertips. "I shredded everything I had. The only copy of any of this is right here. The phone taps are off, and the phone company has no record that they were ever there. There's a disk in here, boot it up and follow the directions and it'll clean out the spyware our chickenhearted friend put on your hard drive. It's important you should do that, God forbid somebody comes looking later on, you don't want anything there for them to see." She cleared her throat. "Listen, I know it's none of my business . . ."

He looked at her. "But."

She nodded. "Don't be too hard on her. Everybody makes mistakes."

"Yeah, well." He could hear his own pulse thundering in his ears. "I guess I made plenty."

"We all do, love. I hired a photographer. The pictures are in the white envelope. Eight-by-tens. But, one thing . . ."

"Yeah?"

"Don't look at them here. Take them home, do it in private."

"Okay." Stoney could feel his world resolving itself into black-and-white stills, becoming clearer, less complicated. Benny was right, he would know what to do when the time came.

"This gets worse," she said.

"Jesus Christ, now what?"

"She worked for an escort service, too. I can't say exactly what she did for them. Everything I do know is in that report."

He leaned back as the room swam in a slow circle around him. His head seemed ripped in two separate directions as his relief over his wife's loyalty competed with his distress over his daughter. What, exactly, had been her problem with Charles David Prior? "What's the name of the escort service?"

"Perfect Angels."

"All right," he said, after a minute. "Listen, Tina, you did great. There's just a couple of things we gotta cover."

"Yes? My fee, for one, I know you're too polite to mention it, but since this yutz you hired has taken a powder . . ."

"Don't worry, I'll take care of you, but that's not what I meant. Is there any way, say someone was looking for information, is there some way to tie you to this kid who is not your boss who took off on me?"

"No," she said. "You told me before, he was looking into someone named Prior for you. Is he the one you're worried about?"

"Yeah." He told her about the dead security guard.

"Now I see why he ran away. Such a schmuck," she said. "Well, I guess it was the smart thing. And no, honey, you don't need to worry about me, my deal with him is strictly cash." She smiled. "My ex-husband's lawyers take such an interest in my career, I can't tell you. But the stupid kid and his computer, sometimes you gotta shut the thing off and go look for yourself already. Microsoft Golf, he can beat Tiger Woods, but a real golf club, he don't know which end to hang on to."

"Well, if this guy Prior has already killed one person to protect his privacy, I don't want anything else to go wrong."

"That's so nice, you worrying about me. Why don't you tell me about this Prior individual."

He shook his head. "I really think—"

"Honey," she said, interrupting him. "Look, the best place to hide is always in plain sight. You wanna look into someone else's dirty laundry on a computer, you go to the library and use a public machine. Even if somebody should come looking, what are they gonna do, sit there all day long to see if you come back? You want my help or not?"

He looked at her, thought it over for a minute. "All right," he said finally. "As long as you're sure he can't get back to you. The guy lives up on the hill in Alpine, rides a bike, a real beauty . . ." She pulled a pad out of her bag and started taking notes.

She looked up when he was done. "That it?"

"No," he said. "First, I want to be absolutely sure you can do this without endangering yourself."

"Don't worry," she said. "I didn't stay alive this long by being stupid."

"Fine. But if you mess up, if you feel uncomfortable, you even see the wrong guy in the rearview mirror, you call me."

"Done."

"Okay. Second, forget about where he lives, where he goes, and all that. Here's what I really want you to find out. . . ."

Stoney sat in his car in the parking lot behind the diner, watching the cars next door lining up for the car wash. It took a while, but when he felt ready, he called Donna on her cell phone.

"I got a favor to ask," he said when she came on the line.

"Yes? What would that be?" She sounded strangely detached.

"A couple of favors, actually."

"Why not?" she said calmly. "I've got no life anyway, I was just sitting here waiting for someone to call me and give me something to do."

He ignored that. "First," he said, "stay home tonight. And second, keep Marisa home with you."

"She'll be so thrilled," Donna said. "After the fight the two of us had this morning, she gets a chance to spend another evening at home with Mom. What could be more exciting?" Donna exhaled fatigue into the phone. "Your friend from Brooklyn brought her home early this morning," she said. "We had it out. She and I. She told me everything."

"Everything? What everything?"

"I don't want to do this on the telephone."

"Man, you really know how to torture me, you know that?"

"You're a big boy. You can take it."

"God."

"This hasn't been easy for me, either, you know."

"Okay," he said. "You're right. Doing this on the phone is a bad idea. How about we meet tomorrow morning, before you go to work."

"All right," she said. "Seven o'clock. Where?"

"Westwood Pancake House," he said. "That's the diner across the street from the hospital."

"I'll be there," she said, and she hung up. Stoney looked at his phone for a minute, then dialed Tuco's cell number.

"Yeah." Tuco sounded groggy.

"What's up?" Stoney asked him.

"Nothing. Your daughter's at home."

"Yeah, I know that." Why are you holding out on me, you

little fuck? He wanted to ask, but he held it in. He could feel the fury building up inside, it had started when he first looked at the pictures Tina had given him. "Anything else I should know about?"

"The world is fulla shit you should probably know about."

"Tuco, what the fuck happened last night?"

"Look, Stoney, you trust me? You trust me or what?"

"Fuck that," Stoney said. "I wanna know what the fuck is going on."

"Stoney, you want me to keep her safe, am I right? I did that. Right now she is safe at home, probably up in her bed. I did what you axed me to do."

Stoney swallowed his anger. The kid actually did more than I asked him to, he thought. And ratting somebody out, even to me, goes against everything he grew up believing. Still . . . "All right," Stoney said. "I'll talk to you later."

TWELVE

Five o'clock in the fucking morning, and after a sleepless night. You gotta be kidding me. . . . Stoney parked on a quiet street in Englewood, New Jersey, and walked back to the arena. It was a small block building just inside the edge of the park. The water tower that cooled the refrigeration system sat on the corner of the roof, blowing water vapor into the predawn sky. He heard the referee's whistle just as he went through the side door. He found a spot by the rail just in time to see a guy in a striped shirt escort some kid off the ice. It was obvious the kid was angry, he slammed his stick to the ground and threw himself into the plastic chair that served as the penalty box. The ref stood by the rail and talked to the kid for a few seconds. Calming him down, Stoney thought. Telling him what he did wrong. He did it quietly, too, without yelling at the kid. Stoney watched the guy. Tall, a little paunchy, thinning hair, late thirties. Jesus, Stoney thought. I get up early one time to come down here and I'm all pissed off. Wonder how many times this guy's done it? And for what? So that a bunch of thirteen-year-old carpet rats can have a hockey league. Yeah, sure, one of them is probably his, but still.

The penalty made the team from Closter shorthanded. The father who was coaching them sent four fresh bodies onto the ice. One of them was a little shorter than the other kids, and he skated around in a couple of quick circles to warm up. Even with the helmet, the pads, the gloves, and all the rest of it, Stoney knew the kid was his son, Dennis.

Stoney felt the weight of an elephant sitting on his chest, wondered briefly if he might not be having a heart attack, but it was just the kid, just his fear that he'd lost him, or worse, messed him up somehow. He had always operated under the conceit that his behavior hadn't hurt anyone but himself, that he paid his own way, that he'd never walked away owing anybody, but it came to him right there, leaning on the rail watching his kid skate, that he'd been hiding from the truth, believing his own bullshit so that he could do what he needed to do. He wondered, then, what kind of price this kid was going to have to pay for his father's misdeeds. Dennis went at things with a single-minded focus and drive that was very reminiscent of the monomania which Stoney had noticed was very common among addicts.

He couldn't think of anything to do about it.

The father in the striped shirt blew his whistle, and they got the game started again. Stoney had bought Dennis a pair of street skates and some lessons, back before he and Donna had split. The kid had practiced in the driveway with feverish determination, starting as soon as the two of them had gotten home from the store. Now he was a much better skater than he'd been the last time Stoney had seen him. The Closter team's penalty-killing strategy consisted of the five kids from the other team chasing Dennis around. The kid was quick, it was hard to get a clean hit on him, and he handled the puck well. After a little better than a minute, they boxed him in down in one corner of his own end, and he passed the puck out to one of his teammates. They gave it back to him soon enough, though, and as the penalty ended, he charged through center ice and rushed the opposing goalie. He didn't get a shot off, one of their defensemen knocked him off the puck, but by then, Closter was back at full strength.

Yeah, sure, Stoney thought. These other guys come out here every week for the little bastards, and you think you did something good because you bought the kid a pair of skates. They had "No Smoking" signs up all over the place, so Stoney went over by the door and lit up. It's no good telling yourself that you're doing the best you can, he thought. You've done more harm than good.

He'd opened Tina Finbury's white envelope the day before, looked at the pictures before reading the report. New Jersey was one of those states that had a lot of regulations about what can and cannot take place inside a strip joint. As a result of that, a girl in a bikini was basically all you got to look at. The bar was called the Jupiter Club, it was in South Hackensack, down by the Teterboro Airport. There was one shot of the exterior. The inside of the place looked like they all did: he could practically smell it. There were two dancers in most of the rest of the pictures. One of them was Marisa. She wore a tiny metallic-silver thong bikini, and she had the usual garter strap around one upper thigh, a bunch of paper money stuck underneath it. Her skin was ghostly white in the spotlights, and the angle of the shots made her look taller, and older, than she was in real life. There were enough pictures to give Stoney more information than he really needed. She was squatting down in one, legs apart, holding the garter strap open so that one of the patrons could show his appreciation while she watched disdainfully. The guy might have been Charles David Prior, but he had his back to the camera, and Stoney couldn't be sure. Maybe he was adding two and two and coming up with five, but he figured he didn't need Einstein's brain to figure out why she'd told him that Donna was seeing Prior. So assume the guy in the strip club with his back to the camera really is Prior, Marisa tells me that Donna is seeing the guy, probably thought I'd kill him, Stoney thought. I'm her trump card, and she's betting I can end the game. Why would she want Prior dead? What had he done?

In another shot, she had her back to the edge of the stage, and she was bent over, stiff-legged, her palms flat on the floor. There were others, too, as well as the written report that went with them. Jesus, why couldn't she have taken after her mother? He asked himself that for the umpteenth time. He glanced through the rest of the pictures quickly, just to make sure they held no more surprises, skimmed through the report. There had been some ugly stuff there, the part about the escort service had been worse than the pictures, really, almost more than he could handle.

The other team scored a goal. The players on that team cheered, along with some of the fathers. The kids skated around high-fiving one another. Two of them fell down, occasioning some laughter and name-calling. Stoney had not been following the game, he didn't know if Dennis had been on the ice for the goal or not. Pay more attention, he told himself. Isn't that what this is supposed to be about? It was hard, though. Even without everything else he had on his mind, the fact was, he'd never played hockey, never watched any of the games, and he couldn't get into it. Bunch of kids with sticks skating around in circles, knocking one another down . . .

Marisa wore the same expression in all of the shots where

you could see her face. It was a lot like the one favored by the broad across the hall from Mrs. Cho's place; a little bit of euphoria, a little bit more of contempt, and some bemused indulgence. The woman knows what she's got, and she knows what we'll do to get it. Now it appeared that Marisa had discovered that, as well. Having the power was one thing, though. Knowing how to use it without getting yourself jammed up was something else.

He'd been sick, at first, he remembered feeling the same way, years ago, when they told him his mother was dying of cancer. Sick, helpless, disbelieving. The rage passed over him in recurring waves, for five or ten seconds at a time he was capable of any destructive act his mind could conjure up, but the waves seemed to recede as quickly as they came. So far. After some of the shock had worn off, mostly what he felt was sorrow. Kids, even smart ones, can be so stupid. . . .

He wondered how Donna was going to take it. He had talked it over with Benny, at Fat Tommy's insistence, the previous afternoon.

"Who took the pictures?" Benny wanted to know. It was hard to tell Benny the parts you wanted and leave the rest out. Evasive action was no good with him, he was worse than a fucking lawyer.

Stoney sighed. "This investigator I hired."

"You hired a detective? Why?"

God, dealing with this guy was like having another wife. "I thought Donna was stepping out on me."

"Why did you think that?"

"I got the impression, talking to Marisa."

"Oh. Was she?"

"No."

"So how come the investigator was following Marisa?"

"I guess she smelled a rat."

"All right, fine. So your seventeen-year-old daughter is dancing in a club." Benny stared at him. "Now you wanna go kill someone. Safe assumption?"

Stoney looked at Benny for a long count. "Is this conversation privileged?"

"You oughta know by now if you can trust me or not."

"All right, yeah, I'm thinking I should torch the place," Stoney said. "Or the guy who owns it. Or both."

Benny looked at him, unblinking. "You know, I believe you could do it."

"Fucking right I could do it."

"So say you burn the place down, and a fireman gets killed fighting the fire. How you gonna feel, then?"

Stoney shook his head, then shrugged. "He's supposed to know better."

"C'mon, man, some putz is trying to do his job and he gets roasted alive because you want to inconvenience some asshole who's had the temerity to pay your daughter for doing something she apparently wants to do, of her own volition. I didn't see anybody holding a gun to her head."

Stoney kept his voice calm. "She's underage, Benny."

"Fine, she's underage. You could go to the cops, rat the guy out, you could probably get him shut down. So what?"

"What do you mean, 'So what?'"

"So fucking what? You think this place is the only strip joint around? You told me Marisa's seventeen, that means she's gonna be eighteen in a matter of months. What's to stop her from going right back out to this place the day after her birthday? Or another one just like it? Or worse?"

"Me, that's what. I'll kill her."

"Sure you will. Look, you asked my opinion, here it is. You and your wife been doing the addict-codependant mambo ever since you got married. Who do you think has been raising these two kids of yours? The other kids they hang with, the shit they watch on television, and maybe a teacher or two, if you're lucky. Is it any wonder they're a little bit fucked up?" He waited for his words to sink in a little, then continued. "There's only one person involved in this mess whose behavior you have any control over." He stopped then, and waited.

"Yeah, all right," Stoney said, gritting his teeth. "Me."

"Yeah, you. Maybe. You go off on this kid, okay, you start yelling and making all kinda threats, you go whack the guy owns the strip club, and I promise you, a year from now, she'll be taking it off in some other joint." He waited, again, let the weight of that settle on Stoney's shoulders. "I promise you. And you know where it goes from there."

"Yeah." He didn't want to even think it, let alone say it out loud.

Benny was not one to pull his punches. "Yeah. She'll be doing the horizontal boogaloo with whoever has the price of the dance. Let me ask you one thing. What's your objective in this? What do you really want?"

It took him a few seconds. "I want to get her out of it."

"Are you sure? Because if you just want to get back at somebody, okay, if you just want to hit somebody so you can feel better about yourself, I can't help you. I'm guessing you already know how to do that."

"Look, I'm not gonna lie to you, Benny, I want the guy's dick in my pocket. But not as bad as I want to get Marisa out."

"All right. Start by admitting that you can't control what she does. Not for long, anyhow. Try to look at it this way: your daughter's in trouble, and she needs your help. Maybe you can show her how to make smarter decisions, but you've got to start by making smarter ones yourself. You know what they say, Stoney."

"What's that?"

"Do what you always did, you'll get what you always got."

"I understand that. But I gotta tell her something, Benny."

"Yeah, you do. Just remember, you'll be walking a fine line. Lose your balance, you might lose your daughter, too."

The kids were cheering again, the Closter team had scored a goal, but they were still behind, and they were running out of time. There was another group of kids, even younger, down at the end of the building, waiting their turn. Stoney didn't know if Dennis had noticed him or not, the kid had given no sign, but when the game ended, he skated over.

"Hi, Dad." The kid kept his voice low, and he avoided eye contact.

"Hey. Good game, kid."

"We lost, Dad."

"Yeah, I saw that. But I saw how you killed that penalty, too. You played a good game."

Dennis looked down at the ice. "Thanks," he said, after a few seconds. "You coming home soon?"

So easy to tell some reassuring lie. "I don't know," he said. "I will if I can."

The kid looked up at him, then back down at his skates. "I can ask Mom, I can tell her—"

"Don't do it."

Dennis made a face, but did not look up. "Why not?"

"Because you don't need to be worrying about that. You need to worry about school, and about working on your slap shot. Your mom and I need to take care of our own shit."

"All right. Thanks for coming to see the game."

"When do you play again?"

"Friday. Four-thirty."

"In the morning?" Jesus. "Why so early?"

"On Fridays, the old guys have the ice at five." The makings of a grin danced at the corners of his face. "Guys your age."

"Oh yeah?"

The dad who coached the Closter team was calling Dennis. Dennis looked over his shoulder. "I gotta go, Dad."

"All right. I'll see you."

"Okay." Dennis nodded, pushed off, raced across the ice in a flurry of quick, short strides. You don't even know where the kid is going from here, Stoney thought, you don't know if he's going home or to school or what. That's how much involvement you got.

Hey, Stoney thought, take what life gives you. Hard, though, not wanting more.

There are a lot of diners in north Jersey, every little town seems to have at least one, usually owned by Greeks, but not always. The buildings they are in look like they all came from the same Prefabricated Diner Factory: chrome and glass, stone facade, interiors finished with a lot of wood that seems to be designed to look as much like plastic as possible. They may have named it the Westwood Pancake House, but it was still a diner.

He sat at a table in the smoking section and fed his nicotine habit while he waited for her. He was the only person in the place who was smoking, even though there were ashtrays on all the tables in his half of the place. Some old crow looked at him cross-eyed when he lit up, he returned the stare until she looked away. Fuck you, bitch, he thought. Plenty of empty tables over on the other side.

He wanted to stand up when he saw Donna come through the doorway, he wanted to smile, throw his arms around her, ask her to dance, something, anything. He didn't do any of those things, though, he stubbed out his cigarette, closed the red folder, and waited for her to come over and sit down.

"Good morning." She smiled at him, sat down. She looked at the red folder on the table, but she didn't ask what was in it.

"Good morning." He watched her face as she read her menu. He apologized again. "Sorry about, you know, last minute and everything. I'm not getting you in trouble with your boss, am I?"

"No." She shook her head. "That woman is so disorganized, she hardly ever notices what's going on. Do you believe she hadn't been able to find a hairdresser around here that she liked? She knew this woman in London, though, she found her when she was over there on some kind of conference, so she'd been flying over there once a month just to get her hair done."

"You're kidding me."

"Scout's honor."

"Damn. So, you're like her personal assistant? You find her someone over here?"

"Yes, I am, and yes, I did. That was the least of it, Stoney. Her whole life is like that. You wouldn't believe the money she throws away on stupidness."

"Sounds like you're enjoying what you're doing."

She looked at him then, thought about it. "I am," she said,

after a minute. "It feels good, especially after I was so afraid, you know, leaving my little cocoon, and all—"

The waiter came then, interrupting them. They ordered, sat there in silence for a minute after the waiter was gone. She looked at him, not at the red folder. "So," she said, leaning on the table. "I assume this is about Marisa."

He had forgotten, for a few minutes, what it had been that had occasioned this meeting. "Yeah," he said, and he pushed the folder across the table to her. "I don't know what she told you, but this is what I got." He'd gone through it earlier, removed all of the pictures but one. He was still fearful, though, there was no other word for it. He was afraid that this was going to be the last straw, not what their daughter was doing so much as the fact that he'd hired someone to snoop on them.

She sucked her breath in when she saw the picture, went pale, then shook her head and exhaled. "That girl," she said. "God, you know, I could have sworn she was going through something, but I never thought . . ." She put the picture facedown on the table, picked up the top page of the report, scanned it for a few seconds, then looked at Stoney. "What made you . . . how did you find this out?"

He had known that question was coming, had his story ready. "Friend of a friend," he said. There was no way he was telling her the truth about this. "I guess the guy saw her, said, you know, isn't that what's-his-name's girl, told his buddy about it, and his buddy got word back to me. I was afraid to ask you, you know, I didn't want to get something started, especially if none of it was true. So anyway, I hired a someone to look into it."

She stared at him for a few seconds. He couldn't read her expression, couldn't tell if she was buying his story or not. She looked down again, glanced at a few of the other pages. "Who did this?" she asked. "Who was this guy you hired? I don't see his name on this anywhere."

He didn't correct her. Let her think it was a man, he thought. Probably safer that way. "He was just a guy. He came highly recommended."

"A guy. Doesn't he have a name? A letterhead or something?"

"I'm sure he does. I think he figures I am going to do something rash about this. He didn't want his name on it anywhere. That copy you're looking at is the only one there is."

"You?" she said, in mock surprise. "Do something rash?" Then she added, almost under her breath, "Where is my husband, and what have you done to him?" She shook her head. "Do you mind if I read this?"

"No," he said. "Go ahead."

She had surprised him again. He hadn't known what to expect, so he'd expected the worst, but Donna seemed to be taking the whole thing in without hysteria. Their food came while she was reading, and Stoney was astonished to see her begin to attack her breakfast while she read. She stopped once, looked over at him, shook her head. "Unbelievable," she muttered, then went back to the report. She must have gotten to the part about the escort service, Stoney thought. That got a reaction. It had certainly gotten one out of him. Funny, though, how she would toss her cookies over the slightest thing, sometimes, but then something big goes down, she takes it in stride.

There was an address for Perfect Angels, the escort service, plus a phone number and some names, but no pictures. There was also a description of the nature of their business, mercifully brief. Role-playing, fantasy fulfillment, fetishes, shit like that. Stoney hadn't told Benny about the escort service, he still held out on the guy sometimes. Maybe Benny would have had the same opinion about it, maybe he would have given Stoney the same advice. To Stoney, though, the escort service was in a whole different category. Yeah, all right, she did what she did in the strip club, if he could get her to walk away from that, fine, but that other thing was some sick shit. Guy had to know she was underage, sent her out there anyway, Stoney was not about to let that go.

Donna finished the report and her breakfast at about the same time. She put the pages down and looked over at him. "You didn't eat," she said.

"You're taking this very calmly." He speared a piece of French toast and put it in his mouth.

"Me?" She looked at him in disbelief. "Me? You have got to be kidding. Why aren't you raving and throwing things? Why didn't you call me from the Hackensack Annex?"

The Annex was the common term for the Bergen County jail. "Benny talked me down. Him and Tommy."

"I see. And when did that happen?"

"Yesterday afternoon."

She stared at him. "I'd love to meet this guy Benny someday."

"Anytime."

"You know, I would have expected one of two reactions out of you. The most likely would have been—" She stopped for the space of three breaths. "Off-the-wall," she finally said, and then she said it again, in a quieter tone. "Off-the-wall. The second would have been for you to dump this all in my lap and walk away. Make it my problem."

He didn't know what to say to that, so he kept quiet.

She stared at him, he could feel her measuring him. "What are you going to do about these places where she worked? I am truly surprised to see you sitting here talking about this and not . . ." She shivered. "How come you haven't blown up? How come you're not off hitting the guy who owns Perfect Angels in the head with a hammer or something? Honestly, Stoney, sometimes I'm not sure I know you anymore."

If she only knew, he thought. If she knew that Marisa let me think you were sleeping with Prior . . . He thought about how to answer her, looked up to see her waiting. "All right, I won't lie to you, I am going to have a conversation with whoever is calling the shots at Perfect Angels. But the more immediate question is what to do about Marisa." He raised one hand in a gesture of helplessness, then wiped his face. "Benny says . . ." He noticed the change in her expression, but he continued anyway. "Benny says that overreacting would just drive Marisa away from us. He said, if I, you know, go making threats and shit, she'd just be more likely to get pissed off, maybe go back to doing this stuff just to get back at me. To show me, you know, be independent and all that. I mean, I don't know what to say about Marisa. Or to her. But she has to know, this shit's gotta stop." He looked down at his plate. "Other than that, I don't know. I mean, yeah, I'm gonna deal with this escort-service guy, I ain't having that. But I don't know if that will have any effect on Marisa, or on what she does from here on out."

Donna was not all that interested in the escort-service guy. "Well, your friend Benny is right." He could tell she didn't like saying that. "We don't want to drive Marisa away. She's jeopardizing her future over a, a, a silly experiment, but she probably doesn't really appreciate that. Marisa does understand reality. Sometimes better than I do." She picked the picture up, looked at it again. "Is this the only picture?"

"No," he said. "But it seemed like enough."

"Were the other ones worse than this?"

"Worse? Oh, I get it. No, not really. In Jersey, the girls aren't supposed to take off more than what you see there."

"And you know this because . . ."

How did we get back around to me? he wondered. "I asked."

"So you don't go to these places." He could hear the skepticism in her voice, and the challenge. He looked at her, counted to ten before he answered.

"I never wanted anybody but you."

She stared back, leaving him to wonder what she was thinking. "Can I keep this picture?"

"Yeah, sure," he said, his heart sinking.

"All right," she said. "We are going to have a talk with Marisa. Let her know that this is unacceptable behavior." She pursed her lips in distaste. "You should probably let her know that if it continues, you aren't going to pay her tuition. She's a smart girl, she'll recognize how much she's risking."

She still hasn't gotten over that, Stoney thought, she's still hung up on the money thing. "All right."

"What comes next? What do we do about Marisa? Aside from just talking to her, I mean. Do you think she's in any danger from these people she's been around at these places?"

"It's possible." He still wasn't sure he wanted to tell her about Prior. "I had Tuco tailing Marisa for a day or two. He's watching the house now."

"I was wrong about Tuco," she said, doubtful. Tuco had never been one of her favorite people. "I'm glad he was there, yesterday morning. Marisa is a different person when he's around. Can he handle . . . Can he . . ."

"Tuco is very capable. I'm coming over, late this afternoon. Marisa and I can discuss her future. You can speak to Tuco, if you want. Address whatever concerns about him you might still have. And you can do whatever you want with Marisa. Ground her until she's thirty, or something. Is that okay?"

"Fine." She glanced at her watch. "I really have to go," she said. She stood up, picked up the picture, glanced at the image one more time before she put it into her bag. "Eat your breakfast," she said.

THIRTEEN

Hard to believe that people went through this shit every day. Stoney was sitting in his car in the southbound lanes of the Palisades Parkway, which runs down the western side of the Hudson River to the George Washington Bridge. The road was one of the nicer-looking highways in the area, lots of trees, hills, grass, and very few buildings or houses visible from the roadway until you got near the southern end, down by the bridge. It was hard to care about that, though, because the line of cars he was in crept glacially forward. Stoney watched as drivers got into the lane for the service station and parking lot which occupied a long stretch of the median strip, drove past the pumps and the parked cars, and got into the clogged lane that exited back onto the highway, all in an effort to gain a fifteen or twenty car-length advantage. The frustrated drivers in the left lane of the road apparently felt like they were being screwed, and they dueled with the cars coming back onto the highway from the service area, trying to freeze them out. The air carried the noise of bleating horns, frustration, and testosterone in Stoney's direction. This is all I needed, he thought. The delay to the bridge was at least another hour, and then he still had to get across, fight his way downtown, and find a place to park the car.

He fished out his cell phone and called Benny. It was against the law, they had a rule against driving and talking on a handheld phone at the same time, but you could hardly call what he was doing driving, and besides, there were no police cars in sight, and no way for a cop to get to him unless he was on horseback, or walking.

Benny was home.

"Hey, Benny."

"Hello, kid. How did it go?"

"She was rational, Benny, she was so calm it was fucking scary."

"You tell her about the P.I.?"

"Yeah, well, sorta. I gave her one of the pictures, and I let her read some of the pages that were about Marisa. I let her think I hired someone just to do that."

"She believe that?"

"Who the hell knows. I'm not sure. Maybe. If she had any doubts, she kept them to herself."

"All right. So now what?"

Now I'm gonna find the scumbag that runs the escort service I didn't tell you about, and I'm gonna strangle him with his own guts. "I don't know, Benny. Donna says she's gonna have a conversation with Marisa, all about unacceptable behavior and all that shit. Plus, Marisa keeps it up, no tuition money. Hopefully, if guilt doesn't work, self-interest will."

"Sounds good so far. What about you?"

"I don't know, Benny. I don't know what else I should do."

"You'll know what the right thing is when the time comes, Stoney, people usually do, they just don't want to face up to it. They'd rather concentrate on getting what they want. But what I meant was, how are you doing?"

"I'm all right, Benny. I'm still sober, I haven't picked up anything over this. Not yet, anyhow."

"Good. Nothing is so bad that you can't make it worse by getting fucked up. You going to a meeting tonight?"

"I'm not sure. I will if I can, but I got this thing I gotta do out here in Jersey."

"Yeah?" Stoney heard the note of amused skepticism in Benny's voice. I can't fool this guy, he thought. He knows I didn't tell him the whole story. "All right, kid. Call me anytime."

Stoney flipped the phone shut, ending the call, and inched his car forward. He'd made about twenty feet while talking to Benny. He looked at the back of the hand that held the steering wheel, remembering something he'd read about one of the Indian tribes of the Great Plains. The first person you met after you died, according to one of their legends, was an old woman called the Hag. One of the Hag's functions was to eat your scars, sending you clean into the next world, but if you didn't have any scars, she would eat your eyes instead, and you would live your next life blind. I'm safe, Stoney thought. The skin on his palms was soft and clear, but his knuckles were covered with a fine lacy network of pale white lines. There were other scars, too, hidden from view, pale reminders of mishaps past, miscalculations, and the price he'd had to pay to achieve his objectives. I've got plenty for the Hag's appetite, he thought. Wherever I go from here, I'll be able to see. . . .

It came to him, how he might productively spend an hour or two. He turned the thought over in his mind a couple times, and it felt right. It was another half mile to the next exit, but now the wait didn't seem so pointless.

Perfect Angels was run out of a second-floor suite in a red-brick building on Main Street in Lodi, New Jersey. Stoney could

not remember ever being in Lodi before, only knew the name
of the town due to the periodic flooding of the Passaic River,
which occasionally put part of Lodi underwater and earned the
place a mention on the six o'clock news. It was a blue-collar
town, houses and small industrial buildings mixed together
and jammed close, with shared driveways, postage-stamp
lawns, and potholed streets. Stoney wandered around for a
while before he found the right address. The red-brick building
looked like it might have once been a mill or a factory, it stood
back off the street behind a large parking lot. Stoney found a
space and parked in the far corner of the lot.

There were some retail stores on the ground level of the
building, a donut shop, nail salon, karate studio, convenience
store and a place that dealt in electronic equipment, along
with a few empty storefronts. There was no sign for Perfect
Angels, but the address was right, so Stoney got out of the car
and walked through the door that led to the upper floors. He
checked the row of mailboxes in the entryway, and there was
no mention of Perfect Angels on any of those, either, but the
mailbox stamped with the right suite number had a label stuck
to it that read P.A. INC. Gotta be the place, Stoney thought, and
he walked up the stairs.

The second-floor hallway was paved with a shiny brown
carpet that looked like it had been beaten into submission
by decades of dirty shoes. Flimsy pale brown wooden doors
fronted each of the office suites. A few had light and noise
leaking underneath them into the hallway, but the crack under
the door to P.A. Inc was dark. Stoney tried the knob on his
way past, but it was locked. The place was in the front of the
building, though, and if the offices had windows, they should
front onto the parking lot. Stoney walked to the end of the

hallway and looked out, trying to orient himself so he could be sure which windows would belong to P.A. Inc. After a minute he gave up and cracked the hallway window with his elbow. Ought to be able to pick it out now . . .

Back downstairs, he stopped in the donut shop for a couple of cups of coffee, went back across the lot to sit in his car and wait. "You'll know what to do." That's what Benny had told him. We'll find out, he thought, we'll find out soon enough if I know what the right thing is, or not.

He watched the people come and go, went into the convenience store, bought the New York papers, sat in his car and read them twice, used the bathroom in the donut shop. He played a game with himself, tried to guess what the operators of Perfect Angels would look like. He put his money on a tired-looking guy in a brown suit and scuffed shoes, lost when the guy went inside and the windows for P.A. Inc. stayed dark.

They showed up shortly after noon. Made sense, Stoney thought, the escort business being a nighttime enterprise. They drove up in a shiny new black GMC pickup truck, a four-door, four-wheel-drive monster with dual rear wheels, tinted windows, and what looked like every conceivable option bolted to it. It took two parking spots end to end to contain the thing, if the guy had used one space, the truck's ass would have protruded far out into the lane behind it.

The driver stood about six inches over six feet, he was overweight, probably went about three hundred fifty pounds, had tattoos on his forearms. He carried his extra weight well, though, didn't waddle the way a lot of fat guys do when he crossed the parking lot. The guy riding shotgun was younger, thinner, and in better shape, wore cowboy boots, jeans, shades, and a wife-beater under a leather jacket. It seemed to Stoney that there was a bit of extra bulk under the left arm of the jacket. One young guy, Stoney thought, carrying, probably makes his living with his hands, and an older guy, might be past his prime, but you never knew. Guy like that might be able to dance with you for about forty-five seconds, he might even make your day if he got lucky. He picked up his cell phone and dialed Fat Tommy's number.

Fat Tommy always answered the phone in the same distinct way. "Yello?"

"Hey, Tommy."

"Stoney. Whattayoudo?"

"Something I wanna take care of, over in Jersey, and I might need somebody to hold my jacket. You busy? Spare me a couple hours?"

"On my way," Tommy said.

It would take Tommy, generally a deliberate driver, at least an hour to drive from his garage in SoHo out to Lodi, New Jersey. Stoney sat and watched the people come and go, wondering who they were, what kind of lives they led, what made them choose to make their homes in this particular piece of the world. Then again, he lived in the hive of Manhattan's Lower East Side, had never in his life lived more than twenty miles from Columbus Circle, and could not really explain why. It was a fantasy he often entertained, though, this idea of striking out for someplace new, leaving his problems and obligations behind, reinventing himself as a new man unencumbered by reputation and history. It couldn't be what he really wanted, though, could it? He was still here, after all.

He watched a woman walk diagonally across the parking lot. She didn't look like she belonged among the suburban women who had been coming and going all morning long. She was thinner than most of them, and her blond hair was a little too blond, her lips a little too red, her nails a little too long. Plenty of parking spots, Stoney thought, but she didn't drive in here, she walked. Must have taken the bus. Public transportation in New Jersey is about as popular as herpes. . . .

She stood next to the door that led to the upper floors and examined her reflection in one of the big glass storefronts. Stoney watched her try to throw off her fatigue, square her shoulders, stick her chest out. She must be interviewing, he thought, and she's not going for secretary, either. She's gonna go up and talk to that fat slob with the pickup truck. She wants to be an escort.

She was still inside when Tommy's Mercedes eased into the lot and parked about six spots away. Tommy emerged from the car, walked over casually, and got into the passenger side of Stoney's Lexus. "Thanks for coming out," Stoney said.

Tommy nodded. "What's the drill?"

"You see that broken window on the second floor over there? Above the nail salon, couple of windows to the left."

Tommy peered at the building. "Got it."

"All right. The windows just to the left of the broken one belong to a place called Perfect Angels. I want to clear up a misunderstanding between me and the guy running it."

"Okay." Fat Tommy did not ask for explanations. "What'sa the inside look like?"

"I don't know. I've never been up there."

"I see." Tommy glanced over at him. "And the, ahh, gentleman inside, he gonna go home inna box?"

"I don't think that will be necessary. I think he and I can arrive at an understanding."

"That'sa nice." Tommy glanced over again. "How urgent is this? We have time to take a nice look uppastairs? You don' gonna like it, you go in there and get a surprise."

"We might not have to do a recon." He told Tommy about the blond.

"Okay, good," Tommy said. "I gonna talka to her. You stay here, nice, quiet. I get her settled down, nice, nice, then I gonna call you."

It was annoying to admit it, but Tommy was right, he'd do a much better job with the woman than Stoney. "All right."

"What happen with that guy?" Tommy leaned back in the passenger seat. "You hear from that private cop you wasa hire?"

"I found out a couple of things," Stoney told him.

"What?"

Stoney reached into his backseat, fished out the pile of paperwork that constituted everything the two investigators had given him on Prior. He didn't bother to edit out Marisa's pictures.

Fat Tommy paged through, reading quickly. It didn't take him long to see the shape of things. "Poor Marisa," he said.

"Poor Marisa?" Stoney stared at him, incredulous. "Poor Marisa? She's the one got all this shit started to begin with."

"C'mon, Stoney. Think about—"

"That's all I been doing, Tommy, and let me tell you, it ain't helping."

"Not like that, Stoney. Listen, not easy to be a woman. You wake up one day, still just a girl, and you realize that you carry a loaded weapon with you everywhere you go. Point it at a man, shake the trigger, bang, down he goes, all fucked up inna head. How she suppose to learn how to use? And now she got this guy, sneak around, hide inna bush, call onna phone . . . And who's she suppose to tell? Her mother? You? Goddam, she tell you the truth, you gonna go off like a cannon. She gonna be very scare, right about now."

"She ought to be fucking scared."

"Easy, Stoney. Remember what it was like, you were seventeen."

"I know, Tommy. I'm trying."

"Of course. Anyhow, maybe we still gonna find out something about Prior. Jack Harman is still looking into him."

"Hope you told him to watch his ass."

"Naturally."

"How far you trust this guy Harman? Something about him makes me a little nervous."

Tommy shrugged. "I trust him to be what he is. Listen, you go to the doctor, you don't worry about his character, you just pay for what he'sa have between the ears. That's whatta we do with Jack. Don' worry, everything gonna come good. So tell me, where is Marisa right now?"

"I got Tuco tailing her."

Tommy nodded, relieved. "All right," Tommy said. "Everything gonna come together, you watch.. That woman, just come out over there. She your girl?"

"Yeah, that's her."

"Okay." Tommy opened his door. "Gimme five, ten minute. I gonna call you."

Tommy had her settled in a booth at a little breakfast joint about two blocks away. She had looked nice from across the parking lot, but up close, she was stunning. She could have been anything from sixteen to twenty-five, and when she turned and looked at Stoney, the rest of the room seemed to go dark. The only thing was, her blue eyes were set just a little too close together in her face; it gave Stoney the impression that she might not be the most intellectually gifted female he'd ever met. Tommy slid over in the booth so that Stoney could sit next to him. He doesn't want me to box her in, Stoney thought. He's making her comfortable. He sat down, cramming Tommy into the corner.

"Stoney, meet Tiffany."

"Hello, Tiffany." Stoney held out a hand. She looked at it before reaching out with hers.

"Hi."

"You maybe recognize Tiffany's face," Tommy said. "She used to be a model."

She smiled at Tommy, then glanced over at Stoney. "Long time ago," she said.

"You don't look old enough for long time ago," Stoney said. "You really wanna work for that fat fucking slob?" Tommy sighed, closed his eyes, pinched the bridge of his nose.

"I need the money," Tiffany said, looking down into her lap. "I'm trying to get out of hock. I want to be a good mom to my daughter, she's five, and she has special needs." She clamped her lips together, biting down hard on whatever she was feeling. She looked up at Tommy. "I never hadda worry about money before. But I'm trying to make it on my own. I'm sick of always having some guy pay my way." Tommy nodded, reached across the table, and took one of her hands in his. Stoney watched the muscles in the side of her jaw working. "I go to school in the mornings," she said, a touch of defiance in her voice. "I'm learning to be a seamstress." She glanced over at Stoney. "I know it isn't rocket science, okay, but I'm doing good, and I think I can get a real job when I graduate. But I still got bills in the meantime. Tuition isn't free."

"I didn't mean anything bad, Tiffany," Stoney said. "I apologize. It's just that this guy seems like a scumbag, you ask me."

She pulled her hand out of Tommy's. "Fuckin' cheesedick bastard," she said. "I fuckin' hate him. But if he'd put me on for a lousy six months, and didn't tell my parole officer, I could finish school, I could get my daughter back, and I could finally get clear of this fuckin' shit." Her face was angry and hard. "He made me blow him," she said coldly, staring at Stoney. "He made me suck his cock, and then he told me to call back next week, and he might have something for me. Might." She was clearly furious. There was a clear space of silence all around them in the little restaurant.

"I can't believe it," Stoney said. "You gotta be kidding me, with your looks, how come he didn't grab you?"

"Because he knows I'm in trouble," she said.

Stoney played a hunch. "How long you been clean?"

She stared at him, her mouth open. "Jesus, is it that obvious?"

"Probably not," he said. "I got eight months."

"I got four," she said. "Welcome to the real world, right? My parents tossed me when I got out of rehab, and the state took my daughter. I can't get her back unless I have a job and a stable address, and I can't get a job because of my record. My sister's letting me sleep on her couch. If it wasn't for her . . . Everybody keeps telling me it'll get better, but I gotta tell ya, it ain't happened yet. Even that fat fuck at Perfect Angels is waiting to see how hard he can squeeze me."

"What's the guy's name?" Stoney asked her.

"Dylan," she said.

"Thomas or Zimmerman, do you suppose?" Tommy muttered.

"I don't know his last name," she said. "It's probably just some shit he made up, anyhow."

"Tiffany, what's your daughter's name?" Stoney asked.

"Sarah," she said. "It was my grandmother's name." And then, with a squeak in her voice, "Would you like to see her picture?"

"Yeah." Tiffany pursed her lips and swallowed while she dug out a wallet and extracted a picture. The little girl resembled Tiffany, but she carried the unmistakable stamp of Down's syndrome on her face. Stoney looked at it and handed the picture back. "She's beautiful."

"Thank you." She stowed it away again. "I gotta get her back. You know what I mean? I gotta."

"I know what you mean. Where's her father?"

"My stepfather, you mean? Who the hell knows."

"You're kidding me."

"I was sixteen. He's not the present one, he was the one before this. I actually thought . . . I thought I liked him."

"Nobody can do it to you like your family," Stoney said. "But if you stay clean, I promise you, a year from now you won't even remember what this felt like."

She nodded. "I keep hoping."

Fat Tommy cleared his throat. "Tiffany," he asked her, "how about the other guy in that place? You remember his name?"

"Carlo," she said. "Carlo Innocenti."

Tommy looked over at Stoney. "Related, you suppose?" Carlo Innocenti was a prominent crime figure in New Jersey, not well known to the general public, but still prominent. The Carlo Innocenti that Tommy and Stoney knew about, however, was in his early seventies.

"Gotta be," Stoney said. "This kid's probably a grandson or something."

"That gonna be a problem?"

Stoney shook his head. "Nah. I don't think so. No way the old man knows the kid is doing this." He'd never let one of his own grow up to be a pimp, Stoney thought. He almost said it, but he looked across the booth into the pinched face and watery eyes of the woman sitting there and reconsidered. "The kid's got to be doing this on his own. Carlo will think we did him a favor. Anyway, it's the other guy I want. I wanna break it off in his ass."

Tiffany cleared her throat. "Do you really? 'Cause I have a friend who'd like that, too. His name is Jason."

Stoney walked Tiffany out to her bus stop. He took some money out of his pocket, counted off a hundred for himself, and handed the rest to her. "Thank you for your trouble," he said. "Ain't none of my business, but you could go do something else for six months. Waitress, receptionist, anything. I bet lots of places would love to have you."

She looked down at the money in her hand. "You'd lose your bet," she said. "It's too easy to do background checks, twelve bucks on the Internet and they've got your whole life. Even the freakin' diners check you out six ways to Sunday before they hire you."

"Be creative," he told her. "Make up a new name. Keep trying."

"Yeah, all right." She salted the money away, then looked

up at him. "I tell you what," she said. "You promise me you won't wimp out when Jason gets here, okay, and I'll apply for a bunch more waitress jobs."

"You really do hate this guy, don't you?"

"You damn right I hate him."

"All right, it's a deal. You can check with Jason, later."

"Okay," she said. "I will." She grinned, her smile made beautiful by the touch of evil in it. "Wish I could stay to watch," she said. "That fat bastard really has it coming."

"Good luck." He didn't know what else to say, so he walked away, left her standing on the corner.

Tiffany had given them the layout before she left. The place consisted of an inner and an outer room. Dylan, the fat guy, took care of business from behind a desk in the inner office. Carlo Innocenti spent most of his time watching television in the outer office. He was sprawled on the couch with his boots up on a low coffee table watching a black-and-white cowboy movie on AMC when Stoney eased through the outer door. Carlo didn't look up right away, and when he did, it was too late. Stoney, six inches taller than Innocenti and a good hundred pounds of muscle heavier, sat down right next to Innocenti, a finger to his lips. He draped an arm over the kid's shoulders as Carlo put his boots down on the floor. Innocenti didn't have a chance, and the look on his face said he knew it.

"Shhh," Stoney whispered, and he reached across Carlo's body and relieved him of his pistol. He stood up, then, and backed slowly toward the door, motioning Carlo to follow him. Carlo stood up, looking like he didn't know what to do with his hands, and glanced uncertainly over at the inner door, the one that led to the inner office.

Stoney shook his head. "Be smart, Carlo," he whispered. The younger man swallowed once, then followed Stoney through the outer door into the hallway. He froze when he saw Fat Tommy leaning against the opposite wall.

"Carlo," Tommy said, his voice low and sad. "Carlo. What'sa your momma gonna say when she find out you're understudy to a fucking pimp?"

"Did my father send you guys?" Carlo looked from one face to the other, fear plain in his eyes. "Anyhow, I ain't studyin' shit, I swear, I just work for the fuckin' guy." His voice was rising, tinged with a note of panic. Stoney held a finger back to his lips. "Sorry," Carlo said. "Listen, guys, my parents think I'm still going to Bergen Community. When they find out I dropped out again they're gonna kill me. Did my father send you, for real?"

Fat Tommy smiled. "Let's just say, friend of a friend. You understand? Somebody wanna give you one more chance to do the right thing."

"Oh, shit," Carlo exhaled, kicking at the carpet. "Oh, Jesus Christ."

"Not everyone gets a second chance, Carlo," Stoney said. "You still got a shot to pull this out. My friend here is gonna give you a ride home. But listen to me, okay? Tell your parents the truth. Things might not go this easy, next time around."

Carlo, looking at the floor, nodded his head. His hands were trembling slightly. Kid's old man is probably gonna beat the crap out of him, Stoney thought. Might be just what he needs, anyhow. Carlo glanced back at the office door. "What about Dylan?"

"Don't you worry about him," Stoney said. "You got your own problems."

Fat Tommy stepped up close to whisper in Stoney's ear. "You want me to put this kid in a taxi? I could be back here in ten minutes."

"No. You better check in on Harman, find out if he's getting anywhere. I got this motherfucker. Call me later on and let me know how things went."

"I will."

He had taken to wearing running shoes since he'd moved back into the city, so he didn't make a sound as he slipped back into the outer office of P.A. Inc. He could feel his heartbeat accelerating, his body getting ready for what was to come. But I don't even know what I'm gonna do yet, he thought. He stared at the door to Dylan's office. Benny told you you'd know, he told himself, so just go with that. He opened the door and stepped through.

Dylan was on the telephone, and he looked up, irritated. "Hold on," he said to the telephone, then put his hand over the mouthpiece. "I know you? You from the limo service? You know I got nothing for you guys this early in the day. . . ." He craned his neck, peering past Stoney through the open door. "Carlo? Goddammit, Carlo . . ."

Stoney walked up to the petitioner's side of the desk, stuck a finger down on the phone cradle, and ended Dylan's call. "I hear," he said, "I wanna fuck a cheerleader, you're the guy to talk to. That right?"

"Oh, buddy," Dylan said, putting the phone down, leaning back in the chair, hands out, shaking his head. "Buddy, you don't know how much shit you're in. You ain't just dealing with me, you understand? I'm not the guy you gotta worry about, I don't own this place, I just run the show. You know the name Rocco Parisi? Because you're gonna, my friend . . ."

Stoney had never heard of Parisi. "Yeah," Stoney said. "And he knows me, and believe me, he's not gonna take me on over a fat piece of shit like you. You think he wants to see his name in the paper? 'Parisi now catering to babyfuckers.' He'll chop your fat ass into little pieces first. Now answer my question. I wanna fuck a high-school girl, you hear me?" He could feel it building up inside, and his voice began to rise. "I bet you got pictures, right? Show me some pictures. You know the kind I want. Show me some schoolgirls, Dylan."

Dylan's eyes gave him away, because he glanced at the desk drawer before he went for it. Guy was quick, though, he got the drawer open and his hand inside just as Stoney turned the desk over on him. The big silver automatic came flying out of the drawer, Stoney watched the black hole at the end of the barrel spin past as Dylan lost his balance and went over backward. The desk tipped over, and the edge of it landed on Dylan's ankle just as the back of the fat man's head hit the floor.

"Aaaaagh!" The pistol landed a few feet away. Stoney vaulted the upended desk and landed on Dylan's stomach with both knees. Dylan rolled to one side, further wrenching his ankle, and began throwing up convulsively, burying his pistol with vomit. Stoney knelt down next to him, waited until he stopped squalling, and then whispered in his ear.

"I wanna fuck a little girl, Dylan. C'mon, you help me out, okay? Hmm? When Parisi finds out you been running underage girls outta here, you know what he's gonna do to you? You fucking piece of shit . . ."

Dylan's eyes were squeezed shut. "What are you gonna do?"

"Me? Nothing. But your past has come back to bite you in the ass, Dylan. . . ."

FOURTEEN

Stoney parked his car in front of the house where he'd lived with Donna for so many years, got out, walked up to the front door, rang the bell. It was supposed to go *bing-bong,* but it didn't, it only went *bing.* It had been that way for a decade, but he'd never gotten around to fixing it. He waited about ten seconds, then started banging on the door with a fist.

Donna opened it, stared at him. "What are you going to do?"

"She here?"

"Yes, she's upstairs. I told you, I grounded her."

"Where's Dennis?"

"Hockey practice." Stoney walked past her, into the house. Donna, white-faced, stood back to let him by, then closed the door behind him.

"Get her down here," he said.

She brushed past him, went to stand between Stoney and the stairs to the second floor. "Are you sure you know what you're doing?"

"Get her down here," he said.

Donna stared at him, making up her mind. Finally, she turned and shouted up the stairs. "Marisa! I need you downstairs. Right now, please." Stoney stood silent, unmoving, listening to the sounds of someone stirring on the floor above. "Today, please, Marisa," Donna said, and then she took one step to the side.

Marisa came down the stairs, stopped halfway when she saw her father standing there. "What . . ."

Stoney stared at her, wishing he knew her well enough to read her face and her body language. She came the rest of the way down, but slowly, stood on the bottom step with one hand on the baluster. "Hi, Daddy."

"Why did you lie to me?"

Her face cracked, she glanced at her mother, then down at her feet.

He had been afraid that he would lose control, afraid of what his temper would make him say or do, but now that the moment had arrived he felt overwhelmed with sorrow. Marisa looked small, standing in front of him, insubstantial, impossibly young, too frail to even look his way. If you had been around, he told himself, maybe none of this would have happened. . . . "Why did you lie to me?" She stood there, quaking, silent. "I still can't believe you put me through it. That was a really rotten thing to do."

She didn't take it the way he thought she would. She exhaled, sat down on the steps. "I was in trouble." Her voice was a plaintive squeak. She stared down at the bottom step her feet were resting on. "I needed your help, but . . ." She glanced over at Donna again, but her mother gave her no sign. "I thought if I told you the truth, you'd kill me."

"So you let me think this guy Prior was sleeping with your mother, so that I'd kill him instead."

"What?" Donna said, going pale. "What? Who's Prior?"

Marisa nodded her head, but she still didn't look at him. "I didn't know what else to do." The tears started down her face. "Dad, Mom, I'm sorry. . . ."

"Sorry don't cut it." Am I really being too tough on her, he wondered, or not tough enough? He had no idea. Am I getting to her or is she just one damned fine actress?

Donna sounded like she was having trouble breathing. She stared at Marisa. "You told him I was sleeping with someone else?"

"I didn't say it," Marisa told her, staring at the floor. "But I let him think it. I thought he would go and scare Prior away, and then, you know, I could get out of it, and get back to my real life, without—"

"All right," Stoney said. "I'm gonna ask you some questions. I want straight answers, you hear me? And if I find out you're bullshitting me again, you will not enjoy the consequences, I promise you. Are we clear on this?"

"Daddy, I'm so sorry. . . ."

He closed his eyes, held up a hand to stop her, asked his question again, three words, each one separate and distinct. "Are. We. Clear." He could hear her sniffing, pulling herself together. Or staying in character.

"Yes," she said.

"How did this shit get started?"

"It was about six months ago," she said. There was still no spirit in her voice, just resignation. "I had just broken up with my boyfriend, you were gone, Mom was all worried about losing the house, and I was broke. My girlfriend Jeannette had danced at the Jupiter Club once when they had an amateur night and she said she'd made some nice money, and she wanted to do it again. You know, for laughs. She said she loved it, she got a real rush from all the guys sitting there with their tongues hanging out. She said it was a fun way to make a few bucks. At first I said no, but you know, after a while I started to think about it. I went with her once to watch, and it didn't seem like that big a deal. I mean, she never, like, showed anything for real, you see more skin at the beach—"

"Oh, yeah?"

She looked up at him for a few seconds. She's wondering how much I know, Stoney thought. Let's see if she turns on the tears again.

She didn't, though. "Well, almost. She wore this bikini, and she, like, held it open a little bit, but that's as far as it went."

"How old is Jeannette?"

"She's almost seventeen."

"Great. All right, so then you started doing it."

"Yes." She was almost inaudible.

"And?"

She sighed. "Then Jeannette met this guy, Dylan, he said we were settling for pocket change. He said he could help us make a lot more money, doing the same thing we were doing in the bar, just like, you know, in private, for rich guys who didn't want to go to those places." She sighed again. "I was never in love with the bar. You know, some of the guys really wanted you, but some of them got drunk and yelled things. So I thought, doing this for one person is probably better than doing it for a whole crowd."

"How many times did you work for Dylan?"

"Three," she said. He noticed that she wasn't looking over at her mother anymore. "The first time, Jeannette and I went together, and after that, I went by myself."

"How many times did you do Prior?"

She took her time answering. "The last two," she finally said. "He got weird. He was calling Dylan every day, offering him all kinds of money if I would, you know, do this or that. Then he got my cell number. I got it changed once, but he got the new number the very next day. He still won't leave me alone."

"What did you do for Prior?"

She didn't answer, so he asked again, louder. "What did you do for—"

"I stripped for him, okay?" Her voice finally rose above the subdued mumble she'd used from the beginning. "All right? Are you happy now?" She was staring at him, angry. Maybe at last we're getting to something real, Stoney thought.

"Yeah, I'm thrilled." Stop now, he told himself, you already know what you need to know. He couldn't do it, though. "So this guy Prior never touched you."

"No." He wondered if she was lying, but he couldn't be sure.

"Bullshit." He let that lie there for a minute. "Do you really want out of this or not? You want to go back to what you were before all this?"

"I don't know what I want."

Probably the second true thing she's said, he thought. "Did you fuck this guy?"

"No!" She shouted it, outraged.

"You blow him?"

"No!" She looked like she'd been slapped in the face.

"What, then? Why don't you just tell me the truth? Because I'm gonna get it out of Prior, I guarantee it."

The air went out of her. "It doesn't matter what I tell you anymore." She sounded resigned again, like she had given up pretending. Either that, or she was taking it to the next level. "You'll never believe me, no matter what I say."

Great job, Dad, he told himself. And maybe it doesn't really matter now, whether she touched the guy or not. Knowing one way or the other wouldn't change much.

"What are you going to do?"

"What do you think I should do? You want me to kill this guy, just to get him out of your hair?"

"I don't know. . . ."

It was his turn to get quiet. She looked up at him, her face wet. "All right," he finally said. "Here's what's gonna happen. You're gonna set him up for me. Tommy and I are gonna bleed him, and at the end of it, Prior will have two choices: he can come after you, or he can run. And if he runs, we're gonna let him go. If he comes after you, then what happens next is on him. Either way, when it's over, he won't bother you again."

"What do I have to do?"

"You're gonna have to talk to him on the phone. When Prior calls you, does he always call from the same number?"

She cried for a minute or two before she answered him. "He usually calls from the phone in his house. Once in a while he uses his cell phone."

"Any particular time of day?"

"Usually around four . . . in the afternoon."

"Do you talk to him when he calls?"

She nodded. "Sometimes."

"All right. Don't talk to him again until I tell you to, and then, you only say what I tell you to say, no more. From now on, write down how many times he calls, and what time."

"Okay."

Stop now, he told himself again, stop before you make this worse. . . . Again, he couldn't hold back. "Listen to me. This other asshole, Dylan, you ever see him again, you ever talk to

him, you even look at him, I'll give you his fucking skull, you
hear me?"

"Yes."

"You go back to that strip joint again, and I'll burn it to
the ground, and I'll bury whoever—"

"Look," she said, her voice rising slightly, "you can't call
me any names that Eddie, your pet bulldog, didn't already
use on me." She looked back down at the floor, and her voice
went back to that quiet, defeated tone. "I'm not going back. I
promised Mom, and I promised Eddie, too. It's over."

You promised Eddie? Oh yeah, Tuco. My pet bulldog. He
wondered what the kid had said to her. You might as well say
it, he thought. You've gone this far. "If you do, you better find
a new place to sleep first."

She was crying silently, looking exactly like a broken little
girl. He shook his head. How can you ever know for sure,
when they're telling you the truth and when they're playing
you? He stared at her. "Also, from now on, you stay with Tuco.
He'll pick you up in the morning, he'll go where you go, he'll
bring you home at night. You don't leave this house without
him, is that clear?"

She nodded.

"This is important, Marisa. This guy Prior already put one
man in the ground over this. I don't want you to be next." He
watched her face, but he couldn't tell if he had gotten to her
or not.

"All right." She let a few seconds pass. "Daddy?"

"Yeah."

"I really didn't mean for any of this to happen. I'm sorry."

He hoped it was the truth, but how could he know? "So
am I." And now what? he wondered. "Marisa?"

"Yes, Daddy."

"You don't have to let this ruin everything. Do you understand that?"

She didn't answer. She didn't need me for this, he thought, I'm not even the period on the end of the sentence. She was beaten before I even stepped foot in this place. It probably doesn't matter what I do or say here, at all. He felt smaller than he had in a while. He wondered what Tuco had said to her, what he had done, but he decided he wasn't at all sure he really wanted to know. "Where's Tuco now?"

Donna started to answer, but Marisa beat her to it. "He's asleep on your couch in the back room," she said, and for the first time she sounded like someone he knew. "You've had the poor guy up for days. He was so tired, I had to drive us most of the way back from Brooklyn."

Brooklyn? Stoney's mouth opened, but Donna put her hand on his shoulder, and he closed it without speaking. "Thank you, Marisa," Donna said. The two of them watched as Marisa stood up and trudged back to the second floor. Donna waited until her daughter was out of sight. She stood there looking at the empty staircase. "Did you believe her? Did you really think I was sleeping around?"

I'm walking in a minefield, here, Stoney thought. I better tread carefully. "She played me like a fiddle," he said. "I didn't know what to think."

Donna shook her head. "I can't believe how much you held out on me. Why didn't you just come to me after she told you all this? Why couldn't you just talk to me?"

The truth came out before he could clean it up. "I was afraid."

The tears in his wife's eyes were almost more than he could

bear to look at. "We're never gonna make it," she told him, "not if we can't even talk to each other. That investigator you hired. He was watching me, wasn't he? To see what I did."

"Her, not him." You weren't even straight with her about that. "I didn't tell her what to look for," he said. "I just told her to look."

Donna chewed on that for a minute. "Well," she finally said, "you should probably go. Go and do what you need to do."

Do we still have a chance? He wanted to ask her, but she looked like she was teetering on the brink, and he was afraid anything he said would just push her over.

He had Benny on the telephone before he got to the end of the block.

There was a midnight meeting at a church out in Queens. Stoney and Benny sat in the Lexus in the parking lot. It had gotten too complicated for Stoney to keep it all separated, so he wound up copping to everything. "My God," Benny kept saying. "My God." Stoney ignored that and told his story. "Christ Almighty," Benny said, after Stoney finished. "Well, this guy, Dylan, did you kill him? Is he all right?"

"I didn't kill him," Stoney said. "I guess he's okay. A little sore, maybe. The guy is a shitbag, Benny, he deserves more than what I gave him. Motherfucker had handcuffs, rope, leather harnesses, all kinds of weird shit in that place."

"Well, what did you do?" Benny said. "Exactly."

"I think I broke his ankle, but that was kind of an accident. He's laying on the floor moaning, right, this kid shows up, Tiffany's friend Jason. Jason has this dude with him. I guess the guy is his business manager or something. Anyhow, Dylan owed them some money for something he hired Jason to do, right, I didn't want to know what it was, but Dylan didn't pay up. So Jason and his buddy hoist the fat bastard up, okay, Jason bends him over the desk, which is kind of like, on its side, Dylan's half out of it, but he wakes up when Jason starts stripping the guy's pants off him. 'Hold him, hold him,' Jason says to his guy, and all of a sudden, I don't wanna be in the room anymore. Dylan is howling, last thing I saw was Jason stuffing the man's own boxer shorts into his mouth to keep him quiet. Jesus, I hope they were clean this morning. . . . Anyway, they didn't help a whole lot, I could still hear the guy right through the boxers, all the way out in the other room."

"Christ Almighty," Benny said, horrified. "Are you saying they corn-holed the poor bastard? Is that what you're saying?"

"Well, I can't say, Benny, I was in Philadelphia at the time. What can I tell you? They gave him some of his own medicine."

"Why didn't you just call the police on him? If he was doing what you say, you could have had him put in jail!"

"I'm sure the guy's been in jail before, Benny. Pretty safe bet he'll wind up back there, sooner or later. Guys like Dylan ain't afraid of jail, it's part of the life. But this way, every time the motherfucker takes a shit, he's gonna remember me. You know what I mean?"

Benny was shaking his head. "I don't understand how your mind works," he said. "You would rather have this guy out walking around than in prison, where he belongs?"

"Benny, if the cops wanted the fucking guy in jail, he'd be there already. But he ain't."

"Well," he said, "that's the way it's supposed to work."

"In what alternate universe? Get real, Benny. This asshole

runs an ad in the local paper, for chrissake. Got a picture of some girl, she looks like a high-school cheerleader, except she's wearing less clothes. You think she's gonna come over your house and give you a Swedish massage? The only things she's gonna squeeze is your dick and your wallet, and not in that order. And the funny thing is, his ad ain't the only one in there, okay? There's a whole shitload of 'em, they got a special section in the want ads for whorehouses, they just don't call it that. Cops read the papers, too, don't they? Some of them must."

Benny was silent, staring at him.

"Don't be a politician," Stoney said. "Don't talk out of both sides of your mouth. Prostitution and cocaine are both illegal, right? So how come every twelve-year-old kid in this city knows where he can get an eight ball and a hooker, right in his own neighborhood?"

"Yeah, I know, I know." Benny sat and thought about it for a minute. "All right, then," he said finally, "are you finished with Dylan?"

"Yeah, I guess."

"So what are you gonna do about this guy Prior? The one that keeps calling your daughter."

"He's next. Tommy and I are gonna run a game on him."

"What the hell are you talking about? Isn't this man going to be expecting something like this? Isn't he just sitting there behind his moat waiting for someone like you to come along?"

"Reasonable assumption," Stoney told him. "But, Benny, a man's greatest strength is also his greatest weakness."

"So what are you going to do?"

"My partner, Tommy, says the key to breaking anybody is, you gotta find a crack, first. Once you do that, you stick your screwdriver in the crack and you pry. From there on, it's just a question of torque. What we're doing now, we're looking for the right crack."

"What if he doesn't have one?"

"If he's human, he's got plenty."

"All right, fine. So what happens at the end of this game you're planning? Are you going to kill this man? Do you think you have enough justification for murder?"

"He's after my daughter, Benny. There's no jury in the world that would convict."

"That wasn't my question. Do you think you have the right to kill this guy?"

"If I thought that, I'd kill him tonight." He was silent for a minute. "I'm gonna give him the chance to run. He does that, okay, it's over, I won't chase him, he can be someone else's problem. But if he comes after Marisa, I'm gonna put him in the ground."

Benny started to say something, then swallowed it, kept silent for the space of three breaths. "I guess I'd feel the same way," he finally said. "What about Marisa? How's she holding up?"

Stoney shook his head. "That's the thing, Benny. The whole time I was talking to her, I had the feeling that it was over already. I wasn't even a footnote. I shouldn't have even opened my mouth. I don't think anything I said meant a thing."

"You never know," Benny told him. "Besides, ain't it kind of a relief, not being the General Manager of the Fucking Universe? Ain't it a lot easier, just being you?"

Stoney thought about it. "I'll let you know," he said.

FIFTEEN

Georgie Cho led Tommy Bagadonuts down a long corridor. He opened a door at the end and the two of them stepped into a large room. The walls, floor, and ceiling were painted flat black. There was a mock living room set up on a raised platform at one end of the room. It had a thickly upholstered yellow couch, end tables, television, and a fake window with venetian blinds and frilly lace curtains. The wall behind the couch was covered with flowery wallpaper. Two large television cameras were aimed at the couch, and thick cables ran across the floor. Banks of lights hung from the ceiling. A guy with a shoulder-held camera was bent over, aiming the thing at a diminutive blonde who sat on the couch smoking a cigarette. Georgie Cho, ignoring it all, ushered Tommy to a door on the far side of the room, down another corridor to his office. It looked more like a control room than an office, filled with monitors and electronic equipment. There was a desk in the middle of it all. It was a very orderly room, no loose paper or clutter on the desk. The trash basket was empty.

"Have a seat," Georgie said, gesturing at the client chair next to the desk. Georgie was tall for a Chinese guy, tall and thin, with long black hair flowing loose around his shoulders. He didn't look like he was long out of college.

Tommy watched one of the monitors behind Georgie. The blonde on the couch was making out fiercely with another woman. "Georgie," Tommy said. "You gotta that stuff going on over here alla time? How you gonna get any work done?"

Georgie looked over his shoulder and shrugged. "Network's all set up, Tommy," he said. "We've gotten all the bugs worked out of the system, and there's really not a lot for me to do around here anymore. Besides, after a while, you don't even notice. I mean, after you've seen everything there is to see, over and over again, it all starts to look the same. I'm beginning to think this place is ruining me." He looked back at Tommy and shook his head. "You want me to turn those off?"

"Spoil my concentration," Tommy told him. "Maybe you better."

Georgie rolled his chair over to a console under the bank of monitors and dimmed them all. "So," he said. "What can I do for you?"

Fat Tommy smiled. "Something good," he said. "You ever hear of something whatta you call a hedge fund?"

"Sure," Georgie said. "Investment vehicles for rich people."

"Yeah," Tommy said. "Usually isa run by a young guy. Arrogant, abrasive, aggressive, crooked. Master of the Universe. Biggest cock inna the henhouse. We need you to be this guy for maybe coupla day. And here's why. . . ." Tommy didn't try to sell it, Georgie was too smart for that. He just laid it out, and then he shut up and let the kid think about it.

"Damn," Georgie said finally. "Damn."

"You see everything?" Tommy asked him.

"Oh yeah, but are you sure you guys want me? I don't know if I . . . I mean, wouldn't you be better off with a professional? Or you could hire an actor."

"No good," Tommy told him. "Actor don' gonna have the guts. We can't have some guy, gonna get escare, go craze right in the middle of this."

"Well, what about a pro? You must know somebody, hell, you probably know a dozen guys that could do this. I mean, a real, you know . . ."

"Criminal?" Tommy asked him, grinning. "Also no good. The problem with most of those guy, they wanna go shoot each other at the end, one guy take all the money. Too much trouble, we no need. Me and Stoney, we think you gonna be the right guy, Georgie. You look right, just the right age, and smart enough to pull it off. Lotta money onna table."

"Yeah. Well . . ." Georgie leaned back in his chair. "I mean, I don't know anything about, ahh . . ." He shook his head. "I can probably tell lies as well as the next guy, Tommy, but I don't know if that's going to be good enough."

"No," Tommy said. "You gonna do more than that, but we gonna show you everything. Don't worry, Georgie, everything gonna come good. You gonna like."

As soon as Tuco stepped into the kitchen, he seemed to suck all of the oxygen out of the room. She had eyes for nothing else. "Morning," she said.

"Hey. Where is everybody?"

"My mother went to work. My brother is in school. My father's on his way over."

"Wow," Tuco said. "You musta did good, they trusting you already."

She shook her head. "It's you they trust, not me."

"Wonder what I did to deserve that."

She didn't answer. "You want coffee?"

"Yeah. Thanks."

She went to get him a cup. "If you want breakfast, you're sort of out of luck. Unless you want toaster waffles. I could probably handle that."

Tuco shook his head. "Too early for me," he said. "Coffee's fine."

She set it in front of him. "Talk to me, Eddie. All I know about you is that you know how to fight."

He eyed her warily. "You seen where I come from."

"So? Tell me about it. Tell me who you are."

He shrugged. "Nuyorican," he said, and he looked around the room. "Dropout." He stared at her. "I don't fit, out here. I don't talk right, don't dress right, don't got the right haircut."

Defensive, she thought. He's afraid of what I think about him. "Never mind all that. Tell me where you live now. Tell me what you do when you're not working for my father."

She could tell he didn't like those questions, either, but after a minute, he answered her anyway. "I live in Brooklyn Heights," he said.

"I don't know where that is."

"It's on the East River, right up by the Brooklyn Bridge."

"Oh. So you're, like, one stop from Manhattan on the subway. Do you go into the city a lot?"

"Yeah. I guess I do."

"You're so lucky," she said. "It's so dead out here. Nothing ever happens. Sometimes I go in and walk around like a tourist, looking at stuff."

"Your parents let you go to Manhattan by yourself?"

"Let?" she asked him. "Listen, up until yesterday, I could have poured gasoline all over myself and set myself on fire in the front yard and they wouldn't nave noticed a thing until the landscaper came and asked them what they wanted him to do with the big lump of charcoal in the middle of the lawn."

He snorted. "Guess you woke them up."

"I guess I did. So how come you don't live with your mom? You can't be that much older than me."

"Well . . ." He shrugged. "She started going with this guy a while back. Year and a half ago, maybe. Deacon in her church. He don't like me much, and I don't like him. So then Fat Tommy . . . You know Tommy Bagadonuts?"

"Of course," she said.

"Yeah, so Fat Tommy found me this place in the Heights." He hesitated, looked off out the window. He didn't look like he wanted to continue, but after a few seconds, he did. "They needed a super for the building," he said. "The job came with an apartment."

He was staring at her again. He's waiting to see if I cop an attitude about that, she thought. He doesn't like being a super. "How come you don't go to school?"

"Maybe someday," he said. "What about you? You gonna go?"

"To college? I was planning on it, but that was before all this. I guess I bitched things up pretty good."

He shook his head. "Stoney will still send you," he said.

He knows my father better than I do, she thought, and that realization made her sad, but she gave no sign. "Why do you say that?"

"Because it's the right thing," he said. "He'll do it, after he calms down awhile. He'll just probably break your balls about it for like the next year or so."

She heard a car roll up outside, and moments later, the sound of footsteps on the front porch. "Eddie? I didn't thank you for . . . you know. Bailing me out. You were awesome."

He colored slightly. "You weren't so bad, yourself. You hadn't grabbed that guy's piece when you did, things might not have went so smooth."

She shook her head. "I owe you, Eddie."

He looked down at the table. "Glad I was there."

They were waiting for him when he got there. Tuco came out of the house with Marisa by his side, walked her over to Stoney's car, closed her in on the passenger side, then walked around to Stoney's window. "Everything all right?" Stoney asked him.

"Yeah."

"You look beat," Stoney said. "Why don't you go home? I got her today. You can pick her up in the morning."

Tuco nodded. "Okay."

"I'll call you tonight."

Stoney got into the car, watched Tuco get into the Beemer and drive away. He didn't look at his daughter.

"Daddy, I'm so sorry."

It sounded more genuine to him this time, but he realized that he still didn't know her well enough to tell for sure. He didn't start the car. "Everybody makes mistakes," he said, still not looking at her. "Smart people don't make the same ones over and over. If you're done with this one, it can be finished. You know what I mean? I don't need to keep hitting you with it."

"But Mom said . . ." Whatever it was, Marisa couldn't repeat it.

Stoney did not want to bash Donna. "Give her time."

"Yeah." There was a touch of anger there, and he wondered if she was letting it show for his benefit. Divide and conquer? "Sometimes I wonder," she went on, "what kind of world Mom thinks she lives in."

Stoney shook out a cigarette and lit it. "No way to tell for sure what another person is thinking," he said, and he blew smoke out the window.

"Do you want to know why I did it?" she asked him, her voice quiet.

No, he thought, I don't. Why do women love doing emotional autopsies? Just when you think the shit's done with, they're digging up the body for a postmortem, and you gotta go through the whole fucking thing all over again. He glanced over at her, but she was staring at the floor. "You don't have to explain anything to me."

"I have to. I couldn't talk to Mom about it. I don't have anybody else, Dad. You're it."

"Go ahead, then."

She sat quiet for a minute, still staring at the floor. "At first, it was just a dare, you know, 'I will if you will, you don't have the guts,' one of those things. Like wearing a bikini at the beach for the first time. I was with my girlfriend. She seemed cool with it, but I was so afraid. . . . When we got to the Jupiter Club, and when I, um, when I went out there, everyone in the whole place was looking at me, all the guys, the waitresses, the bartender, everybody, they were all clapping. It was the first time in my life that had ever happened. I'm a lousy dancer, so I just . . . you know. I just did it. They were all screaming. I wouldn't get close enough for any of them to do that dollar-bill thing, so they started to throw money up on the stage." She paused, but Stoney didn't trust himself enough to even look at her, let alone say anything. "It was the biggest rush I ever got in my life," she said. "I never felt anything like it before, ever. It was like I'd never really felt anything at all before that, I felt like I had just been let out of prison or something. I didn't want to stop. When it was over, I couldn't wait to go back."

Great, he thought. Wonderful. He glanced over at her, finally. She had more color in her face than he'd ever seen there before. "What about now?"

She shook her head. "It wasn't the same, the second time. It wasn't as much fun. By the fourth or fifth time, it was no fun at all. It was just . . . sticky." She looked over at him. "Is this what it's like, knowing you can never get high again? That it was the biggest thing that ever happened to you, and now it's over, and you can never have it again."

"That ain't how it works."

"Why not?"

"Because I'm not strong enough for never again. I can't do forever, so I just do right now. When tomorrow gets here, I'll worry about tomorrow."

"I don't know if I can do that." She looked out her window. "You know, the idea that I'll never . . . that I can't . . ."

Don't blow this, he told himself. You say the wrong thing now, you might never get this close again. "The two situations are not exactly parallel."

"Why not?" She wasn't looking at him, she was staring out her window, out into space.

"Because if I wanna have any kind of a life, I gotta stay totally away from shit that fucks with my brain chemistry. You don't have to go through life without taking your clothes off. You just have to pick your venues a little more carefully."

She turned and looked at him, scowling. "What do you mean?"

He took a last drag on his cigarette and flicked it away, held the smoke in his lungs for a few seconds before blowing it out. Just like a joint, he thought, except it doesn't get you off. "Your mother and I used to like going to the movies, back in the day. We had this running joke. We had to take turns picking the movie, because if there was a lot of talking, she was gonna like it and I was gonna hate it, and if there was a lot of violence and nudity, I was gonna like it and she was gonna hate it. So I ain't gonna be a hypocrite, okay? I always been in favor of naked women. I just never thought you were gonna be one of 'em."

She looked away from him, stared down at the floor between her feet. She looks worse than ever, he thought. It was too late, though, he couldn't go back now.

"There's a lot of that stuff around. You know, they got clubs in the city like the one you were in. And there's magazines, and videos, and the Playboy Channel on TV. Okay? So I probably seen a thousand naked women in my life. Maybe more. The thing is, if any one of 'em walked past right now, I wouldn't know her. So all of those times, whether they were stripping for the camera or just for me, you know, it didn't mean a damn thing. It was just a bodily function, you wanna know the truth. Instinct, nothing more than that. Not much different than taking a piss."

She didn't answer, she didn't even look like she was breathing.

"What I'm trying to say is, it ought to mean something. It ought to mean more than . . . hormones. I believe the right guy is out there, you just gotta find him. You find the right guy, none of this makes any difference anymore. The problem is, you gotta work for it. And you ain't gonna find him at the Jupiter Club."

She pursed her lips, then, and nodded her head.

"Now you do understand, I ain't saying you gotta run right out and start beating the fucking bushes looking for the son of a bitch. . . ." She got up out of her seat, climbed halfway across the center console, and wrapped herself around him. He could smell the faint scent of the perfume that she wore. It seemed like forever before she spoke, but it was probably just a minute or so.

"Do you know," she said, her voice muffled by his shirt, "that's the most words you've ever said to me at one time? Without yelling, anyhow."

He wanted to capture that feeling of her draped across his shoulders, the texture of her hair on his face, the smell of the shampoo she used, the sensation of her hands clamped around his arms, hold it somewhere up in his head where he could take it out, once in a while, when he was feeling low. "Did seem like a lot."

She let go of him, bussed him on the cheek, subsided back into her seat, and wiped her face. "What do we do now?"

He looked out the window. He thought briefly about all the things he had done wrong at her age, but there was no profit in that. "Events have been put in motion," he told her. "Things are happening. What we do in the meantime is keep you safe. You're gonna have to stay out sick for a few days. Basically, I want you where I can see you, or at least know where you're at." He looked over at her. "That means you're gonna have to see some things. And you're gonna have to put up with some shit. You're gonna have to sit quiet, be bored, not make trouble. Can you handle that?"

"Whatever you say."

He just stared at her.

"Really," she said.

"All right. You getting along with Tuco okay?"

"Fine," she said. "Why do you call him that? His name is Eddie."

He put his foot on the brake, started the car, stuck it in reverse.

"Dad?"

"What."

"Can you put your seat belt on?"

"I fucking hate seat belts."

"Do it for me," she said. "Please."

"All right, all right." He jammed the gearshift back into park and yanked on the seat belt. Women, he thought. They're never happy unless they're running your life.

SIXTEEN

If it hadn't been for Tommy's newspapers, Marisa would have gone crazy. Tommy always read the *News* and the *Times,* and they kept her busy for the first couple of hours.

The house was huge. It was one of seven houses, each uglier and more pretentious than the next, a microdevelopment built around the perimeter of a hole in the woods up on the hill in Alpine, off in the middle of nowhere. It looked like it was the brainchild of some half-mad Arab potentate who was trying to house all of his wives, somewhere isolated, but where he wouldn't have to drive too far when he was going from one to the other. She got up and walked through the house again, wandering the empty rooms, lying down for a nap on the carpet in one of the upstairs bedrooms, rising at the sound of a car to see what the sultan's mistress drove.

Downstairs in the kitchen, Fat Tommy and her father were rehearsing some kid, and she half listened to the sounds of their voices. The kid was a tall, twentyish Chinese dude, basic computer nerd. They were apparently trying to teach him how to act like an asshole, but he was having a hard time with it.

Hard to believe.

He kept apologizing, for one thing, and he had this

annoying bray, a sort of nervous laugh. She was sorry they hadn't introduced her. Imagine a guy, you have to coach him on how to act like a jerk, for God's sake, and he doesn't get it. That was a switch. Most of the males in her life, man and boy, seemed to have an absolute gift for being dickheads.

There was no television in the house. Actually, there was nothing at all, no furniture, not even a chair. They hadn't needed to tell her why they were using the place: it was right down the road from Prior's house. She shivered at the thought of him so close. She wondered if he'd call today. Her father hadn't yet said anything other than 'Don't talk to him until I tell you to.' If he decided he wanted her to talk to Prior today, he had plenty of time to tell her what to say, Prior usually didn't call until around four. His number showed up on her caller ID almost every afternoon. Sometimes he left a message, sometimes he didn't, but it didn't matter, she knew what he wanted. He'd already promised her the world, trying to get it. She looked at her watch, immediately sorry she'd done so, it wasn't even eleven in the morning yet, but it seemed like she'd been stuck in the empty house for an absolute eternity.

She thought about Eddie, wondered what he was doing. God, the guy was so buff! Usually she wasn't attracted to the jocks, but Eddie had an intensity the rest of them all seemed to lack. They were so dim, next to him, and so dull. They don't call them "ironheads" for nothing, she told herself. But Eddie was different, she felt it, she sensed a depth in him, a dark and unexplored dominion that even he didn't know of, and she wondered if he would ever let her get close, or, if having once seen her at the Jupiter, he would always see her there.

She wandered back downstairs to look at Tommy's newspapers again. There would be nothing new in either of them, of course, and she'd already done the crossword in the *Times*, but one of the puzzles in the *News* had stumped her about halfway through.

She paused in the kitchen doorway. The acting troupe was taking a break. Her father was on his phone, and the kid was apologizing to Fat Tommy again. "Maybe I'm not right for this, Tommy," he was saying. "Maybe I'm just no good at this. Maybe I don't have the performer's gene. That's probably why I work all by myself every day, in front of a computer screen. I'm really sorry—"

"No, Georgie," Tommy said. "Don' give up, you gonna do fine, you wait and see." He saw Marisa standing there and he brightened. "Marisa, come in, meet Georgie Cho. Nice'a boy, very smart. Georgie, Marisa, Stoney's daughter." She stepped forward to shake his hand. Her father turned and looked at her as she did, his face a total blank.

Georgie dweebed.

"I, ahh, nice to, umm, hi. Nice to meet you." His face reddened.

"We try to teach Georgie the alpha-male voice," Tommy said. "He'sa don' get it yet, because he'sa nice boy, but he gonna do fine. Don' worry, Georgie."

"You're doing it wrong," Marisa said.

Tommy looked down at the counter where the pages of dialogue they'd written up for Georgie were lying. "What?" Her father ended his call and turned to watch. "Whatta we do wrong?" Tommy asked.

She shook her head. "You're doing everything wrong," she said. "Besides, it's not in his voice, anyhow. Are you guys, like, on coffee break?"

Tommy shrugged. "I guess."

She held her hand out to Cho. "Come with me," she said. "There's a swing out on the back porch. It's the only place to sit down in this whole freakin' house. Come on."

Georgie looked uncertainly at Tommy. "We'll, ahh, we'll be right, I mean, I'll be right back." She led him toward the back of the house as her father and Fat Tommy stared, first at her, then at each other.

Georgie choked on his tongue for a couple minutes, but then he calmed down. "They're trying to teach me to be aggressive and stuff," he said. "I'm not good at it, though. I sound phony, even to myself. Because I've never been like that, you know what I mean? No one in my family was ever, like, a shouter or anything."

"You're doing fine, George," she said. "I was listening. But those two are not helping you. Did you happen to catch that thing on *Nova* a couple of nights ago? About baboons."

He blinked. "Baboons? Oh, that was 'Apes of Gibraltar,' or something like that."

"Yeah."

"I missed it, but it was a repeat. I've seen it before."

"It was a repeat," she agreed. "I've seen it before, too. One of the things they showed was the way the baboons compete for the females. Did you catch that?"

He didn't look at her. "They, um, they fight? For dominance, I mean."

She was shaking her head. "It looks like that's what they're doing," she said, "but they're not. The theory goes, if the big males fought each other every time they were going to, you know, get some, pretty soon they all would have killed each other off, and then the little guys would be the ones passing on their genes, and that would weaken the tribe. Do you buy that?"

He nodded. "Makes sense," he said, "from an evolutionary point of view."

"I was very disappointed," she said. "I wanted the females to choose. You know what I mean? Like, pick the one with the cutest hair, or something."

Georgie smiled. "Maybe that's why they're so ugly."

"You're right," she said. "I have to learn to look at these things from an evolutionary point of view. Anyhow, the way the male baboons compete for dominance is by throwing temper tantrums."

"I'm sorry?"

"Well, that's what it looks like to me. One of them loses his temper, or he pretends to, and he just starts screaming. He starts throwing things around, pounding his fists on the ground, and breaking things, and shaking the trees, and screaming, and he keeps it up until all of the other males go away, and then . . ." She wiggled her eyebrows at him. "He's the winner."

Georgie looked troubled. "You mean, all I have to, I mean, if I want . . . But . . . Don't women want to be with a nice guy? I mean . . ."

"Hey, George, this is baboons we're talking, here."

"Sorry."

"Stop saying that. But a lady baboon, she has to feel like this guy is gonna stand up for her, and keep all of the other baboons off of her and shit. Still being around tomorrow is important, too, and the next day, and not losing her telephone number, and not talking bad about her to the other baboons, but those things are not at the top of the list. So if you want to be an alpha male—"

"I always tried to be a nice guy. You know, civilized. That's what you guys always say you want."

"You can't believe everything you read, George. I'm not saying that being a nice guy is a bad thing. I'm just saying it won't work. Not in the pursuit of certain objectives."

"But we're, you know, we're not monkeys. We're, um, *Homo sapiens.* Shouldn't we be more . . ."

She was shaking her head. "Something like ninety-eight and a half percent of the DNA is identical," she said. "According to the guy on *Nova,* anyhow. Do you want to know the reason I remembered all of this?"

He nodded.

"The next night, they had this show, it was on E!, I think. A camera crew was following Ted Turner around, right? Would you like to take a stab at how he acted when he didn't get what he wanted?"

"No. Really?"

She nodded. "Pitched a fit. Screamed, threw things at people, broke stuff. At first I thought he was acting like a six-year-old, but I was wrong. He wasn't."

"Baboon, um, baboon behavior."

"Dominant-male baboon behavior. He might have been a bit better-looking, but he was doing all of the same stuff. And it was working."

George sat there on the swing, considering. "You know," he said finally, "you're putting a different spin on it. I guess if I want to be successful in, um, life—"

"And in love," she interrupted.

"Yeah. That, too." He sat quiet a moment longer, and then he stood up. "Thanks, Marisa," he said. "I'm gonna go back, um, I have to go try again."

"Have fun," she told him. She sat there for a while, and presently they started in rehearsing again. She listened to the noise of Georgie's voice over the sounds of slamming doors. The place is empty, she thought. Not much to throw. She got up and walked back inside, just in time to hear her father interrupt Cho. "But I thought—"

"Who the fuck asked you?" Georgie yelled, his voice cracking. "Do you get paid for thinking? I don't fucking think so."

She paused in the kitchen doorway. Georgie winked at her.

"Much better," Tommy said. "Beautiful."

Her father came out looking for her a short time later. "I don't know what you did to Georgie," he said, "but it worked. Good job."

"Thanks," she said.

"I gotta go out for a little while," he said. "You gonna be okay here?"

"I'll be fine."

"All right. Listen, you gotta promise me you'll turn Georgie back into himself again, after this is all over. We can't have him walking around like this."

"No problem," she said. "I'll just wave my magic wand."

Westwood, New Jersey, had a small noisy downtown scattered carelessly across a dozen small streets surrounding a central green. An old woman stood on the sidewalk and watched Stoney park his Lexus behind a Porsche Cayenne. She wore a shapeless pair of pink sweatpants, running shoes, and a long brown mink coat, buttoned up to her chin. Looking slightly dazed, she watched him as he got out of his car and fed the meter. You ought to ask her if she's okay, he told himself. She looks lost. She doddered off unsteadily, pausing to peer into the store windows as she passed. Stoney walked in the opposite direction, but he stopped when he got to the corner and looked back. The old woman was still going, her sails seemed to have filled, and she was tacking off down the sidewalk, picking up speed. As he stood there, a middle-aged guy with permed orange hair came out of one of the buildings, got into the Porsche, fired it up, and roared away. I should get one of those, Stoney thought. Maybe that sound would satisfy me, maybe then I could stop all this crazy shit. Find out what a normal life feels like.

Tina Finbury's office was on the third floor of one of the downtown buildings. "Over a jewelry store," she'd told him, so he walked down the main street, looking at the buildings. He passed a pet store, one that didn't sell dogs or cats, just the accoutrements that you apparently needed when you got one, and then an art gallery/framing shop, and a place that only sold chocolates. He was standing in front of a newsstand when he saw the jewelry store. It occupied the ground floor of a large, square, flat-roofed three-story building. The place was a hodgepodge of yellow brick, cinder block, and poured concrete. The upstairs windows were all soot gray, but the ground-floor windows sparkled brightly from the harsh white lights inside that glared down on the shiny bits of polished metal and stone carefully arranged on black velvet. Stoney went over and looked, thinking that he ought to buy Donna something, just so she'd know he thought of her now and then, but then he continued on past.

When you were out on the sidewalk, the gold watches and diamond rings held your attention, but when you went inside, you could feel how tired the place was. Stoney climbed the stairs, the metal tread plates worn shiny in the center, and then he walked down the third-floor hallway, looking for Tina's

office. When he found it, the heavy oak door was slightly ajar.
He rapped on it with his knuckles.

"Tina?"

Hearing no response, he pushed the door open wide and
stepped inside. Something tickled at the lining of his stomach.
Wish I was carrying, he thought, and he came fully awake as
he walked carefully through the outer office.

"Tina?" Then, louder, "Hello?" You should turn around
and leave now, he told himself, but instead he opened the
door marked PRIVATE and stuck his head inside. Tina Finbury
was inside, at least what was left of her. Her body was tied to
her wooden office chair with lamp cord. Tough old broad, he
thought, she must have resisted, she made the guy work for it,
whatever it was he wanted, because one of her ears and three of
the fingers on her right hand were missing.

"Goddammit, Tina . . . I told you to be careful." The guy
had finished up by cutting her throat, making her look like
she was wearing a red apron. The desk drawers were open,
so were the ones in the filing cabinet, but the place wasn't
trashed, nothing broken or strewn around. There was a copy
of *Hemmings Motor News* on the corner of the desk. She never
struck me as someone who'd geek out over old rust buckets,
Stoney thought, and he looked closer at the familiar brown
paper cover. "March," he read. "Four years old." He looked
around the room, and seeing nothing else that looked out of
place, he backed slowly out of the room. Got to get out of here,
he thought. What did I touch, where did I leave prints . . . ?

He heard a noise behind him, and he turned to see a short,
broad man dressed in jeans, a work shirt, and construction
boots. The guy was trying to peer past Stoney. "Mom?" Stoney
kicked the inner door closed before he could think of what

to do. "Mom?" The man's eyes went from the closed door to Stoney's face. "Who are you? Is she all right? Mom?" He tried to step past Stoney, and Stoney bear-hugged him. "Hey!" Tina's son, if that was who he was, might have been short, but he was built like a bull and he was enormously strong. It was all Stoney could do to hang on to him, but he did it. The guy was a construction worker, not a fighter, so Stoney easily avoided the guy's attempted head butts and knees to the groin. Tina's son, Stoney thought, his head swimming. What kind of trouble was he in now? He waited until the guy quit struggling and shouting. There were more noises out in the hallway. No way I'm walking away from this one, he thought. Jesus. He eased up his grip, looked the guy in the eyes.

"She's dead," he said.

"She can't be. She's only . . . Mom? Let me go, man, I have to see her."

Stoney stood in front of the guy and held him by the shoulders. "Listen to me. There's nothing anybody can do for her now. Do you hear me? I know this is hard, but she's gone. And you can't go in there. She would never want you to see her like this." There were white faces in the outer doorway, eyes watching the two of them.

"What are you talking about? What happened? Get outta the way, man, I gotta . . ."

Stoney shook the guy. "Listen to me. You go in there, you'll never be able to think of her again, not in the right way." The guy strained to look past Stoney, as though he could penetrate the closed wooden door by force of will. "Look at me. I knew your mother, she was a good woman. You wanna do something for her? Stay the fuck out of there. Call the cops. Here, you can use my phone."

"I got my own goddam phone," the guy said.

"Gentlemen?" It was one of the oglers from the outer doorway. "I'm a lawyer? And if this is a crime scene, you shouldn't be in there? So come out into the hallway. Please? The police are already on their way."

This is great, Stoney thought. This is just great.

The Westwood chief of police was an older guy, he had gray hair over a tired, lined face. "Sir," he said, when he finally came down out of the building and out onto the sidewalk where they were holding Stoney, "thank you for waiting. Do you have some ID?"

Stoney fished his New York license out of his wallet. His Jersey license had been yanked several years back. The cop looked at the picture on the little plastic card. "This your current address? You live in Manhattan?"

Stoney was aware of how careful he needed to be. He'd done nothing for the past half hour but think of what to tell this guy. It was Prior who had done it, he knew that. And all his warnings to Tina to stay clear of the man did nothing to make him feel less responsible. But he couldn't tell the cops about Prior. He suspected that they'd never be able to prove the man's guilt anyhow, even if they knew he was the murderer. "Yeah."

"And what brought you out here today?"

"I had an appointment to see Tina," he said.

"What was the nature of your business with her?"

"She was looking into something for me," Stoney said, his mind racing. You can't say a word about Donna, he thought, you can't even hint at who you used to be. "My partner and I are thinking about putting some money into commercial real estate out here, and we asked Tina to look around for us."

"Why not go directly to a real estate agent? Why hire an investigator?"

"When you're asking whether or not you ought to buy something," he said, "you can't take the word of a guy who makes his money by selling it to you. And we don't know the towns or the players out here, so we thought we'd start with an objective viewpoint. We'll get to an agent eventually, if we decide to go forward."

"I see." The cop handed Stoney back his license. "Did you go into her office, upstairs? Or did you just see her from the hallway?"

"I went in."

"You touch anything?"

"Pushed on the outside door to open it. It wasn't latched. Turned the knob on the inner door."

"Anybody see you when you got here this morning? Besides the people who were upstairs, I mean. Anybody see you park your car? Anybody see you before you went inside the building? Did you stop for a cup of coffee or a newspaper? Anything at all?"

"No," Stoney said, but then he remembered the woman in the mink coat.

"She's not gonna remember you," the cop said. "We're gonna have to take a formal statement."

It was a couple more hours before they let him go. They were very thorough. They had him go over exactly what he had done and seen several times before they codified it all into a written statement, which he signed. It might have turned out to be a lucky morning for me after all, he thought, even though it didn't start out looking that way. On his way out to New Jersey, the traffic had been backed up all the way down the Harlem River Drive. Stoney, typically impatient, had detoured over the Triborough Bridge and up the Deegan. It was a little longer, probably not any quicker, but at least it had been moving, which fostered the illusion that he was getting somewhere. The detour had necessitated the payment of a toll on the Triborough, where he'd gotten a time-stamped receipt for his contribution to the greater good of the Metropolitan Transit Authority, and that receipt seemed to allay the suspicions of the Westwood cops.

Tina Finbury's son was in the police station while they were questioning Stoney. Stoney heard rather than saw the man. It took the cops some time and effort to calm him down. The police chief, who had gone off to deal with the guy, apologized for the interruption when he returned. "It's her son," he told Stoney. "The man's pretty upset. It's understandable. Wouldn't you be?"

"Yeah."

The cop looked at him for a second. "Listen," he said, "the man wants to talk to you. You're certainly under no obligation, but if you agree to speak to him, I'd prefer the meeting take place right here. Mr. Finbury is very upset, and I don't need anything else to go wrong."

They met in an interior hallway at the station. Finbury was shaking with rage and sorrow. He broke down when he saw Stoney walking in his direction, he stood there and wept openly and without apology. Stoney yielded to impulse and waved the cops away, he put an arm around the guy's shoulder and led him down to the end of the corridor where two chairs sat under a window. Stoney sat across from the guy and waited for him to recover. It took a while.

"I owe you an apology," Finbury said finally. "They told me you couldn't have done it. They said you were in the city at the probable time"—he swallowed—"when she was killed. And they told me to thank you for identifying . . . the body. I'm sorry if I . . ."

"Forget it," Stoney told him.

"Did you . . . did you know my mother?"

"I met her twice before," Stoney said. "She seemed very nice."

"She was." Finbury replied through gritted teeth. "Whoever did this to her, I want to find him and cut his balls off."

"Yeah," Stoney said. "I understand. Look, I'm gonna give you my cell-phone number. Why don't you give me yours? I'd love to get my hands on the guy who did this, believe me."

SEVENTEEN

Her mother had been strangely silent the night before, she had asked none of the myriad questions Marisa had anticipated. She didn't even want the normal details, where were you, who else was there, what did you do, what did everybody say, none of that. She'd asked one question.

"Were you with your father all day?"

"Only for the morning," Marisa told her. "He had to do something in the afternoon, so he left me with Tommy." She looked at her mother. "Didn't you notice? It was Tommy who dropped me off."

"I didn't see the car."

That was it, that was the end of the conversation. Donna usually didn't miss a trick, and Marisa began cataloging the possible reasons for this change of attitude. Was she still mad at Stoney? Absolutely. Was she jealous of the time Marisa spent with him? Hard to believe that. Afraid Stoney would turn Marisa against her? Marisa couldn't believe that one, either. Afraid Marisa might get in harm's way? But they weren't doing anything, they were only talking about it, her mother had to know that. Worried that she and Eddie were getting too comfortable? She kicked that one around for a while. She had sensed that her mother was not overly fond of Eddie, but that only made him one more member of an expanding fraternity. That's her job, Marisa thought, she's supposed to be tough on young guys. . . . But it didn't feel right. Donna's distrust of Eddie might be part of it, but it wasn't the whole story. There had to be something more.

And what had she done yesterday, anyhow? Sat around reading the paper and listening to Tommy, her father, and George. God, it had been duller than an all-day calculus lecture. Jesus, didn't they have computers for all that now? And why on earth did they waste everyone's time trying to drill all of that arcane crap into your head, especially when everyone knew that you were never going to actually do anything with it?

I was there all day long, and all I did was watch them getting ready to do what it was that they did. . . .

Yeah, she thought. Yeah. That had to be it.

Her mother had always maintained a sort of willful ignorance of her father's life. She had her house out in the burbs, she had her kids, and her stuff, her car and all of that, but what Stoney did all day long, why he went into the city every day, that was a whole separate thing, Donna kept a wall up between herself and all that. And now I've been over the wall, my innocence is gone, and hers is threatened. And then there was the issue of Marisa's dancing career, her mother totally could not get with it, she kept saying, over and over, that she could never understand why any self-respecting person would ever . . .

Everyone thinks less of me now, Marisa thought. They all think I'm president of Future Sluts of America or something. Jesus.

Her mother came down the stairs looking tired and grim just as Eddie pulled up outside. Marisa went and looked out the window to make sure it was him. "I gotta go, Mom," she said, and she grabbed her bag. She was going to be better equipped today, she'd packed a couple of books, some seltzer water, and even her brother Dennis's old Game Boy, he'd surprised her and let her take it.

Donna came back out of the kitchen, looking haggard. "Be careful," she said. "Call me."

"I didn't know how you took your coffee," Tuco said. "I got it with cream, sugar's inside the bag."

Marisa didn't drink coffee. "Thank you," she told him, accepting the cup. "This is fine. You didn't have to do that."

"S'okay." He backed out of the driveway. His own cup was wedged into one of the Beemer's cup holders, a small hole torn in the lid. Marisa tore hers open and took a sip. "You miss me?" he said.

She didn't know if he was serious or not, the guy almost never smiled, although she supposed she hadn't given him much cause. "Yeah," she said, admitting it to herself. "I did. What did you do yesterday? Did you sleep all day?"

"About half," he said. "Stoney says you know where this place is at."

"I do," she said. "Left at the end of the street, then right at the light. What else did you do?" God, I'm just like my mother, I'm interrogating this poor guy.

"Caught up on stuff," he said. "Pissed off one of the tenants."

"How'd you manage that?"

He glanced at her, then quickly looked away. "Oh, you'd be amazed at what some of these people think you got to do for them."

• • •

Everybody had something to do except her. Tommy and her father were still working with George, although, thankfully, they were done with the part of his job that required temper tantrums and had moved on to more esoteric matters. It seemed to be more in Tommy's court now, with long discussions about the stock market. They didn't seem to mind her listening in, but it bored her to tears. Eddie was down in the basement with some new guy, Jack Harman. She had been instinctively wary, when they'd been introduced, ready to dislike the guy, though she couldn't have said why. He'd held her hand gently instead of shaking it, bowed slightly, saying how pleased he was to meet her, and he wore a smile that signaled how desperately he needed her to approve of him and said nothing about what he really felt inside. That's how it seemed to her, anyhow. She had observed him as the day had gone on, and that smile never slipped, his carefully managed appearance always stood between the world and what Jack Harman really was.

She went downstairs, sat at the bottom of the cellar steps, and watched as Harman picked the locks on the safe-room door, with Eddie watching intently. "It's a useful skill," Harman said, his ever-present smile telling her that it was all in fun. "Sort of like playing the piano. You never know when you're going to be called into service." He opened the door when he was done, then closed it and relocked one of the locks. "Your turn, Tuco," he said. Eddie took the tools from him and started in. It took some time. Eddie was on his knees in front of the door, a far-off expression on his face as he worked, cocking his head to Harman's instructions. He finally got it open, and Harman took the lock apart to show Eddie how it worked.

It bothered her.

She didn't know why it should. These guys were not choirboys, she knew that, and Eddie had been too quick and too efficient in the parking lot the other night to have spent all his life working at a regular job someplace. Harman took the cylinder out and handed it to Eddie. Eddie began using Harman's picks as he listened to Harman's explanation of how you used them to feel for the pins. Would you rather see him learning how to be an accountant? she asked herself. George had been right, the day before. Men were not baboons, but still, part of the reason you like him is because he's bad enough. . . .

She left them there, went back up to one of the upstairs bedrooms, intending to take refuge in one of her books, but she couldn't get into it. Would you seriously go out with a guy who mops hallways and takes out the garbage for a living? Yeah, but, that interior voice said. Yeah, but. That's only what he's doing right now. You have to start someplace, don't you? He might become an engineer, or a mathematician, or . . .

Right. The dude is downstairs learning how to be a guy who can open locked doors without using a key. This is just great, she told herself. An apprentice thief and a former stripper. She put her book down and began crying softly.

"So tell me," Harman said. "Where did you guys come up with XRC Technologies? Can't Prior just look them up?"

"We've had our eye on it for a year or two," Stoney said. "Tommy found the stock. It's one of those companies that has possibilities, because they make good stuff, but they're not going anywhere. I mean, they're not quite dead in the water, but they're close. The CEO is this Italian guy, he's gotta be ninety years old, but he keeps hanging on. His son is the CFO, he's the guy that's actually running the company. He's the guy Tommy is supposed to be. That's what makes them so interesting."

204   NORMAN GREEN

"Anthony Bonanno," Harman said. "So it's all real, if Prior does any research."

"He can find them listed," Stoney said. "He'll see their peak share price two years ago of eighty-six and change, and he'll see how they've been dragging along the bottom at ten or twelve bucks for the past six months. Their bonds are junk, and they've got two superfund sites dragging down their balance sheet. Plus, they've got an attitude problem. If Prior calls them up, he won't find a single person at XRC who will talk to him. They're perfect."

"What if he looks at their Web site? Isn't the real Bonanno's picture on it somewhere?"

"It used to be," Georgie said, and he snickered. "I fragged it. Try and look at their site now, you get bounced to a porn site, and the only way to get loose is to log off and reboot. I can't imagine anyone trying that more than once."

"So we're covered, then."

"Jack," Tommy said. "Whaddayou worry about? Everything is under control."

"Sounds like it," Harman said. "But it's my nature to sweat the details. It's an occupational hazard: I like to know everything before I go in. There's a lot at stake."

"That's okay," Tommy told him. "In case it'sa make you feel better, go ahead and sweat."

"Thanks, I will. So what does XRC really do?"

"Tell him, Georgie," Tommy said.

"Chemicals," Georgie said. "Industrial batteries, like for golf carts and forklifts. They make electrical components in Italy, those are mostly marketed overseas. And they have an automotive-products division, which is the part of the company that makes the most money. But it's pretty boring stuff."

"So how are you going to get Prior interested in a dog like that?"

"If you could get rid of the morons in charge," Georgie said, "XRC would really be a nice company, they've got decent market share, their stock is undervalued, and they do a lot of cutting-edge research in their field, but you've got that senile old goat and his half-wit son sitting in the driver's seat. The two big problems with batteries, and believe me, everyone in the business is working on this, they're heavy and they take too long to recharge. Now imagine this: What if someone at XRC came up with a battery that was half the weight of the ones we use now, and that would recharge from flat to full in, say, a half hour?"

Harman shrugged. "So what? You wouldn't have to leave your golf cart plugged in all night. Who cares? What am I missing?"

"Actually, you're not far off," Georgie told him. "We can build an electric car right now that has a range of something like two hundred miles. The problem is, once you've gone that distance, you're done, you can't move for another eight hours or so."

Harman was nodding his head. "Okay. Okay."

"And since our mythical new battery is half the weight, now our range is closer to three hundred miles. So you go on a road trip in your new XRC Electrocoupe, you drive for, say, five hours, and then you pull in at a rest stop. You plug your car in, and in the time it takes you to have a piss, a cup of coffee, and a candy bar, you're ready for another five. And all of this happens with no big changes to the infrastructure."

"No helium, then."

"Hydrogen, you mean. You know, everyone's talking about

hydrogen power as though we could start using it next year, but the fact is, we're decades away. There are all sorts of technical problems we haven't begun to solve, not to mention refueling, or big tanker trucks of the stuff running around to resupply gas stations." Georgie was getting excited, waving his arms around. "Or detonate when the truck driver falls asleep and runs off the road. It's like Reagan and SDI. Oh yeah, let's build a fucking laser so we can shoot down incoming missiles with it. These people have been watching too much science fiction. So, yeah, batteries are dull and boring, but compared to hydrogen, they're easy. Imagine it: overnight you cut air pollution and greenhouse gas emissions in half."

"Wouldn't you still have to burn oil to generate the electricity to recharge the batteries?"

"Sure, initially, but power plants don't have to be oil-fired. We've still got coal and nuclear. And if your car is parked most of the time, like most cars are, you could use solar cells."

"There's no way anybody's building another nuclear plant in this country," Harman said.

"Maybe not," Georgie said. "But just because we're a bunch of science-phobic, PC, brain-dead weenies, it doesn't mean that the rest of the world is, too. And given the choice between nuclear and selling your soul for oil, I think a lot of people would reconsider their opinions. Anyhow, for our purposes, none of that matters. Even if we never sold a single one of our mythical batteries in this country, the market world-wide would be enormous. XRC wouldn't have to ever produce another thing, all they'd have to do is license the technology and count their money. They'd be like Eskimo Pie. They could get rich selling the name and the wrappers."

"All right," Harman said. "So the pitch is, XRC came up with this new battery, but what? They're sitting on it?"

"Well, not exactly. We're saying that they still have to commit some serious development money to bring this to market, and they don't have it. They'd be gambling whatever equity they've got left in the company that this would work, and the ossified management team doesn't realize what they have, so they aren't moving on it. So we come along, we take over, chop them up, sell the pieces, and keep their breakthrough for ourselves. Once the smoke clears, anyone holding a stake would be disgustingly wealthy."

"Wow," Harman said. "Makes me sorry to know that this is all phony."

"Doesn't it? Funny thing is, it's gonna happen, you wait and see."

Marisa woke up a couple of hours later. She lay where she was for a while, feeling drained, listening to the murmur of voices from the first floor. She thought about what she'd felt earlier and wondered if it meant anything. You hardly know him, she thought. Why are you so concerned about what he thinks, anyhow? Besides, he's never given you any indication. Not after that first night. Not after Brooklyn. What makes you think he cares about you at all?

Get over yourself.

She got up, stretched the kinks out of her back. She checked her messages on her cell phone. There were three, none of them from Prior. It was too early for him to call, anyhow. She shut her phone back off and wandered down the stairs.

"One more time," she heard Tommy say. "Start with the question about mutual funds."

"Okay," George said. "Look, dude, you can't play poker with scared money." She could picture the sneer on his face, just from his tone of voice. He sounded like a completely different person from the guy she'd met yesterday. "I'm about making money, okay? I'm not about minimizing risk, I'm not about giving you three percent over the S&P or any of that shit. I ain't running a mutual fund here, fucking mutual-fund managers, they all buy and sell the same two hundred stocks anyhow. You could train a chimpanzee to do it. Look, if you are uncomfortable with risk, do us both a favor. Take your money, go buy an index fund, and get it over with. You can watch the Dow with all the rest of the tourists, okay, you can cry when it goes down and jerk off when it goes up, and in the long run, you'll probably do all right.

"I'm gonna tell you one fucking time what I do, so listen up. I get four or five great ideas in an average year. You get on the boat with me, here's what you get to do: you get to sit in the boat with your mouth shut while we row ashore in the dark. We attack the village while everyone is still asleep, we kill the men, we rape the women, we take whatever we want, then we get back in the boat and we row away. You get it? But you have to be clear on one thing, this only works about three times out of four. The fourth time, King Arthur is waiting in the weeds and he kicks our ass. We take some casualties, and we run away licking our wounds. That's the chance you take.

"Here's what you do not get to do: you do not get to give me suggestions. You do not get to register your opinion. You do not get to ask for status reports, you do not get to call me on the fucking phone or otherwise render yourself a pain in my ass. I run your money for you, and you go do whatever the fuck it is that made you the money in the first place, and both of us will get richer.

"*Comprendo?*"

"Yeah," she heard her father say. "That little thing at the end, like you think he's got an IQ of about sixty, that's perfect."

Marisa walked past the kitchen without looking at them, out into the vaulted front entryway. Her footsteps echoed in the empty space. This is a cold house, she told herself. I'll be glad when we don't have to come here anymore. . . . She kicked her shoes off and walked barefoot into one of the rooms off the entryway at the front of the house. Formal dining room, she thought. More wasted space, a museum for someone's furniture. She passed out of that room and into another one. Library, she thought, looking at the built-in bookcases. Or an office. Or a place to display your Hummels . . . There was a bathroom off the library, and an empty bedroom beyond it. This must be like the guest wing, she thought. Who would want to live in a house like this anyway? Isn't life already lonely enough? You'd need radar or something, just to know where the other person was. She went into the bathroom, sat down, and looked out the window. She could hear voices again, but these ones weren't coming from the kitchen. One voice was soft, the other louder, and with a Brooklyn lilt. On the wall in front of her was a small metal door marked LAUNDRY. She cracked it open and the voices became more distinct. They're in the basement, she thought, and the washing machine is down there, too. You must throw your dirty stuff down this chute. That's why I can hear them. She glanced at the bathroom door, then got up and locked it before returning to kneel in front of the little door.

"I know you think these guys are your friends." It was Harman's voice. Somehow she knew that, this one time, he would not be smiling.

"Where you going with this, man?" Tuco said.

"Don't take it the wrong way. I'm just saying, you seem like a nice kid, and I'd hate to see you make the same mistakes I did when I was your age."

"Yeah? Like what?"

"This kind of thing is great in the planning stages," Harman answered him. "Everybody's on the same page, everybody's deciding how they're going to spend the money they haven't made yet. Millions, right? Then the job goes down, and even if everything falls exactly the way you've got it figured, which never happens, and even if everybody walks away clean, which doesn't happen either, you still have to survive the split. You have to hope nobody gets too hungry and takes you out so they can have yours."

"I ain't worried about that," Tuco said. "Not with these guys."

"All right, fine," Harman said. "Assuming you're right, and I'm not convinced you are. It's all good, right? Wrong. It isn't over yet, my friend, especially if the job has a big payoff, because all it takes is one jerk to go get toasted in a bar and start running his mouth about how smart he is. I can tell you what comes next, because I lived through it. Somebody in the bar goes to the cops and rats out the genius, someone always does, and then the cops pick up the genius. And they sit the guy down in a small room, and they say, 'We got you, asshole, we got you, you're in the box for the next twenty years unless you start singing. You give us the other guys, and we'll let you walk out of here a free man.' So maybe your guy will think about it for a while, but put yourself in that chair. Twenty years can be half your life, man, what are you, twenty? So you'd be a used-up middle-aged con when you got out, and your head would be all screwed up from all that time in the animal farm, you'd be lucky if you could find a job bagging groceries."

"That what happened to you?"

"Almost. I went inside twice. Both times, it was one of my friends put me there. All I'm saying is, if you get out of this with a few bucks, get away from this garbage and go back to school."

"I hate school," Tuco said.

"I did, too. You know what I'd give for the chance to go back and do it again? I'm not saying you have go to Harvard, okay? But you really ought to check out some kind of technical school, engineering or something like that, because you've got a great pair of hands. I've never seen anybody pick up anything so quick, you're almost as good as I am with those locks, and you've been at it less than half a day. The real crime here is if you don't start using the brain that's attached to those hands."

There was silence then. Marisa shifted to a more comfortable position.

"Well, if this is all true," Tuco finally said, "then why are you here?"

"Truth? I shouldn't be. Chalk it up to a weakness of character. As it is, I am definitely not going to do anything on this one that I can even get indicted for. I mean, technically, impersonation is probably against the law, but nobody's going to bother with that. Conspiracy, maybe, but that's a mother to prove. Cops and D.A.s are like everybody else, dude, they're lazy. Unless you piss them off too much, they like to take the guy who's easy, they'll grab whoever has blood dripping off his fingers, and they'll close the case and walk away happy. But the thing is, you stay in this racket too long, sooner or later your luck runs out. I just think you ought to think about your other options while you still got 'em."

Tuco's voice came back quiet. "I don't know if school would work. I'm dyslexic. I never learned shit in school."

"That's not as rare as you think," Harman said. "I know an architect up in Toronto who is dyslexic, can't read worth beans. He claims that most dyslexics are above average, and I haven't seen anything out of you to make me doubt it. There's a way to get this done, Tuco."

Tuco's voice was still quiet. "So are you gonna quit again, when this is all over?"

Harman was silent for a moment. "Here's the lie: I already quit, I don't need the money, I'm only consulting here."

"So what's the truth?"

Harman let ten seconds go by before answering, and when he did, Marisa could hardly hear him. "The truth is, I stayed too long at the party. I can't help myself anymore. There's nothing else left for me now."

"All right," Tuco said. "I know I ought to be doing something else, but I'm not."

"I can ask my buddy, up in Toronto, you know, how he got past it. I'm sure the dude would talk to you, at the very least."

"Okay. But can we get back to this job? Because I already told Stoney I'd do it."

"Sure. But will you talk to this guy? He's a good guy, I'm sure he'd be happy to help you out."

"Yeah," Tuco said. "Okay."

"All right. I'll set it up, then. You'll talk to him, right?"

"Yeah. Yeah, I will."

"Good. Okay, back to business. We need to talk about the dogs."

"Dogs?"

"Yeah. Guard dogs. They can smell you a mile off, and they're usually smarter than the uniform hanging on to the other end of the leash, believe it or not. The thing is, dogs love McDonald's."

"Really?"

"Oh yeah. Quarter Pounders with Cheese, babe. You lace them with a little sleeping powder, chuck them over the fence, you're in. The dog knows the sleeping powder is there, too, but he can't resist . . ."

Marisa got up and pushed the metal door closed. It made a loud click when it latched. She got up on her feet and headed back upstairs.

Her phone rang. She took it out and looked at the screen, recognized Prior's number. She looked around, then opened the phone and took the call. "Hello?"

"Oh, it's really you," he said. "Today must be my lucky day, I get to hear the real girl and not just her recorded voice. God, this makes me so happy." He sounded genuinely pleased.

"I shouldn't talk to you," she said. "Why did you have that gorilla come after me in the parking lot the other night? How is that supposed to make me feel?"

"I apologize for that, honestly, Dwayne was completely out of line. He totally misunderstood my instructions to him. He was supposed to ask you, in the nicest way possible, if you'd deign to have a conversation with me, nothing more. Honey, I can't be more sorry about that than I am. I hope you'll allow me to demonstrate—"

"I don't know why you keep him around," Marisa said. "He's an animal. If my friend hadn't been there . . ."

"Nothing would have happened," Prior said firmly. "I promise you on my mother's grave. I'd have reprimanded Dwayne, which I did in any case, for stepping over the line. And I would have done my best to make it up to you. Will you consider—"

"I have to go," Marisa said.

"Oh, no, no, not yet," Prior said. "Please. Just a minute longer. I would love to meet with you, just so we could talk face-to-face. You wouldn't believe how much I miss being around you. We could meet anywhere you like, really. Somewhere public, if that reassures you. Honestly, I just want to see you."

"I don't know," she said. She kept firmly in mind what she wanted her voice to make her sound like: spoiled, easy, clueless. "I'm so busy lately."

"So who was that boy you were with? The one who slapped Dwayne around? He must be very tough. You wouldn't believe how angry Dwayne is about that. Is he your boyfriend?"

"Really," Marisa said, "I have to go now. Good-bye." She snapped the phone closed, cutting him off in midsentence.

She was sitting out on the back porch swing when he came out to tell her they would be leaving soon. "Hello, Jack," she said. "Tell me. Is that your real name?"

"Ah, well," he said, his "please like me" look fixed firmly in place. "What's a name, anyhow? Something your parents chose to call you, or something you choose to call yourself. Doesn't mean much."

"I guess that means no," she said. "What did your parents choose to call you?"

He glanced back over his shoulder before he answered, as though someone might be lurking there to overhear him. "Between you and me?"

"Sure."

"I was born Nathan Moore," he said.

She nodded her head. "I can see that. It fits you much better than Jack Harman."

"Jack Harman is much better for business," he said. "All-American, isn't it? Blue eyes, apple pie, golly and gee whiz, pardon me, ma'am, you dropped your wallet." His smile went wider.

"Ah, I see. You think the name makes people trust you."

"Well, not by itself, but it reinforces the image. Think about it: your father could be the most upright man in the world, right, but when Joe Average looks at him, what does he see? A big, dark, brooding guy smoking a cigarette, usually with his fists clenched. He's memorable, and he's intimidating. I'm shooting for the other end of the spectrum."

My father is twice the man you are, she thought. "You want to be the lead salesman in an infomercial."

He nodded. "Exactly. 'You can trust me. And you should buy these pots and pans.'"

"So you used to be a burglar," she said. "And now you're not?"

He shrugged. "I used to be a lot of things. The difficulty is that it's hard to change into something new after the paint has already dried. Sometimes I think I'm born to this kind of life, and no matter how hard I'm trying to be something else, it's almost as if I'm wearing another man's clothes, and when I take them off, nothing is really different."

She looked at his face, trying hard to ignore that manufactured look, trying to hold on to the image of the man she'd overheard talking to Eddie. She swallowed, gathering her courage. "Is it that hard? Can Eddie change, if he wants to, or is he stuck, too?"

"Eddie? Oh, you mean Tuco." He looked at her then, and something in his eyes told her he had just figured out the purpose of the conversation. "You like him? He seems to be a good kid. Smart as hell, too, despite, ahh, some of what he carries around. And he's lucky. No record, yet, no juvie arrests, he's clean, but he's standing right on the brink. Every time he rolls the dice, he comes a little closer to crossing over for good." Harman reached out and took her hand in both of his. "I'm not sure I can help him," he said, his face suddenly earnest, "but maybe you can. If Tuco wants to be different, he's going have to do some hard things. And I'm not saying you could change him, or anything like that. But some people have a way of giving a guy a reason to want to be better than what he's been. Maybe you could give him reason enough to do the hard thing, and not the easy one."

It was a daunting prospect. I don't know if I can do that, she wanted to say, I just want to go home to my bedroom. . . . But it struck her then that she had turned that page the moment she'd stepped on the stage at the Jupiter. It was a terrifying thought, and she held her breath. Don't you cry, she told herself, don't you dare cry, not here, not now, not in front of this guy.

"I'm working on something for Tuco," Harman said. "It would probably involve him coming up to Toronto. I've been wondering how hard I should push him. I wasn't really sure he would put himself through it. But maybe you and I together, if we manipulated him carefully . . ." He was grinning. "Maybe we could shove him in the right direction."

Marisa pulled her hand out of his and resumed breathing. Even when the guy is trying to do something good, he's so creepy. "Is that where you live?" she asked him. "Toronto?"

He hesitated a half second before answering. "Yes."

"When are you going home?"

"Couple more days."

This is stupid, she thought, you can't trust this guy. . . .

"You better give me your number," she told him, and she reached for her phone. "I think I'm gonna need your help on this." They were still punching the buttons on their respective cell phones when Stoney opened the back door and stuck his head out. "Yo," he said. "Time to go. Chop-chop."

"Did Prior call you today?"

Marisa sat in the passenger seat of her father's Lexus and stared out the window. Are you using Eddie, she wanted to ask him, what are you going to have him doing, is he going to be okay? She didn't, though, and she knew it was because she was afraid of the answers. "Yes," she said.

"What time?"

"Ten after four."

"Did you talk to him?"

"I did just what you told me to." She turned and glanced at Stoney. "Where did everybody go?" Where is Eddie, that's what she really wanted to know, and why are you taking me home instead of him?

"Tommy went home. He took Georgie with him. Tuco and Jack have something to do tonight."

I knew it, she thought. "Like what?"

He looked at her, and she tried to read his expression. Was he laughing at her, maybe just a little? "If you're worried about Tuco," he said, "you're wasting your time."

"I never said I was worried about anyone. And if I was, why would it be a waste?"

"You need to worry about yourself," he told her. "You ever hear what they tell you on airline flights? In case the oxygen masks come down, you gotta put your own on first. You can't help anyone else if you're passed out yourself."

"I'll try to remember that," she said. "So you don't think something could go wrong? You don't wonder if you or Tommy or Georgie or Eddie or even Jack might get hurt?"

He shrugged. "There's a chance. We work hard to make sure it's a small chance."

"So there is a possibility that something could happen."

"Of course. Hey, there's a chance the two of us will get killed before we get back to the house. I could hit a deer, or the car could blow up, or we could get hit by a meteorite. You can't stay in the house for the rest of your life just because you think something might happen to you." He glanced at her again, and that look was back on his face. "Although in your case, it might not be a bad idea, at least for the next year or so."

"Great," she said. "Very funny. Who's going to pick me up in the morning?"

"Nobody," he told her. "Tuco will be there in the morning before your mother leaves for work. You can hang out with him for the day. I would prefer it if you stayed home, out of sight."

"All right," she said. Anything was better than sitting in that empty house all day long.

"Matter of fact," he said, "you could do something for me. You ever hear of *Hemmings Motor News*?"

"No."

"Well, it's a fat book of ads for antique cars. Comes out every month, I think. I'm looking for a particular issue, March, four years ago. Go on eBay, or used-book sites, and get me one. Can you do that?"

"Sure."

"Good. Get 'em to ship it overnight."

EIGHTEEN

Harman slouched in his chair in the front corner of the waiting room, his feet up on a coffee table. He paged through a two-year-old copy of *Sports Illustrated,* pretending to look at the pictures as he watched the street outside the window. It was early morning, downtown Haworth, New Jersey. As a downtown, it was hardly worth the name, it was one block-long street occupied by a convenience store, a drugstore, a couple of real estate joints, and a small office building. There was a police station at one end and a post office at the other. The sign in the window where Harman sat read EMIL BARTON, FINANCIAL SERVICES. Outside on the street, it was very quiet.

Harman saw a limousine turn the corner at the end of the block. "All right, he's coming," he called, without moving out of his chair. "Fire it up!" A few seconds later, he heard indistinct sounds of loud and heated conversation from an inner office as the limo slid to a stop at the curb in front of the office building. Prior got out of the backseat on the street side and walked around to the sidewalk. He was a tall guy with gray hair, and he moved with the grace of an athlete. He's had this routine for a while, Harman thought, because he's not looking around, he's coming straight in. But Prior seemed to spot him then, because he stopped, stood there on the sidewalk looking at Jack through the front window. Prior then took two steps back to his car and rapped on the roof with his knuckles. A second later, a large bald guy emerged from the driver's seat and hurried around to join Prior. The two of them walked up to the door of the building, out of Harman's line of sight. A moment later the bald guy opened the door to Emil Barton's office, filling the doorway, and stood there, looking at Harman. Harman glanced at him, then went back to his magazine.

Prior must have decided that Harman was not a threat, because he shouldered his way past the bald guy and stepped into the waiting room. He looked around, cocking an ear to the sounds of arguing that came from the back. Without looking, he waved a hand at the bald guy, who turned on his heel and left without saying a word. Prior stood there looking at Harman. "Good morning," he said.

"Hey," Harman said, and he put a touch of Brooklyn into his voice. "Wassup?"

"Either I'm early," Prior said, looking at his watch, "or you're late, assuming you are with whoever that is making all that racket back there."

"I'm just the driver," Harman said. "Don't worry, they won't be long."

Prior's jaw muscles bunched in the sides of his face. "The reason I come here at this hour," he said through gritted teeth, "is so that I don't have to wait. But I suppose that's not your problem."

"Nope." Harman dropped his feet to the floor and sat up a little straighter. "But I'm telling ya, couple minutes more. You ain't gonna be waiting long."

Prior grimaced, then took a seat next to the door. "I have a standing appointment with Barton at this hour," he said, "and my prerogatives are important to me. Who the hell is in there with him?"

"Mr. Gregory Ahn."

"Who might he be?"

Harman sighed. "My boss. Wall Street whiz kid. He's in there with his lawyer and Barton. They're tag-teaming some poor schmuck that runs a big chemical company." Harman could hear Fat Tommy's voice then, angry and strident. A moment later he was shouted down by Georgie, who yelled loud enough for his words to be discernible out in the waiting room.

"The party's over!" Georgie screamed. "Get it through your fat fucking skull! You work for me now!" Fat Tommy yelled back, but not as loud, and whatever he said got swallowed up by the voices of the other men.

"So, this Gregory Ahn," Prior said. "What does he do?"

"He runs a hedge fund," Harman said. "It's kind of like a mutual fund, except it's private, which means he don't have to answer to nobody. The guy's a fucking pirate, you wanna know the truth."

"How big is his fund?"

Harman's attention still seemed to be centered mostly on his magazine. "I dunno," he said. "Couple billion, give or take. Something like that."

"He any good?"

Harman finally looked up. "You kidding? He's a legend. He's averaged forty-three percent return for the past four years. The little shit shorted Enron back when everyone else couldn't get enough of it. He's so good he's fucking scary."

"So who's this guy they're working over in there?"

Harman finally tossed his magazine aside and sat up

straight. "Hey, listen," he said. "I'm just the Neanderthal. I'm not supposed to understand how any of this works, you know what I'm saying? My job is just to drive the little cocksucker around and keep the people he insults on a daily basis from kicking his fucking ass. Everybody I know hates the son of a bitch. But you know what? I ain't as dumb as he thinks I am. I hear things." He tapped his temple with a forefinger. "This guy they got in there, his name is Anthony Bonanno. His company is something called XRC Technologies. Ahn has been buying his paper for a couple months now. The stock is what they call a 'teenager,' because it used to trade in the eighties and nineties, and now it's busted all the way down to thirteen, fourteen bucks a share. It was down to eight, but it came back up a little. Bonanno thinks it's because he has things turned around, but Ahn says the rise in price ain't nothing but a dead cat bounce."

"Just a recoil," Prior said.

"Yeah," Harman said. "Don't mean shit. Gonna head right back down in a week or so."

"So why is Ahn buying into it?"

Harman shrugged. "I dunno. I mean, I got this much just from eavesdropping. XRC must have something Ahn wants. If this goes the way these things usually do, Gregory will keep on buying on the dips until he can force his way onto the board. Once he gets control, he'll break the company up, sell off the pieces, and keep the parts he wants."

"Putting Bonanno and all his people out of work," Prior said.

"Well, yeah," Harman said. "The whole point is to grab all the money and keep it for himself. And for the people in his fund. That's what he does."

"Interesting. You buying a little of XRC on your own?"

"Piggyback on Ahn's play, you mean? Hell, no. I buy into XRC, I become what Gregory calls a 'stuckholder.' There's no way you can ride this guy's coattails, he's got more moves than an epileptic prostitute. Ahn takes care of me, anyhow. You know what I mean? He pays me more than I'm worth, and we both know it. That way, I chauffeur him around, I eat his shit every day, and I keep him out of trouble. It's better than I would get anywhere else. If I can stand the little bastard for another year or so, I can prolly retire."

An inner door opened, then banged shut again. Fat Tommy stormed out into the waiting room. He stopped when he saw the two men sitting there. He shook a handkerchief out of a coat pocket and wiped his face. He stowed it when he was done, glanced at Prior, then pointed a thick finger at Harman. "That fucka piece a shit," he hissed. "You tella that lilla prick, him and his fucking lawyer, I wasa no build uppa this business just to hand it to a asshole like him! He don' watcha his fucka mouth, he gonna wind up down in the bottom of the Hackensack River. You tell him! You hear me?"

Harman nodded. "Yes, sir."

Tommy jerked the door open and exited. Prior turned and watched him go. "Bonanno, you said his name was. He related? You think he could put a hit out on your boss?"

"Related to the crime family Bonannos?" Harman asked. "Nah, I don't think so. He was, they'da raped his business a long time ago."

"I suppose. So you aren't taking his threats seriously, then."

Harman shrugged. "You think it would make any difference if he was connected? You think Gregory is any less ruthless than those guys? He wanted to take Bonanno out the old-fashioned way, believe me, they'd be digging the hole right now."

"How about that," Prior said.

The inner door opened again, and Stoney's voice, pitched low, floated down the hallway. "I think you might have been a little rough on him."

"Look," Georgie's voice said. "The day I start paying attention to what you think is the day I have Martin out there shoot me in the fucking head."

"Fellas," a third voice chimed in. "C'mon, fellas. . . ."

Prior quickly relocated himself to the chair next to Harman. "Martin," he said softly. "That you?"

"Yep."

"Big dog's coming, Martin. You got a business card?"

"Sure." Harman took a thin silver case out of an inner pocket, broke it open, fished out a card, and handed it to Prior. "He won't even take your phone call for less than five million."

"That doesn't surprise me," Prior said, pocketing the card. Georgie Cho, Stoney, and Emil Barton, the broker, entered the room. Harman watched Prior stiffen when he saw Georgie, who glared back at him. If they were dogs, Harman thought, they'd be growling and trying to sniff each other's butts already.

"Up off your ass, Slick," Georgie said, still staring at Prior. "You ain't making me a fucking cent sitting there."

Harman sighed, nodded to Prior, then got up and followed Georgie and Stoney out of the room.

"You must have been tired," Marisa said.

"Sorry," Tuco told her. "Guess I ain't been much company. I worked late last night. Is that coffee?"

"Yes," she said, and she walked across the kitchen to get him a cup. "I'll have to nuke it for you. Did you work late with

my father or are you still doing your regular stuff in Brooklyn?"
She remembered that he had been reluctant to lie to her father,
and she was curious to see how he would answer her now.

"I got a guy to cover the building for me," he told her. She
waited for more but she did not get it. He was looking out
through the window, across the green lawn of the backyard to
the trees at the rear of the property. "Very pretty out here," he
said. "Quiet."

"I suppose." She glanced out at the yard. She couldn't
remember the last occasion she'd spent any time out there.
"You're a strange guy, Eddie."

"Maybe." His voice was quiet. He was still looking out the
window. "Maybe I just look that way. 'Cause, like, from my
neighborhood, where I grew up at, I think I'm a pretty average
dude."

"I don't think so, Eddie." The microwave dinged, she got
his coffee out and handed it to him. "Cream's in the fridge. I
don't think you're average, not in any way."

"Not like the other baboons?" He actually smiled.

"Oh, who told you about that?"

"Georgie told me."

"I was just trying to help him out. It doesn't mean that I
think all men are baboons."

"Georgie's a nice guy," he said.

"Yes, he is."

"Way smart. He's got some kinda engineering degree.
Taller than me, too."

"We're not talking about George, Eddie."

"No? What are we talking about?"

"You," she said.

"Oh."

"What's going to happen to you? Do you ever wonder?"

He opened the fridge, busied himself pouring cream into his coffee, then took it to the far side of the room and sat over by the window. Marisa leaned on the counter. "When I first got the job from Fat Tommy," he said, not looking at her, "back in that junkyard him and your father used to have, it was like I hit the lottery. You know what I'm saying? Even if I had problems, and whatnot . . . I was very happy. They had this old guy working there, his name was Pete. Pete taught me things, you know, like welding, and how to use a torch, that kind of stuff. I was always pretty good with a wrench, but Pete taught me the way to understand how things are supposed to work. If I could have stayed in that junkyard for the rest of my life, I think I would have done that." He glanced over at her. "I never thought there could be anything more for somebody like me. I don't know, maybe it's wrong, but when you finally find a comfortable place, you just want to stay there."

"I don't know either," she said.

"Maybe I'm just not, what did Georgie call them? One of the big baboons."

"Dominant males," she said. "There was more to that story, Eddie. More than I told George."

"Yeah?"

"Yes," she said. "Would you like to hear it?"

"Sure."

"All right," she said. "These baboons live in a sort of tribe, and they have their own customs and all of that, and since these particular baboons are close to civilization, they're easy to watch, so scientists have been studying them for a long time. Okay? Now, it so happens, there's a garbage dump in their territory. The dominant males eat the garbage, and they won't let any of the other baboons near the place, not even the ones from their own tribe. You know what I mean?"

"Pigs," he said.

She shook her head. "Dominant males."

"Okay."

"All right. Now what happened, just by accident somebody threw something into the dump that was very poisonous. Since the dominant males were the only ones who ate there, they died. All of them."

"Ah."

"Yeah. Now, what I thought, I figured the next echelon, you know, the next rank of males, would just move up a notch, right, and everything would go along just the way it always had." She stopped, looked at him expectantly.

"And it didn't?"

"No. And the thing is, the scientists had been watching this tribe forever, and they had been keeping track of everything that happened. You know, 'Today we had six confrontations, four that just involved screaming, two with physical contact, and one that involved biting,' and so on. So they were able to measure exactly what happened after the big males all died. And what happened was that the whole tribe became less violent, more peaceful, more nurturing. Infant mortality went down, life span increased, the baboons shared food with one another, everything got better. And it stayed that way, you know what I mean? Even after enough time had passed for three or four generations of baboons to come and go, even after new males had grown up, the ones who would have been fighting for dominance before, they were all still quieter, still less violent, they were still better off."

"How about that. So you want to change the world, all

you got to do is kill the dominant males, is that what you're saying? And then everybody would be happier."

"With the baboons," she said, "it happened by accident."

"Yeah," he said. "But you could still do it, right? The politics of assassination. Somebody starts getting too pushy, you just whack him. I wonder if it would work."

"I don't think so," she said. "Human males are much more devious than baboon males."

"Yeah," he said. "The females, too."

She colored slightly. "Maybe. But what I'm saying is, maybe you can pick out what you want for yourself. Not everybody has to be like Prior, or like Fat Tommy and my father."

"Maybe not," he said. "But sometimes you gotta do what you gotta do. To get by, you know what I'm saying? To live another day. Your father came up the hard way, he didn't come from a place like this."

"I'm not attacking him, Eddie. You don't need to defend him, not to me. I'm just saying, you don't live down by Mario and those guys anymore. You made it out."

"I still miss it sometimes," he said.

"Do you really? Why?"

He didn't answer her question. "Maybe you and me are not so different," he said. "Maybe we a little bit alike, after all."

Stoney picked up the tail on his way back down to the city. He was trying to learn to drive like a civilized human being and having a tough time with it. I'll only go ten over the limit, he told himself, but his resolve would melt after a few minutes and he'd start asking himself what he was doing over in the right lane with the grandmothers, and the next thing he knew, he'd be doing eighty or ninety, dueling with the rest of the maniacs, at which point he'd remember his earlier resolution and slow back down again. A blue Volvo 850 station wagon kept pace with him, speeding up and slowing down when he did. You gotta be kidding me, he thought, looking at the thing sitting three cars back. A Volvo? He got off at Central Avenue in Yonkers. Sure enough, the Volvo did, too, it followed him as he drove west through the town. Stoney wasn't particularly hungry, but he stopped at a Wendy's. The Volvo drove on past and pulled into a Dunkin' Donuts parking lot about a hundred yards farther on.

No way, he told himself. No way anybody works for Prior is driving a goddamn Volvo station wagon. Fucking thing looks like a shoe box on wheels, for chrissake. Hard to imagine a cop driving it, either, but you never knew with cops, sometimes they did things that were hard to figure. Maybe they seized the thing from some old lady for dealing cocaine out of her co-op in Fort Lee. Stranger things had happened. And if it was the police, they might be listening in on his phone calls, too, he didn't doubt that they could do it, and would if they were taken by the notion. He got in line, bought a burger and a cup of coffee, and went and sat down at a table. He ate half the burger, then stuffed the napkin in his mouth, took his coffee, and went over to the pay phone by the door. He made his call, listened to Fat Tommy's prerecorded voice, waited for his beep.

"Thisa Roberto," he said, spitting the words out through the soggy napkin. "Veddy seek. I don' coming to work tomorrow. But don' tell nobody, hogay? Isa nobody's goddamn bidness." A short black kid holding a skateboard that was almost as big as he was watched, openmouthed, from a few feet away. Stoney winked at the kid, fished the napkin out and threw it away, and went back out to the car.

He got back out on Central, drove straight across to where it connected with the Deegan, and took the Deegan southbound. The Volvo did, too, hanging a bit farther back than before. Suspicious, maybe. Stoney wondered if he ought to try to take it easy. But you alter your pattern too much, he told himself, the guy will know something's up. It didn't matter anyway, he held his speed down for a mile or two, but then he wound up doing what he always did, hammering down the left lane like his ass was on fire.

He found a parking spot on his block. The only reason he got the spot, typical Manhattan bullshit, there were four signs on one pole, you had to sort through all of them to figure out if the spot was legal or not, and what it boiled down to was you had to move the car before seven the next morning, and no way you were finding a legal spot at that hour. The Volvo parked by a hydrant at the far end of the block.

Stoney went into his building, went upstairs long enough to turn a light on, then went back down and exited by the back door of the building. There was an alley that led you out to Thirteenth Street. He stuck his head out, didn't see anything too strange. He went down Thirteenth, turned at the end of the block, and went to have a quick look at the Volvo driver.

White guy, blond hair in a buzz cut, motherfucker was looking through a pair of binoculars. He had a newspaper and a cup of coffee on the dashboard. Wasn't a Dunkin' Donuts cup, either, he'd stopped at a 7–Eleven. The man came prepared, Stoney thought.

Jersey plates on the Volvo.

Night was falling on Alphabet City. I could wait an hour or two, Stoney thought, come back, yank that guy out of the car, dance him up and down Twelfth Street until he tells me what's going on . . .

I really needed this, he thought. What a pain in the dick.

Roberto's Deli was across the street from Fat Tommy's loft. There was a joint next to Roberto's, down in the cellar, they had live jazz six nights a week, five if you didn't count open mike night. They also had a lot of other things, the bartender could hook you up with almost any poison you preferred. Stoney bought a ginger ale, found a booth in a dark corner, and waited.

Tommy came in about an hour later, made a slow circuit around the room before he sat down across the table from Stoney. A six-piece band was playing, three white guys on brass, brothers on bass and piano, and a sister behind the drums. She used a brush and a stick, she and the bass player worked together like they were joined at the hip. The piano tinkled softly in the background while the horns carried on a hushed conversation of their own. Stoney and Tommy sat and listened. Forty-five minutes later, the band took a break.

"You wasa have a lilla problem?" Tommy asked.

"I'm burned," Stoney said, and he told Fat Tommy about the Volvo.

"Damn," Fat Tommy said. "Bad timing."

"I know. You didn't say anything?"

"No. Didn't tell nobody." Tommy leaned on the table. "So now you wanna pulla the plug?"

"We're too close, Tommy. Besides, I want Prior. I been through too much on this one."

"I know whatta you mean. Still . . ."

"You don't have to tell me. If somebody's onto us, we could all be up shit creek. Son of a bitch."

Tommy shrugged. "Maybe Prior don' gonna call."

Stoney shook his head. "He's on the hook. Five gets you ten he calls Jack before noon tomorrow."

"Make him wait," Tommy suggested. "Jerk him around a couple day."

"I don't like it," Stoney said. "It's the wrong way to play this guy. What I'm wondering is how much they've got. If they've got me, do they have the rest of you? Do they have our phones, too? If Prior calls Jack tomorrow, what will Jack say when he calls you?"

"Don' worry," Tommy said. "Smart boy. He don' gonna say much onna phone. 'Hey, Uncle Tommy, you wanna buy me lunch?' Something like that."

"Goddammit," Stoney said. "I know the smart play is to close up shop and walk away, Tommy, but I want this guy bad. I gotta do this."

Tommy leaned back in the booth, sipped at his drink while he looked out across the dimly lit room. The band members were drifting slowly back to their places. "My call," Tommy said, and he stood up. "Don' do a thing. Wait until you hear from me."

NINETEEN

Marisa had paid for early delivery, next day air, so it came before her mother had left for work. "Something for Dad," Marisa told her, and she tore the cardboard carton open. It had cost her four bucks from an online used-book dealer, who charged another ten for shipping. It was a four-year-old copy of *Hemmings Motor News*. Stoney had not, initially, told her why he wanted it, but she had gotten it out of him. Marisa had never met Tina Finbury; neither the name nor Stoney's description of her rang any bells. When Stoney told her he was sure the woman had been murdered by Prior, and why, Marisa made up her mind that Prior was going to pay. She'd never thought of herself as a vindictive person, but she became one that moment, she could feel it.

She sat down with the book and began leafing idly through it. She found a picture of a fat, middle-aged guy standing in front of something identified as a Delahaye, an ugly little half-century-old car that looked like it might have been drawn for some cartoon character to drive. As a matter of fact, the guy standing so proudly in the picture did bear more than a passing resemblance to Elmer Fudd. Guys are so weird, she thought, they get all wrapped up in the strangest things. She had once dated a boy whose father owned a Corvette from the early sixties. The guy had kept the car closed up in a garage that looked like a museum. The floor was tiled, the walls were painted white, and the tool cabinets against the wall were new, undented, and clean. The car was parked on four little square pieces of carpet so that the tires did not even touch the floor, and it was draped with some special kind of soft-cloth cover. It took the guy fifteen minutes of fussing just to give you a look at it. And God forbid you should ask a question, if you got him started you had to stand there for an hour while he told you stories about the stupid thing. He kept promising her a ride in it, which she'd never gotten because she broke up with his son while the weather was still cold and the guy never took his baby out unless the day was perfect. Amazing, she thought, that some people had nothing worthwhile to bother themselves about.

Focus, she told herself. Try to pay attention to what you're doing, for chrissake.

She didn't know what anything in the book could possibly have to do with Prior. The man didn't even drive, the only cars he had were limos, and he always rode in the back. Do it anyhow, she told herself, just go through the book and see what jumps out at you. If it had a connection to Prior, this Finbury lady must have found it, and if she can do it, you can, too.

She got lost in the book. God, didn't anybody ever throw anything away? Maybe the Delahaye was ugly, but there were plenty of cars listed that weren't, everything from old MGs and Triumphs to World War II jeeps, and how cool would it be to drive up to your prom in this guy's '61 T-bird convertible, only twenty-two grand, she couldn't remember ever seeing a car that beautiful. Or that little Cobra, oh yeah, a hundred and forty-five grand the guy wanted. In your dreams, buddy . . . It took a couple of hours to get to the end of the book, and she saw nothing in that time that said "Prior" to her.

Stoney's phone rang early in the morning. It was Fat Tommy. "Come on down to my place," he said. "I gonna buy you breakfast. Take the train."

"Okay," Stoney said, and Fat Tommy, for once in his life, apparently had nothing else to say, and he hung up. Stoney stood in his apartment, a coffee cup in one hand and the phone in the other. Take the train? Why the hell would Bagadonuts want him to ride the subway? And that's what he wanted, Stoney had no doubt of it, otherwise Tommy would never have mentioned it. He shrugged, cradled the phone. Whatever you say, he thought.

The Volvo guy was still there, although he was no longer parked by the hydrant. Someone must have moved a car during the night, and the guy had grabbed the spot. He had another guy with him now, sitting shotgun in the car. Stoney ignored them both and walked up to Fourteenth to catch the L. He wasn't sure if they followed him or not, the platform was too crowded with morning commuters, and Stoney didn't want to appear too curious. The train rattled into the station and he shouldered his way on with everyone else.

Fat Tommy wound up cooking breakfast, and of course he made a production out of it: poached eggs, cob-smoked bacon that he mail-ordered from Georgia, Italian-roast coffee, toast made with bread he drove all the way out to Staten Island to buy, and so on. Stoney held in his questions and watched. Tommy's joy in the ordinary things of his life was something that Stoney could see but did not understand. He tried to remember a time when he was as fully present in the moment. . . .

Tommy set his table for three. "I wasa call Jack Harman last night," he said.

"Okay."

"Don' worry," Tommy said. "In case this thing falls apart, we still find a way to take care of your friend Prior."

Harman rang Tommy's doorbell a short time later. Stoney hardly recognized him when he stepped through the door. He was wearing ancient sneakers with no laces, ragged pants, a long, stained woolen overcoat, and a stocking cap pulled low across his forehead.

"Well," Stoney said, watching as Harman stripped off the hat and coat, "nobody's gonna pick you out in that getup."

"I sincerely hope not," Harman said, grinning. "You didn't."

"What?"

"I was camped out on the stoop on Twelfth Street, right next door to your place. You came out this morning, walked right past me, didn't say hello or anything. I was going to ask you for a quarter."

"Jesus. You were there? I didn't notice you at all."

"Well, that's the idea. I was just another East Village train wreck, just one more lost dog. No reason to notice. Those two goobers shadowing you didn't notice me, either."

"Okay," Stoney said, nodding. "So? What did they do?"

"They had an argument. The one guy is over here in his wife's car, and it sounded like she was pretty pissed off about it."

"You're kidding me. The Volvo guy?"

"Yep. The two of them got out and tailed you from your place to the subway station, but then the Volvo guy got all nervous and jerky about the car, he was afraid to leave it parked there. They argued for a while. The other guy was steamed,

'How the fuck am I supposed to do this all by myself, I gotta get back to Jersey in time for my shift,' and on and on. He finally went down into the subway station, but he didn't have a Metrocard, and by the time he figured out how to use the machine, he missed the train and you were gone. He went back over to Twelfth Street and the two of them yelled at each other some more. I left right after that, so I don't know where they are now, or what they're doing."

"Sound like Tweedledum and Tweedledope," Tommy said.

"They do," Harman said. "Definitely not varsity. But they did kind of look like cops."

"I guess that's a relief," Stoney said. "Either one of you two guys notice anyone watching you?"

"Not a soul," Harman said.

Tommy shook his head. "Nope."

"All right," Stoney said. "Well, keep your eyes open. Unless we pick up someone else, let's assume those two are only targeting me. From now on, be careful what you say when you call me, and if I have something important to talk about, I'll find a pay phone."

"Forget that," Harman said. "I'll pick up one of those prepaid jobs for you."

"All right," Stoney said.

"Tell me one more time what they look like," Tommy said.

"They looked like cops to me," Harman said. "You know, short hair, white faces, you can tell they've hoisted some iron, you know, Young Republicans of America."

"From Jersey," Tommy said.

"Their car was, anyhow. Why?"

"I'ma no like this," Tommy said. "I think I know what to do."

"Whatever," Stoney said. "In the meantime, we're still on. At least until the next bump in the road."

"So we're still waiting for Prior to call," Harman said. "There an over-under on him?"

"Before noon," Stoney said.

Tommy thought about it. "By two o'clock."

"I'll be the pessimist," Harman said. "I'll take four-thirty this afternoon. Make it five, give him a while to think it over after the market closes. If it's a down day, we got him."

She went back at it after Tuco showed up. He watched for a while, then asked what she was doing. She wasn't sure how much he knew, or how much she was supposed to say, but in the end she decided that if he didn't know what was going on, he ought to, and she told him what she knew about Tina Finbury and Prior. Tuco sat and listened without showing much emotion.

"Okay," he said when she was done. "So I guess you didn't find a picture of Prior in that book anywhere."

"If it's there, I didn't see it," she said. "Besides, it's mostly cars. There's only a few pictures of people."

"Oh. And he isn't into cars, that what you said, right? You sure he ain't got an old Jag under a tarp in the corner of his garage?"

"No," she said. "He has a couple of limousines and a van, that's all."

"Well, there has to be a connection. Does he sell insurance? Like on antique cars?"

"No, Eddie," she said. "The guy's rich, he doesn't do anything."

"You're sure he's not, like, partners with someone in the

old-car business? Some guy doing restorations, maybe, or some other rich guy with a car museum, something like that?"

She was shaking her head. "I never once heard him even mention a car, his or anyone else's. I never got the impression that he cared about them at all. To him, they were just transportation appliances."

"No kidding. Well, nobody's gonna buy *Hemmings* if they're not into old iron in a big way. Look through again, sometimes they take pictures of a car parked in front of someone's house. Look at the backgrounds, not the cars, see if anything looks familiar."

"All right." She did it, she did it until she was sick to death of everything automotive. "Nothing," she told him.

"There's gotta be something," he said. "Okay, let's try something else. Talk to me about this guy Prior."

"Do I have to?"

"I think so."

She closed her eyes. She didn't like thinking about Prior, didn't like remembering what she had felt like when she was inside his house, and she sure as hell didn't want to talk about it in front of Tuco. She heard him get up and walk over, felt his hand on her shoulder. "It's all right, Mar," he said. "Just talk about the guy. Talk about what you know."

"Okay." She didn't want to look at Tuco while she talked, so she stared out the window. "He loves women. I mean, all of us, but he's crazy about young girls. When he wants something from you, he talks to you, and he, he like, looks at you as if there's nobody else in the world, just you and him. Once he gets what he wants, he doesn't want to see you or hear you, he just wants you to go away. I think he's got a lot of money, but I never saw him throw it around or try to impress anybody

with it. I don't think he cares at all what other people think.
He, ahh, he thinks he's smarter than he really is, but I don't
suppose that makes him any different. He plays golf, he's got
a lot of golf magazines laying around, and he has this big net
thing in his backyard that he hits golf balls into. And he has
these other things, they're a cross between golf balls and Wiffle
balls, and he hits them from one side of his yard to the other.
He hates the dogs. The dogs are afraid of him. I don't know if
he has any friends. He works out a lot, he has a punching bag
hanging in the room where his pool table is. Ahh, I don't know.
What else?"

"What's he do for excitement?"

"He flies an ultralight, it's like a hang glider with an engine.
He goes parachuting, somewhere up in Connecticut. He says
he used to be a mountain climber. . . ." She looked over at
Tuco, who had taken the book and was sitting down looking
at it. "Gimme that," she said. He got up, walked back over,
handed her the book.

"What?" he said.

It was up near the front of the book, a two-page ad for an
auction in Montreal. COLLECTIBLE CAR AUCTION, the banner
read, but there was a picture of a motorcycle in one corner.
"That's his bike," Marisa said, pointing at it. "You made me
think of it when you asked what he did for excitement. I mean,
he talked about all those other things, but the only thing I
actually saw him do for fun is ride that thing."

"Are you sure?" Tuco looked at the picture. "That's pretty
exotic. Not exactly a Harley-Davidson."

"I'm positive," she said. "I've never seen another one like
it. He must have gotten it at this auction. Oh look, it says 'call
for provenance.' That must mean they know the history of this

thing, like where it came from and all that. The auction house has a Web site, let's go look." She looked at him. "I think we got him, Eddie."

"You got him," Tuco said. "I don't know if the auction house will have the details on a sale from four years ago on their Web site."

"Maybe not," she said. "But the Internet is freak central, all we have to do is find somebody who's nuts about that particular kind of bike. If we Google that bike, I promise you we'll come up with six guys who know where they bought the screws when they built the thing, and if they don't know about that exact auction, they'll know how to find out about it. Ducati, right?"

Fat Tommy won the bet by thirty-seven minutes.

Harman's phone warbled, he opened it and held it to his ear. "Wassup?" Tommy and Stoney came to point, listening to his end of the conversation. "Yeah, it's me," he said. "Yeah, I remember you." His voice changed, and he didn't sound like Jack Harman any more, he sounded like Martin from Brooklyn. "Okay. Yeah? Do I think he really wouldn't talk to you for five million? Believe it or not, that's not a fortune anymore, my friend. But I'll see what I can do. Just, like, be ready to move, this guy doesn't fuck around. Yeah, like a cashier's check or something like that. You got to what? What?" He listened in silence for a minute. "No, wait," he said. "No. Don't do that. Yeah, I'm sure. Why? Because the bigger crook Ahn thinks you are, the more he's gonna like you. You was an ax murderer who pried the gold out of dead people's teeth, he'd love you. Gregory's queer for that kinda shit. It's a locker-room thing, you know what I'm saying? He thinks hanging around hard

cases makes him some kinda player. Okay, listen, I'll tell you
what I'm gonna do, I'm gonna run this past Gregory's lawyer.
No, forget it, don't worry about that, the guy's as big a crook
as they come. Didn't I say he was a lawyer? Anyhow, he's better
at manipulating Gregory than I am. He can probably get Greg
all wound up about your story, Ahn will be so hot to meet you,
he'll be coming all over himself. No, there's no commission, no,
no, no, Jesus Christ, don't even think about that, I ain't taking
nothing from you. Because I get mine from Gregory Ahn. You
know what I'm saying? He believes I'm loyal to him, I get to
ride this gravy train awhile longer. He thinks I'm working him
to make a few extra bucks for myself, I'll wind up sucking mud
somewhere down in the bottom of the Meadowlands. Okay?
So here's what's gonna happen: this guy is gonna call you, you
meet with him, and he'll tell you how he wants to approach
it with Gregory. Yeah. This number you called me from, that
where you're gonna be at? Okay, good. No, figure tomorrow
morning. All right. Yeah, ciao, baby." He snapped the phone
closed, ending the call.

"What happened?" Stoney said.

Harman's smile and voice were back. "Diamonds. He was
going to, how'd he put it? 'Take some of my holdings over to
Forty-seventh Street and get liquid enough to do this.' He's got
his money in diamonds."

"Oh, boy," Tommy said, rubbing his hands together briskly.
"Oh, boy." He walked over to his house phone, picked it up,
dialed a number. "Moses Wartensky," he said. "Please. Tell him
it's his old friend Tommy."

It was hard for Stoney to believe, but Tuco and Marisa sounded
sure when they called him, so he borrowed Tommy's car and

drove out to meet them at a coffeehouse in one of the big malls on Route 4, not far from the George Washington Bridge. Go figure, he thought. After all this, the kids wind up nailing the son of a bitch.

"So who is he?"

"His real name is Wayne Plotnik," Marisa said. She glanced from her father's face to Tuco's. "He was right in that old car catalog. I never would have seen it if it wasn't for Eddie."

Stoney looked at Tuco, who shook his head, denying his contribution. "Okay. Great job. So go ahead and gimme his story."

"You tell him, Eddie," she said. "You were the one who found him." She sat there looking at Tuco. Stoney tried to read her expression and Tuco just tried to look blank. Jesus Christ, Stoney thought. What's going on with these two? He'd never seen his daughter defer to anyone like that. Let it go, he told himself. You got no time for this now. . . .

"All right," Tuco said. "The guy was in the RCMP—"

"What? He was a fucking Mountie?"

He nodded. "Listen to the story. This guy isn't some schlub in a red jacket riding through Central Park on a horse. Somewhere in the early nineties, okay, a special unit in the RCMP was absorbed into something called JTF-2. They're Canadian special forces, and Wayne Plotnik was one of the first."

"Never heard of 'em."

"The Canadian government seems to like it that way. But just to give you an idea what these people are like, let me tell you one thing we found out. In Bosnia, the Serbs took some Canadian diplomats hostage. A JTF-2 team was sent in to get them back, and when the Serbs heard who was coming, they let the hostages go."

"Holy shit."

"That's what I thought. There's not a lot of hard information on what else JTF-2 has done, but they're supposed to have been in places like Kosovo, Rwanda, Zaire, Haiti . . . All the garden spots. Most recently, some Canadian citizens were captured by a band of Peruvian guerrillas, and a JTF-2 team went in and got them out. Apparently not many of the guerrillas survived. So you know, okay? These guys don't play."

"I get it."

"Wayne Plotnik was cashiered out of the service in '96. We never found out why, but there was a story in a Toronto newspaper that if you had three captives who wouldn't talk, you gave them to Plotnik, and a while later you would get two of them back, and they would be happy to answer all of your questions."

Stoney rubbed his chin. He'd run into guys like that before, guys who liked turning the screws a little too much. Nobody trusted them, even in the underworld they wound up ostracized.

"Anyhow, after they threw him out, he went to work for a Belgian security company that, quote, provided arms and tactical training for suppression of insurrectionary forces, unquote."

"Mercenary."

"I thought those guys only existed in the movies. Anyway, he worked for the Belgians for two years. He was in Italy on vacation when two of the directors of something called Banco Calvino were taken hostage. After Plotnik sprang the directors, some bodies turned up in the Po River, no IDs, cause of death was massive trauma. So two and two add up to four, except if you're in Italy and a large and powerful bank finds it in their heart to show gratitude, in which case nobody looks too close. After that, Plotnik went to work full-time for Banco Calvino. What he did for the bank, your guess is as good as mine, but they didn't have any more problems with kidnappers. Anyhow, Banco Calvino was a very interesting enterprise. Even in a down market, they promised, and supposedly delivered, excellent returns for people and entities who had a relationship with them. Anybody who was anybody in Italy had money in Calvino, from the Sicilian mob all the way up to the Vatican."

"Not a place where I could get a check cashed. And how did you find all of this out?"

"When the scandal hit, there were stories everywhere. We found them in a half-dozen newspaper archive sites."

"We had to join up, here and there, you know, to access the stories," Marisa said, grinning. "I used your American Express card. Hope you don't mind."

Stoney glanced at Tuco, who was working hard at keeping his face expressionless. Christ, Stoney thought. "We'll talk about my credit card later. What scandal?"

"In '99," Tuco said, "Banco Calvino went under. The scandal was, what happened to all the money?"

"So? What happened to the money?"

"One of the directors dropped out of sight, along with Plotnik and a couple zillion lira."

"How much in real money?"

"Forty-two million, U.S. Four months later, the director was found hanging in a stairwell in a hotel in Amsterdam. When they cut him down, he had a fish in his mouth."

"Which means," Stoney said, "the Sicilians got him."

"That's what everybody thought. But nobody found any of the money, and Wayne Plotnik is still missing."

"Ah."

Marisa produced two sheets of paper, laid one of them on the table in front of Stoney. "This picture," she said, "is from a story in one of the local Jersey papers about Charles David Prior when he bought the house in Alpine." She laid the second next to it. "This one is from an Italian newspaper, right after the bank closed."

Stoney picked up the two pictures. "Cheekbones are a little more prominent, and it looks like he got a chin implant, but it's the same guy. Definitely. How'd you put all this together?"

"We traced his motorcycle," she said.

"What?"

Tuco nodded. "He bought it at an auction. That old copy of *Hemmings* had an ad run by the auction house the month before the sale, and there was a picture of his bike in the ad. When we looked at the auctioneer's Web site, they had all the stuff from their old sales posted. We had to pay to look at that, too. Anyhow, that's where Prior got the bike. In Canada. The seller was a Canadian collector. The auctioneer thought it was one of a kind, historically significant, it ought to be in a museum, and on and on. You figure they were just trying to pimp the price, but anyhow, they gave a history of who rode it in such and such a race, who owned it, and from when to when. Like with a painting by Rembrandt or one of those guys, they tell you the whole history of the stupid thing to convince you it isn't phony. Anyway, Prior bought it at auction, and he had to bid against some motorcycle museum on the West Coast. The guy who was trying to buy the bike for the museum wrote an article about it for some bike collectors' magazine, that was online, too. But the guy who sold the bike to the Canadian collector, you're gonna be so surprised, was a man named Wayne Plotnik. That happened about six months before Calvino went under."

"He probably knew the shit was coming. He wanted to keep the bike, so he made a deal with the collector in Canada. 'I sell this to you, you hang on to it until I'm ready to take it back.'" Stoney picked up the two pictures, folded them, and put them in his pocket. "You guys did a great job. Now what I want you to do is forget that you ever heard the name Plotnik, and I want you to stay out of sight. He's still calling you, right?"

She glanced at Tuco, then looked down at the floor. "Yes."

"You know what to do, right?"

"Yes, Daddy." She looked almost angelic. Drop it, he told himself. Leave them alone.

"All right. Just a few more days, and this ought to be all over."

"You never told me any of this," Benny said.

"Yeah, well, that's why I'm telling you now." Benny and Stoney were sitting in Stoney's Lexus in the parking lot of a church in Bronxville.

"This is supposed to be an honest program," Benny said.

"I know, Benny," Stoney said. "That's why I'm telling you the truth."

"Jesus Christ," Benny said. "You're telling me the truth about you being a crook."

"Yeah," Stoney said. "You told me once, back in the beginning, that if I was a horse thief, you guys would make me a better one. You remember that?"

"I said that?" Benny shook his head. "Sounds like something I'd say. So it's as easy as that? This guy is just gonna walk up and hand you his money."

"I said it was simple, Benny, I didn't say it was easy."

"Well, who dreamed this up, that's what I wanna know."

"It's based on an old scam they used to call 'the Wire.' You ever see that movie, *The Sting*?"

"Robert Redford and Paul Newman," Benny said. "And old-time music. That's all I remember."

"Oh. Well, they based the movie on the same scam. The way it worked, you had a phony betting parlor, like for sports and horse races and all that. They used to run them out of a regular storefront. In a town like Chicago, they were practically institutions, they'd run the same games in the same locations for years. Anyhow, you had a guy who would go find a mark, he was called 'the runner.' He would spot some rich guy who was a little bit crooked. Those were the only two qualifications necessary, money and greed. The runner would introduce his mark to a second guy, who was known as 'the insider.' The insider would be a guy pretending to be connected, right, he was posing as a guy whose job was to place bets for a syndicate that fixed horse races. The insider would tell the mark, 'Oh, this horse, Rusty Nails, is gonna win this race,' and he would place this big bet on Rusty Nails, and sure enough, Rusty would pay off."

"How did he know which horse would win?"

"Stay with me, Benny, the gaming place is phony, they're running everything on a tape delay. You got the guy calling the race and all that, but it really happened an hour or so previous. And if this is in New York City, you don't use a race at Aqueduct, you use Churchill Downs or some shit. Some racetrack far enough away so that the results ain't gonna be in the *Post* the next morning. 'Course, that was back before the Internet."

"All right," Benny said. "So after a while, your mark starts believing that this second guy really does know what horse is gonna win."

"Right. And you do this two or three more times, and you let your mark have a little taste. You know what I mean? You let him win a few bucks. When the guy is ready, the insider tells the mark, 'Hey, these people I work for treat me like shit. They watch me like a hawk. I'm making them all this money, but they're not taking very good care of me. Next week, they got this horse going off at eleven or twelve to one, and I wanna make something for myself, but I don't dare make the bet on my own, because if they find out I did it, they'll kill me. Now, I can scrape together fifty grand. I'll tell you what. I'll give you the money, and you can have your friend make the bet for me. He's known here, and they'll take a big bet like that from him without questioning it.' By *friend*, he means the runner, the guy who found the mark to begin with. And he says, 'Hey, if you wanna put fifty of your own with mine, I don't care.' So now, if you played the guy right, he sees dollar bills dancing everywhere, and he goes off to dig up as much money as he can. So the day of the race, the runner, the insider, and the mark all show up at the phony storefront. The insider gives the mark the name of the horse, the mark tells the runner, and the runner places the bet just before the race goes off. Now, say the horse's name is Quaker's Dance. The runner fucks up, he puts the money on a horse called Baker's Chance. The mark shows the tickets to the insider, the insider sees the mistake, he blows a cork. The two of them rush back to the window to change the bet, but it's too late, the horses are already running. The insider pulls out a gun, got to be something big and impressive, right, something that looks like a fucking cannon, and he shoots the runner, bang, the runner's dead. Now, naturally, the gun's loaded with blanks, and the runner is fitted up with a bladder full of pig's blood, but it all looks real as hell. So now the insider pretends to panic, because the cops are coming and all that. Him and the mark take off running, the mark goes home minus his money, but he's not thinking he's been robbed, he's thinking, 'Goddam, I was this close!' And if the guy was greedy enough, sometimes they'd work the same game on him all over again."

"And this actually worked?"

"Are you kidding me? The Wire was found money. Sometimes they'd have two or three marks in and out of the same storefront on the same day. And it wouldn't necessarily have to be fifty large, either. They were taking guys for that much all the way back in the thirties."

"Jesus. And the con artists would take turns being the insider," Benny said, shaking his head.

"No," Stoney told him. "Usually guys would specialize. Like a doctor. You get all used to doing bunions, right, you don't wanna have to carve up some guy's hemorrhoids."

"Whatever," Benny said. "But that's what you guys are going to do to Prior."

"Kinda," Stoney told him. "Variation on a theme."

"I get it," Benny said, a little agitated. "You don't have to lay it all out, not that I'd expect you to. There's no racetrack, no phony betting parlor, but you and your partner, you go find yourself some poor schlub, and you build him up until he's ready to mortgage his house on your say-so, and then you take his goddam money."

"First of all," Stoney said, "if he's really a poor schlub, he's got nothing to worry about from me. You know what I'm saying? I don't want the guy's house. And if he's the least bit honest, I can't touch him anyhow."

"Why not?"

"Because the game don't work on a guy who's not a thief himself. We don't just go pick some guy out of the phone book, anyhow. You got to have the right guy. The way it works . . ." He thought about it for a minute. "It's like jujitsu. You ever heard of it?"

"I heard of it," Benny said, "but I can't say I know what the hell it is."

"It's a form of self-defense," Stoney said. "Japanese. It's based on the theory that someone who attacks you is fundamentally off balance. Just by being the aggressor, he's irrational, he's unbalanced. Okay? Jujitsu capitalizes on that imbalance, it uses the guy's own negative energy to knock him on his ass. You get it? So if the guy's pile of blocks is already leaning, you don't even have to kick 'em over, you just tickle the guy's nuts with a feather and he'll do it himself."

"We're gonna miss the meeting," Benny said, glancing at his watch. "So you, you just go around looking for a thief with a big pile of blocks. . . ."

"That's me," Stoney said. "I'm the guy with the feather." He looked at his friend. "I didn't go looking for this guy, Benny. I'm just looking after my own. Is that a bad thing?"

"I don't know," Benny said. "You gotta figure that out yourself."

TWENTY

Stoney examined his fingernails while he waited.

"Forty million," Harman said, after a minute.

"Probably don't have anything like that left," Stoney said. "We can't be sure how much he pried out of the banker before he killed the guy, and we don't know how much of that he's already spent. Bound to be a lot less."

"Maybe," Harman said. "Maybe not. There are lots of ways to make money when you've got that kind of capital and you aren't overburdened with scruples. And Prior has to be a smart son of a gun to have survived this long. But even if you're right, so what? Suppose there's only twenty? Or ten? Still a lot of money. How many ways you plan on splitting this?"

"That depends," Stoney said. "There's the three of us, plus Georgie Cho. Then there's Emil Barton, the broker, we gotta give him something. And there's gonna be two or three more players before this is all over, they're all gonna want theirs."

"Still could turn out to be a very nice score. But there's a couple of things you haven't thought about. First, there's no way a guy like Prior, or Plotnik, is in this country without the State Department knowing about him."

"You kidding?" Tommy said. "They lucky they finda they shoe under the bed in the morning."

Harman was shaking his head. "Don't you believe it. That's just for public consumption. Whoever it was let him in, they might have neglected to inform the FBI or whatever, but you can bet your last nickle that somebody on a federal level gave this guy safe harbor. If he was working in Europe before that bank thing went down, he must have had something to sell. Probably something in the Balkans. Maybe he knows where Milosevic hid his money, or some shit. But they know he's here."

"Suppose you're right. You think they're still watching him?"

"Who knows? After a couple years, you would think they've probably loosened up on his leash a little bit, but I would guess they haven't forgotten about him."

"All right. So the feds are a wild card. What's the second thing?"

"You still haven't told me why you hate this guy. He kick your dog or what?"

Stoney's face darkened. "Prior has a thing for my daughter."

"Your daughter? Marisa? Oh my God. That bastard."

"She's seventeen," Stoney said.

"Yeah, I know. Where is she right now?"

"Tuco is watching out for her."

"He's just a kid. He's probably overmatched, you know that?"

"I wouldn't count on it."

"Come on, man, these guys are pros, and there's three of them, counting Prior. Who's that good?"

"Tuco is. . . ."

"No way, man. No, listen, forget that. That's why you had her here before, am I right? You have to bring her in, I ain't kidding, dude, you gotta put her butt right in this kitchen where you can eyeball her. You need to know where she is, for real, and you need to know where Prior is, and you have to be damn sure that never the twain shall meet, especially after this game gets rolling, because if anything happens to her, you are going to come unglued right in the middle of this, and you'll take all of us down with you."

Stoney looked at Fat Tommy, who was nodding in agreement. "He's right," Tommy said.

"I thought she'd be okay," Stoney said. "I mean, nothing happened so far."

"Nothing you know about," Harman said.

Stoney stared at him.

"Hey, sorry," Harman said, holding his hands up in surrender. "But listen, I'm closer to her age than you are. I remember what seventeen was like better than you do."

"All right. Okay, we'll bring her in." He patted his shirt pocket. "I gotta go have a cigarette."

Tommy and Harman watched him go. Harman waited until he heard the back door close. "Tommy, was I out of line?"

Tommy shook his head. "No," he said. "You know something, when you see someone every day, you become blind. Stoney's daughter, she's so smart, she look so good, you know, I never wasa think she gonna do anything, you know . . ." He searched for the right word.

"Human?" Harman offered.

"Yeah," Tommy said. "Anyway, maybe you wasa see something Stoney and I wasa no see."

"Maybe. While we're on the topic . . ."

"Yeah?"

"Tommy, you sure your buddy out there is gonna be able

to keep it together? I think he really just wants to kill this guy Prior. And if that's what he's really after, he should just do it. If he goes into this with a bad enough case of testosterone poisoning, he could wind up getting all of us jammed up."

Tommy looked in the direction of the back door. "Used to be a lot worse," he said. "I tell you something, this happen maybe one year ago, we don't gonna be sitting here talking about. Still, I understand whatta you say."

"Maybe you're right, Tommy." He shook his head. "My real problem is, my heart just isn't in it anymore. I thought I was bored, up in Toronto, but you know what? I miss my house, and I miss my boring life." He put his arm around Fat Tommy's shoulders. "I thank you for one thing, Tommy. This job has cured me. I lived my whole life seeing how close to the edge I could get, but when I'm done with this, I'm done. I don't want to go to jail, Tommy. I just want to go home."

"Nobody wanna go to jail," Tommy said. "Let'sa say in this way: we gonna keep you out of trouble. Know what I mean? Sit near the door. You feel like you gotta go, you just leave. No hard feeling."

Harman was shaking his head. "My part of this is just about done, isn't it? Would you feel like I was running out on you if I decided I had enough?"

"Don' worry," Tommy told him. "When you finish to talka to Prior, go on home. No hard feeling."

"All right. I'll check the flights when I get back to the hotel tonight."

"Fine," Tommy said. "You calla me in the morning, let me know how you feel. Anyway, everything here gonna come good. You'll see."

• • •

Stoney made the call from the back porch. He pitched his voice low and soft, in the manner of a man whose head hurts him when he talks too loud. "Hello," he said, when Prior came on the line. "My friend Martin tells me you'd like to see me."

"You the lawyer?" Prior asked, without preamble.

"Yes," Stoney said.

"Your employer caught my interest when I happened to run into the three of you yesterday," Prior told him. "In subsequent conversation with Martin, it seems that there might be an investment opportunity here for me."

"This is a private fund," Stoney said. "You do understand that. You can't just buy or sell it on an exchange."

"I know who Gregory Ahn is and I know what he does," Prior said. "I also know that anyone who is as big an asshole as he appears to be has to have the chops, or someone would have stepped on him before now."

"Very well," Stoney said. "Martin also said that you are holding . . ."

"I don't wish to go into that on the phone," Prior said. "When and where can we get together?"

Stoney pretended to think it over. "I have some time this afternoon," he said. "If it's convenient for you, why don't you meet me at Emil Barton's office at five-thirty."

"I'll be there," Prior said, and he hung up.

Stoney went back inside. "We have achieved liftoff," he said.

"This is not exactly 'staying out of sight,'" Tuco said. He was following Marisa through the giant Willowbrook Mall in Wayne, New Jersey. She wasn't paying much attention to the stores, she seemed more interested in the people streaming through the corridors. This place, Tuco thought, is Jersey's version of Thirty-fourth Street. Something to look at everywhere you turn.

"I know," she said, and she touched his elbow, sending a charge up and down his nervous system. Relax, he told himself. She's just letting you know she wants to stop over here. "I'll go nuts if I have to sit home all the time," she said. She steered him over to the side of the hallway.

About twenty-five feet away, a young woman stood next to a kiosk that sold newspapers and lottery tickets. She had two children with her, one imprisoned and half asleep in a baby stroller and another who was zooming through the crowds in an erratic orbit around her. The woman was working her way through a pile of scratch-off tickets. Whenever she hit a winner, she traded it in for more tickets and added them to the bottom of her pile. Every so often, the kid who was ping-ponging through the general vicinity would stop by. "Are we going yet?" he would ask. "C'mon. . . ."

"In a minute," she kept saying, intent on her tickets, and he would exhale in frustration and resume his irregular journeys.

"She looks like she's got it bad," Marisa said.

"Yeah," Tuco said. "Everybody got something. That's what your father says."

She glanced his way. "I feel jealous of you sometimes," she said.

It was the last thing he would have expected her to say. "Of me? Why? What do I got that anybody would want?"

"Contact," she said.

"What do you mean?"

"You and him," she said. "You and my father. The two of you seem very cool with each other. I see the way you mess with him. Like, yesterday when he told you to do something, I forget what it was, you said, 'Yassuh, boss.' If I did that, he'd have a fit."

"Yeah, well, I ain't his kid," Tuco said. "That makes it different."

"Maybe so," she said. "But to me, it just feels like I'm a lot farther away from him than you are."

"I probably spent more time with him than you," Tuco said. "When I was working at that junkyard that him and Tommy were running for a while, we would be together a lot. And the two of them, they, ahh, they like adopted me. You know what I'm saying? I was like this stray dog, and they felt sorry for me and they fed me, and after that I wouldn't go away." That didn't come out exactly the way he had intended, but it was too late to get it back.

"I don't believe that," she said. "Check this guy out, white guy with the shaved head, by the jewelry store, walking in our direction." The guy was about five foot five, he looked like a doughy three hundred pounds, but he was all duded up in the tough guy uniform of the day, voluminous shorts that hung almost to his ankles, two-hundred-dollar sneakers, skirt-length basketball shirt. He wore a goatee. The guy was almost a parody of gangsta cliché, on top of being overweight and out of shape, he had to be at least thirty. "What do you suppose he was thinking?" Marisa wanted to know. Just then the man seemed to sense the attention Marisa had directed his way, and he glared at Tuco and Marisa as he lumbered toward them, but Marisa just stared vacantly off down the hallway.

"I guess you don't come here for the stores," Tuco said.

"Sometimes I do," she admitted. "But not always. You have to dress just right at my high school. If you wear the right clothes, it doesn't much matter what else you do." The overweight tough guy passed them by, throwing them what had to be his best hard stare on his way past. Tuco didn't look at the guy, and Marisa simply ignored him. "So you hooked up with Fat Tommy and my dad," she said, continuing to gaze off down into the distance. "And that was a good thing, 'cause it got you out of that neighborhood. Right? But are you, ahh, are you gonna stay with them now? Do what they do?"

She was trying for an offhand tone when she asked her question, but it seemed to Tuco that she didn't quite nail it. My answer means more to her than she wants me to know, he thought. He considered his reply carefully. "That's what I thought," he said. "I worked hard to get them to, you know, have some confidence in me. But that was back when they were my only shot. I didn't have nothing else."

"I understand that," she said, still not looking at him.

"But I'm learning, you know what I'm saying? I'm finding out new things. I think that a new door is gonna open up someplace for me."

Her cell phone rang, startling her. She dug it out of her bag and looked at the caller's number on the little screen. "Is it that guy?" Tuco asked her. "Is it him?"

"No," she said. "Too early for him. It's my father."

"Don't answer it yet," he told her. "Let's get out of here first, that way you can tell him that we're riding around in the car."

She nodded, put her arm in his, and turned them for the exit. Jesus, Tuco thought, does she know what she's doing to me when she does that? I bet she does. . . . "I'm getting you to lie to him again," she said. "You said you'd only do it once. I'm sorry. I don't know why I keep doing this."

"Doing what?"

She looked away when she answered. "Coloring outside the lines," she said. "I was the one who wouldn't go home, like I was supposed to. I had to come here instead."

"You know what your problem is?" Tuco asked her. He didn't wait for an answer. "You got something," he told her, his heart thudding in his chest. You are stepping in it now, you idiot, he told himself, but he went on anyway. "You know you got it, but you don't know what it is. You gotta keep trying it out. You gotta keep stepping on the gas."

"What are you talking about?"

"Come on, you know what I mean. You always gotta push. Like with that fat guy just now. You knew you could mess with his head, just by looking at him a little too long, so you did it. I know the guy looked all fucked up, but he's doing the best he can, right? You know what I'm saying? But you stripped him just a little bit more naked than he was. He knows he don't measure up, and you rubbed his face in it. You gotta learn how to be more careful." She slid her arm out of his, hooked his elbow to stop him, stared intently into his face. "Have a little mercy on us," he said. "We know what we are."

"No, you don't," she said, and she slid her arm around his waist, giving his nervous system another jolt. He felt the pressure of her hand on his hip, urging him forward. They walked in silence a couple of steps. "I'll try to watch myself," she said.

The makeup girl in the salon in Oradell said she was twenty-two, but she seemed even younger than Marisa. She giggled when he told her what he wanted. "Well, whyncha just go get 'faced?" she asked him. "I don't get it."

"I don't want a real hangover," Stoney told her. "I just want to look like I got one. And it can't look like makeup, either. It has to be subtle enough to fool a very smart guy, up close."

She shrugged. "Enkay," she said. "No problem."

It only took her a couple of minutes, but the effect was, when he walked into Emil Barton's office in Haworth for his meeting with Prior, he looked like a beaten man. His face was pale, his hair was not quite right, and he had dark circles under his eyes. His hands trembled, too. He had achieved that by drinking four cups of coffee. Barton came out, looking almost as bad, although Stoney figured that Barton's case of the shakes was probably well earned. Barton ushered Stoney into his inner office, where Prior and his guard were waiting. Prior was seated at a conference table. His guard stood against the back wall, silent, his hands crossed in front of himself.

Prior stood up, held out his hand. "We didn't have the opportunity to meet, last time," he said. The makeup worked: Stoney knew from the look on Prior's face that the man saw him, not as a threat, but as someone who had accepted his lot in life and was resigned to the choices he had made. Prior's grip was fierce. Stoney returned the squeeze, but just barely. The first impressions are the strongest, and Stoney knew that from now on, Prior would think of him as a lush, a loser, a man defeated by life.

"No, we didn't," Stoney said, and he sat down carefully, in the manner of a person whose bones were made out of chalk. I spent half my life feeling like this, he told himself. What a waste.

"So," Prior said. "Does Gregory Ahn take his lawyer and his bodyguard with him everywhere he goes?" Prior was feeling it, Stoney was sure. The man was practically itching with the need to prove he had a bigger dick than all the other dogs.

"Generally," Stoney said.

Prior continued probing. "Can you tell me why that is?"

Stoney leaned back slowly and sighed. "Gregory Ahn," he said, "is a man of singular capabilities, but peaceful coexistence is not one of them. You don't need to like him, Mr. Prior. You only need to tolerate him. And he will make money for you."

"So I'm told," Prior said. "Is that what he's done for you?" His tone insinuated that the cost of Ahn's largesse, in Stoney's case, might have been too high.

"I do well enough," Stoney said. "And I only have the one client to worry about."

"What about Martin?" Prior said, speaking of Harman's character. "What's his story?"

"Martin is very good at what he does."

"And that is . . ."

Stoney grimaced. "He defuses situations, when that seems possible. He discourages, ahh, the more impulsive among Gregory's business associates. And he keeps Gregory out of trouble and Gregory's name out of the newspaper. And he is very well compensated for his services."

"He's the designated adult, then."

Stoney managed a brief, painful smile. "It does seem that way at times."

Prior stared at Stoney. "Please forgive the inquisition," he said. "I like to know something about the people I do business with, and intel on Gregory Ahn is remarkably sparse."

"That's not an accident, Mr. Prior."

"I understand. Well, when I last spoke to Martin, I mentioned that I would need to get more liquid if I were to decide to invest with Ahn. In my case, for reasons we do not need to go into, that involves selling some diamonds."

"Martin told me that," Stoney said.

"Martin said not to do it," Prior said. "He seemed to think that Gregory Ahn would be interested in buying my diamonds himself. Would you care to tell me why that is? Because I have to tell you, from what little I know about him, it seems a safe bet that I would come out on the losing end of any transaction I might conduct with Mr. Ahn."

"That is a consideration," Stoney said. "Martin mentioned the sum of five million."

Prior nodded. "I thought I would start small, and see how things progressed."

"Understandable," Stoney said. "All right. Here's my suggestion: take your merchandise and have it appraised by someone you trust. Separate out the five million dollars' worth you were thinking of selling. Mr. Ahn, Martin, and myself will meet you in a diamond broker's office in Manhattan, who, acting in Mr. Ahn's interest, will appraise them as well. Once you and Mr. Ahn have mutually agreed on a value, you can choose whether to proceed or withdraw. Does that sound fair to you?"

Prior stared at him for a minute. "I have certain security procedures," he said.

"Whatever," Stoney said. "Do what you need to do to make yourself comfortable. There's just one other thing."

"And that is?"

"This is more in the way of a suggestion. Mr. Ahn is going to be fascinated with your story. If I were you, I would resist the impulse to tell it. I would allow Mr. Ahn's imagination to fill in the blanks, that way he'll be less tempted to initiate a pissing contest. Dealing with Mr. Ahn can sometimes be problematic, and the more mysterious you are, the more pliable he is likely to remain."

Prior leaned on the table. "I've seen his type before," he said. "It's a sickness. Has nothing to do with how brilliant Ahn may or may not be, the fact is, his predatory instinct is so overpowering, he can't control it. If there's another living thing in his sights, he can't rest until he's killed it."

Stoney nodded. "Killed it or fucked it."

"And the more time you spend with him, the more he tears at you."

Harman was right, Stoney thought. This guy already hates Cho so much, he can't keep from engaging. Why is it, he thought, that the moth always winds up with his wings on fire . . . ? "You could look at it that way," he said.

"How do you stand working for him? Is the money he's paying you worth the damage he does?"

Stoney closed his eyes, pretending that his head was throbbing, then he opened them and looked at Prior. "It's just a job, Mr. Prior. When it ends, and however it ends, I'm sure I'll find another one."

"Lawyers," Prior said. He stood up, looked at Stoney with a half smile on his face. "I could never understand the way you people think. All right. I can have five million in diamonds ready to go tomorrow."

"That soon?" Stoney massaged his forehead. "I'll try to get the meeting set up for tomorrow afternoon."

Bernard Finbury stared at Stoney, a sour expression on his thin face. "Took you long enough," he said, after a minute.

"Yeah, well, you ain't the only blip on the screen, Bern. I been busy. But you know, you got shit locks on your doors."

"You went inside?" There was a hint of outrage in Finbury's voice. Stoney was sitting in a white plastic chair on the front porch of Finbury's house in the exclusive East Hill section of Demarest, New Jersey. "That's breaking and entering! I got you for unlawful entry, I got—"

"You got *en gatz en a culo*," Stoney said calmly, and the end of his cigarette glowed orange in the gathering dark. "That's what you got. Why don't you sit down?" He shoved one of the other plastic chairs in Finbury's direction. Finbury looked at it for a minute, then climbed up on the porch, pushed the chair around so it faced Stoney, and sat down in it.

"What does that mean, anyhow?" he said. "I always wondered."

"A dick in the ass," Stoney told him. "Listen, I don't know if I said it before or not, but I'm sorry about your mother."

Finbury thought about that for a while. "Thank you," he said finally. "Your parents alive?"

"No." Stoney sucked on his cigarette. "I was a great disappointment to my mother," he said.

"So was I," Finbury said.

"You're kidding me."

"No. She never understood why I wanted to work with my hands. She wanted what all Jewish mothers want, she wanted me to be a doctor. So I build houses, and I make more money than most doctors, but she could never get it. She only saw the work clothes instead of the suit. She tried not to show it, though."

"You build this house?" Stoney had taken a quick tour of the place after he disabled the alarm. It was big, new, and it had all the modern conveniences, but it had the soul of a Holiday Inn.

"Yeah. After the divorce." Finbury shook his head. "Just had to have a bigger place than the ex. Stupid. You come here about those two guys I had shadowing you?"

"Yeah. I'm guessing they were unofficial, right? Friends of yours."

Finbury shrugged. "They're from the Tenafly PD. I couldn't think of anything else to do, so I gave them a few bucks to watch you," he said. "I'm not sure how good those guys in Westwood are. You're all I got."

"That's what I thought."

"She didn't deserve to die that way."

"No, she didn't."

"I'll pull those guys off," Finbury said. "They were getting pretty sick of you, anyhow."

"You'll probably have to go bail on them, first," Stoney said.

"What? What happened?"

"New York's finest showed up while your guys were out front and carted their asses away. I would guess weapons charges. Something like that."

"Oh, fuck. How did you pull that off?"

"My partner knows this guy on the Job in Midtown. The guy's brother got bagged at a DUI checkpoint in Fort Lee a couple of weeks ago. He seemed to think all Jersey cops are a bunch of hard-ons."

"Shit. Am I gonna have to try and do something about the DUI?"

"Probably."

Finbury sighed. "What are those things you're smoking?"

"Kools."

"Gimme one."

Stoney passed one over, along with his lighter. Finbury stuck the cigarette in his mouth, lit it up, then inhaled, eyes closed. "God," he said, exhaling. "God, I missed these things." He inhaled again. "You know who did it, don't you?"

It was Stoney's turn to think for a minute. "Yeah," he finally said. "I got a pretty good idea."

"You gonna give him up to me? Look, maybe you look at me and you see 'carpenter,' okay, but I got connections. You don't get to be a successful contractor in Jersey without knowing how to solve problems, if you get my drift."

"You'll never find anybody good enough to take him down," Stoney said. "You'll only get your guy killed. This dude is a pro." He told Finbury a little about Prior's background, but without giving him a name. "Matter of fact," he said, "you get the cops to investigate the guy, the feds will come in and shut you down. Then they'll move our boy, and neither one of us will be able to get him."

"Why you after this guy?" Finbury said. "And don't tell me it's because you were such great friends with my mother."

Stoney contemplated the dwindling end of his cigarette. "Let's just say I owe him. Okay? And I hired your mother to look into the guy. And for that, I am truly sorry. But I needed to know what I was up against."

The veins stood out on Finbury's neck, the man clenched his jaw and stared at Stoney, and for a moment Stoney thought coming to this place might have been a mistake, but then Finbury swallowed whatever he'd been feeling. "What on earth could my mother have done that would justify him killing her?" he said.

Stoney shrugged. "Invaded his privacy, maybe."

"That doesn't make any sense."

"Not to you. Not to me, either. But it's hard to figure how this guy's mind works."

"You sound like you feel sorry for the son of a bitch."

"What can I tell you," Stoney said. "I don't always trust

my instincts. You know what I'm saying? My first thought was like, just whack the guy, but then I started to wonder. You tell me, Bern. I mean, no offense, but you look like a regular guy. You got this house in the burbs, you got your business, and you build things for a living." He glanced over his shoulder at the darkened house. "I'm guessing, some guy hires you to build him a house, you try to do the right thing by the guy. Am I right?"

Finbury exhaled as he examined his fingernails. "Pretty boring life."

"You know what I'm saying. Suppose you know for a fact this guy did your mother, but he walks. Okay? Now you're out driving, you see the guy, he's walking down the side of the road, there's nobody else around, just you and him. What do you do?"

Finbury leaned forward and stared at Stoney. "He cut off her goddamned ear," he said, his voice cracking. "He cut off her fingers! You wanna know what I'd fucking do? I'd run over the cocksucker, that's what I'd fucking do, and then I'd back up and do it again just to make sure. And you know what? If she was your mother, you'd do it, too."

"Maybe I would."

"Look. You give me this bastard's name, I don't care who the fuck he is, and I promise you he will never give you any trouble again. Word of honor."

Stoney looked at Bernard Finbury. You never knew, just because a guy was on the small side, didn't mean the guy couldn't cut it. "I tell you what, Bern," he said, wondering how far he could trust the man. "I got a better idea. . . ."

TWENTY-ONE

Stoney decided to show up at the house early that morning. Tuco had beaten him there, clearly, because the Beemer was already parked at the curb. Unless the little bastard stayed the night . . . The hood was still warm, though, when he felt it on his way past. What are you worrying about? he asked himself. Donna is way tougher with the kids than you, anyhow.

He knocked on the front door. Donna didn't look surprised when she opened it and saw him standing there. "Morning," she said. "Have your coffee yet?"

"No."

"Well, you may as well come in." She stood back out of the way and let him pass. "Go on in the kitchen, I'll get your coffee. Marisa's not ready yet."

He preceded her into the kitchen and sat at the counter. "Where's Tuco?"

"He's upstairs," she said, "playing Nintendo hockey with Dennis."

"That right?" Stoney glanced upward, as though he ought to be able to see through the wood and plaster to confirm that Tuco was, indeed, sitting in Dennis's room, and not Marisa's. Donna saw him do it, and she smiled.

"Your turn to worry," she said.

"You're not worrying? You sure there's nothing going on with those two?"

"Oh, there's something going on, all right," she said. "You want to know what I think, Marisa's in awe. Whether it turns into something else, your guess is as good as mine, but I don't think anything's happened yet."

"I see." Stoney hoped his relief didn't show too much. "What do you think of him?"

She handed him a coffee cup. "Tuco? Well, he's an uneducated inner-city kid with issues, his English is not great, his Spanish is worse, he has no sense of humor, and he doesn't have a job. What's not to like?" She snorted. "Actually, he's a nice kid. He's polite, he's been good to Dennis, plus he gets along fine with Marisa, and you know what a trial she can be. Why do you ask? I thought he was your friend."

"He is my friend. And he does have a job. It's just, you know, at his age, with the hormones and all that, I was just wondering."

"Is that so."

"Yeah. But Tuco's not like most kids. And he's got a few bucks salted away, how rare is that for someone his age?"

"How much?"

"Couple hundred thou," Stoney told her. "I think Tommy helped him put it into some condos in Brooklyn."

"Whatever," she said. "The question with Tuco is, what is he going to do with himself? What kind of life is he going to put together?"

"I don't know," Stoney said. "But this will all be over soon. Maybe today, I don't know for sure. Then Tuco can go back to Brooklyn, and you can have Marisa fitted for a chastity belt."

Donna laughed. "I wouldn't dream of it," she said.

"No?"

"Of course not. She's too smart, for one thing. If she really wants Tuco, I question how much you or I could do to dissuade her. Marisa is the oldest seventeen-year-old I know. I'm afraid she's already past the point of letting her parents make her decisions for her."

"Maybe," Stoney said. "Man, I'll be glad to get this thing wrapped up, I'll tell you that."

"Today, you said."

"Yeah. If things break right."

"Come home, after," she said.

His mind reeled. He struggled for words "Do you, ahh, are you sure that you, ahh, you want me back here?"

"I don't want to think about it," she said, her voice husky. "I don't know what I mean. I can't believe I'm just making up my mind about this right now, or that I'm talking to you about it already, but I want you home. That's all I know for sure."

"That's good enough for me." He stood up, took an uncertain step toward her. She crossed the kitchen floor and hugged him, squeezed him until he thought he would crack.

The voice on the phone filled him with dread. "I know who you really are." Harman felt as though he was going to throw up, and he rolled over to the edge of the hotel bed and hung his head over the side. It was Prior, and Harman could hear him gloating. "That hospital your sister is in has the worst security I've ever seen."

Harman's head swam. "My sister has nothing to do with anything," he said.

"For my purposes, it hardly makes any difference."

Harman fought to regain control. He looked at his shaking hand. "I suppose not."

"All right, here's what's going to happen. You're going to call in sick today. There's a diner on Lemoine Avenue in Fort Lee. There will be a car in front of the place in an hour. Be there."

"And if I'm not?"

"If you're not concerned about your own safety, you should at least be worried about your sister. The one who hasn't done anything."

"Okay. Okay. I'll be waiting."

"Great. And if you're smart, Martin, or should I call you Nathan? If you're smart, you won't make any phone calls about this. If you keep this between you and I, you can still come out of this with a whole skin." He was chuckling as he ended the call. Harman thought about calling Fat Tommy, but Prior's last statement kept ringing in his head, and he decided against it. You can always call him later, he told himself. What would I say to him, anyhow?

Harman looked at the approaching car and debated the wisdom of getting in. He was standing on the sidewalk in front of the diner on the main drag in Fort Lee, New Jersey, just as Prior had instructed him. I should have called Fat Tommy, he thought, I should have told someone what was going on. . . . You left it too late, he told himself, but then he shoved his hand into his pocket, feeling for the cell phone. Green button, he thought, all by itself, on the left side. He pushed the button twice, which would tell the thing to redial whoever he had talked with last. Too bad he couldn't remember who that had been.

Prior's car pulled up at the curb, and one of Prior's guards held the rear door open for him. Harman looked at the guy. "Hey, what's happening," he said, thinking that he had to make enough noise to keep his phone call going. Got someone's voice mail, he thought, because he didn't hear any noises coming from his pocket. "You Prior's guy?" I could never handle him, he thought, let alone him and the driver, too. Not that it mattered. I should have never listened to Bagadonuts, he thought, I should never have gotten involved in this. I should have stuck to the plan and taken the next plane back to Toronto. Should have caught the red-eye, should have flown out last night.

He got in.

The guard closed him in, walked around the rear of the car and got in on the other side. The man looked over at him and smiled. Yeah, up yours, too, Harman thought. "You enjoying this?"

"Not yet," the man said.

"Well, you might as well take me to see Prior. Let's find out what's on his mind." Harman wondered if the voice mail had cut him off yet, and then he wondered who it was he had called, and what they would make of his message, if anything. You gave it your best shot, he told himself. Put it out of your mind.

They drove him a short distance away, to a motel in Fort Lee that lay right in the shadow of the George Washington Bridge, not thirty feet from the roar of traffic. The place was called the Toll Gate Motel. Big neon signs on the side of the building proclaimed AIR CONDITIONED! and CABLE TV! The place was two stories high, cut into the hillside. It had a second-floor veranda that served as an exterior hallway, which looked like it was threatening to fall off. There was a row of filled garbage cans between the end of the building and the ripped chain-link

fence that delineated the end of the property, and stacks of used
two-by-fours and sheets of plywood were turning gray in the
sun in the corner of the parking lot. The windows of the office
on the first floor were boarded up, but the white door was open.
The whole thing was a bilious yellow orange, something akin to
the color of vodka sauce, with the trim painted a nice contrast
of baby-shit brown. Amazing, Harman thought, the place was
overshadowed by new office buildings, yet no one had torn
this shithole down to build another one. . . . Always a market
for a hot-sheet house. It was the kind of motel where most of
the patrons generally got their business taken care of and got
gone within a half hour of their arrival. From the parking lot
Harman could see Prior leaning on the railing of the second-
floor balcony. There were three other cars and a step-van parked
in the lot. Prior's driver parked next to the step-van, then came
around and opened the door for him. The man had a sick half
smile on his face. "Right upstairs," he said.

Prior watched Harman come down the hallway the way a
cat watches a mouse. "I want to thank you for agreeing to see
me on such short notice," he said.

"You didn't give me much choice."

"I guess not," Prior said. "Step inside. Room 202."

Harman watched as Prior plucked a semiautomatic out of
his pocket. "Is that really necessary?"

Prior didn't answer, he simply gestured with the pistol.
Harman sighed and stepped into the room. It was standard
motel issue: queen-size bed, television bolted to a metal bracket
that was screwed into the ceiling, a bureau and a couple of
chairs. There was something that looked like an automobile
battery charger, the kind you bought at Sears, sitting in a corner.
The room smelled faintly of vomit. Prior's second guard stood

in a corner of the room, impassive. The bald chauffeur came into the room behind Prior and stood with his back to the door, blocking the only exit. Prior remained behind Harman. "You ever do cocaine?" Prior asked.

"Cocaine?" Harman was surprised at the question. "I suppose I've done a lot of things that I regret." Like coming here, he thought. "What's that got to do with anything?"

"Take a look in the bathroom," Prior told him. "Go on, take a look."

Harman walked over to the bathroom doorway and looked inside. Emil Barton, the stockbroker from Haworth, fully dressed, lay in the tub. His face was ashen gray, his eyes were open and so was his mouth. He had one sleeve rolled up, and the pale skin of his forearm was rotten with needle tracks. Harman tried to read the expression on the man's face, but it was impossible to say if Barton's last emotion had been ecstasy or horror.

"Terrible drug, cocaine," Prior said. Harman turned and looked at him. Prior was pointing his pistol straight at Harman's chest. "When they can't snort enough to get high anymore, they start mainlining it. And the doses get higher and higher, until it kills them. Did you know that Barton was a cokehead?"

Harman shook his head. "No."

Prior clucked his tongue in disapproval. "Sloppy," he said. "That doesn't inspire confidence. You really need to check these things out."

Harman's mind worked furiously. He found out who you are, he thought, but he can't know the rest of the scam. If he did, you'd be dead by now. Hang on to as much of the lie as you can, because it's probably the only thing that's keeping you alive. "Not my department," he said. "Mr. Ahn has other people to handle that sort of thing."

"Well, he should have known, then," Prior said. "I'm actually sort of sorry to see the man dead, but I suppose he's served his purpose."

"He OD?"

"You might say that. He was kind enough to answer some questions, first," Prior said. He gestured with his pistol again, directing Harman to one of the chairs. "Have a seat."

The chair was too low to the ground to get out of quickly. Harman sat there with his feet straight out in front of him. I'm screwed, he thought, no way can I jump fast enough to even try for this guy. Prior's guard was behind the chair, out of Harman's line of sight. Well, play along, Harman told himself. It's your best option. Your only one, right now . . . "That why you were doing business with the guy? So you could whack him if you felt the need? Then dump him in a joint like this one?"

Prior snickered. "You catch on quick," he said. "Another drug addict, overdosed in another cheesy motel room. What could be more natural?" He sat down on the bed a short distance away, looked around the room. "The cops will probably figure a hooker did him, shot him up, then walked off with his money and his dope. Hookers and cocaine go together like peanut butter and jelly. . . . Of course, I won't be able to use this place anymore. Pity. I've had a lot of fun in this room." His pistol was still pointed at Harman's chest, and he caught Harman looking at it. "I'm very good with this thing," he said, "so don't do anything stupid. If you stay calm, and if your employer, if that's what he really is, isn't trying to rip me off, then we'll all go home happy, soon enough."

"All of us, except Emil Barton."

"Emil's with God, now," Prior said, and he snickered. "Listen, Barton was beyond happiness. He wasn't sorry to see the end, believe me. Anyhow, Gregory Ahn's lawyer gave me the green light to do this."

"What? Are you serious?"

"Completely. I told him I had certain security concerns, and he told me to go ahead and do whatever I needed to do to make myself comfortable. 'Five million is not a fortune,' that's what he said yesterday, or was that you? I suppose it may not be to everyone, but it is a lot of money from my perspective, so I am taking precautions. I needed to find out what Barton knew. Now I need to find out what you know. So tell me, is Gregory Ahn aware of who you really are?"

You have to preserve the illusion of Gregory Ahn's omnipotence, Harman thought. "Yes."

"Just out of curiosity, why did you agree to work for him? According to the copy of your rap sheet that I saw, you ought to be set for life."

"Set for life," Harman said, his voice bitter. "Yeah, sure, providing I don't live more than another five years or so." The man's in the same position I am, he thought. He's made it out, he's sitting on his money, but it's all he'll ever have. Is he as bored, here, as I was in Toronto? Or is he running low? Is he watching those numbers come back lower and lower with every bank statement? Is he doing the arithmetic, figuring how long it will be before he has to start wondering how he's going to hang on to his new life? "Do you know how much was left, by the time I got to a safe harbor? Not enough, my friend. Not nearly enough. So when Gregory Ahn told me he could double it in three years, I listened. You bet your ass I listened."

"So? Is he doing it? How good is he?"

Harman thrust his chin out. "At whatever you used to be, how good were you?"

"At the top of my game, there was nobody even close to me." Prior's lips parted. That's not a smile, Harman thought. He's just showing his teeth. "I am the best interrogator this continent has produced in a century."

"Fine," Harman said. "That's how good Ahn is. Maybe better."

"You know, it's a funny thing," Prior said. "Everyone thinks that the most effective tool in my business is torture. Castration, disembowelment, the imaginative application of pain. My personal favorite is shock therapy. But as much fun as those things can be, we both know there are other things that are stronger, don't we?"

"Yeah, we do."

"What am I talking about, Nathan? You don't mind if I use your real name, do you?"

"We're talking about my sister."

"Exactly. Very good, Nathan. I imagine she would miss you a lot."

"Hard to tell."

"I'd hate for anything untoward to happen to her," Prior said. "Really. Every man draws the line in a different place. I myself never truly harmed an innocent person unless there was an important reason for it. Such as my own safety, or my financial well-being. How old is she?"

"She's twenty-eight, chronologically."

"And about six, mentally? That's what I was told. Now, please believe me, Nathan. I wish nothing but a long and uneventful life for your sister." He paused, letting his words sink in. "Dwayne, behind you, there, is a horse of a different color. Aren't you, Dwayne?" Harman did not turn to look at the guard, and the guard did not answer. "Dwayne has some peculiar appetites. It's probably not his fault. I imagine he was born that way." Prior turned and glanced at his other guard, the bald chauffeur. "We indulge Dwayne from time to time, don't we?" The chauffeur said nothing, either, he just smiled. "Tiresome, though," Prior said, turning back to face Harman. "And if your sister did survive, she'd never be the same. Do you get the picture, Nathan?"

You'd better make sure I never get loose, Harman thought. It was then that he realized that he was dead. This guy is never going to let me walk, he told himself. The best outcome he could hope for was that his sister would be left alone. Prior stepped up closer and pointed the gun at Harman's forehead. "Please be very still," he said. "Dwayne is going to secure you to the chair."

Harman sensed the other man behind him. Dwayne's head came into view as he knelt down next to the chair. He had a handful of plastic cable ties. They had been invented for electricians to fasten bundles of wires together, but they made great handcuffs. Harman watched as Dwayne made liberal use of them to fasten his forearms to the chair, first on one side and then the other. Once that was done, he repeated the process, securing Harman's legs to the chair legs. Prior relaxed, then, tossed his pistol onto the bed. "Tip him back," he said. Harman felt his chair lean backward, raising his feet off the floor, and Prior removed Harman's shoes and socks. "Put him back down." He walked over and fetched the battery charger, if that's what it was, from the corner of the room. Harman could see the driver, over by the door, a wide smile on his face.

"You may think I'm doing this strictly for my own enjoyment," Prior said, "but I'm not. Dwayne, take a sheet off that bed and wrap it around his head. Make it tight." A few minutes later, Harman could not hear, see, or speak, he could barely breathe. He felt something bite into the flesh of his right foot and hang on. Seconds later, the same thing happened to his left. Then his whole body convulsed as electricity coursed through his body, he bit down hard on the cloth covering his face and strained against his bonds. He had never felt anything like it in his life, the sensation was halfway between being shaken violently from his feet and being thrown into a hot frying pan. It stopped, finally, and he tried to catch his breath, tried to talk around the mouthful of bedsheet, tried to tell Prior to stop, but he couldn't manage any of that. The current hit him again, and in spite of himself he screamed into the muffling cloth, strained against the cable ties until he was sure he'd tear his muscles loose from the bone. It stopped again, and more to himself than out of any hope Prior would hear him, he mumbled into the sheet. "Ask me something," he said. "Ask me anything." That didn't happen, though, Prior gave it to him again, and again after that. Finally, merciful darkness descended, and he lost consciousness.

The sheet was gone when he came to, but the machine was still clipped to his feet. Prior was sitting on the bed, he had the slide jacked back on his pistol, the clip removed, and he was peering at the inner workings. He glanced up at Harman. "Back with us, I see." He reassembled the gun and laid it aside. "Are you convinced of how serious I am?"

"Completely." Harman could barely get the word out.

"Good. That's good. You should know I took it easy on you. With the leads fastened to your feet, you don't really get the full effect, but I didn't want to worry about stopping your heart. It happens sometimes, if you use the hands instead. The current goes right through your chest that way."

"Thanks." Harman could not have said whether he was serious or not.

"I just want you to understand, it can get much, much worse. Now I'm going to ask some questions, and you will want to be forthright with me. This meeting I am going to this afternoon, carrying my five million like a sap, am I going to be held up on my way there? Is this a setup?"

I probably can't save myself, Harman thought. But Prior seems to want this illusion of Gregory Ahn to be real, and the longer I can keep the lie alive, the longer I might survive, and if I'm alive, anything can happen. Give Fat Tommy and Stoney a shot at this guy, he thought. It's the best you can do. . . . "No," he said

"Who is the target, then?"

"Anthony Bonanno. XRC Technologies."

"You disappoint me," Prior said. "I'd appreciate it if you told me the truth. It will be better for both of us, truly." He gestured at the bathroom with his pistol. "I didn't get much time with our friend, in there. One little jolt and he was screaming like a girl. I feel like I got cheated. I wonder if the man's addiction may have made his nerve endings more sensitive. . . ." He looked back at Harman. "Now imagine how much worse it would feel to your sister, who is really just a child. No one heard Barton squalling. They didn't hear you, either. They won't hear your sister. Think about what you're risking." He leaned in close, dropped his voice. "I know you can take it. I respect that. But your sister can't. Don't make me hurt her, too."

Harman sighed. "No need for that."

"That's good, be sensible. Who's the target?"

"XRC, for real."

"Look, don't try my patience," Prior said harshly. He stared intently at Harman. "If you continue to lie to me, Nathan, I'll bring your sister down here, and I'll give her to Dwayne. And I'll force you to watch. When we're done, I'll kill you and I'll put your sister out on the street. Just think about the kind of life she'll have. Will you think about that?" Prior sounded like he were the one in pain, and Harman the tormentor. "Please, Nathan. Now, I had XRC checked out. They're a nothing company, they're already on the balls of their ass, they aren't worth shit. Tell me the real target, and tell me right now."

"Fire your researcher," Harman said calmly. His outward demeanor belied his inner turmoil. "You are mostly right about XRC, but they do have one thing worth taking. Something very valuable . . ." He told Prior the story of XRC's fictional breakthrough. Prior saw the potential immediately.

"Wow," he said. He relaxed, leaned back, and lost some of his intensity.

Got pretty close to the edge this time, haven't you, Harman thought.

"Wow," Prior said again. "All right. Yeah. Goddam. Is that why Ahn needs my five million?"

"Gregory Ahn does not need your money. Gregory Ahn is going to do this whether you decide to invest with him or not."

Prior considered that. "Ah. Well, that's good to hear, believe it or not." He stood up. "I'm afraid you're going to be sitting there for a while. Just until I return safely from my meeting with Ahn and his sot of a lawyer." He shook his head in mock sorrow. "I'm sorry, but you look too capable for my taste, and I don't want to have to worry about you. Tie the sheet around him again, Dwayne, but give him room enough to breathe. And you leave him alone while I'm gone. Do you hear me, Dwayne? Don't you touch him until I get back."

"You wasa get a message from Jack this morning?"

Stoney looked at Fat Tommy with a blank expression on his face. "A message? Oh, on voice mail. I haven't checked. Nobody leaves me messages."

"When I went to his motel this morning," Tommy said, "he wasa no there. He wasa no call me, either. Check and see, maybe he say something to you onna machine."

"Shit." Stoney took out his phone and stood there staring at it. "I'm not even sure I remember the code for this piece of shit." It took him a couple of minutes, but he finally got it. "No," he said, holding the phone to his ear. "No new messages."

"Call his cell," Tommy said. "See if he'sa pick up."

Stoney tried it. "No answer. You want me to leave a message for him?"

"No."

"Do you think he bailed? Where's that leave us?"

"Still on," Tommy said. "Jack wasa start to get homesick. Go home, I tolla him, you wanna go, go ahead. No hard feeling. But you wanna know the truth, I am surprise he went."

"Maybe the two of you got your wires crossed," Stoney said. "He probably took a car service to the airport. He might be flying home right now."

Georgie Cho had been standing in the McMansion kitchen, watching Tuco and Marisa through the window, but he managed to focus in on the conversation. "Wait a minute," he said. "That doesn't sound right. If he was going to leave, wouldn't he say that? He'd have said something to somebody."

"No necessary," Tommy said. "I wasa talk to him last night, he wasa say he maybe gonna go home. Anyhow, we no need Jack, really. We can just go ahead anyhow. All set up, no reason to hold back now. We don' gonna walk away from this yet. Just, you know, take extra care."

"Maybe he did take off," Stoney said. "Or maybe Prior caught on to him. And if that's the call, Prior will work on him until he knows what's going on, in which case we'll never hear from Prior again. He'll lock his diamonds away and we'll have to go to plan B. But in the meantime, if Prior shows up at Wartensky's, then we can safely assume that Jack went home. Okay?" He looked around, saw general agreement in their faces.

"Now, Georgie, when we go into this meeting with Prior, you're already suspicious. When you meet Prior, you act like a new dog is walking up your front steps, because that's what he'll act like. The two of you are gonna do this little dance until you've established that you have the upper hand. Prior won't be happy with that, and he'll push back, so you let him get under your skin for, say, ten minutes or so, and then you go off on him. Be careful not to overdo it, though. You understand? You have to react the way Gregory Ahn really would, but you don't want to mess up our play."

"I'm all ready," Georgie said.

"Okay," Tommy said. "Right now we got some time, and I don' got nothing to do, so I'm gonna drive back up to the motel where Jack wasa stay, checka to see if anybody'sa see something."

"All right," Stoney said. "If you don't find anything, you can get on the horn and find out if Jack was on any of the flights to Toronto last night or this morning."

"Okay," Tommy said. "I gonna do. Marisa knows what to do?"

"By now, everybody better know what to do," Stoney said. "When Prior calls her this afternoon, she knows what to say. Until then, Tuco is gonna keep her out of sight." He glanced through the window at Tuco and his daughter in the backyard. "This is it. No more phone calls unless something is coming apart."

Moses Wartensky's place of business was located in a narrow, run-down building on the west side of Manhattan, in the jewelry district. The exterior of the building was dirty white. Stoney and Georgie Cho walked into the lobby, empty except for a directory on one wall and a security guard who sat in a booth opposite the elevators. The man had a copy of the *New York Post,* open to the sports section. "Wartensky," Stoney said, walking past him.

The guard did not look up from his paper. "Twelfth floor," he said. Stoney pushed the button for the elevator, then turned and looked at Georgie, who was up on the balls of his feet, bouncing a little bit, looking like a very thin welterweight, standing in his corner, psyching himself up.

Neither of them spoke as the elevator rattled them up to Wartensky's floor. It jerked to a stop and the two of them stepped out into the hallway, the floorboards creaking underfoot as they made their way to the correct metal door. Stoney rang the bell, then yanked the door open when he heard the buzzer. They both stepped into the small, dark vestibule, and after the door closed behind them, the inner door buzzed, and they were in.

Moses Wartensky had once been a tall man, but time had rounded his shoulders and bent his spine. He had puffy white hair, blue eyes, and a wispy goatee. "Come in, come in," he said, hobbling across the floor. "You're letting all the heat out." Stoney pushed the door shut behind him.

The place looked like it hadn't been painted since the Depression. A long, high, L-shaped counter blocked off most of the space inside, and three dark-haired men sat at tables behind the counter, working. They did not look up as Stoney and Georgie entered. There was a massive metal safe down at the end of the room, its heavy doors open. The thing looked like it was ready to go through the floor any minute. On the public side of the counter, a couple of ancient, stained, mismatched armchairs and a table gave a place for Wartensky's less squeamish customers to wait while business was being conducted. "Our boy here yet?" Stoney wanted to know.

"Yeah, he got here about forty-five minutes ago," Wartensky said.

"Really? Where is he?"

"Waiting in the stairwell, like a schmuck."

"You're kidding. You see him?"

"What?" Moses said. "You think just because I'm old I should be blind also?" He shook a long, thin finger in Stoney's direction. "I haven't lost my mind yet. I got a closed-circuit camera watching the hallway. Forty-five minutes ago, the elevator door opens, two apes get out. They walk past my door, pretending not to look, then they go to the end of the corridor. Only thing down there is the office of a guy, used to make zippers. All his business has went to China, poor bastard. So they go through the stairwell door, and it locks behind them. What do they know? There's no sign. There ought to be a sign, don't you think? You could complain to the landlord, but would he listen to you? He would not. So they can't get back in, they have to walk all the way down the steps, then the doorman calls to tell me they're on their way back up. So here they come again, they repeat the whole performance, except now one of them has his foot in the door like an encyclopedia salesman. Which nobody buys anymore, because now we have the Internet. Who needs a book?"

"We all ready, Mose?"

"What kinda question is that, of course I'm ready, you think I been standing around all day long with my thumb in my ass?"

"Easy, Mose. I was just asking."

"Well, I'm ready. Are you ready, that's what you need to worry about."

Four minutes later, Stoney watched Prior on Wartensky's black-and-white television screen as the man stood outside the door. Prior's bald chauffeur stood right behind him. A bell sounded, and Wartensky buzzed the men inside. Georgie Cho stood up, wadded his bony fists, and started bouncing up and down again.

Prior opened the door, took one step inside, and seeing Cho, held out his hand. He was wearing black silk pants, white tee, silver jacket over the tee. "Gregory Ahn?" he said.

"Come in, come in," Wartensky said, hobbling arthritically across the floor. "You're letting all the heat out."

Cho ignored Prior's outstretched hand. "Give him your shit."

Prior scowled, pulled his hand back, and motioned to his driver with the other hand. The man stepped forward with a thin attaché. Prior opened it, took out a black velvet bag the size and shape of a large burrito, and handed it to Wartensky. "In a sock, he brings it," Wartensky muttered. "You wanna watch, come with me."

Prior looked at his driver for the first time since they'd entered the room, but he still didn't say anything to the man, he just nodded to him, and the driver followed Wartensky back behind the counter. "You and you," Wartensky said, designating two of his three assistants. "Each of you take half of this. I want a good wholesale number."

"Hey, wait a minute," Prior said. He walked over to the edge of the counter. "Who said anything about wholesale?"

"What?" Moses didn't even look at him. He watched as one of his assistants spilled the diamonds out of the bag onto a metal tray and began dividing them into two piles. "You want the goy price? What the hell good will that do you? You won't get that kinda money from anyone, not unless you open up a store and start selling earrings, and believe me, by the time you absorb your overhead, pay your taxes, and your workers steal a little something for themselves, how much difference will there really be? Better you should sell wholesale, you don't gotta listen to a bunch of asshole customers." He put on a high, thin, nasal voice. "'Mr. Wartensky, don't you think this one is a little yellow? It don't really match the other one, you think maybe you could do something about the price?'" He turned and looked at Prior. "Hey, just let us give you a number, okay? Then you and the big macher can hondle each other all you want."

"Yeah," Prior said, and he tore his attention away from the diamonds. He made brief eye contact with his chauffeur, who nodded and settled in to watch the two jewelers.

"Where did you get this shit, anyway?" Georgie said. "I decide to take them off your hands, am I gonna have trouble unloading them?" He turned to Stoney. "What was that thing with diamonds everybody was yelling about a couple years back? Do you know what I'm talking about?"

Stoney closed his eyes and pretended his head was aching. "The Congo basin," he said. "Rebels held the miners in virtual slavery. They were selling the diamonds to finance their wars." Stoney walked over to one of the armchairs and dropped himself into it. Georgie, tall, thin, long-haired, stood with a hand on his hip, staring at Stoney with a mixture of pity and disdain. Prior, as tall as Georgie but older, better-looking in a Waspy sort of way, and in far better shape, stood by looking uneasy. By any rational measure, Stoney thought, Prior ought to have all the advantages. He could probably snap Cho in two if he desired, and he had years of real-world experience on the kid. Whatever else the man was, he was a survivor, but it was obvious from his posture that he had given in to the classic jock's inferiority complex: I am a meathead, I may be stronger and quicker, but this guy really is smarter than I am. Prior stood with his hands clasped in front of his belt buckle, his elbows pinched in close to his body, his feet together and shoulders slightly stooped. He's not even conscious of it, Stoney thought, but he's making himself as small as he can, while Georgie, never quite still, turned, put his elbows on the counter, watched the jewelers for a moment, looked at Wartensky, then turned back to Prior. Georgie's taking up as much space and attention as he can manage, Stoney thought. Dominant male. Stoney willed himself to shrink smaller into his chair.

"Prior, is that what your name is? Where'd you get these fucking things? Huh?"

Prior exhaled like a man who had been holding his breath. "They're not conflict diamonds," he said, and he rubbed his face. "Not to my knowledge. They came out of the De Beers vaults in Amsterdam. They were purchased at one of the annual auctions that De Beers holds." He glanced at Wartensky. "Is that the goy price?"

"Not unless you're a moron," Wartensky muttered.

"Purchased by who?" Georgie demanded. "By you?"

"Not directly." Prior took a breath. "Maybe you should tell me what's bothering you, Mr. Ahn."

"What I wanna know," Georgie said, "is whether or not the real owner is gonna come looking."

"They're not hot. The man who bought them from De Beers died in Europe a couple of years ago. I was given to understand that he met his end via an unfortunate reaction to a fish dinner. He apparently didn't make it to the hospital in time. I was able to obtain the gems from his heirs." He looked at Wartensky. "For cash. I await your judgment as to whether the price I paid was fair or not."

"I don't know from fair," Wartensky said. "I can only tell you wholesale."

"Oh, please," Georgie said. "Let me try and translate, okay? Let me sift through that line of bullshit you just handed me and see if I can't come a little closer to reality. Some unnamed and probably unlamented jerk-off makes a large investment in ice, but then he steps off into the great by-and-by. Something like that. Or did someone push him? No matter, somehow or other he transforms himself into a sidewalk pizza. Am I close? And before the pepperonis are even cold, you swoop in and you make your grab. Maybe you did pay off the widow and orphans, maybe you didn't, but the end result is, you're here with a bunch of rocks in your hands, and you would just love to get out of the jewelry business and into the market, and oh yeah, you need to do it quietly. No need to alarm the local IRS storm troopers. Isn't that a bit closer to the truth? You are nothing but a fucking shark, but you would rather look like a retired schoolteacher. Am I right?"

Prior's face got a little rosy. "Shark?" His voice began to rise. "Who are you to call me a shark?"

Wartensky looked at them from the other side of the counter. Prior's chauffeur glanced their way, too. "Hey," Wartensky said. "You come to fight or to do business? 'Cause if you wanna fight, you're gonna have to take it outside." Georgie waved him off without even glancing in his direction.

"Come on," Georgie said. "Get off it. I need to know something. There are two kinds of shark, okay? There's the kind that swallows its prey whole, and there's the kind that bites off a piece and swims away. Which kind are you?"

"Let me tell you something, you little turd," Prior said, thrusting his chin forward. "I served my country and my employers with honor, and all I got out of it was the right to eat shit."

"Current market value for honor sucks," Georgie told him.

"So?" Prior demanded. "So if I saw an opportunity and I jumped on it, how does that make me any different from you? You really think you're that much better than me?"

"Yeah," Georgie said, "I do. I didn't get stuck with a depreciating asset, for one thing. Did you know that the De Beers monopoly ain't what it used to be? Their market share drops every year. Another ten years, that shit will be worth half of what it is right now."

"What?" Wartensky asked, his mouth agape. "What did you say?"

"Ah, what do you care?" Georgie asked him. "You'll never make another ten years anyhow."

Moses Wartensky closed his mouth, and he seemed to shrivel, like a turtle withdrawing into its shell. He shook his head and turned away.

Prior looked at the other people in the room before turning back to Georgie. "Man, you are really something," he said. "I have dealt with some cast-iron pricks in my time, but you gotta be the blue ribbon dick, you know that? So tell me something, genius. If diamonds are a depreciating asset, why the hell do you want 'em? Huh?" The two men were getting closer to each other, one slow millimeter at a time. Stoney readied himself, and he noticed Prior's guard in the background, who was watching, and doing the same.

"Well, that depends on how bad you wanna get rid of 'em," Georgie said, sneering. "Seems to me you wanna cash in the Queen's jewels, but you don't want the Queen to hear about it. And then you think you wanna maybe make some money. Okay? And you ain't gonna take your shit down to the local pawnshop, can we agree on that? You gotta deal with someone like me. And you know what? There ain't anybody like me. There's just me. So if Moses says your shit's tagged at five large, I'll give you three and a half. Take it or fucking leave it."

Prior was turning purple. "Three and a half?" he shouted, outraged. "Three and a half? Fuck you! Fuck you, you little cocksucker! You ain't gonna—"

Georgie got right up into Prior's face and shouted back. "Fuck me? Is that what you said? Fuck me? I'm trying to do you a favor, you asshole! Fuck you! What do you think the feds are gonna think about your little stash, huh? You fucking piece of shit . . ."

Everybody moved at once. Moses Wartensky backed away as Prior made a grab for Georgie Cho's throat, missing narrowly. Georgie ducked, tucking the thumb on his right hand and driving four stiff fingers into Prior's abdomen just under the ribs as hard as he could. Prior, grunting, made another grab and got Cho just as his chauffeur cleared the counter. The guard wrapped himself around Prior as Stoney jammed his body in between Prior and Georgie and broke Prior's hold. All four men wound up on the floor, with Prior and Georgie still bellowing at each other. Prior, red-faced, regained his feet first, but by then Wartensky had an old .357 in a shaking fist. The end of the barrel described an unsteady circle. "Stop it!" he shouted. "Stop it, goddammit! Don't make me shoot somebody!"

Prior looked at Wartensky and laughed, and all the steam went out of him. "That's a double-action piece," he said. "You wanna shoot someone, you gotta cock the hammer back. No, all the way. Gimme that." He reached out and plucked the revolver out of Wartensky's hand. He looked at the gun. "Be helpful if you cleaned this thing once in a while. You pull this trigger, this thing would probably blow up in your face. Pack my belongings back in the bag, please, I'm leaving." He pointed the revolver in Georgie's general direction. "You breathe a word of this to anyone, my friend, and you'll live to regret it, but not for long."

"All right, all right," Georgie said, still sitting. "I'll go three and three quarters, but not a cent more."

Prior shook his head. "Unbelievable," he said. He turned and watched Wartensky's assistants as they poured a river of glittering silver back into the black velvet bag. Wartensky, his dismay writ large on his lined face, accepted the refilled bag, then handed it over to Prior with obvious reluctance. Prior looked at the bag, then down at Georgie. "Go fuck yourself," he said.

"Are you kidding me?" Georgie shouted. He was up on one knee, and his voice was a little hoarse. "I can't go four! That's ridiculous! Three-nine is my absolute highest offer!"

Prior uncocked Wartensky's cannon and laid it carefully on the counter. "Clean that," he said to Moses, then, bag in hand, he walked over to the exit. Wartensky leaned on the buzzer. Prior, followed by his chauffeur, who held the empty briefcase, went through the inner door, and then the outer one.

Georgie waited until the outer door closed, then cleared his throat. "Was that too over-the-top?" he asked.

Stoney and Wartensky just stared at him.

TWENTY-TWO

Tommy Bagadonuts watched Prior stalk out of Wartensky's building, followed by his driver. Prior, Tommy thought, is either extremely pissed off, or else he all of a sudden grew an underbite. "Oh, boy," Tommy said. He itched with the desire to call Stoney and find out how everything had gone, but he did not. His job now was to tail Prior and see where the man went, and he did not need his attention compromised. And if he lost track of Prior while he was on the phone with Stoney, he would never hear the end of it. Prior and his driver got into a black stretch Lincoln Town Car that was parked in a commercial-vehicles-only parking spot just up the block. Just the two of them, Tommy thought, noting that Prior got into the back and the other guy got in behind the wheel. He wondered where the other guard was. Prior had two guards, and he often traveled with them both. Wouldn't it make sense, Tommy asked himself, to take the two of them along when you are transporting five million dollars' worth of gems? He saw the Town Car's front wheels angling away from the curb, so he dropped his Mercedes into gear and prepared to follow. A car coming down the block behind him saw the Mercedes ease forward and stopped to let him out. Tommy knew that it wasn't courtesy, the guy wanted the space. That was the only way you ever found a parking spot in midtown. Just up the block, the same thing happened, a commercial van stopped to let the Town Car out into traffic. Tommy couldn't get past the van until the guy had it parked, but it was no sweat. The light up at the corner was red, and the van driver had himself over next to the curb in one shot. New Yorkers, Tommy thought, may not be able to drive for shit, but they are world-champion parkers.

Marisa listened to the voice mails on her phone, deleting them one by one. "Sheesh," she said, after sitting through one particularly long message. "Someone must have dialed me by mistake. I can't hear what they were saying."

"Voices in the background?" Tuco asked.

"Yeah, but far away. Can't make out the words."

"Probably hit a button by mistake," Tuco said. "Who was it?"

She looked at the little screen. "Oh, shit."

"What?"

"It was Jack."

"Lemme listen to it." She handed him the phone and he held it to his ear, but he couldn't make out any words, either.

"I don't know what to tell you," he said. "Think you ought to call him back?"

"Tommy and my father already tried to reach him," she said. "Besides, my father said no more calls unless it was an emergency."

"I guess we leave it alone, then."

"I don't like it," she told him. "I got a funny feeling."

"Call him back, if you want."

She shook her head. "I think I'm gonna do what they told me to do, for once. He can always call me."

Prior called her a short time later, at almost exactly four. Marisa jumped, but Tuco didn't react to it right away because Marisa's phone had been ringing off and on throughout the afternoon. She had been very quiet, most of the day. He left her alone, respecting her silence.

"It's him," she said, looking at Tuco. He was sitting on the counter in the kitchen in the McMansion in Alpine, New Jersey. "Are we ready?"

"Are you ready?" he asked her.

She nodded, pushed the button, held the phone to her hear. "Hello?"

Tuco listened hard, he could hear the caller's voice but couldn't make out the words.

"Yeah? You missed me? How much did you miss me? You liar . . . I'm not there anymore. I went back to the Jupiter Club. Because I'm not a perfect angel. Besides, I got tired of Dylan. He was rude and he smelled funny. Why don't you give me the money you were gonna pay him, you and I can open a new place. We'll call it 'Fallen Angels.' Probably do a lot more business. Anyway, I like the Jupiter, that's where I'm at now. I'm dancing tonight. Yeah, tonight. I don't know what time, there's a lot of girls here tonight. Maybe in about an hour."

Marisa wasn't sticking exactly to the script Stoney had written for her, but Tuco wasn't worried. He figured Marisa was smarter than any of the others realized, and she probably knew better than any of them how to play Prior, and besides, there was only one more thing that it was critical for her to say.

"I don't know if I can do that," she said, and Tuco could see her changing, becoming a different creature right there in front of him. He could see it in the way she stood, the height of her chin, the set of her lips. "Because I'm busy, that's why." She glanced at Tuco and colored slightly, turned away from him. "Maybe I don't need your money," she said. "And no, I don't care. Well, it's the truth. Wouldn't you rather know the truth? No? All right, I'll lie to you, then. Is that what you want?" Tuco realized that his fists were clenched, he was gritting his teeth, and his whole body was rigid. He made a conscious effort to relax.

"Let's do it over the phone. No, right now. Right now. Where are you? In your car? Where, in your car? Oh, in the city . . . Is anyone with you? No? Well, have your driver swing down the West Side Highway and get off by the Lincoln Tunnel entrance, you can probably pick up a girl down there. She can get you off while you talk to me. No? You don't want that?" She took a few steps away, turned, came back, but she was into it now, Tuco had the feeling that she didn't really see him anymore. "Well, I don't know how I can help you, then. Hey, can't you close the privacy glass in the car? Nobody can see you then, right? Go ahead, then, close it. Okay, now strip. Stop being a jerk, or I won't talk to you anymore. Strip, I said." Her voice had taken on a commanding tone. "Are you doing it? I'll wait. Yes. I said I would, didn't I?" She turned away again, paced slowly over to the kitchen window, turned, came back. "Yeah, I'm still here. Okay, tell me, then. Tell me. Is that right? Is that what you want?"

Tuco felt homicidal, he was sorry this was all taking place over the phone, he was angrier than he had been since the night he left his mother's house. He gripped the edge of the counter he was sitting on, feeling his hands around Prior's throat.

"Wait," Marisa was saying. "Wait. Hold up. Yes, you can, you can stop. Because I have to ask you something first. Are you ready?" Tuco watched Marisa's face. It was costing her to do this in front of him, he realized that, but then it dawned on him that she wanted Prior as bad as he did. And maybe she wanted something else, too. Maybe she wanted to see if he would treat her any differently after seeing her do this. . . . He could see in her eyes that she had reached the best part, the part when you've got the knife out, you know you're going to stick the guy with it, and he hasn't seen it yet. She glanced down at the piece of paper lying on the kitchen counter.

"Wayne?" she said sweetly. "That's who you really are, right? What kind of a name is Plotnik?"

The voice coming through the tiny speaker on her telephone got louder then, but Tuco still couldn't make out any individual words. Maybe there weren't any. . . .

"Oh, I thought they were your friends," she said, her voice dripping with phony concern. "They told me they'd missed you so much, they were going to throw you a surprise party. Besides, they told me you've got money stashed in a safe-deposit box, and they said I could keep it. I guess they have to give all the rest of your money back to whoever you stole it from." She looked over at Tuco, mouthed a silent question: "Okay?"

He nodded.

"Hey, fuck you, Wayne," she said. "I hope they get you." She snapped the phone closed, ending the call, and turned away, head down, shoulders slumped. Tuco hopped down off the counter.

"You were perfect," he said.

She crossed the space between the two of them, wrapped herself around him, and buried her face in his chest. "Thanks," she said, and she held him for a long time. Tuco didn't say anything, he just held on to her, breathing her air, feeling her heat and her strength. "I have to go to the bathroom," she finally said. "I want to wash my mouth out with soap." She released him. "Will he do it? Will he go to the Jupiter?"

Tuco looked at her, thought of how completely her face, her voice, and her touch filled his head. "That's his choice. If he's smart, he'll run," he said. "But I'm betting he'll be there."

The Town Car headed west across Manhattan. Tommy had his car radio tuned to a news station so that he could listen to the traffic reports. Just catching one or two of them rarely did you any good, but if you caught three or four in a row, sometimes you could hear news of a tie-up in time to figure out an alternate route. It was too late in the day to get a trouble-free ride out of Manhattan, for that you had to hit one of the bridges or tunnels no later than three in the afternoon. Sure enough, some putz got a flat tire on the lower level of the George Washington Bridge, and when he got out of his car to look at it, he got pranged by a passing car. Police, ambulance, and tow trucks were en route to the scene, but the George was done for, all of the outbound approaches were backing up already. The domino effect was going to mess up the Lincoln Tunnel as well, Tommy knew that, but they were close to the Lincoln and they could probably beat the crowds. Tommy wondered if Prior's driver was smart enough to have caught the news, and when they hit the West Side Highway, it did look, for a moment, like Prior was going to head downtown toward the tunnel entrance. Out-of-towner, Tommy thought, watching as the black car seemed to think about heading south, but then turned north toward the bridge instead. So much for that, Tommy thought. He relaxed, reaching for his phone. No chance Prior would be able to lose him in this . . .

• • •

It turned out not to be that bad, after all. The Town Car, with Tommy's Mercedes a half-dozen cars behind it, made it all the way up to the sanitation plant before they ran into the tail end of the backup, and even then it wasn't horrible. Traffic never really stopped, everyone crept along, so it looked like the accident was only going to add a half hour or so onto the commute. Miraculous, Tommy thought. He followed the progress at the George on the radio. The Port Authority handled the whole thing with unexpected competence: cops, tow trucks, and an ambulance from the Fort Lee side of the bridge got to the site in minutes. A short time later, they had both cars yanked off the bridge, with the first driver on his way to the hospital and the second guy on his way to jail for driving under the influence of a controlled substance. The radio announcers reacted with appropriate shock and affront, amusing Tommy. Yeah, sure, he thought. Like you've never done it . . .

Prior surprised him by taking the second exit on the Jersey side, the one that dumped you onto the local streets in Fort Lee. Tommy followed, uncomfortably close now, with only one car between his Mercedes and the limo. Prior's driver turned right at the stop sign, and the next driver turned left, leaving no one between Prior and Tommy. This is not good, Tommy thought, and he hung back as far as he dared. The limo headed into the little warren of one-way streets that lay just north of the bridge, and Tommy lost sight of them for a moment. He came out at a stop sign, turned right just because it was easier than going left, and he was driving past a crumbling motel when he caught sight of the front of Prior's Town Car as it parked in the motel lot. He couldn't stop, he had to keep going, and he thought it was just as well, anyhow, he didn't want to risk raising Prior's hackles by following too close. He went around the block, pulling into the underground parking lot of the office building that was off to one side and slightly behind the motel. The lot was just below grade, and a row of openings along ground level let in some light. Tommy left his car in the first empty spot and walked over and stood in the dark space just to one side of the opening closest to the motel. He could see Prior walking across the lot. The man was briefly lost to view, but he was just climbing the stairs to the second floor, because he reappeared on the balcony. Tommy had to move to a different opening to get a better view, but it seemed to him that Prior went into the last room on the second level. He didn't stay long, he came back out in little over a minute and headed back to his car. Tommy hustled back to his Mercedes and exited the lot. Due to the one-way streets, there was only one way Prior's car could go. Tommy found a place to park and ducked down as the limo passed him by. He reached for his phone while he waited for the Town Car to get a reasonable distance ahead of him.

"Tuco," he said. "Whattayou do?"

"Nothing, Tommy," came the answer.

Tommy told Tuco the name and location of the motel, as well as the underground parking lot of the office building next door. "Listen," he said. "All you gotta do is watch, okay? Keep Marisa out of sight. It'sa the last room onna top, inna front. Just see, anybody'sa go in or out. Okay?"

"Yeah, Tommy, no problem. We can probably be there in about twenty minutes."

"Good. Don't do nothing, okay? Just watch. I would do it myself, but I gotta stay on Prior."

"Okay. It was just Prior that went in? Where's his guards?"

"One driving. I'ma no see the other guy."

"Okay. What am I watching for?"

"I'ma no sure. But it'sa don' fit, him stopping here in this place. Stay outta sight, see what's gonna happen."

"Okay, Tommy."

TWENTY-THREE

Stoney paid his money at the door, signed his name on the form the doorman handed him, half listened to the man's spiel about his signature verifying that he'd joined a private club. The sweet smell of stale beer and sweat that washed out through the doorway compromised his attention. "I'm sorry," he said to the guy. "What did you say?"

"Doesn't matter," the guy told him. "Just a new wrinkle in the cabaret law. All it means is that the girls can take it all off now, because this ain't a public joint. You got to be a member to get in."

"How about that," Stoney said. "Since when?"

"Couple days," the guy said. "Another week, tops, and they'll close the loophole."

"And then your lawyers will have to find another one."

The guy shrugged. "That's business. Change or die."

Inside, it was the same old thing, flat black everywhere, spots on the half-moon stage, muted lighting everywhere else, bar with mirrors and a wall of bottles behind it against one wall. The dim room was about half full, the crowd ranging from hard hats in jeans and work boots to coiffed and manicured suits. A couple of half-naked girls worked the room, you want to buy me a champagne cocktail, honey? Lap dances in the

VIP room in the back, baby, and you know you want me. . . .
Stoney made his slow way across the room and found a spot at
the far end of the stage. A sound system with blown speakers
blared fuzzy disco music, obliterating all other sounds.

Stoney watched the waitress, she was short, stocky,
strawberry-blond hair, midtwenties. She wore white terrycloth
shorts and a flimsy halter top. She had a black leather fanny
pack fastened loosely around her waist, and she carried a tray
in one hand. The fanny pack tried to work its way down over
her hips as she walked, taking her shorts south with it, and
every now and then she would stop and tug them back up into
place. Just part of the show, Stoney thought. She came over,
stood by his elbow, and waited. "One Diet Coke," he said. He
had to shout to be heard, she had to lean in to hear him. "Just
one, okay?" He handed her a fifty. "Keep the change."

She looked at him and nodded. She understood. Bring me
the drink and then leave me alone.

On the far side of the stage the dancer up on the stage
was baiting one of the patrons. He was a young guy, sat at a
table with three other guys, they all looked like construction
workers. He and the dancer carried on a shouted conversation
that Stoney could not hear. The dancer was a butch-looking
female, brush cut dark red hair, Oriental tattoos on one arm,
very muscular. She was down to a string bikini bottom and
the ever-present garter, and she gyrated slowly to the music,
she never stopped moving as she continued her exchange with
the young man. It looked like she was challenging him, she
sneered at him, held out one hand, curled her fingers as she
undulated slowly, come on, come on . . . One of the club's
bouncers hovered uncertainly in the background. Finally the
young man stood up, red-faced, to shouts and cheers from his

friends and the surrounding crowd. The bouncer took a step closer, but the crowd pushed back away from the kid, giving him room. He dropped to the floor, assumed the push-up position, then raised one hand and put it behind his back. When he was sure of his balance, he looked up, watched as the butch stripper did the same.

Stoney had to smile. One-handed push-up contest. The kid nodded at the redhead, dipped to the floor, pushed himself back up. Everyone in the place shouted "One!" No way the kid wins, Stoney thought, he's probably in decent shape, but he's a little heavy, and the redhead was ripped. "Two!" The count went on until it got to seven. People were standing around the kid now, Stoney could no longer see him, but apparently he faltered. His friends howled and jeered at him, and the redhead began cranking out repetitions in quick succession. She quit when she got to twenty, a ragged cheer went up, and the men went back to their tables. About half of them paused to pay their respects, and the stripper nodded to each one as she accepted the money they proffered. The kid was last, he acknowledged defeat to a smattering of applause, counted out the bills he had wagered. She squatted in front of him, held the garter out from her thigh, snapped it shut on his money, and blew him a kiss. The push-up contest had been as close to real as the two of them would ever get, he knew it and she knew it. That understanding robbed the whole transaction of whatever sexual tension might have otherwise been present, because everybody knew you were never going to score inside the Jupiter Club. It was funny, really, everyone came to watch naked women dance, but when you got right down to it, the place was all about masturbation and the lies men tell themselves.

The redhead stood up, turned her back, untied the bikini strings at her waist, and slowly pulled the scrap of fabric between her legs and tossed it aside. She mooned the kid she'd beaten once, then moved on. Show's almost over, Stoney thought, she's got nothing left to take off. . . . She worked her way across the width of the stage, milking her admirers for whatever she could get. Stoney half rose out of his chair when she got to him, slipped a twenty in with the rest, nodded his respect. He didn't know how many one-handed push-ups he could do, but she hadn't looked like she was slowing down when she hit twenty.

Someone slipped into the chair behind his, the redhead glanced at the guy but he wasn't forthcoming, so she stood up, waved to the crowd, and walked off as the music ended, pausing to gather up the discarded bits of her costume.

Stoney sat back down, half turned to look at the new guy. It was Prior, or Plotnik. He was wearing the same clothes he'd had on at Wartensky's, but now he had a silver pistol to match the jacket. "Eyes front," he said, holding the jacket open just long enough for Stoney to see the gun he held in his right hand. "You just keep your eyes on the bitches." Stoney shrugged, watched as the redhead waved good-bye one last time and went behind the curtain. Yeah, honey, he thought, you are beautiful in your own way, but I'm sorry it came to this. You look smart enough to have figured out a better gig. . . .

He heard Prior's voice in his ear. "Who are they? Where are the shooters?"

"Don't use 'em."

"Yeah, sure. All right. Whoever they are, I hope they like you, because if anybody moves on me, I'm taking you out first."

"Relax," Stoney told him. "My partners love me."

"They'd better. It was me, right? It was me all along you were after. There's no hedge fund, no XRC takeover."

"Sorry," Stoney said.

"You fucked up, you should have taken me down at that place in the city. You had your chance, and you blew it. I should have seen it coming. I should have known, especially after I had to take care of those two, earlier," he said. "You had people poking into my business. They yours?"

"Yeah," Stoney said.

"You gotta take better care of your people than that," Prior said. "You guys suck, you know that? Better men than you have tried. . . . But that Chinese kid, he was fucking good, man, he really got under my skin. Fucking little bastard . . ." He looked around. "Is she here?"

"Who?"

"You know who, that skinny little bitch that set me up. Brother, when I'm done with you, I am gonna fuck her raw. . . . You can believe that."

Stoney sighed. "Yeah, she's here." Onstage, someone stood behind the edge of the curtain. The music kicked in again. "She'll be out after this one, I think."

"Shut up and watch," Prior said. "Eyes front."

The new stripper was called Tiffany. She looked much younger than the redhead, and she couldn't dance a lick. She looked lost, slightly dazed, fragile. Her blond hair shone bright over her pale skin. She was coltish on her high heels. She wore a frilly, lacy, feathery negligee, and she took her time with it, fumbling with the buttons as she wandered across the edge of the stage, staring out over the heads of the men watching. They were into the second song by the time she got the thing off, dropped it to the side, and writhed awkwardly in a filmy bra and panties.

Stoney shifted slightly in his seat, just enough to get a feel for what Prior was doing. Thought so, he told himself. The guy was rapt, Tiffany looked exactly like Prior's kind of girl, beautiful, but too young to know anything. Still the guy had that pistol in his right hand, hidden under his jacket, and there was no way Stoney could make a move. Stoney caught a glimpse of Prior's bald driver leaning against the bar.

She lost the bra first, walked around topless for the space of another two more songs, then she stepped out of the panties. There was a G-string under those, and she gyrated around in it for a while before finally taking it off. She began accepting money at the edge of the stage, taking it from the men watching without looking at them, seemingly as disinterested as if she were selling newspapers. When she got to their end of the stage, she squatted down and looked directly at Prior. "Hi," she said.

"Hey, sugar," he said, his voice hoarse. He handed a C-note to Stoney. "Pass it up to her," he said.

"Hey, wow, thanks," she said, smiling. "Thanks a lot." She stood back up then, stooped to grab her clothes, then paused to wave before wandering back behind the curtain.

Prior switched the gun to his left hand, stuck it into his jacket pocket, and jabbed Stoney in the back. "I'm not waiting any longer," he said. "We're gonna go backstage, and that little whore better be back there. Get moving."

Stoney got up, made his way slowly across the floor toward the bar. There was a corridor at the far end of the stage, it led back past a couple of restrooms to a gray door with a sign proclaiming AUTHORIZED PERSONNEL ONLY.

Behind them, the music stopped and the bartender's voice boomed out of the PA system as he announced the next dancer. The waitress came up the corridor behind them, tugging her shorts up. "Hi, guys," she said. "You gonna hit the VIP room?"

Prior nodded in the general direction of the bar. "Yeah," he said. "I talked to the guy at the door, Mac. He said it would be okay."

"Hey, whatever," she said, and she reached past the two of them and jerked the door open, held it for them to precede her through. "Mac makes the rules, I just carry the drinks." Prior jabbed Stoney again, and the two of them walked through the doorway. They both stopped when they saw Tiffany standing there. She had the pieces of her costume in one hand, and she was wrestling with one of her high heels with the other. "God," she said. "I hate these freakin' shoes." She looked at Prior. "Did you come back here for me?"

It was just about dark when they got there. Tuco parked the Beemer in an empty spot in the parking garage Tommy had told him about. The spot was marked RESERVED, and that was the sort of thing that would normally bother Tuco, but it was closing time and the building's occupants were all going home. He did wonder whose spot it was, though, and decided that he would move without protest if the rightful owners showed up. Why do you worry about this crap, he asked himself, but he knew that he was funny about certain things. He liked to know that he belonged, that nobody could come along and tell him he needed to get out.

The motel was, by then, just a dark shape against the flickering backdrop of the flood of headlights streaming by on the George Washington Bridge. The darkness hid most of the motel's more distinctive features, but it seemed obvious to both of them what kind of place it was. "What a dump," Marisa said.

"Yeah," Tuco said. "Two stars in the *Fleabag Gazette*."

She didn't laugh. "Tell me again why we're here."

"Tommy said he was tailing Prior back from the city, and the guy stopped in here for a couple of minutes. Tommy said he went into that last room on the top, down by the end."

"So what are we supposed to do, sit here and watch the motel-room door? What good will that do?"

"Listen, the first thing we are supposed to do is keep you out of trouble."

"Yeah, yeah," she said. "Save Marisa from herself." They sat and watched in silence for a few minutes. A few more people from the office building came downstairs, got into their cars, and left. As far as Tuco could tell, none of them appeared to give the Beemer a second glance. "We don't know what Prior was doing here, or where he went when he left, am I right?" Marisa said.

"No, we don't. He probably headed for the Jupiter, looking for you, but we don't know that for sure. Maybe he stopped here to buy coke or something."

She shook her head. "Drugs are not his thing, he's a kink. Did he have both of his guys with him?"

"Tommy said it was just Prior and his driver, the bald guy. We don't know where the other one is." Tuco looked over at her. She looked like a dog that smelled a stray cat. She was leaning forward in her seat, peering out at the darkened building, a scowl on her face. "What?" he said. "What is it?"

She sat there on point for a minute before she answered

him. "You guys don't know what a shit Prior is," she finally said. "If he stopped in here, he had a reason for it, he didn't come to look at the wallpaper. And we don't know what happened to Jack, either."

"He went home. Isn't that what everyone decided?"

Marisa did not look convinced. "He would have told someone," she said.

"You think so?"

"I think he would have said good-bye. And then there was that strange voice mail he left me." She lapsed into silence. About five minutes later, a figure appeared at the balcony railing, down at the end, by the room they were watching. It was impossible to tell, in the dark and at that distance, who it was. Seconds later, a match flared.

"Cigarette," Tuco said.

"Yeah," Marisa said. "Something's up, Eddie. Is there a way to kill that dome light?"

"What? What are you talking about?"

"The car's dome light is gonna go on when I open this door. I wanna go see who that is."

"Hey, no way," Tuco said. "If anything happens to you your father will kill me."

"We can't just sit here, Eddie."

"Marisa, your father said—"

"Fuck that," she said. She opened her door and got out.

Tuco jumped out of the car and got around in front of her, spreading his arms out to stop her. "Marisa," he said. "Come on. You gotta be kidding me."

"Eddie, why do you think Tommy asked us to come down here? We need to have a look in that room."

"Listen, Marisa, your father—"

"My father is not here. And if he was, you know what he'd do, he'd go up there and check that room out."

"Yeah, okay, but he'd make you wait in the car."

"Eddie, I'm going. I'm just gonna go see if that's Prior's guy. His name is Dwayne, he's the guy who tackled you in the Jupiter parking lot. So get out of my way."

"You think I can't stop you?"

"I think you won't. Come on, you know I'm right. Dwayne is one sick piece of shit, and if Prior left him here, something bad is going on up in that room. There's no one else to do this, they're all busy. It's up to you and me, Eddie."

"Whatever happened to doing what they told you to do?"

"Let's not go crazy with that."

He dropped his arms, admitting defeat. "Jesus Christ."

"Look, stop worrying. If we go along that retaining wall by the street, he won't even know anyone is there. We'll go down to the end, and you can boost me up high enough to see over the wall. Okay? And if it's not Dwayne, I'll come back and sit in the car, I promise."

They did it just like she said. He helped her climb up onto his shoulders, stood there holding her, thinking how light she was. Behind them, the occasional car rolled past on the street without comment. After a minute she jumped down. "It's him."

"Shhhh."

"He went back in. Come on."

"Hold up." She surprised him by stopping to listen. "This guy is not the kind of person you can sneak up on in the dark. I think he's too good for that. We go up there in the dark and wait for him to come back out, that's exactly the kind of thing he'd expect."

"You got a better idea?"

"Yeah."

The motel office had the sharp, sour stink of a man who had not bathed in a long time. The guy behind the front desk did not even look at the two of them, he just took the money Tuco gave him and slid a key across the counter. "Gimme a room on the second floor," Tuco told him. "Down at the end." The guy pulled the key back, substituted another one without comment. Marisa turned to go, and the guy watched her rear end until Tuco caught him doing it, then he turned away.

It seemed like forever. Marisa had told him it would be twenty minutes, tops, before Dwayne would come back outside for another cigarette, but Tuco could swear he'd waited at least an hour before the guy finally reappeared. Exhaling in relief, Tuco stepped around the corner at the end of the balcony and walked slowly in the direction of the orange glowing end of Dwayne's cigarette. He stopped once, halfway down, leaned out over the railing to peer at the number on the little plastic tag attached to his room key, then continued on his way. He stopped at the second-to-last door and tried to look confused, looking at the door and then at his key. He turned and looked at Dwayne, visible now in the light coming through the open door to the motel room. He took a tentative step in Dwayne's direction and glanced through into the room. He could see the front end of a chair, with two denim-clad legs fastened to the chair legs with thick white plastic cable ties, the long ends sticking out. The feet were bare.

"It's my room, shithead," Dwayne said, and he stepped into Tuco's line of sight so that the legs were no longer visible. "Get lost."

"They musta give me the wrong key," Tuco mumbled, and he tried to peer around Dwayne.

"Hey," Dwayne said, "Hey, wait a minute. I know you." He took two steps toward Tuco, reaching for something at his belt line behind him. He came up with a revolver and aimed it at Tuco's face. "You were with that little bitch at the Jupiter the other night." He reached his thumb for the hammer.

Tuco raised his hands. "It wasn't me," he said, trying to sound drunk and scared. It wasn't hard. "I never seen you before in my life, I swear it."

"Bullshit. I remember you."

Tuco's mouth went dry, and suddenly it became very hard to breathe. He could feel his heart pounding in his chest. You took one chance too many, he thought, and he wondered how much it was going to hurt when the bullet hit. He could hardly hear Marisa in the background. She had slipped up the stairs behind Dwayne. "Hey, asshole," she said.

Dwayne half turned to look behind him and the hand holding the pistol followed him around, and for a moment the revolver pointed out into the night, east, in the general direction of Washington Heights, the New York City neighborhood on the other side of the Hudson River. I should make a grab for that thing, Tuco thought, but his body was not yet ready to listen to instructions.

Marisa was holding a three-foot piece of galvanized pipe, the kind plumbers use to run gas lines. Tuco could see the muscles in her upper arms as she swung it, not like a ballplayer, but like a golfer, and the end of the pipe caught Dwayne's gun-hand forearm midway between wrist and elbow. The pistol went flying out of his hand, out into the air and down over the railing to the parking lot below.

Dwayne bellowed in pain and rage as he turned to lunge at Marisa, completely ignoring Tuco. "You fucking little whore! I am gonna fucking kill you!" Tuco felt mildly insulted. The connection between his mind and his muscles reestablished itself, and he leaped at Dwayne, grabbing the man by his hair and his belt. He heaved him out over the railing, not stopping to think that the man's pistol was down there somewhere, too, and that it might not have been his best option. . . .

He needn't have worried. When he went to the balcony railing to look over, he could see Dwayne on the tarmac below, his head twisted up underneath his body at an impossible angle. Dwayne's legs and feet were thrumming rapidly in the manner of someone having a seizure, but after a minute, they went still.

Marisa was already inside the room. "My God, Jack, what did they do to you?" By the time Tuco got to the door, she had just finished removing the sheet that had been wrapped around Harman's head.

"I'm all right," Harman said, but he didn't sound it, he sounded weak and shaky. "Cut me loose, but watch where you put your hands. Don't leave any prints."

"Should I get you some water?"

"No!" He sounded a little stronger. "No, stay out of the bathroom. Just get me loose, we can stop somewhere on the way."

Marisa told him that Dwayne usually carried a knife, so Tuco looked for it while she went for the Beemer. Once he had the knife, Tuco went back up and sawed through the tough nylon cable ties that held Harman fast, then helped Jack to his feet. Harman was heavy and his entire body shook badly, but Tuco got him up and together they made it down the stairs. Harman hit his head on the roof of the Beemer as he lowered himself into the passenger seat, but he barely noticed. "You gotta put Dwayne in the trunk," he said. "We can't leave him here."

Tuco didn't know why not, but he didn't question it, he went and did it as Marisa got into the backseat. A moment later, they were moving. "Shit," Tuco said, slapping his pants pocket. "I forgot to leave the room key."

"Don't worry about it," Harman told him. "Head north. Next town up, they got a park, down by the river. There's a boat ramp there, should be empty this time of year."

Tuco waded out into the freezing water, pushing Dwayne's lifeless body in front of him. He got out waist-deep, out where he could feel the current tugging at him, he stopped there, and he pushed Dwayne out into deeper water. The man's body hung just beneath the surface, hardly visible at all as it floated slowly south toward the bright lights of the bridge. Tuco stood there for a minute, watching it go. The body began moving a little faster now, as the currents pulled it farther from the shore. Could have been you, just as easy, Tuco thought. He took the motel key out of his pocket, wiped it off, tossed it as far out into the river as he could. He turned to head back to shore, saw her darkened outline. She stood ankle-deep in the Hudson, waiting for him. She embraced him when he got to her, wrapped her arms around him, and when she kissed him, his resistance melted, he felt that old feeling again, the one he thought had been lost forever. God, he thought, I'm jumping off this cliff, this one right here, please don't let me hit the ground too hard. . . .

"We have to go," he croaked, as soon as he had the chance.

"Eddie," she whispered, her mouth up next to his ear. "Tell me you feel it, too. Tell me it's not just me."

"You had me almost from the beginning," he said, feeling the shape of her back underneath his hands. "I been so afraid. . . . I didn't think I should say anything. I didn't think, you know . . ." She buried her face in his chest, her body shaking. He wondered if she was crying, and why, but then, just as suddenly, she was squeezing him with a fierce and surprising strength.

"My parents are gonna freak," she said.

"Not if we do this right," he said. "Come on, let's go."

Prior stood in the hallway, behind and slightly to one side of Stoney. The door swung shut behind him. The hand holding the pistol was inside one of the pockets of his silk jacket. He stared at Tiffany, who smiled and stared back. The look on her face said, "Friendly, but only two numbers in my IQ, neither of them a nine."

"No, miss," he said. "We didn't come back here for you, but that does sound very nice. Do you suppose we could use a private room for a few minutes?"

"Sure," she said, cheerful as hell. "But I come with the room. Package deal, you know what I'm saying? House rules."

"Oh, of course," Prior said, and he poked Stoney in the back with the pistol, prodding him forward. "We'll be more than happy to pay whatever the charge might be. Plus something for yourself, of course. Where's the room?"

"Straight down the hall," she said. "On the left. I think they're all empty, it's early, yet. Would you like me to go arrange something for us to drink?"

"Yeah. Champagne, I know they love for you to sell that, right? So get us a couple of bottles. Just give me ten minutes to finish up a little business with my friend, here."

"Okay. I'll go find the waitress." She bounced off down the hall.

"You heard the lady," Prior said, after Tiffany was gone. "Up ahead, on the left."

The room had apparently been decorated by the same guy who'd done the rest of the club, but there was a couch, a couple of hard chairs, some posters on the wall, a large square of industrial carpet in the middle of the floor, a large-screen television. Prior stopped Stoney just inside the door, held his pistol at Stoney's head while he patted him down with the other hand. "On the couch," he said, after he finished. Stoney complied, and Prior pulled one of the hard chairs over and sat in it, facing him. He returned the pistol to the pocket of his jacket. "Did you think this scam was really gonna work?" he asked.

"How long have you known?" Stoney asked him.

"I suspected as soon as I found out someone was trying to look into my background," Prior said. "I thought I had it taken care of. Then you people showed up at my broker's office. It made me wonder. It was me you were after all along. Right? There was nothing with XRC."

"It was you," Stoney said.

Prior shook his head, looking disappointed. "How about that," he said. "Why didn't you rob me, earlier today?"

"That didn't come off entirely the way I wanted it to," Stoney said.

"Too bad for you. That Oriental kid was good, though. Little bastard really got to me. That's how it was going to work, wasn't it? Nothing ever changes, I guess. All of these schemes work on sleight of hand, when you get right down to it. I'm so engaged with him that I forget to watch the rest of you."

"Something like that."

"And there was never any breakthrough at XRC," Prior said. Stoney laughed, and Prior's eyes glittered with anger. "And you went through all of this just to get to this point? Just to get me alone? You should have brought some backup. Why this way? I don't understand your angle. Unless you simply suffer from overconfidence."

Stoney watched him. "You remember the power company bucket truck on the street outside your house a few nights ago?" There had been no truck, but Stoney saw a flicker of doubt in Prior's eyes. "Fifty-caliber with a telescopic sight, I could have just shot you then and there, it would have been the smart play. Would have taken your head right off your shoulders. But I didn't like how it felt, you know what I mean? I wanted to give you the chance to walk away."

"Walk away?" Prior stared at Stoney. "From you? Or from that little bitch you used to set me up?"

"I needed to give you a choice," Stoney told him.

Prior stared in incomprehension. Just then, the door to the room opened, startling him, but he calmed down when he saw that it was just Tiffany. She had put her costume back on. Prior glanced her way. "Ten minutes, honey, you were going to give me ten minutes, remember?"

"Sorry," she said. "I need to run your credit card."

Prior nodded. "Always get the money first."

Stoney watched Prior. The guy is good, he had to admit it, he never let himself get too distracted. He did keep glancing Tiffany's way, though, and she was certainly easy to look at. I could try when he reaches for his wallet, Stoney thought, I could probably kick him hard enough to take him down if I caught the meridian on the outside of his thigh. . . . Prior stood up, though, walked over and stood next to Tiffany, faced Stoney while he took out his wallet. "Why don't we do this in cash?" he said.

"Works for me," she told him. They agreed on the price, and she accepted the bills.

"Just give me a couple more minutes," Prior told her. "My friend will be leaving soon."

"Okay," she said. "I'll go pay the house."

"All right," Prior said, and he peered out into the hallway, checking in both directions. Then he closed the door, walked back over, and sat in his chair again. "I'm not walking away from anything," he said.

"Your call," Stoney said. "I didn't really think you would. It's always your appetites that take you down, isn't it?"

"I wouldn't know," Prior said. "I'm not like you, I'm just a soldier, I'm not a con artist."

"You haven't been a soldier for a while. What are you now?"

"I am the winner, and you are the loser." Stoney could see it in the man's posture, he had made his decision, and now he was moving on it. "Here's how this is going to work. I have a man in the outer room. I'm going to call him on his cell phone, he's going to come in here, and he's going to escort you out to my car. I'm going to stay here and take my pleasure with the young lady. After that, we're going to go somewhere where you and I can have an extended conversation. Now, I need to warn you, my man taught hand-to-hand at Quantico, and he is very, very good. He's almost as good as I am." Behind him, the door opened up again and the waitress entered carrying a tray with the wine and three glasses.

Prior stared at Stoney. "Stay where you are."

"Whatever you say," Stoney said. Prior took out his phone, made his call, murmuring briefly into the mouthpiece

"This won't take a second," the waitress said. She was the same girl who'd been working the front of the room, the strawberry blonde with the terrycloth shorts, halter top, and the fanny pack that kept trying to pull her pants down. Stoney actually found her more attractive than the other women in the place because she looked more like a real person than they did. She crossed the room, put the tray down on the end table next to the couch. She took one of the champagne bottles and opened it, firing the plastic stopper across the room with a loud pop, then poured two glasses full, carried one of them over to Prior. "Anything else?" she said.

Prior's guard opened the door, stepped into the room, and closed the door behind him. He was smiling, his attention split between Stoney and the waitress.

"Why don't you pour one for yourself?" Prior said.

"Against the rules," she told him, but then she reconsidered. "You know, I could use a belt." She crossed back over to the tray, stood between Stoney and Prior, leaned over for the other glass. Her halter top was right in Stoney's face, and her fanny pack slid low on her hip. The zipper on the thing was open. She picked up the other glass, stood back erect, and chugged the wine. The sweet, slightly acrid smell of the stuff filled Stoney's head. "God, I needed that. Thanks," she said. She pulled her shorts back up again.

"Why do they make you wear those stupid pants?" Prior asked her. "They look like they're more trouble than they're worth. You ought to just lose them."

"I'm not a dancer," she told him, doubt in her voice. "I'm really just a waitress. I got two left feet. I don't know how to, you know . . ." Her voice trailed off as she watched Prior reach for his wallet. "What do you, um, want me to do?"

"You really don't need to do a thing," Prior told her, and he smiled. He handed her a hundred, and she stuffed it in her fanny pack. "My friends, here, they're both leaving, and maybe you could just keep me company until Tiffany gets back."

"Sure," she said. "But you really ought to get something for your money. I hate to see anyone get gypped." She stepped over in front of the television, hooked her thumbs on the waistband of her shorts, and slid them artlessly down over her hips. Prior glanced at Stoney, then leaned back in his chair, smiling. He had his hand on his pistol, inside the jacket pocket, but the jacket was unbuttoned and it hung open, exposing the shirt beneath. That's where Stoney pointed the .22, the one he had taken out of the waitress's fanny pack when she was pouring the wine.

Prior saw it, his mouth dropped open as he struggled to comprehend, but then he jerked his body sideways out of his chair, the hand holding the silver automatic coming out of his jacket as his body hit the floor. "Down," Stoney said, and the waitress dropped straight to the ground. Stoney adjusted his aim, and the .22 spit three times, then three times again when he shifted his aim to Prior's bodyguard, who, transfixed by the half-naked woman on the floor, hesitated for one fatal second before groping for his own weapon. Hit by a head shot, he was dead before he hit the floor. It wasn't luck, Stoney thought, not entirely, but the other two shots he had fired at the bald man had gone through the ceiling and out into the night.

Prior was hit twice high in the chest and once through the neck. His eyes and jaw both gaped wide, then he struggled to swallow the blood that began filling his mouth. Stoney held the .22 on him, steady as Prior looked once at the gun in his own hand, but a few seconds later, his grip relaxed, his fingers went slack, and the gun lay there in his open hand. Prior's mouth worked, as though he were trying to say something, but his airways were filling with blood. He coughed a red spray of it out onto the rug. He looked up at Stoney as the waitress got back up off the floor, pulling her terrycloth shorts back up. "You all right?" Stoney asked her.

"I'm fine," she said, and she watched Prior. "The only part of this that bothered me was that Brazilian wax job Tiff made me get. Hurt like a bastard." She glanced over at Stoney. "Tommy says he'll help us get Tiff's daughter back. Can he really do it?"

"If anybody can," Stoney said, "it's Tommy."

She nodded, then stepped over a puddle of champagne on the floor, around the lifeless bodyguard, and walked out of the room. Prior coughed again, weakly, tried to swallow the blood. His eyes never wavered from Stoney's face. How quickly you become a footnote, Stoney thought. One minute you're invincible, the next minute the waitress doesn't even see you anymore. He watched silent as Prior died, marshaling his justifications for what he had just done. The man killed a security guard whom he could have just as easily spared, he murdered Tina Finbury, who surely deserved better, and he was stalking your own daughter. And those are just the ones you know about . . . But he was sorry, still and all, he regretted the pain he saw in Prior's eyes even as it faded to a cold gray. It's on you, he wanted to say that to Prior's lifeless face, but whether it was true or not, it didn't seem to matter anymore.

The truck was so big it shook the ground when it drove around to the back of the Jupiter. FINBURY CONSTRUCTION, the sign on the door read. HOMES OF DISTINCTION. There was a huge container on the back, it was filled with rubble that had recently been a house. The house had been a knockdown, a nice building whose crime had been its exclusive location, and Finbury had bought the place and torn it down to make way for another McMansion. Prior and his bodyguard were both in the container on the back of the truck, rolled up in the carpet from the VIP room. Finbury had his arm out the driver's window, his face silver in the glare of the parking lot floodlights. He said something to Stoney, but Stoney couldn't hear him over the clatter of the big diesel. Finbury declined to shout, he clambered down off the truck. "Watch the news," he said. "Couple days from now, someone will find him and his rocks somewhere down in the Meadowlands." Then he climbed back up, jammed the truck into gear with a grinding thump, and roared away.

TWENTY-FOUR

It was a new rule, proposed, vetoed, overridden, debated, finally agreed to with reluctance by both parties: no smoking in the house. Donna, having lived in a smoke-free environment for the better part of a year, did not want Stoney smoking anywhere, at any time, while he had done his best to explain why that was not possible, maybe not even desirable, not here, not yet. There was a small screened porch at the back of the house, now home to a ratty couch and an ashtray. He came out of the house, sat down in the dark, shirtless, night breeze cool on his skin, the only light the glow at the end of his cigarette.

It had been well past midnight by the time they'd gotten everything sorted out. Stoney wondered if Finbury would really leave Prior's little velvet bag with the body. Not that it mattered anyhow, the stuff was only ice. Cubic zirconias, switched for the real thing by Moses Wartensky and his sons during the little dance they had done in his office. Wartensky had agreed to liquidate Prior's diamonds, for a cut, of course. Stoney wasn't sure he trusted the man, but the guy was Tommy's problem now. Maybe the hand is quicker than the eye after all, Stoney thought. Even when you're looking for the play, you miss it. . . .

Jack Harman was sleeping in the spare bedroom, and Tuco

was sacked out on the couch. Prior's Doberman ws curled up next to the sofa. Tuco and Jack had made one last trip throught the woods up in Alpine, and they had found three more velvet bags, just like the one Prior had carried to Wartensky's. So far, no one but Stoney and the two of them knew about it. Tuco had brought the Dobie back with him. Kids, Stoney thought. What could you do? At least he hadn't brought the Rottweiler, too.

Tuco and Marisa were locked into a mutual orbit, Stoney could sense the pull of gravity between the two of them. Tiffany and her sister, the strawberry-blond waitress, had both gone home with Fat Tommy. Stoney shook his head. I don't know how the man does it . . . He thought about calling Benny, but it would wait. No use waking him up, they would probably see each other later in the day.

Somewhere in the trees behind the house, a frog cried out for a mate, his metallic croak sounding like someone hitting a galvanized pipe with a hammer.

Pank.

Pank.

I'm here. Is anybody there?

The door opened behind him, she came out into the night. "Are you okay?"

"Yeah, I'm fine." That old lie came smoothly: I'm all right, really. Leave me be.

"Why don't you come back inside?"

"Nice out here."

"Yes, it is," she said. He felt her hands soft on his skin. He was surprised, because he could still sense the vague and unspoken resentments that lay between the two of them. Tell me, he wanted to say, tell me what you want me to say, what you want me to be, but he held his tongue.

"Tell me we're not keeping that dog," she said.

He chuckled. "It's Tuco's."

She ran her hands through his hair, rubbed his bristled cheeks, kissed him. He touched her, hesitant, because it was no longer second nature to have his hands on her, he wanted to be sure of his welcome first. A moment later, she drew away from him, and he heard whatever she'd been wearing slip to the floor. For the first time in his memory, it seemed that she was the aggressor, and he was left to wonder what he really wanted. He didn't know what to think, and presently he quit trying, went with his gut instead.

Pank.

Pank.

The frog was still searching.

Stoney felt for him.

It's hell, being alone.

BOOKS BY NORMAN GREEN

DEAD CAT BOUNCE

ISBN 0-06-085169-4 (paperback)

Norman Green's first crime thriller, *Shooting Dr. Jack*, introduced three unforgettable characters: Stoney, "Fat Tommy," and Tuco. Now they're back in an exciting story of greed, murder, and revenge.

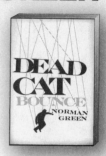

THE ANGEL OF MONTAGUE STREET
A Novel

ISBN 0-06-093411-5 (paperback)

In the fall of '73, Brooklyn, New York, is home to worn-down hotels, wiseguys, immigrants, the disturbed, the disenfranchised, and a few people just trying to make an honest buck. When Silvano Iurata's troubled brother, Noonie, goes missing, Silvano returns to a place he swore he'd never set foot in again.

SHOOTING DR. JACK
A Novel

ISBN 0-06-088830-X (mass market)
ISBN 0-06-093413-1 (paperback)

"Norman Green writes with a voice that bites like razor wire. A gritty, dark, and totally original debut."
—Harlan Coben, author of *Tell No One* and *Darkest Fear*

WAY PAST LEGAL

ISBN 0-06-079130-6 (mass market)

"Twists on top of twists." —*Kirkus Reviews*

"Tension and suspense abound. . . . Way past terrific."

—*Booklist* (starred review)